To my wife and daughter. You inspire me to be better.

Chapter 1

The Exodus Seed

Villa Hause Ende - Herdecke, Germany

April 1945

The collapse of the Third Reich is inevitable, taking with it the Kaiser Wilhelm Society. Now, 37 years after its creation, the many institutions making up the infamous society have been reduced to rubble by continuous Allied bombing or are working at a significantly reduced capacity due to a lack of personnel and resources. After heavy German losses at the Battle of the Bulge and Stalingrad, Allied troops will soon begin their push toward Berlin with little resistance.

Even now on this spring day, Albert Völger, politician, industrialist, entrepreneur, and the last President of the Kaiser Wilhelm Society, can hear the sound of bombs falling in the distance. Moments later, another louder explosion can be heard as he feverishly continues combing through years of documents, deciding which must not fall into enemy hands. He hears a knock on the door as his secretary enters the room. Without looking up, he issues more orders to his young assistant.

"Excellent, Otto, come in. I have more papers for the fireplace."

Otto hesitates as he stands at attention next to Vögler. Vögler notices an envelope in his hand. Otto extends the note, snapping to attention as he was taught to do in Hitler's Youth program.

"Sir, a memo has arrived from Headquarters."

Otto hands the envelope to Vögler and begins collecting the documents he will add to the fireplace. Völger, picking up the letter, notices it is from Bernard Rust, Minister of Science, Education, and National Culture for the Nazi Party. Rust appointed Völger as

President of the Kaiser Wilhelm Society in 1941. He hand-picked him to oversee a top-secret project that could alter warfare forever. Völger looks down and begins reading as Otto exits the room.

Herr Vögler,

With profound regret, I must inform

you that French Resistance fighters

have intercepted the Exodus Seed

research while in transit to Austria.

This tremendous loss means that you

and I are the last to know of the

project's existence. It is an

unfortunate end to this journey. I trust

you will do what must be done.

Bernard Rust, Minister

Völger falls back into his chair as the weight of the lost research sets in. He looks up at the window to the park fronting his office window, slowly rising from his chair, and walks over to a wall safe, discreetly hidden behind a tapestry. He removes a folder stamped "Streng Geheim" (Top Secret) and reviews its contents. He thumbs through the remaining few pages in the file and realizes it is inadequate to continue moving the Exodus Seed project forward. He recalls the conversation with Minister Rust, in which he convinced him he had the necessary skills to complete the project. Skills developed while President of a multinational agricultural company focusing on plant breeding and seed production. He returns to the moment and verbalizes his regret.

"The Exodus Seed project was the future of warfare and would have secured a top position for me in the Third Reich. Such a waste."

Vögler returns to his desk and places a call he never thought he would have to make. After a few moments, the operator begins speaking.

"Yes, Herr Vögler."

"Connect me to The Curtain Group. I need to speak with the ranking member immediately."

"Yes, Herr Vögler. I will ring you once I have them on the line."

Vögler, feeling the weight of his despair, replaces the receiver and sits back. His only hope is that The Curtain Group can somehow extract him to their headquarters in Austria. Minutes pass until the phone rings, snapping him out of his malaise as the operator speaks.

"Herr Vögler. I have Herr Liton on the line. Connecting the call now."

The voice of an Englishman begins speaking.

"Mr. Vögler. My name is Liton. I am on the Board of The Curtain Group. I understand you are fluent in English. Is this correct?"

Vögler hesitates as his mind tries to make sense of the British-sounding man. Liton continues.

"Mr Vögler. Allow me to put your mind at ease. I already know you speak English. I also know of the letter you received from Minister Rust. I know this because I placed an asset in your employ a few years ago. You know him as Otto."

Vögler's mind begins spinning as the Englishman continues speaking.

"Albert. The Curtain Group knows that the French have captured the Exodus Seed research. It is, therefore, paramount that you hand over all Exodus Seed documentation to Otto. The information is vital to continue the project."

Confused, Vögler begins to stammer.

"But, but, but you are British..."

Liton interrupts.

"Let me stop you there, Albert. We are on the clock and have it on good authority that a specialized Allied Army unit will soon arrive to take you into custody. We must conclude our business promptly."

At that moment, Otto returns to Vögler's office without knocking. He walks up to Vögler, takes the telephone from him, and scans the file Vögler retrieved from the safe. Vögler looks at Otto as though it is the first time he is seeing him. Otto begins reporting his findings to Liton.

"Herr Liton, there's not much here other than progress reports and a few supply manifests for equipment and chemicals. Hold on for a moment..."

Otto puts down the phone to examine the documents more thoroughly. Then, he quickly picks up the receiver again.

"Sir, I can confirm that there are detailed notes from plant geneticist Carl Correns on the initial discovery. It would seem Herr Vögler thought them important enough to keep to himself."

Vögler, realizing his error in judgment, quickly takes back the receiver from Otto.

"Mr Liton. These notes belong to the Kaiser Wilhelm Society. I suggest that you..."

Vögler cannot finish his statement as Otto removes his 9mm Luger P08 pistol and points it at Völger's face. Liton returns to speaking while Vögler stares down the gun barrel.

"Listen, Albert. The Kaiser Wilhelm Society was an experiment. It proved that privatized scientific discovery could be monetized and exploited globally. We chose you because you have a history of maximizing profits. A job that you have done very well. However, the research created by the KWS is the sole property of those who have funded the Society. I need not remind you that protecting

KWS's intellectual property is exactly why The Curtain Group was created.'"

Listening to Liton's words, Vögler finally realizes the nature of the work. He was, after all, an ardent industrialist whose sole focus was maximizing profits. Liton continues as Otto lowers his gun and begins gathering the papers on the Exodus Seed project.

"The Exodus Seed project is important, but much work is still to be done before it can become operational, let alone profitable. You can rest well knowing that the notes you squirreled away could benefit the cause. Now, we have run out of time as there is, most certainly, armed military personnel on their way to take you into custody."

Vögler's attention is distracted as Otto hands him a small ampoule with a clear liquid inside it. Vögler accepts it hesitantly as Liton continues speaking.

"What Otto is likely handing you will allow you a clean death without pain. Swallow the liquid, and before you can count to 10, your problems will be painlessly solved. Imprisonment or the gallows will no longer be your worry. "

Otto takes back the phone from Vögler.

"Sir, I can hear armored vehicles nearby. I will leave now and meet at the rendezvous location."

Liton's response is urgent.

"Do not fail, Otto. Protect those documents at all costs. We must get the Exodus Seed project back on track."

With resolve, Otto responds.

"I will not fail Herr Liton."

Otto puts the phone back on the cradle and notices a deep melancholy on Vögler's face. He hears boots outside the office and starts to leave the study through the servant's entrance, but the Exodus Seed folder begins to slip from his hand, and a few pages fall to the floor. He turns to pick them up just as the door to Vögler's office is kicked in. Otto goes through the servant's door, and a unit of Allied soldiers approaches Vögler with guns drawn.

At that moment, Vögler's thoughts are about his role as the last President of the Kaiser Wilhelm Society. An institution that produced the most horrific science the world had ever seen, all in the name of profit, and all of it will be laid at his feet. He quickly realizes that he will likely be hanged for the suffering and death caused by the Nazi controlled Kaiser Wilhelm Society.

Moments later, as soldiers begin leading Vögler to a waiting troop carrier, he opens the ampoule and drinks the liquid. Ironically, the liquid is another scientific discovery by the Society's Institute of Chemistry. Vögler collapses dead before he can count to 5.

The Alsos Mission - April 1945

Captain Wayne Stanard of the Alsos Mission wasn't looking forward to the call with his commanding officer, Lieutenant Colonel Pash. His unit, comprised of four Naval counterintelligence agents, four interpreters, and four scientists, was the brainchild of US Army Chief of Staff General George Marshall. Their mission was to investigate and collect intelligence on the Nazi's scientific research, especially anything relating to the Nazi's *nuclear* research program. Today's objective at Villa Hause Ende was to detain Albert Vögler and retrieve all scientific documentation. It was to be a simple interrogation, but that didn't mean it would be easy. When Alsos soldiers kicked in the door, they realized Vögler knew they were coming. The radio operator hands Captain Stanard the receiver.

"Sir, I have Lieutenant Colonel Pash."

Captain Stanard rolls his eyes and begins his report.

"Sir, I am afraid our effort to detain Albert Vögler was unsuccessful. He swallowed poison as we were preparing for his transport back to HQ. "

Stanard's radio operator can hear Lieutenant Colonel Pash's displeasure at the news through the receiver. Captain Stanard begins looking for a silver lining to this cluster fuck of a situation.

"Sir, Vogler's safe was already cleared out before we arrived, and we were unable to find any documents relating to the Nazi's nuclear program. We did, however, find a document that captured the attention of one of our eggheads, Dr. Johnson. Something to do with what they called "The Exodus Seed Project." He's pretty fired up about it, but to be clear, it has nothing to do with Nazi nuclear science."

Captain Stanard pulls the receiver away from his ear as Lieutenant Colonel Pash begins another of his signature tirades. Eventually, he finds an opening while his Commanding Officer takes a breath.

"Sir. Dr. Johnson is here with me now. I am handing the receiver over to him."

Captain Stanard waves over the waiting Dr. Johnson and hands the phone to the Cornell graduate with double doctorates in physics and plant biology.

"Yes, sir. This is Dr. Johnson. Sir, I came across a single page of a report prepared in 1913 by Carl Correns, a plant geneticist who directed the Kaiser Wilhelm Society Institute of Biology. In the document, Correns refers to discovering a plant mutation that could cause widespread crop failure."

Dr. Johnson pulls the receiver away from his ear as he listens to Pash's loud, frustration-laced rant. Captain Stanard cannot help but hide a smile. Dr. Johnson continues.

"No, sir. There is no connection to nuclear materials. [he pauses again as Pash continues yelling] Yes, sir. I understand, sir...but if I may, this program seemed to merit the attention of the President of the Kaiser Wilhelm Society.

Dr. Johnson's face was a mixture of fear and anger as he received more shouting from Pash. His patience is beginning to wear thin.

"All due respect, sir. I was brought on to discover Nazi *scientific* projects, not just the ones that offer promotions to those who push them up the chain of command."

Within earshot of the conversation, Captain Stanard has a newfound respect for Dr. Johnson for speaking to the Lieutenant

Colonel that way. Dr. Johnson leans into his point and interrupts Pash.

"*Excuse* me, sir. Have you ever heard of the Irish Potato Famine of 1845? Millions of people either starved to death or were forced to leave their country because of a blight that killed off their food supply. If the Nazis were working to weaponize a similar biological pathogen, they wouldn't need a nuclear bomb to wipe out an enemy. All they'd need to do is drop some seeds into an enemy's food supply."

Dr. Johnson's face drops as he listens to his orders.

"Yes, sir. I understand, sir. I will send this document to the Department of Agriculture for their assessment...[He pauses while Pash begins screaming again] OK. I understand. Yes, sir. I am handing you back to Captain Stanard."

Captain Stanard takes the handset and watches Dr. Johnson storm off toward Vögler's former office. As he enters it, his friend Dr. James (Jim) Fisk of MIT looks up and notices his colleague's demeanor.

"It is how we both imagined it would go, Johnny. They're not interested in anything other than nuclear discoveries."

Fisk's words do little to console him as he drops the slightly crumpled paper back onto Vögler's desk. Fisk reaches over and re-examines the paper.

"Johnny-boy, it probably didn't help your argument that this report is over three decades old. Shouldn't the project have been completed by now?"

Dr. Johnson displays a "serious as death" look at his colleague.

"For a millennium, humanity has been altering the genetic makeup of nearly every organism on this planet. Mostly to make it more resilient to disease. Dr. Corren's discovery could, in theory, genetically weaponize those enhancements. It could take decades or longer to figure out the exact science and replicate the discovery."

Dr. Johnson takes the paper from Fisk, wads it up, and throws it toward the still-smoldering fireplace. He then starts waving his arms around as if displaying the room.

"And the fact that the report was in Vögler's office makes me believe it was more than a pipe dream."

Dr. Fisk looks outside Vögler's office window and sees Captain Stanard finishing his call with Lt Colonel Pash.

"I hope for your sake, Johnny, that they aren't talking about replacing you on this team...or jailing you for insubordination."

Dr. Johnson thinks for a moment.

"No offense, Fisk. But I've had enough of this mission, and it's nuclear bullshit."

Chapter 2

The King of Chefs

Carlton Hotel, London, England - 20 June 1914

"You would be wise, my dear Auguste, to not tempt fate."

Escoffier looks at his wife, Delphine, through the corner of his eye.

"Delphine, it is clear you are unhappy. Would it not be best for us to talk about it before I leave?"

Delphine pauses in silence, knowing her dear husband is correct. She stops and looks deeply into his well-aged eyes.

"I am worried, Auguste. I worry about the talk of an impending war with Germany. I worry about our son and his desire to fight if called upon. I worry that you are spending precious time away from our family. I could go on, but my worry remains even when you return from this voyage."

Escoffier takes his wife's hand and lightly kisses it.

"My dearest, you know it is my fondest desire to retire."

Delphine rolls her eyes at her beloved as tears begin to show.

Another moment later, a sharp whistle signals to Escoffier that the bellman has finished loading his luggage onto the horse-drawn carriage. Turning back to Delphine, he brings her close and kisses her cheek.

"My dearest, I will return in a week."

It is a short trip to Waterloo Station as the porter takes Escoffier's bags to his first-class cabin. Within a few minutes, he relaxes with a Rye Whiskey and begins reviewing his itinerary.

"Two hours to Dover Port and another two and a half days to reach Hamburg by ship. I'll then have a day to review the kitchen and staff with Chef Scotto on the SS Imperator before departing for Heligoland."

His thoughts are interrupted as he remembers the parting with his dear Delphine. He cannot shake a feeling of dread coming over him.

Ocean Liner S.S. Imperator - 23 June 1914

After his journey from London, Escoffier is eager to explore the deck of the S.S. Imperator. However, upon settling into his accommodations, he finds it takes nearly 15 minutes to walk from his cabin to the kitchen three decks below. The trip is lengthened further by his preference for the elevator, which is located at the ship's forward section, while his cabin is near the stern. As he approaches the kitchen, he glances at his watch, thinking:

"This is not the day to keep the Kaiser of Germany waiting."

Escoffier quickens his pace.

Bridge, Ocean Liner S.S. Imperator

It is a calm summer evening aboard the SS Imperator. The Hamburg-Amerikan Ocean liner, named after Kaiser Wilhelm II, is the only male-named ship of its day. Commodore Theo Kier is well-seasoned, and a slight smile creases his sea-washed face as he looks out over the ship's bow. After departing from its mooring in Hamburg, the SS Imperator slowly navigates the Elbe River and is now beginning to enter the North Sea. It is on an overnight cruise to the Isles of Heligoland to commemorate the silver anniversary of its namesake, Kaiser Wilhelm II.

Under a waxing gibbous moon, Commodore Kier turns his attention to managing the crowded shipping lane of the Elbe River as it turns into the brackish water of the estuary. Soon thereafter, there is open water in the North Sea, then another three hours to Heligoland. He gives the order to increase speed.

"Helmsman. Engines to two-thirds."

The Helmsman telegraphs the speed increase to the engine room. After quickly receiving a reply message, he responds to Commodore Kier.

Engines to two-thirds. Commodore!"

Commodore Keir is eager to lose sight of land. He rises from the bridge chair, checks the compass, and moves to the helm to read the barometric report updated just as they entered the estuary. From this vantage point, he observes streaks of light dancing across the quiet, dark surface of the water. This streaking effect is created by the dorsal fins of various fish breaking through the phosphorescence at the water's surface, giving the illusion of bolts of electricity.

As he gazes out the bridge window, Commodore Kier notes that barometric pressure is rising, meaning there will be plenty of good weather for guests to enjoy as they stroll the decks after dinner. His First Officer, Hans Luber, quietly approaches from behind and stands at attention, patiently waiting for his Captain to finish his thoughts and acknowledge him. Hans Luber has served under his command for nearly a decade, making him an invaluable asset. Hans subtly relaxes his posture. Commodore Kier's voice conveys a mix of commanding authority and calm familiarity.

"Yes, Hans."

First Officer Hans Luber walks closer to his stoic Commodore.

"Sir, we have received word that His Majesty will soon depart the Imperial quarters. He will arrive at the main dining salon at 2100 hours (9 pm)."

Commodore Kier delivers the order to relinquish command authority to the First Officer.

"Thank you, Hans. I stand relieved until midnight. First Officer Luber has the helm!"

Hans quickly resumes, standing at full attention. The crew on the bridge responded in unison.

"Aye, sir!"

Commodore Kier walks toward the aft hatch leading directly to the main dining salon, knowing he will arrive at the table well before the Kaiser. As he moves down the passage, his thoughts drift to the upcoming dinner and his earlier conversation with the famous Chef Escoffier, who assured him that the newly renovated galley was operating at peak efficiency and under his strict and watchful supervision. The captain's brow reveals the slightest crease of worry, betraying his stoic appearance. This dinner must be nothing less than perfect. Commodore Kier quickens his pace to ensure he arrives well ahead of Kaiser Wilhelm II.

Ritz-Carlton Kitchen - S.S. Imperator

Seventeen minutes later, Escoffier is greeted by the kitchen manager, Gaston.

"Good afternoon, Chef!"

As a reflex, both Chef Scotto and Escoffier turn their heads. Gaston chuckles.

"I've always wanted to do that. It is rare to have two Chefs in the same kitchen!"

Escoffier walks over to his protégé, Chef Charles Scotto, who hands him a copy of the menu. Escoffier mentions naming the dessert after the Kaiser. Chef Scotto smiles, knowing that changing the dessert's name will yield greater praise for the dinner. Escoffier takes out his Art Deco Wakl-Eversharp pencil, a gift from Australian opera singer, Nellie Melba (whom he named his famous dessert "Peach Melba" after), and begins reviewing the menu.

Molosso Caviar
Lighted Salted Premium Russian Caviar served on ice with buckwheat blini (a small pancake), chopped onions, and créme frâiche.

Chicken Cream Chicago with Terrapine Maryland
Turtle Soup in a "Chicago" chicken stock is a nod to Chicken Vesuvio, a classic dish from the Chicago area that shares some

similarities with French cream sauces, particularly in its finish. (Escoffier discovered it while traveling in America.)

Fillet of Sole à la Payssane

Delicate sole fillets cooked and served with a rustic, "country-style" vegetable garnish.

Venison Cutlet Rominten style

Recipe originated in the Rominten Heath, once a royal hunting ground in East Prussia.

Punch a l'Americaine

A category of fruit-and-spirit-based drinks historically served in large bowls.

Fresh Asparagus with Sauce Mousseline

A classic French side dish. The sauce is a light and airy hollandaise folded with whipped cream.

Broiled Chicken with Lettuce Salad

Fragrant herbs of Provence, whole chicken, pan-seared before finishing under the broiler.

Maraschino Parfait with Fruits

Maraschino Cherries in vanilla cream and various fruits.

Fraises Wilhelmine

Large strawberries with caster sugar, orange juice, and brandy, named in honor of Kaiser Wilhelm II. (His favorite dessert)

After Escoffier and Scotto finish the preparations, Escoffier takes one last walk around the kitchen to review each food preparation station. Satisfied that everything is in order, he checks his watch, returns to Chef Scotto, shakes his hand, and exits the kitchen. In the last moment before exiting through the door, Escoffier stops abruptly and turns around, facing the kitchen staff.

"When I began my career in the culinary arts, I worked in unorganized and unsanitary kitchens. Seeing each of you working as part of the same unit has proven that discipline and organization are the keys to ensuring that those eating our food are delighted beyond compare. You honor yourselves, your honor your chef de cuisine, and you honor me. Most of all, you honor our guest, Kaiser Wilhelm II."

As Escoffier walks through the door to greet the Kaiser, you can hear a pin drop. With a snap of Chef Scotto's finger, the team begins preparations for the service.

SS Imperator, North Sea - Next Day

Escoffier is stirred by a rapping on his stateroom door. He thinks he might be dreaming for a moment, but as the knocking persists, he realizes otherwise. Escoffier's eyes open reluctantly as he reaches for his glasses to check the wall clock at the foot of his bed. The light streaming through the gaps in the porthole window indicates it is already well into the morning. His head aches, and his ears throb in time with his heartbeat. Escoffier scolds himself.

"Last night's dinner was undoubtedly on a pantagruelian level."

Escoffier's ancient reference is to Pantagruel, the jovial drunkard character from the scandalous story by French author François Rabelais, written in the 16th century. The character Pantagruel was renowned for hosting extravagant multicourse meals that began in the late afternoon and continued well into the following day. Escoffier smiles, grateful that the Kaiser's dinner lasted only until 2 am. He rises and sits on the edge of the bed as the rapping on the door persists. Escoffier's loud voice fills the room.

"Yes, yes! I heard you! Everyone aboard this ship has heard you!"

Squinting his eyes, Escoffier tries to focus on the clock across the room as he rises to retrieve his housecoat. It takes him a few moments to make his way to the door. When he opens it, he is confronted by a man in a formal military uniform. The man bows quickly and extends his hand, holding an envelope with the Royal Seal.

"Good morning, Herr Escoffier. The Kaiser extends his apologies for waking you. His Royal Highness has asked to spend a moment with you before the breakfast meal is served."

Taking the envelope, Escoffier raises his reading glasses as the acheté bows and turns militarily, leaving Escoffier at the door. Breaking the royal seal, Escoffier begins reading the letter.

Monsieur Escoffier,

The meal you prepared last night was beyond reproach. Your talent in the culinary arts is without equal. I received no less than fifty notes of accolades this morning. Each spoke of the level at which the meal progressed and the finale, where you were so kind as to name the dessert after me. I request the pleasure of your company at breakfast to thank you personally and to speak about another matter of some importance.

KWII

Puzzled by the breakfast invitation, Escoffier pauses to consider its significance. He glances at the clock, realizing he has less than an hour before breakfast service begins. Quickly dressed in attire suitable for meeting Emperor Wilhelm II, Escoffier exits his room and heads to the kitchen, where he finds Chef Scotto and the other sous chefs busy with morning meal preparations. Escoffier pulls Chef Scotto aside.

"I have been invited to breakfast with the Kaiser this morning."

Chef Scotto's face is one of surprise.

Escoffier observes the precision already established in the kitchen and smiles at Chef Scotto, recognizing his commitment to Escoffier's culinary organization and cleanliness standards. He then approaches Scotto to oversee the preparation of the morning meal.

"You are a good man, Charles, and an even better Chef de Cuisine."

Chef Scotto takes a moment to wipe his hands on a flour sack hanging from his shoulder.

"That means a lot to me coming from you, Auguste. Thank you."

The two men exchange a quiet moment as they scan the room and watch with precision as the sous chefs quietly work at the various stations. It is like clockwork, a purposeful and precise movement that never falters. Escoffier is brought back to the moment. He looks back at Chef Scotto and smiles.

"I am off to the Imperial Suite. Ensure the kitchen does not burn down before I return. I would hate to be thrown off the boat before we return to port."

Imperial Suite, SS Imperator, North Sea

Escoffier makes his way to the outer room surrounding the Kaiser's Imperial suite. He is greeted by a man in his mid-40s, dressed formally in a starched collar, jacket, and military-style trousers—the same man who delivered the note to him earlier. Ribbons hang from both sides of his uniform, and the royal sash of Germany does as well. He stands at attention as Escoffier enters the room. After seeing him a second time, Escoffier quickly concludes that the man standing before him has never encountered the working end of a rifle in his entire life. Nevertheless, Escoffier extends the courtesy of a head bow while holding the letter he received from the Kaiser, ensuring the royal seal is visible. Even though the two had seen each other earlier, Escoffier needed to adhere to protocol when visiting the Kaiser.

"I am Monsieur Escoffier with an appointment for breakfast with the Kaiser."

The man in uniform looks down his nose, rebuking Escoffier for his tardiness.

"You were to be here 2 minutes ago."

He turns away and walks towards a door at the back of the room. He raps on it twice, and within moments, it opens to reveal another man in full uniform. This one is wearing a decisively larger quantity of medals and ribbons. Escoffier notes that it is the same man from the dining table after the conclusion of last night's meal. He was the one whispering and looking at Escoffier. Escoffier smiles as he wonders how much the medals weigh in percentage to the man's overall weight. The two men exchange introductions, and Escoffier is then escorted into the next chamber.

"Monsieur Esccofier, you are lucky. The Kaiser is also running late. Please come with me."

As the door opens and he is led into the room, the only word that comes to Escoffier's mind is luxury, which only begins to describe the space he has entered. Technically, it is a drawing room where guests are welcomed, and the host will sit with them, separate from other areas of the suite. On the SS Imperator, the "Imperial" suite was the most exquisite accommodation of its time, featuring a dining room, drawing room, bedroom, and bathroom designed by the German decorator Johann Poppe in his signature Baroque revival style. Poppe's design employs furnishings and decor that create contrast, where movement, exuberant detail, deep color, grandeur, and surprise evoke a sense of awe. Escoffier feels a profound sense of wonder at the decor and would later recall to friends as he sat in an overstuffed chair made from the finest velvet, gazing up at the 20-foot stained glass ceiling and gilded columns.

Moments later, the Kaiser enters the room, smiling. Escoffier immediately rises to a formal standing position. As protocol dictates, the Kaiser speaks first. His French is heavy with a thick German accent, which assaults Escoffier's ears, yet his demeanor betrays nothing of his thoughts.

"Monsieur Escoffier. Last evening's feast was beyond reproach. Your skills and those of your protege are unmatched! I am the Emperor of Kings, but you, Monsieur Escoffier, are the King of Chefs!"

Escoffier is surprised by the personal nature of the statement. The Kaiser gestures for him to sit back in the chair and then takes the seat closest to him.

"Monsieur Escoffier, shall we continue in French, or would you prefer English?"

Escoffier smiles.

"Your Imperial Highness is too kind. English will be fine."

The Kaiser leans in towards Escoffier.

"I'm still receiving congratulatory messages from everyone who attended last evening's dinner. Your staff exceeded expectations, and I don't say that lightly. With each meal, you continue to elevate the culinary arts to new heights. I was particularly pleased with the dessert, and my compliments to you for naming it after me. You've made me feel like a celebrity, just as you did for the opera singer after whom your Peach Melba is named."

Escoffier begins to squirm in his chair with the compliments, and the Kaiser notices the letter he still holds. The conversation abruptly changes.

"Excellent! I see you received my note. I want to discuss a matter related to my Scientific Society."

Escoffier places the letter in his jacket pocket and sits back in his chair.

"I serve at your Imperial Highness' pleasure. How may I be of service?"

The Kaiser reclines in his chair as a kitchen steward delivers a coffee service through a private service door. After taking his first sip, the Kaiser gazes up at Escoffier.

"It is my understanding that you will soon be retiring. Is this true?"

Escoffier's response is direct, as is his commitment to his retirement.

"Yes, Your Royal Highness. It is true. I still have much work to do on my culinary book, but my kitchen duties have already been handed over to Chef Scotto. To be completely transparent, he prepared last evening's meal."

"The praise for your staff is admirable. However, it's well known that the precision with which your kitchen operates results from the military-like organization you alone established. This is undoubtedly due to your time as Chef de Cuisine in the Army during the Franco-Prussian War. Am I wrong?"

The Franco-Prussian War of 1870 was relatively recent, and the Kaiser paused to measure Escoffier's stoic demeanor. Escoffier is well-seasoned when it comes to dealing with nobility.

"Your Imperial Highness. What you say is true. When a kitchen is run properly, it can replicate success with precision. How can I be of service?"

The Kaiser relaxes and is happy with Escoffier's response.

"Let me be direct. We have drawn several prominent scientists since founding the Kaiser Wilhelm Society."

Escoffier's interest is piqued, and he nods to the Kaiser in the affirmative.

"My Society " is the pinnacle any scientist could hope to achieve. It provides everything they need without consideration of cost.

The Kaiser pauses for dramatic effect.

"Everything save a kitchen capable of producing food to match their status. This is a detail that was overlooked when the Society was established. A detail I would like you to repair."

The Kaiser relaxes back into his chair, allowing Escoffier to respond.

"Your Royal Highness, I am deeply honored. However..."

The Kaiser interrupts.

"Monsieur Escoffier, I understand you have achieved much in your career. I ask you to do me the honor of designing the most magnificent kitchen the world has ever seen. One worthy of the men whom it will serve."

Escoffier pauses a moment. The Kaiser continues.

"Please do me the honor of coming to Berlin, touring the facility, and meeting the scientists. It will be time well spent. What say you?"

Escoffier sits up in his chair.

"Your Royal Highness, I am at your service. I would be honored. However, I did not account for this change and have not secured train passage for such a trip."

The Kaiser rises, as does Escoffier. The two shake hands.

"I will have my staff see that you accompany me on the Royal Train."

At that moment, another attache enters the room and hands the Kaiser a note.

"It would seem, Monsieur Escoffier, that your kitchen is wondering when we will have our meal."

The Kaiser rises from his chair, and the two men shake hands.

"Excellent! Then it is settled. You will be at the Kaiser Wilhelm Society in Berlin-Dahlem by tomorrow afternoon."

After breakfast, Escoffier finds himself alone on the forward deck contemplating the Kaiser's request to design a kitchen for the Kaiser Wilhelm Society.

"I must telegraph Delphine and let her know I will be delayed. She will not be pleased."

Escoffier cannot shake the same feeling of dread coming over him again. As he looks toward Germany, he notices dark clouds on the horizon, announcing the arrival of an ominous and angry summer storm.

Chapter 3

The Kaiser Wilhelm Society

The Kaiser Wilhelm Society, Berlin-Dahlem Germany

- June 25, 1914

Escoffier's walk from the train platform to the main lobby of the Berlin Gesundbrunnen station was brief, and he quickly noticed the men there to meet him. Escoffier would later recall that each man had a distinctive appearance. Although they weren't wearing identical suits, each sported a white pin with a black Swastika in the center of the lapel. The tallest of the men stepped forward to greet Escoffier. His accent was Prussian, and it was evident from the sound of his voice that he was well-educated. However, his French was clumsy and awkward.

"Monsieur Escoffier, my name is Oscar. We have been asked to escort you to the Kaiser Wilhelm Society."

He extended his hand towards the two other men.

"This way, if you please."

Seeing the questioning look on Escoffier's face, Oscar pauses before approaching the automobile waiting for them.

"Monsieur, your luggage will be taken to your lodgings in Berlin. Throughout your stay, you will be the guest of Adolf von Harnack, President of the Kaiser Wilhelm Society. We are here to escort you to a reception in your honor hosted by the Society's Board of Directors. This way, sir, everyone is waiting."

Escoffier smiles at the precise way of thinking attributed to the German people, though he inwardly wishes their guttural dialect were more Austrian than Prussian. However, he notices that each of the three men is wearing a blue and gold sash beneath their jackets. Escoffier's curiosity gets the better of him.

"Sir, I noticed your sash. What does it signify?"

The man immediately changes his posture and stands at attention, as do the other men now about to enter the car.

"Monsieur, it signifies the Order of the Kaiser, and it is an honor given to those who were part of the founding members of the Kaiser Wilhelm Society. Think of it as his Imperial recognition and blessing."

Well-versed in politics, Escoffier changes his relaxed posture and stands at attention in front of the men, bowing slightly in respect for such an honor.

"Gentlemen. I am at your service."

After the formalities are complete, Escoffier is ushered into the car, and they begin the 30-minute journey to a residential suburb in Berlin-Dahlem. Upon arriving at the Kaiser Wilhelm Society's central facility, Escoffier is astounded by its efficiency and design. Created by the Kaiser's Chief Architect, Ernst von Ihne, it contrasts sharply with the landscape, featuring tall columns and a spired turret, reflecting the Classicism architectural style of the 1800s.

As Escoffier enters the building, he notices that it is nearly empty. The tallest of his three escorts notices his surprise and explains.

"Monsieur Escoffier, we have only recently completed the construction, and our staff is being hired and trained. However, the cooking facility is already in place, and once the reception is over, we can take you on a tour."

The three men direct Escoffier into a large room off the main lobby. Upon entering, he is greeted by the Society's president, Adolf von Harnack. Escoffier notices several men in the room gathered around a dining table. With a proud look on his face, Von Harnack extends his hand.

"Good day to you, Monsieur Escoffier. It is an honor to have such a celebrated Chef in our company. I hope your travels have been pleasant."

The two men shake as von Harnack directs Escoffier to a nearby group of men.

"Monsieur Escoffier, it is my pleasure to introduce you to Klaus Müller, the Chairman of the Board of Trustees."

Klaus turns away from the men around him.

"Yes. Yes. The King of Chefs! How delightful to meet you, sir. We are expecting great things."

Escoffier bows slightly, and the two men shake hands. Escoffier notices the man's sweaty hand and chuckles, giving Klaus a slight wink.

"It is a pleasure to meet you, sir. However, the title is only symbolic. No need to bow."

The men laugh as von Harnack ushers Escoffier to the head of the table. Escoffier observes that each of them knows exactly where to sit as they take their places. In two minutes, several servers enter and start pouring wine for the gathering. Escoffier is seated at the head of the table, to the right of von Harnack, signifying his stature to the other attendees. Once the wine is poured, von Harnack stands with a glass in hand.

"Gentlemen. In these moments, others will reflect on the strength of our commitment to establishing Germany as a leader in the sciences. It is not enough to possess the best minds; we must ensure that every detail, no matter how trivial it may seem, is addressed with the same dedication to excellence. This is why we are honored to have Monsieur Escoffier, the renowned French culinary chef, who will guarantee that our kitchen meets the tastes of the most discerning scientists in our Society."

Von Harmack raises his glass.

"To Georges Auguste Escoffier."

The men around the table stand, and each raises their glass in honor in unison.

"Here! Here!"

Escoffier stands as the men take their seats.

"Gentlemen, I have designed numerous European culinary facilities and would like to share my experiences. I will excel at creating the most efficient and state-of-the-art facility to fuel and inspire the greatest minds in science!"

The men rise again from the chairs in unison.

"Here! Here!"

Lunch arrives soon, and Escoffier quickly notices that the food is German-inspired and well-prepared. Some men rise from the table and gather in small groups of three to five as digestives are served. Von Harmack stands and begins taking Escoffier around the room to introduce him to each group of men. The closest group includes the renowned physics professor Albert Einstein. The two men shake hands. Einstein speaks first, and in a beautiful Austrian French accent.

"Monsieur Escoffier. I have enjoyed several dinners you have prepared. It is an honor to meet you, sir, in person."

Escoffier's face is one of recognition.

"Herr Einstein. I recall each time, and if I may be so bold, I have found that you carry yourself as a man constantly struggling to solve immense puzzles. Even while you are eating, I have always wanted to know if this is true."

Einstein smiles wryly and responds.

"Monsieur Escoffier. If that were true, I would be plagued by continuous indigestion. No sir. When I am eating, especially from your menus, it is a certainty that I am present in the moment."

Everyone within earshot smiles from amusement, except one: a stout man with spectacles that seem to hide the depth of his eyes. He steps forward to shake Escoffier's hand.

"Sir. My name is Carl Correns, and I will soon be taking a position as the Director of the Institute of Biology. My main area of study is plant genetics."

The two men shake hands, and Escoffier, noticing the seriousness of the man's face, decides to lighten his mood.

"It is a pleasure to meet you, Herr Correns. It would seem we have something in common."

Correns cannot conceal the look of surprise on his face. Escoffier explains.

"You, sir, study the science of how plants replicate. I study the science of how plants taste."

The men exchange a quiet laugh, and Correns extends his hand again to Escoffier.

"Monsieur Escoffier. I must leave to continue unpacking and organizing my new laboratory. Perhaps at another time, I can show you the specimens we have been working on to help increase disease resistance."

Escoffier, interested in anything that can help with food production, begins to lean into the conversation with Correns.

"Sir, it would please me greatly to see your work. As you may know, I work with many food producers throughout Europe to source the products for our hotels."

At that point, von Harmack is pulled away by a staff member, so Escoffier takes a moment to follow Correns into the hall leading to his lab.

Correns, seeing Escoffier following, slows, allowing him to catch up. Escoffier quietly smiles and explains.

"It would seem that the welcoming event has changed into several discussions that have nothing to do with the kitchen. Do you mind if I take a look at your lab now?"

Escoffier misinterprets a look of worry on Correns's brow as they continue to walk.

"Sir, if you prefer, I will take my leave and look for the kitchen...I do not want to interrupt your work."

Corren's demeanor changes, casting a smile back at Escoffier.

"Monsieur Escoffier, in full disclosure, I was hoping to spend a few moments with you privately. I think I have something you will find interesting."

Corren allowed the conversation to end, and the two men silently walked through several corridors. Eventually, arriving at an opaque glass-paneled door with the number 12-C painted on it.

Corren takes out a key and enters the room. Inside, Escoffier notices the smell of formaldehyde and the earthy scent of several plants near the windows on the far wall. However, nearly every other surface in the lab is covered with labeled boxes, each arranged in an alphanumeric sequence. Corren closes the door as Escoffier steps inside.

"Excuse the mess. It has taken most of two days to get the boxes cataloged."

Escoffier looks around the room, where numerous boxes are meticulously cataloged and organized. He notes the system Correns uses to manage them and makes a mental note to update his practice of organizing foodstuffs. Correns, now sorting through a research folder on a table across the room, begins speaking while his back is turned to Escoffier.

"Monsieur Escoffier. It is divine providence that you are here. When I heard that you would be visiting the Society, I made certain to speed up my moving process."

Escoffier cannot conceal the questions racing through their mind. Correns continues speaking as though he is the only person in the room.

"Last year, I was approached by von Harnack and others to fill the position of Director for the Institute of Biology. I was indeed honored, and I accepted immediately. Thinking back now, I believe I may have made a hasty decision. I have learned much about the Society that is of concern to me.

Correns pauses and turns toward Escoffiers to assess his facial expression. Satisfied, he continues and turns back to look through his research.

"My good sir, the Kaiser Wilhelm Society is a magnificent institution for advancing science. However, I have recently become aware that it is also being utilized as a research and development facility for the High Command of the German Army."

Without turning around, Correns points to a table next to Escoffier, where an open folder marked Vertraulich

(CONFIDENTIAL) in red is displayed. Intrigued, Escoffier leans over, retrieves his spectacles from his vest pocket, and begins reading the page. Meanwhile, Correns continues to speak.

"I am a plant geneticist, and I am working on decoding how plants propagate. However, I have recently been assigned to oversee a military project."

As Correns' words fill the room, Escoffier's eyes widen, and he stumbles back against a nearby chair and sits in it. Eventually, Correns turns to face Escoffier and allows him to speak the words written on his face.

"Sir, how can this be so? It says that there is a science that could create a plant that could wipe out entire crops..."

Correns' reply is blank, harsh, and scientific.

"Monsieur Escoffier. The pathogen is a mutation of a common blight. It is commonly known to have killed many people in Ireland from starvation and caused millions to flee their native country in the late 19th century. While researching pea plants ' hereditary traits, I discovered a mutated version of the blight."

Escoffier's brilliant mind finally sees the evil truth of the project. He looks up at Correns with a face that resembles a child once they realize there is no Santa Claus. Correns continues to speak without emotion.

The German military has asked that I replicate the discovery and create a pathogen that would allow an army to take over a country without firing a single shot. They call the project "The Exodus Seed."

Escoffier's anger bubbles up to the surface, and he quickly rises to stand directly in front of Correns.

"Why are you telling me this!? What is it that you expect I can do?"

Correns steps back and walks Escoffier back to the door.

"My good sir. Your reputation precedes you, and I only ask that you pass this information to your government."

Outraged, Escoffier turns away from Correns and walks towards the door. He stops and turns.

"Am I to understand that you will continue to work on this project?"

Correns looks back at Escoffier dispassionately.

"In truth, the science is far beyond my capabilities; however, it will still require countermeasures to render it inert if it is to be useful to the military."

Correns turns back to his papers and continues.

"It will take greater minds to see this project through to completion, and it will likely take decades to become a reality."

Correns' tone is again serious.

"Make no mistake. The science will eventually be discovered, and it will become a horrific tool if put in the hands of this or any other government. Therefore, it must be given to all governments."

Escoffier is dumbfounded but understands Correns' motivation. He walks over to the documents and closes the file. He struggles quickly with his conscience and makes his decision.

"Herr Correns, I do not know what will come of this, but I will ensure this information reaches my government."

Correns extends his hand. Escoffier accepts it, and the two men share solemn looks. Correns turns and opens the lab door, showing Escoffier out and directing him toward the kitchen. At the end of the hallway, the two men spot von Harnack, along with two men who picked Escoffier up at the station, approaching them. They arrive with shocked expressions. Von Harnack begins to speak as the two men in dark suits and lapel pins position themselves behind Escoffier.

"There you are, Monsieur Escoffier. We had wondered where you wandered off to."

Correns begins to speak, but Escoffier interrupts. He reaches out his hand to Correns."

"My good man, I am thrilled to hear about your progress in enhancing tomato production. It is truly fascinating, and I hope you will keep me updated. As you are aware, I have established connections with several European agricultural distributors. Just say the word, and I will gladly make the introductions."

Correns smiles back and thanks Escoffier. Von Harnack breaks the train of conversation to escort Escoffier toward the kitchen.

"My good sir, the kitchen is this way. Our chef is waiting, and I can say he is very nervous and excited to meet you."

The group separates, and Escoffier does not look back as Correns returns to his lab. The remaining day was spent in the kitchen discussing design ideas with von Harnack's architect and chef. Later, there was another reception and dinner that even Escoffier had to admit was excellent. As the evening concludes, a rather tall man in a topcoat with a silver-tipped cane approaches Escoffier and hands him a card. He begins speaking in his native French.

"Monsieur Escoffier, my name is F. Devereux. I work on behalf of the Board of Trustees for the Society. My family is also a donor to the Society."

Escoffier immediately recognizes that the man is from Normandy based on his accent. With a casual wink, Escoffier leans into Devereux and jokingly whispers.

"My good man, it is a pleasure to speak actual French. I am afraid German accents tear through our language like a hungry man to a veal chop."

Devereux is not amused, surprising Escoffier.

"Monsieur Chef. Be that as it may, I have been asked to speak with you more about your discussion with Herr Correns."

After spending the remaining afternoon with Von Harnack, probing him about his talk with Correns, Escofiier was in no mood.

"My good sir, I have spoken with von Harnack about this topic to some extent. Unless you wish to learn about tomato production, I must excuse myself, for it has been a long day."

Escoffier bows slightly, turns away, then stops and turns back to Devereux, his anger getting the best of him.

"And if I may offer a word of advice: if I were you, I would spend more time in your home country. Your French sounds like a dog is speaking it. Good night, sir."

Escoffier turns and notices von Harnack's stare across the room. Escoffier finds the maid, who shows him to his room. Once there, he closes the door and notices two men stationed at the end of the hallway. He sits on his bed, reflecting on the knowledge he now possesses.

"What can be done with such information?"

Escoffier changes into his night clothes and falls into a fitful sleep.

Chapter 4

Archduke Ferdinand

Cafe Parkuša, Sarajevo, Austro-Hungarian Province of Bosnia and Herzegovina - 27 June 1914

Just as Escoffier is arriving in Berlin-Dahlem, Gavrilo Princip scans the crowded café and spots Nedjelko and Trifko sitting in a small, dimly lit booth in the back, as expected. Before heading to the bar, he waits to see if anyone is paying the two men unnecessary attention. He smiles inwardly, thinking that the training the three young men recently received from the Black Hand is much more intriguing when applied in real-life situations. The bartender looks up as he approaches and speaks in Hungarian.

"Welcome. What can I get you?"

Gavrilo points to a bottle and places a few kroner (the Serbian currency) on the bar. He then raises his hand with his thumb, index, and middle fingers, signaling he wants three glasses. The bartender returns, collects the money, and sets the bottle and glasses before the serious-looking young Serbian. After one last look around, Gavrilo walks toward the table in the back. Trifko slides over, making room for his comrade to sit. He pours a drink for each of them. They raise their glasses in a silent but meaningful toast.

"The Black Hand."

Gavrilo finishes his drink and brings out a small piece of paper that looks like a map. Trifko and Nedjelko lean in.

"I have received our assignment. By tomorrow, the Archduke will no longer threaten our independence."

Gavrilo points to the Cumurja Bridge on the map. His route from the train station to the town hall will take him over this bridge.

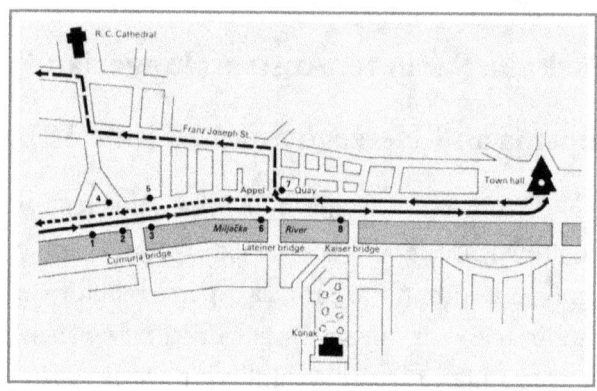

"Nedjelko, you will be stationed here by the bridge. As we were trained, you must throw the grenade just in front of the leading automobile."

He looks over at Trifko, pointing to a different position on the map.

"Trifko, you will be at the Kaiser Bridge here, and I will be between you both here at the Lateinier Bridge."

He looks around and hears loud laughter from a nearby table. He looks back at the others.

"When Nedjelko's grenade stops the automobile, I will shoot the Archduke and his wife. If, for some reason, they do not stop, then Trifko will have another chance to shoot him as they continue to the Town Hall."

Gavrilo pauses, looking each man in the eyes.

"We must be in position by 10 a.m. Make certain to bring a newspaper, have a smoke, and try not to look like you are waiting for something."

Gavrilo pours another drink, and they raise their glasses again to make a silent toast.

The Next Morning - 28 June 1914

It is a pleasant 24°C (75°F) as Archduke Ferdinand and his wife, Sophie Chotek, Duchess of Hohenburg, are driving through the streets of Sarajevo to meet with local dignitaries. As Inspector General of the Austro-Hungarian armed forces, the archduke is visiting Bosnia to oversee military maneuvers and inaugurate a new museum.

As the Archduke's automobile approaches the Cumurja bridge, a loud explosion erupts from behind, causing the trailing car to careen into a nearby tree. Fearing an attack, the driver speeds past Gravrilo and Trifko, neither of whom has a clear shot at the Archduke.

Moments later, the archduke's automobile arrives at the town hall, greeted by a row of dignitaries who appear confused and frightened. The archduke exits the automobile with Sophie and storms past those waiting to greet him. As he enters the anteroom of the town hall, the Mayor approaches him. Archduke Ferdinand is furious.

"So, this is how I am greeted!? With bombs!!"

The Mayor begins humbling himself, vowing to bring those responsible to justice. A few moments later, an aide to the archduke runs into the room.

"There is news of survivors from the attack. They have been taken to a nearby hospital."

At the direction of the Archduke and Duchess, they are escorted to their car, accompanied by a trailing vehicle to take them to the hospital to visit the injured from the explosion. Gavrilo, noticing the opportunity pass, crosses the street and waits for the Archduke's return trip to the museum. After spending 30 minutes waiting near a local tavern, Gavrilo sees the Archduke's cars coming back. As they make the turn, the cars stop. There is confusion about their direction, and the vehicles stall.

Thankful for the opportunity, Gavrilo pulls out his pocket-sized FN Model 1910 pistol and, walking up to the automobile, he shoots the Duchess in the abdomen and the Archduke in the neck. He then flees to the safe house located a few blocks away. The archduke, holding his neck, issues his final command.

"Don't die, darling; live for our children."

It is there that the Archduke and Duchess die of their wounds.

An Hour Later - KWS Institute of Chemistry Berlin-Dahlem - June 28, 1914

Escoffier awakens with a knocking at his bedroom door. It is von Harnack's maid.

"Herr Escoffier. It is time to wake up. There has been an assassination."

Escoffier rises and heads to the armoire to retrieve his change of clothes. The maid knocks again.

"Herr Escoffier..."

With a touch of anger, Escoffier retorts.

"Madame. Please tell your employer I will be along in a few minutes."

Escoffier hears the pitter-patter of feet quickly heading down the hall. Glancing at his pocket watch, Escoffier realizes that it is nearing midday. He had tossed and turned all night after the meeting with Correns, but it only took him a few minutes to wash up and get dressed. Taking one last look in the mirror, he heads downstairs, where he can already hear the voices of many people coming from the parlor.

As he reaches the landing, he senses heightened anxiety from the many voices in the house's main salon. Just then, one of the maids approaches Escoffier, carrying a small, white envelope emblazoned with the initials "ITU" and sealed with wax. Escoffier recognizes the International Telegraph Union logo as the primary and most immediate means of communication between countries. After thanking the maid, he breaks the telegraph's seal and reads.

Auguste Escoffier [stop]

```
Political assassination in Sarajevo

[stop]

War imminent [stop]

A seat on train to Paris is waiting

at the station [stop]

A car is heading your way. Look for

a white rose [stop]

Depart immediately! [stop]

Gaston [stop]
```

Moments later, Escoffier turns toward a loud exchange between von Harnack and several members of the Board of Trustees. Talks of war are already underway. Von Harnack sees Escoffier in the foyer and walks over to him.

"Monsieur Escoffier. I am afraid that there has been an assassination of Archduke Ferdinand, and the threat of war is imminent. I took the liberty of bringing your bags down, and a car awaits you. The driver has strict instructions to take you directly to the train station. It seems our culinary project will have to be put on hold."

Escoffier nods, and the two men shake hands. Escoffier notices that von Harnack's forehead is unusually sweaty. Von Harnack follows Escoffier's stare and wipes his brow with a handkerchief.

"I apologize for my rudeness, but there is much to do with the Society. I hope that we can speak again at some later date. Have a pleasant journey."

Von Harnack turns on his heels and heads back into the salon. The maid has returned with Escoffier's coat, hat, and gloves.

"Sir. Your driver is waiting."

Escoffier follows her in silence, observing the same two men in dark suits with lapel pins—one seated in the driver's seat and the other holding the rear door open. As he approaches the car, Escoffier can't help but notice the sinister expressions on their faces—the man holding open the car door gestures for Escoffier to enter.

"Herr Escoffier. If you please."

Sensing danger, Escoffier stops momentarily as another car arrives in great haste, stopping abruptly in front of the first. He notices that the new car driver is wearing a large white rose on his lapel, which he recognizes as the flower that adorns the lobby of the Carlton hotel. Escoffier understands the signal and excuses himself.

"Gentlemen. My car has just arrived. Please give Von Harnck my sincere thanks for his hospitality."

Leaving his luggage behind, Escoffier quickly moves around Von Harnack's men as they stare at him menacingly. Getting into the waiting car with his satchel, he looks back and urges the driver to start moving.

"My good man. If you please, I am in a hurry."

The driver puts the automobile in gear.

"But what of your luggage?"

Escoffier turns back to the driver.

"Leave it and do your best to get to the train station as quickly as possible."

The driver complies and speeds off, arriving at the train station in record time. Escoffier shakes the driver's hand and hands him an enormous tip. The man will not accept it and instead gives it to a woman escorting five children onto the crowded platform.

"Monsieur. She needs the money more than I do."

Escoffier smiles at the gesture as the two men shake hands. Before departing, Escoffier writes out a note and asks the driver to send a telegram back to Gaston. As Escoffier turns towards the station, he sees the same two men in dark suits walking towards him at the far end of the platform. Too many people are on the platform for the men to see Escoffier. However, because of their height, Escoffier can easily see them.

Thinking quickly, Escoffier removes his hat and asks the woman who just received the money from the driver if he can help her manage the children onto the train. She gladly accepts, and the men in dark suits, searching for a solitary man in a topcoat and hat, pay no attention to the elderly man helping his grandchildren onto the train. As they board, the woman is thankful for the assistance.

"Thank you, kind sir. I was afraid we wouldn't make it on time."

Escoffier shuttles the group of children toward the first-class coach. The mother is noticeably upset.

"Sir. This is for the premier class. Our tickets are for third-class."

Escoffier smiles.

"My dear woman. I am offering you my private suite, which features an additional room for your children. I will take your seat in the 3rd-class coach."

The woman is confused and begins to protest.

"Madame. You will feel differently once the servant puts away your clothes and feeds your children while you relax next to a warm fire with a glass of wine."

The woman immediately moves the children toward the premier-class car, and once Escoffier speaks to the staff about the change in accommodations, he makes his way back to her coach seats. Since the seats were for the woman and her children, Escoffier had the entire row to himself. Once he departs, his mind drifts to the events of the last few days.

"Auguste, you are in it now. How could such seemingly random circumstances come together so?"

He turns to look out the window at the passing German landscape. He thinks of the narrow escape from von Harnack's men. However, he is confident that something nefarious is happening with the Kaiser's Society. His brow furrows, trying to imagine how and to whom he should convey this information, and then it hits him.

"Very shortly, there will be war, and France will likely be dragged into it."

Escoffier's mind races as he thinks of his two boys, one of whom is of enlistment age and would likely answer the call if asked. A parental fear creeps into his thoughts, sending a chill down his spine. His beloved Delphine has likely heard the news and is concerned. However, Escoffier feels more at ease, knowing that the driver would have informed Gaston of his departure, and in turn, Gaston would have contacted Delphine. Escoffier begins to feel the weight of his burden, and leaning back in his seat, he falls into another fitful sleep.

Chapter 5

War Has Begun

Carlton Hotel, London - 14 July 1914

After narrowly escaping Germany with his life, Escoffier now sits in his office at the Carlton Hotel kitchen. He reads the words he fears most on the paper's front page: **WAR HAS BEGUN!** He puts the paper down and recalls the conversation over breakfast, where his son Daniel proudly announced he would soon enlist in the military. However, this is only one of many worries on Escoffier's mind since returning from Germany.

In the three weeks since his return to the comfort of the Carlton Hotel, the usually calm and composed Escoffier has found no peace after learning about the science Correns shared with him in his lab. Now 69 years old, Escoffier increasingly struggles to bear the weight of this knowledge, and his demeanor is beginning to reveal the strain. His mind grapples with the unthinkable as he seeks solace in Correns's comment from the lab.

"I must continue working to discover countermeasures for the blight."

A sharp knock echoes on his office door. Escoffier's kitchen manager, Gaston, peeks in, extending only his head into the room as if any more of him would not be welcome.

"Chef, a man is at the reservation stand asking for you. However, he does not have an invitation. He claims you will recognize him. His name is Devereux."

Escoffier turns his head sharply. Gaston notices a dark cloud forming over Escoffier's demeanor.

"Chef, I will send him away. It is rude of him to impose on you."

As Gaston is about to pull his head back from the door, Escoffier calls after him to seat his guest.

"Gaston, it is a man I met while in Germany. Please let him know that I will be along shortly."

Gaston, taken aback, nods at Escoffier before closing the door. Escoffier rises from his desk, increasingly aware of the tremendous weight on his shoulders. He removes his chef's jacket and dons his formal day coat. He studies his aged face in a nearby mirror and wonders aloud.

"How is it, Auguste, that you are in such a mess?"

Arriving at the reservation stand, Escoffier sees the smug look of Devereux leaning on a silver-tipped cane.

Devereux extends his hand as he approaches, but Escoffier does not accept it. With a relaxed smile, Devereux begins speaking.

"Monsieur Escoffier. I was not certain if you would see me since our last encounter. I hope my French has improved since our last meeting."

Escoffier stands his ground and, without emotion, replies in kind.

"No, sir. It has not. But you must consider the company you are keeping these days."

Devereux's visage turns to stone as he gets to the point.

"Your conversation with Correns has caused great speculation with people in high places."

Escoffier's face is emotionless.

"Nothing could matter less to me than the speculation of the people you are speaking of."

Devereux stares back at Escoffier.

"Monsieur Escoffier. Let us not act as though we are unaware of the information Herr Correns shared. Let us stop this charade. There are dire consequences if we do not come to some agreement."

Escoffier stares at Devereux for a long, uncomfortable moment.

"Sir, perhaps it would be best, if not more efficient, that you simply get to the point of your not-so-veiled threat."

Devereux cast a look back at Escoffier.

"Monsieur Escoff..."

Escoffier raises a hand, interrupting him.

"Sir, this is my restaurant, and here I am called _Le_ Chef. From this moment on, assume that is what I wish to be called."

Devereux is taken aback, and his smile dissolves.

"You are right. You are a busy man, and the dinner hour is fast approaching. I'll get straight to the point. My employers believe Correns shared information of military significance with you. I have been asked to deliver this message to you on their behalf. If you were to disclose such knowledge to anyone, your life would be torn apart. You must consider dear Delphine and your strapping sons."

Escoffier's anger rises when his family is mentioned. He raises his voice so everyone in the room can hear.

"Sir, do you dare to stand here in _my_ restaurant and threaten my family? You would be wise not to underestimate me. Consider _your_ precious family in Normandy and your connection with our German enemy. I would argue that we both can cancel each other's threats. Wouldn't you?"

Devereux's smug smile returns.

"Very well, Chef. If this is how you want to play this out."

Devereux turns to leave and then stops, looking back at Escoffier.

"There's more happening than you realize. It would be wise to think about that, or things may not turn out well for you."

Escoffier turns away from Devereux.

"Gaston, have this man escorted from the premises and notify the staff that he and his family are never welcome here or at any of our restaurants."

Gaston is startled. Whoever this man is to Escoffier has now made himself unwelcome. His demeanor shifts, and he calls security to the reservation desk. Devereux regains his composure.

"Perhaps, Chef, when you have more time, we can find a moment to speak further. I would be distressed to know that your reputation is irrevocably damaged."

Over the years, Escoffier has dealt with many corrupt politicians and purveyors. When he begins chuckling at Devereux, it catches him off guard.

"Monsieur, I have dealt with men like you my entire life. I assure you, the damage you could do to me will pale compared to the havoc I will inflict upon you. Good day to you, sir!"

Escoffier turns and walks back to Gaston. He leans in and whispers.

"I want this man followed."

Gaston recovers and turns to Devereux.

"Monsieur, if you would be so kind as to follow me to the door."

Gaston and Devereux leave the restaurant as an inconspicuous messenger boy across the street looks up with interest. With a hand gesture from Gaston, the boy nods in agreement.

Devereux turns back to Gaston.

"Please inform the chef that I will return if his actions warrant it. Oh, and have that boy refrain from following me. He will only get himself into the kind of trouble from which his mother will never recover."

Devereux hands his card to Gaston, who now has an astonished look on his face.

"You can tell _Le_ Chef he can find me here."

Gaston accepts the card and looks at the company name embossed on the thick linen card—The Curtain Group, Berlin, Paris, London, Hong Kong, and New York. Gaston signals for the boy to stay and goes back to the restaurant, where a waiting Escoffier receives the card and tears it up. He lets out a deep sigh and looks up.

"Gaston, it's best not to worry about this. I've angered some powerful people. I will take a short leave from daily operations to reflect on my situation. You know where to reach me if anything arises. Please inform the kitchen that I expect nothing less than excellence during my absence. I trust operations to your capable hands."

Gaston stands at full attention.

"Yes, Chef!"

Escoffier's walk back to his office is even more difficult than when he left. He needs to devise a plan to deal with this.

Moments Later...

An angry Devereux, unhappy with the meeting's outcome with Escoffier, steps onto the street and hails his car. He scolds himself for allowing his temper to flare at the unyielding Escoffier. He looks around to ensure the young boy has followed his instructions. Devereux's trademark smug smile surfaces as he contemplates his next steps. One thing is clear: Auguste Escoffier will involve others before deciding how to proceed. Lost in thought, he strides into the street as his chauffeur arrives, driving a jet-black 1912 Lorraine-Dietrich 12 HP Torpedo. The driver quickly gets out and opens the door for Devereux.

"I apologize for the delay, Monsieur Devereux. There is an increasing number of automobiles in London each day. I will ensure that this does not happen again."

Devereux responds without looking at the driver. He points his cane towards where the boy is standing.

"Do you see the young boy standing there?"

The driver squints.

"Yes, sir. I do."

Devereux begins pulling on his gloves and stowing his silver-tipped cane inside the car's cabin.

"See to it that he is beaten to death and left on the steps of Nelson's column in Trafalgar Square by tomorrow. And if you are late again picking me up, I will ensure that your boy is also found there."

The driver is horrified and begins to stammer. In the next moment, he is resigned to do as commanded.

"It will be done."

The drive back to Devereux's office is across the Thames River. As he nears his office, Devereux starts to breathe easier. He reflects on his native Normandy, where life is less hectic than in bustling London. He has always favored the open outdoors of his seaside home over any other place. He looks forward to returning as soon as the Escoffier issue is resolved. Devereux expresses his thoughts out loud.

"Monsieur Escoffier. You will either be put under the yoke, or you will be put in the ground."

Upon hearing Devereux's words, his driver feels a deep despair. He must find a way out of this trouble. But for now, he must follow orders. He swallows hard, thinking of his son and what the bastard Devereux would do if he were to betray him.

Nelson's Column, Trafalgar Square, London - Next Morning

Early the next day, a man walking towards the Carlton hotel notices a young boy lying at the base of Nelson's Column.

"You there! Street urchin! You cannot sleep here. Go now before I call a Bobbie!"

As he approaches, he notices blood around the boy's lifeless body and recognizes him as a messenger for the Carlton hotel. Moments later, shouts ring out, and the whistle-blowing from the Bobbies can be heard.

A few moments later, Gaston arrives early, as usual, for his shift and is immediately informed that the boy's body has been discovered. Realizing the gravity of the situation, Gaston sends a telegraph to Escoffier.

```
Georges Escoffier [stop]

Our young messenger was found

dead. [stop]
```

Please advise [stop]

    Miles away in the English countryside of Birmingham, Auguste Escoffier lets the telegram fall to the floor. He bows his head and makes a solemn promise.

    "Devereux, you will not survive this."

Chapter 6

Escoffier's Revenge

The Town of Berkswell, England - 4 Days Later

Escoffier sits dining at a small café in the town of Berkswell just outside Birmingham. It is a cozy, family-owned establishment he frequents when meeting produce purveyors who supply his kitchen at the Carlton Hotel. Inspired by the many culinary influences from such places, Escoffier appreciates their use of fresh ingredients prepared from recipes passed down through generations. His thoughts are interrupted as a close friend, Paulo, spots Escoffier in the café and greets him at his table.

"Auguste Escoffier, it's such a pleasure. I did not receive notice that you were coming. I will have strong words with Gaston for his oversight."

Escoffier rises, and the two exchange a hearty handshake. Escoffier's sour demeanor quickly shifts upon seeing his good friend.

"My dear friend, how are your lovely wife and children? Good, I suspect."

Paulo's smile becomes even brighter.

"She is, and they are...and we also expect another in the spring."

Escoffier extends his hand in a firm handshake and laughs.

"Congratulations, my friend. At this rate, your family will soon make up more than half of Berkswell's population!"

They both laugh heartily as Escoffier offers Paulo a seat. The two men engage in small talk while Escoffier, knowing it's part of Paulo's morning routine. Paulo is not fooled.

"My friend, it is not by chance that you are here."

Escoffier's face turns sour.

"Yes, my friend. It is true. I have been waiting for you. There is much to talk about. I hope you will play along and ensure everyone here sees this as a chance meeting."

Escoffier leans in closer and whispers.

"Please, if you would help me with this ruse and invite me to your farm to inspect the produce, I promise to tell you about my troubles."

Without hesitation, Paulo rises from his seat.

"Monsieur Escoffier, I insist you come to my farm to look at this season's produce. We have two new varieties of squash and onions that I believe would be perfect for your fine restaurant. Let us go."

Escoffier smiles and puts on his jacket, noticing the smiles from others in the café regarding the two men conducting business. The horse-drawn wagon takes about thirty minutes to reach the farm. Once Arthur brings the horse to a stop, Escoffier climbs down and stretches his back.

"My friend. You must invest in an automobile. This transportation is killing my back."

Paulo smiles, and they walk into a field of onions and mustard plants. Escoffier pulls up a mustard plant and smells it in his hands.

"You are a clever businessman, Paulo. This mustard gives your onions their unique flavor and makes my soups a standout in all the kitchens of England."

Paulo's face is set in stone, and he stops walking.

"My friend. I believe you have something to tell me. But before you do, allow me to guess. Does it not have something to do with a man named Devereux?"

The surprise on Escoffier's face does not affect Paulo.

"Paulo, how is it that you know this?"

"My friend, it's the look in your eyes. The Devereux family came to Berkswell 50 years ago. If you look at the horizon in any direction, you'll see properties the Devereux family still owns. Many people in the towns surrounding Birmingham depend on them for their livelihood. Many more attribute their poverty to them, and the looks on their faces now mirror yours."

Paulo spits on the ground.

"Devereux harbors great malice in his heart. If you're coming to see me outside of our usual business, it must concern him and his wretched alliance with Germany. How can I assist you?"

Escoffier pauses to gather his thoughts and bends down to replant the mustard in the onion field. He stands up and brushes the dirt from his hands.

"I have made a powerful and ruthless enemy in Devereux. Since encountering him on a recent trip to Berlin, I have felt the eyes of many following my every move. Recently, I have learned that Devereux has killed a young boy in my employ and left his body at Nelson's Column, beaten to death."

Escoffier has difficulty continuing. Paulo collects his thoughts as the two men look at and beyond each other.

"Auguste, I already know of the boy."

Escoffier swivels his head toward his friend.

"He is the nephew of a close friend here in Berkswell. The boy is just one of many cases like the one you describe."

Paulo diverts his eyes, where tears form, and continues talking.

"Our little village has always been a quiet and charming place, but now it is gripped by fear, always anticipating the next catastrophic event. It feels as if we are cursed by the Devereux family."

Escoffier waits until Paulo turns back to him.

"My friend, I see no way to resolve this other than to ensure Devereux finds a quiet resting place beneath the ground. However, I am unsure how to make that happen. I am not a coward, but I fear for those who could be harmed around me."

Paulo considers Escoffier's words for quite some time.

"You are a good man, Auguste. If this causes you to worry, let us stop it here."

Paulo looks off in the direction of Birmingham.

"There is a man here who has been affected more by the Devereux family than anyone else. He has worked for my family for 30 years, and the boy you spoke of who was killed is his sister's son. He is connected to a local group of thugs out of Birmingham. They call themselves the Peaky Blinders, and I am certain he will answer the call when the time comes for action. However, it will require that he first be released from prison."

Escoffier's face brightens at Paulo's words.

"My friend, I believe I can make that happen. I still know a few people in high places. However, I have some business to take care of before we proceed. When I'm ready, I will send you a cable requesting that you prepare an order for your famous mustard onions. Your response with a delivery date will let me know when the task is to be done."

Paulo cast a wicked smile at Escoffier.

"I believe you will know it is done before I do."

The two men shake hands as Paulo's two children rush out of the house and into their father's open arms. Moments later, Paulo's pregnant wife comes into view, holding a baby in her arms. Paulo calls out to her jokingly.

"My dear. We have a guest for dinner! Bring out the worst wine in the cellar!"

By late evening, Escoffier had returned to his room at a local inn. His heart and stomach were full from the hospitality and love of Pailo and his family, which included more wine than he had intended to drink. Escoffier climbs down from the buckboard and shakes his friend's hand, using a louder voice than usual for this time of night.

"Thank you again for the inspection of the produce. I am looking forward to the delivery."

Paulo smiles and winks in response.

"You are always welcome here, my dear friend. Goodnight, Auguste."

As Paulo drops Escoffier off at his hotel, he notices two men standing across the street. They appear to be enjoying a late evening smoke. The scent of pipe tobacco is strong, and he sees the men looking directly at him. Escoffier tips his hat in their direction to acknowledge them, but neither of the men returns the gesture. Escoffier is certain they are working for Devereux and the Curtain Group.

Escoffier enters the hotel just as the shorter of the two men walks down the street to find a position where he can observe the back door. Looking at the front of the hotel, the taller man waits to see which room window is lit. It takes longer than he expects.

"Hurry up, old man. I need to see your room."

Moments later, a lamp lights up a room just off the main floor. The taller man pulls out a notebook and his pocket watch to record the details of the evening. He takes a long draw from his pipe, then, lifting his leg behind him, taps the pipe bowl against his boot heel to clear out the ashes. As he places the pipe into his jacket, he reveals a metal badge pinned to his vest, which he earned after being released from prison by his new employer, The Curtain Group.

Curtain Group Headquarters - Berlin-Dahlem, Germany

Klaus Müller's son, Heinrich, looks up from his desk as his secretary enters the office.

"Sir. I've been reading Devereux's reports. Escoffier is still under surveillance, is he not?"

Hienrich's demeanor changes, welcoming the initiative of the young man.

"He is. Devereux is developing an asset at the Carlton to keep a closer eye on him. His other assets followed Escoffier to Caen yesterday. He is purchasing produce."

His secretary takes a moment to think.

"Isn't it odd that Escoffier would inspect the produce himself?"

Hienrich's curiosity is piqued. His secretary continues.

"It is also a strange coincidence that the Devereux family has significant land holdings in Berkswell."

Heinrich rises from his desk.

"Remind me again who Escoffier was meeting with?"

His secretary's response is immediate.

"A local farmer named Paulo. Devereux's assets noted that they appear to be long-time friends."

There is a momentary pause as Heinrich absorbs the new information.

"Inform Devereux to have those assets remain in Berkswell and keep track of Paulo."

Uncertain if he should disagree with his boss, Heinrich's secretary offers another option.

"Sir. The investigators are not locals. It will not take long before they are noticed."

Heinrich, appreciating the initiative, alters the plan.

"Have the assets begin looking for property to purchase in Berkswell. This should give them at least a week before anyone takes an interest.

Later that day, a telegram was sent from Devereux to his field agents. It reads:

```
Stay in Caen [stop]

Begin inquiring about

properties to purchase [stop]

Focus on Escoffier's supplier,

Paulo [stop]

Report the unusual [stop]
```

Winson Green Prison - Birmingham, London - Two Weeks Later.

"Arthur, you have a guest."

The prison guard's condescending remark echoes through the narrow, dank hallway leading to the ancient cells of the Winson Green prison. Arthur remains motionless on his cot, pretending to be asleep. He has already anticipated his guest. His friend, Paulo, bribed a friendly guard to deliver the message earlier in the week.

"My friend, the charges you are convicted of will soon be dropped.

It is time to settle your score."

Arthur rises and faces the wall as the guard opens the gate to his cell. Shakling his wrists, he leads him down the hall to the only room near the cells. Once seated, the guard steps back as Paulo enters the room, holding a document. The two men exchange greetings, and before Arthur can sit down, Paulo raises the document toward the guard.

"This man has been released into my custody. He will be on work furlough at my farm for the remainder of his sentence. You can see that the prefect and the warden have signed the release."

The guard takes the letter, reads it, and returns it to Paulo. He then approaches Arthur and unlocks his shackles.

"I will miss your fighting in the yard. I made quite a bit of money betting on you."

Arthur looks at Paulo and smiles while rubbing his wrists. Arthur approaches to shake Arthur's hand, but Arthur pulls him in for a lung-crushing hug. Arthur's sarcasm doesn't go unnoticed by Paulo.

"My friend. What took you so long?"

Paulo smiles, and the men depart the prison. Arthur looks back as they exit the door and spits on the ground.

"Good riddance to this shit hole."

On their journey back to Paulo's farm, Arthur learns about the plan to deal with Devereux. Two days later, Escoffier receives a telegram from Paulo.

```
Escoffier [Stop]

Onions are harvested and on their

way to London. [Stop]

Paulo [Stop}
```

St. James Area - Westminster, London - The Next Week

After leaving Winson Green Prison for London, Arthur sits at the bar of a small restaurant on Conventry Street, nursing a warm beer and a stale sandwich of smoked pork. Having arrived 2 days earlier, Arthur spent his first day settling into his apartment, which is located above a small shop near Devereux's hotel in London.

Arthur looks at himself in the mirror behind the bar. He has lost weight in prison, which has slimmed his face and made his frame appear taller. Having never shaved during his incarceration, he trimmed his beard to make it more presentable for his stay in the city. As he gazes into the mirror, he can hardly recognize himself.

Arthur's cousin arranged a job for him at a local butcher shop in Bull Ring Market near his apartment, allowing him to walk to and from work daily. Arthur's knowledge of knives made the position perfect because he could easily cut a man's throat just as quickly as he could slice the rump of a cow or pig. His job also had the added benefit of allowing him to transport his cutlery in a pouch. Arthur takes another drink of beer and begins contemplating his strategy.

"Devereux is a man who pays attention to details. He will not be easily caught off guard. It will require that I blend into the routine he sees daily near his apartment."

After another five days of his routine, Arthur gets his first view of Devereux as he arrives in a chauffeured car at his apartment. Arthur notices fear in the driver's eyes as he opens the door for the waiting Devereux. He makes a mental note to investigate the man further and find a way to leverage him.

As Devereux exits the car, he gives his driver some instructions. With his situational awareness alert, he instinctively turns his head toward the bar where Arthur stands facing the mirror behind the restaurant's bar. He doesn't flinch or look away from the mirror and begins joking with the bartender with an air of comfort and belonging. Devereux looks away, his situational awareness settling into calm, and thinks to himself.

"Yes, someone new to the block, but a non-threat."

Finishing his drink, Arthur slings his satchel over his shoulder and trudges down the street, resembling a man heading to another day at work. He decides to follow the driver after he drops off Devereux later in the day. As he walks to work, he observes the number of automobiles on the road. Typically, it would not be feasible to follow a car on foot. However, automobile speed was limited due to the amount of horse traffic still in use, especially in the bustling area of Bull Ring. If necessary, Arthur thinks,

"I can easily follow his automobile on foot."

Later that day, Devereux returns to his hotel while the driver takes the car back to a nearby garage that was rented along with the office. After cleaning the car, the driver locks the door before walking toward the Chinese Quarter, where his apartment is. Arthur correctly reasoned that Devereux would want the man nearby in an emergency. As a sign of good fortune, the garage was also in the same direction as Bull Market, where Arthur works.

As expected, the driver made it a habit to stop at a local bar to drink away his fear and contempt for his employer. A short time later, Arthur enters the establishment, sits at the bar beside the driver, and orders a beer. After a while, Arthur started engaging the driver in conversation. The driver was pleased to talk to someone other than Devereux, and Arthur capitalized on that sentiment.

"You have no idea, sir, how much pressure comes with being a chauffeur. My boss is ruthless to the brink of insanity."

Arthur looks at the driver and shrugs.

"Why not simply quit? There must be plenty of jobs around here. If what you say is true, then your boss is worse than most hardened criminals."

The driver takes a long sip from his pint of beer.

"I have no choice. He would harm my family if I were to quit."

Driven by an immense disdain for Devereux, Arthur turns to the driver with a serious look.

"I can see the fear and contempt in your eyes, my friend. You need to be careful. If your boss were to discover how you feel, he won't hesitate to kill you for any number of reasons. I know this because he has done the same to my family."

The driver glances up, struggling to understand what Arthur is saying. Then it hits him, and his hands start to shake visibly.

"Sir, there's nothing I can do. He has threatened to kill my family in front of me, so I have to do whatever he asks."

Arthur pauses and looks squarely into the driver's eyes.

"Men like Devereux have enemies, too. Some are more ruthless than he is. I am one such person, and I can assure you that Devereux will be dead by the end of the week, even if it means I die with him. Only then can our families be safe."

The driver examines Arthur from head to toe.

"What is it that you want from me?"

Arthur looks deeply into the eyes of the driver.

"I want you to stop the car on Haymarket and turn off the engine."

Arthur sees fear in the driver's eyes and understands he wouldn't willingly agree to Arthur's plan. After all, Devereux is the devil the driver knows, while Arthur is not. He adjusts his approach.

"My friend, I can see in your eyes that you are not up for the task I've asked of you. I have misjudged you."

The driver begins to relax, and Arthur offers him his beer.

"You need this more than I do."

The driver grabs the pint and gulps down a substantial amount of it. What he didn't notice was Arthur adding a small amount of opium powder to his beer before handing it to the driver.

"Thank you, sir, but I have to go. Please don't worry. I won't mention this to my employer. You have my word on that."

The driver starts to rise, and his legs grow wobbly. Arthur catches him before he falls. The bartender glances over at the driver.

"Looks like he has had enough."

Arthur takes the driver by the arm and helps him out the door. By then, Arthur is nearly carrying his total weight.

"Why am I feeling so lightheaded?"

The driver's words are slurring. Arthur replies.

"I have drugged you. You will sleep for quite some time. Long enough, I believe, for me to finish the job I came here to do. After that, you will have nothing more to worry about."

Arthur arrives at his apartment and places the driver on his bed, binding his arms and legs. Just as Arthur is about to leave, he takes a scarf from his pocket and gags the driver in case he wakes up sooner than expected.

Early The Next Morning - Arthur's Apartment

Arthur, having slept on the sofa, rinses his face and checks on the driver, who is still unconscious from the opium. He takes a moment to examine the driver's bindings. Satisfied, Arthur looks down at the driver, who is sleeping peacefully.

"I do not envy the headache you will have when you awake."

Grabbing a pair of gloves, his butcher's coat, and the knife satchel, Arthur departs the apartment as though he is once again heading to work. Except today, he has scheduled a detour.

Devereux is staying at a hotel within a few blocks of his office. There is no need to have a car pick him up other than to make him appear important. Arthur is grateful for Devereux's ego and reflects on it to himself.

"Your self-importance, Devereux, will be the end of you."

After days of observing Devereux's routine, Arthur learns his departure schedule. He approaches the garage and unlocks the large barn doors using the driver's keys. Once inside, he starts the car and puts on the driver's hat to create the illusion that he is a chauffeur. He would go unnoticed by anyone other than Devereux.

Pulling out his pocket watch, Arthur notices he has about ten minutes before Devereux leaves the hotel. He parks the car at the hotel entrance, takes a few pounds from his pocket, and, noticing a nearby man who has fallen on hard times, hands him some money. The man's build and hair color resemble Devereux's driver. He gladly accepts Arthur's generosity while leaning against the car, just as the driver has done daily since Arthur observed him. After looking over the man, Arthur is sure it will be enough, thinking:

"By the time Devereux figures it out, my knife will be buried in his back."

Arthur takes a thin, filleting knife from his pouch and slips into the shadows of the building's facade, well out of Devereux's peripheral vision. He has taken particular care in selecting this blade and affirms his choice.

"The filet knife is small and exceptionally sharp; its low-angle edge can slice through even the toughest fish skin and sinew, and once removed, its thin blade will limit blood loss."

Arthur watches the clock above the bank across the street. In the reflections from the bank's windows, he sees Devereux looking out from his hotel room at what he believes is his waiting driver leaning against his car. Devereux puts on his jacket, and with his silver-tipped cane in hand, he heads to the lobby.

Arthur has been counting down the seconds until Devereux exits the building. When the circular door starts to spin, Arthur prepares himself as the departing Devereux heads straight for his car. Arthur waits for Devereux's situational awareness to become confused by the number of out-of-place elements.

- The driver never raises his head.
- The driver's pants and shoes are shabby, and those of a street urchin.
- The car door is already open.

When fed into Devereux's brain, these small pieces of information cause confusion and an ever-so-slight hesitation, providing more than enough time for Arthur to complete his task.

Moving quickly from the shadows, Arthur times his attack just as Devereux realizes his situational awareness has changed. Devereux, now alarmed, has lost valuable time, and enough so that Arthur has already lodged the fillet knife deep inside Devereux's lower vertebrae, severing the nerve bundle to his lower body.

Devereux stumbles forward as Arthur catches him and tosses him into the car, shutting the door behind him. Arthur glances around, quickly realizing that no one has taken an interest in his actions. He gives the vagrant extra money, retrieves the driver's hat, starts the car, and slowly drives away into the thick London traffic.

From the back seat, Devereux cannot feel anything below his waist, but his arms, lungs, heart, brain, and mouth are still working, and his words are filled with venom.

"I thought I saw you across the street the other day. You did well to hide in plain sight. I should have had you killed in prison."

Looking straight ahead, Arthur gives Devereux a moment of silence to consider his thoughts.

"Devereux, you should never have killed my nephew. Leaving his body at Nelson's Column was particularly sadistic, even for you."

Devereux is beginning to feel his life draining from his body. Arthur continues.

"And now that I think about it, you shouldn't have stolen our family's land to build your estate or wrongfully imprison me. I understand why you would pay criminals to kill me in prison, knowing this day would come if I ever got free."

Arthur angles his head slightly and chuckles a merciless laugh.

"You would now be enjoying a leisurely drive with all your limbs functioning properly if just one thought had crossed your evil mind."

Arthur turns to lock eyes with Devereux.

"The devil always comes to collect."

Devereux is starting to feel the impact of blood loss. Arthur pauses for a moment to deliver the final mental blow.

"And if you're wondering where we're going, wait no further. We're headed to Trafalgar Square, to the very column where you had my nephew's body dropped. Waiting there is the boy's mother and the rest of the family. I believe they want to finish the job I started."

Devereux, now resigned to his fate, is filled with fear and begins to plead for his life. Arthur remains unresponsive. As he enters Trafalgar Square, Arthur pulls up to the column and drags Devereux's limp body to the base, propping him up to see the faces of the people who will end his wretched life. Even the Bobbies stand aside while their revenge is delivered.

The following day, an article is printed in the London Journal simply saying. **"Justice Is Served."** Listing the many crimes of an unidentified man, including his brutal death sentence. Those involved in the man's death could not be identified.

Carlton Hotel - The Next Day

Gaston places the newspaper on Escoffier's desk, featuring the headline "Justice Is Served." It takes Escoffier a few days to read the article, and according to comments from people who know him, Escoffier never speaks of Devereux again.

Curtain Group, London Branch - Two Days Later

An administrator removes a folder with Devereux's name and stamps the letters "K.I.A." (Killed In Action) on it. She then sets the folder aside and calls the Chief of Station.

"Sir, this is Administrator Levin. We have learned that our asset, Devereux, has been killed in Birmingham. I thought you should be notified immediately, seeing that his family is on the Board of Directors for the Kaiser Wilhelm Society."

The Chief of Station takes a moment to allow the moment to pass.

"You were right to call me. This is unsettling. What do we know?"

The administrator already had his notes in front of him.

"Sir, the asset recently met with Escoffier about the Correns' leak. It seems he wanted to make a point of his threat and had a messenger boy at the Carlton Hotel killed and left his body at the base of Nelson's Column."

He pauses, allowing the Chief of Station to think. A long moment passes.

"Do we know who killed him?"

"Yes, sir. Arthur Landy. The messenger boy was his nephew. Records show that he was recently furloughed to work on a farm of a former employer outside Birmingham. He never showed up for work."

Again, the Administrator pauses.

"Whose farm was he furloughed to?"

"A man named Paulo Trilch. A Greek immigrant. He alerted the local prison to Arthur's failure to report. However, we found that Paulo's farm provides produce for the Carlton."

"So Escoffier is connected to Devereux's murder."

The Administrator pauses uncharacteristically. The Chief of Station notices.

"Is there more to this?"

"Sir, Arthur Landy is a Peaky Blinder."

The Chief of Station sits back in his chair and contemplates the revelation. The Curtain Group has had run-ins with the Blinders, and it didn't turn out well for the Curtain Group. He considers his options and finds an acceptable solution. If Devereux's family believes it was the Peaky Blinders who killed their son, they will use their political power to eliminate them. With the Blinders' busy fighting the Devereauxs, the Curtain Group could gain a greater foothold in Birmingham.

"I need you to remove all information from the file concerning Escoffier and the farmer Paulo."

The Administrator is puzzled.

"Sir?"

"You have your orders. I will personally make the call to the Devereaux family. If asked..."

The Administrator cuts in.

"This conversation never happened, sir."

"Good man."

"And the other two assets in Berkswell?"

"When they are found by local police with their throats cut, we can blame it on the Blinders."

"Understood, sir."

Chapter 7

Ernest Miller Hemingway

Villa Fernand - Monte Carlo, Principality of Monaco

It has been a decade since Escoffier learned of the plan to weaponize Correns' discovery. At that time, the "War to End All Wars" had come and gone, taking Escoffier's eldest son, Daniel, in its wake. Since learning of Correns' discovery, Escoffier has been under around-the-clock surveillance by the Curtain Group. Even after he retired from the Carlton and moved to Monte-Carlo, he could still feel the weight of their watchful eyes. There is a knock at his study door. The day servant, Juli, peeks her head into the room.

"Sir. Your visitor has arrived."

"Thank you Juli. Show him to the receiving room."

"Very Good, sir."

Escoffier takes a moment to rethink his plan.

"Perhaps my guest can help me ease the burden."

Rising from his desk, he reaches for the silver-tipped cane once owned by F. Devereux—the one Arthur gave to him many years ago when justice needed to be served. He thinks back to his last conversation with Arthur.

"It is only right, Monsieur Escoffier, that you have Devereux's cane. If for no other reason than as a reminder of the danger surrounding you. For me, it serves only as a reminder of my nephew's death."

Arthur's words echo in his memory as tears well up in Escoffier's eyes. He brushes them away with the back of his hand. There was a moment, after the Kaiser abdicated his throne following the loss of World War I, when Escoffier thought the Exodus Seed project was lost for good. However, his hope was in vain. He says the words that he has been dreaming of for years.

"It is time to find someone who can assist me in carrying the weight of this secret before it perishes with me."

Not long after, Escoffier finds someone he believes can share the load. The man is Ernest Miller Hemingway, an American WWI veteran who is a war correspondent and writer in Paris.

As Escoffier enters the receiving room, a tall man stands looking through the volumes of books on the far wall. He turns immediately and extends his hand.

"Monsieur Escoffier. It is an honor to meet you."

Escoffier accepts his hand and offers the man a seat near the window.

"The pleasure is mine, Monsieur Fitzgerald. May I get you something to drink?"

"Yes, that would be nice. And please call me Scott."

Escoffier hands him the drink, and the two settle into their chairs. After a few minutes of idle talking, Fitzgerald changes the conversation.

"August, I must admit that I am in the dark about why you asked to meet."

Escoffier casts him a wry smile.

"Scott. I understand you are friends with Ernest Hemingway. I wish to meet him."

Cafe Deux Magots - Paris, France - 2 Days Later

"Ernest, I can see that you are in the same foul mood I left you in yesterday."

It is midday in the Saint Germain des Prés. As part of his ritual, Hemingway attempts to write while his friend, F. Scott Fitzgerald, has other plans for him. He is seated outside the Café Les Deux Magots, which has been home to literary and artistic greats of the time. The café's Art Deco interiors, adorned with mahogany and velvet, create an atmosphere that feels both luxurious and intimate. Inside, the statues of two Chinese "mandarins" (magicians) harken to the shop's origins as a silk store.

F. Scott Fitzgerald stands by the café table where Ernest Hemingway writes in his journal. Hemingway glances up just long enough to give a nasty glare to his friend and literary rival, including the female companion he has brought along.

"Scott, you know better than anyone that the creative process is personal and not intended to be shared. Perhaps you and your *friend* can find someone else to bother."

"Be careful, Ernest, you are in the presence of a lady. I present the fair Sophia-Claire of the family Mormant of Marseille."

Hemingway is dumbfounded and rises from his chair, casting a foul gaze at Fitzgerald. He takes Sohia's hand and kisses it lightly.

"Mademoiselle Sophie, I apologize for my mood. Even I know of your family, as do most in Paris."

Ernest continues holding her hand, making it clear he is smitten by her beauty. Sophia is blessed with striking auburn hair and a complexion that can only be described as spun ivory. Fitzgerald clears his throat to break the spell she has on Hemingway. Hemingway backs away to the table, looks at Fitzgerald, and then addresses Sophia.

"Please explain how such a creature as you has come into the company of the two most disreputable men in Paris?"

Fitzgerald is insulted, yet Sohia cannot help but laugh. Fitzgerald recovers.

"Ernest. I have been asked to invite you and your wife, Hadley, to Monte Carlo. There is someone who wishes to meet you."

Hemingway sits back in his chair just as the server delivers his order. Sophia's demeanor changes when the words "your wife" are used.

"Monsieur Hemingway. Your favorite. Pommes l'huile. Bon appétit."

Fitzgerald continues to press Hemingway.

"I am certain you will want to meet him, Ernest."

Hemingway begins eating without answering Fitzgerald.

"Fine. I will inform Monsieur Escoffier, "The King of Chefs," that you are not interested in meeting him or joining him for food and drink at the Monte Carlo Casino."

Hemingway jerks his head at the mention of the famed chef. Fitzgerald chooses to tease his friend and fellow writer.

"Oh, so you have heard of the most celebrated chef in Europe?"

Changing the subject, Hemingway takes a bite of the sausage and points his knife toward the Eiffel Tower.

"Scott, have you and the fair Sophia visited the sites of Paris?"

Sophia's face brightens up. Hemingway notices. Fitzgerald gets the conversation back on track.

"Stop trying to change the subject, Ernest."

"Yes. Who hasn't heard of him? He is in the papers nearly every month."

Seeing the sour look on Fitzgerald's face, Hemingway abruptly stops and puts down his cutlery.

"OK, Scott. Why exactly does Escoffier wish to meet with me *and* Hadley?"

Fitzgerald rolls his eyes.

"Ernest. He only wishes to speak to you. I assumed you'd want Hadley to come along with you."

"That doesn't explain why Escoffier wants to meet me."

Fitzgerald's frustration is getting the better of him.

"It isn't enough that the most celebrated chef of our generation is interested in meeting you?"

Hemingway puts his knife down and sits back in his chair, staring at Fitzgerald, waiting for him to continue.

"Ernest. He didn't tell me. He only knows that you and I are friends and asked me to give you the invitation. This is how people in society meet. They use an intermediary."

Hemingway is taken aback by Fitz's comment.

"You think of me as your friend?"

"I do. I also think you are a better writer than I.

Hemingway doesn't know how to respond to Fitzgerald's statement. So he retreats.

"Socializing is your thing, Scott. So, if you both don't mind, I'd like to finish the writing you find more interesting than your own."

Undaunted, Fitzgerald advances.

"Ernest, at the very least, this meeting will grant you access to individuals with wealth—people who support the arts. I know you play the role of the starving artist, but surely, you take it too far. You have talent, and Sylvia would agree you shouldn't thumb your nose at this."

Hemingway reflects on Sylvia Beach, the owner of Shakespeare & Co., a bookstore where he began his career, and someone he deeply admires.

"Despite Sylvia's thoughts, most people in those circles consider my work banal."

The moment goes stale as each has said their piece. Hemingway considers Fitzgerald's compliment.

"Fitz. I appreciate your words. However, I feel there is more to this request than you say."

Changing tactics, Fitzgerald uses brute honesty.

"Ernest, you are correct, there is more. I gave Escoffier my word that you would be there. If you don't come, my reputation will be harmed."

Hemingway sits back in his chair. Fitzgerald squares off with Hemingway and hands him an envelope containing the invitation. Hemingway accepts it.

"Sorry, Scott, I can't make any guarantees."

Hemingway notices a look of disappointment on Sophia's face and decides to change his mind. He rises as does the pace of Sophia's heart. She realizes at that moment she is in love with Hemingway.

"I will come, Scott. I owe you that and much more."

Noticing Sophia's look of anticipation, Fitzgerald gives Hemingway a wry smile.

"And not to worry, Ernest, the food and drinks at this party will come without cost."

Fitzgerald takes Sophia's arm, and the two walk away as Hemingway ponders whether more is happening than it appears. At the very least, he is certain he will see Sophia again, and it improves his mood.

The Casino de Monte-Carlo, Principale de Monaco -

The Following Week

Georges Auguste Escoffier preferred to walk the 800 meters from his Villa to the Casino de Monte-Carlo. However, at 74 years of age, those days are past him. Relaxing in the comfort of the horse-drawn carriage, Escoffier looks out at the tree-lined promenade leading up to the steps of the famed Casino de Monte-Carlo and next to it, the Hotel du Paris. The beautiful summer afternoon is lost to him as he considers the nature of his lunch with Hemingway.

As a man of his word, Fitzgerald confirmed that Hemingway would be there with his wife, Hadley. Directly after, Escoffier contacted the Manager of Hotel du Paris and paid for their lodgings along with a credit at the famed Casino de Monte-Carlo. Rarely a man who would flaunt his celebrity, Escoffier uses it to gain access to the hotel, which is usually booked through the summer months. As the carriage approaches the hotel, he sees Fitzgerald standing there with a ravishing, auburn-haired woman on his arm as the carriage arrives in front of the hotel. A crease of worry finds Escoffier's face as he sees no one else standing with him.

As he exits the carriage, Fitzgerald and Escoffier shake hands. Fitzgerald turns to Sophia.

"Good day, Monsieur Escoffier. May I present Sophia Mormant of the Family Mormant of Marseille?"

Escoffier takes her gloved hand and lightly kisses it.

"Mademoiselle Mormant. It is a divine pleasure to meet such a beautiful creature. You make an old man's heart long for younger days."

Sophia blushes as Escoffier begins looking around. Fitzgerald takes the queue.

"Monsieur Escoffier. It appears that our other guests are still in their room."

In that moment, Hemingway and Hadley come through the hotel's spinning door. Hemingway sees Sophia, and his heart jumps. Hadley notices his reaction and makes a point to stand between him and Sophia. Hemingway extends his hand to Escoffier.

"Monsieur Esccofier, I presume. I am Ernest Hemingway, and this is my wife, Hadley."

The two men shake hands, and Escoffier kisses Hadley's hand. Fitzgerald takes a stab at Hemingway.

"Late as usual, Ernest."

Fitzgerald walks up to Hadley and takes her hand.

"You must be the lovely Hadley I have heard so much about. F. Scott Fitzgerald, madame. At your service. May I present Sophia Mormant? I am acting as her chaperone while she is staying in Paris."

As the group enters the hotel, Sophia tries to steal a look at Hemingway, but Hadley's sharp and angry gaze catches her. Seeing the venom in Hadley's eyes, Escoffier quickly addresses Fitzgerald.

"Monseur Hemingway and I have much to talk about. I have taken the liberty of setting up a luncheon for you and the ladies in the private dining room of this hotel. I understand it has a spectacular view of the Mediterranean."

Taking the two ladies' arms, Fitzgerald turns to Hemingway.

"Ernest. You will not be missed."

As the remaining group is shown to the private dining room, Escoffier leads Hemingway through the Bar Americaine to the far end of the terrace. There, they find a table set for two and a server standing at attention in formal black-and-white attire. Escoffier smiles at the precision of the table and the staff. Hemingway's look is one of discomfort.

"Monseur Escoffier. You have me at a disadvantage."

Escoffier softens the moment.

"Please call me Auguste, and may I call you Ernest?"

Hemingway nods as the servers pull out the chairs for the two men and take their drink order. Hemingway orders first.

"I'll have a Rum St. James."

The server bows. However, before he can ask for Escoffier's preference, he responds.

"Make that two."

"Excellent, sir."

The server retreats through a side door leading to the bar and kitchen. After a short pause, Hemingway begins speaking.

"August, I must admit that I am overwhelmed by the effort you have put into setting up this meeting."

Escoffier smiles through his thick beard and mustache.

"You are Ernest Hemingway—a veteran of WWI, a noteworthy war correspondent, and, from what I've heard from Sylvia Beach, a remarkable writer. However, in truth, I have not read any of your work."

It is then that the two men are interrupted by the returning server carrying a tray of drinks. They both raise their glasses, and Escoffier makes a toast.

"To our respective health and well-being."

Hemingway reflects on the peculiar word choice in Escoffier's toast. He quickly realizes that something more is transpiring, and true to his character, Hemingway gets straight to the point.

"Monsieur Escoffier, while I appreciate your effort in arranging this meeting, I must express my discomfort at sitting here while you have something on your mind."

Escoffer smiles.

"Perhaps, before we get to that, we can enjoy this meal and get to know each other. What say you?"

Hemingway relaxes, sits back in his chair, and smiles. The two men begin their meal by discussing their histories, wishes, desires, and dreams. They talk about politics and war, as well as Europe and America. It takes nearly two hours for them to finish dining together. Hemingway has never consumed so much food or alcohol at once. Yet, he feels neither drunk nor full. Escoffier sees the curious expression on Hemingway's face.

"Ernest, I've spent my life perfecting the art of cuisine, and I will likely leave this existence protecting that which I have created."

Hemingway smiles.

"I think you are trying to tell me something, Auguste. Please, do not mince your words."

Escoffier smiles at the pun and gazes intently at Hemingway. He dabs the corners of his mouth, wiping away crumbs that stubbornly cling to his beard.

"Very well, Ernest. Much of what we perceive in this life is not as it appears. Take me as an example. I am a man of means, well-mannered, and capable. Yet, I am frail and prone to restless sleep filled with troubling dreams. I am racing toward the end of my days, and very soon, I will no longer be here to perform my magic in the kitchen. However, before my time runs out, I must leave something behind: a book that will establish a culinary legacy for others to follow. But I fear even that will not suffice."

Escoffier pauses to collect his thoughts.

"After careful consideration and research, your name has emerged as a person of honor, sharp wit, and a keen awareness of his surroundings. You are also a talented writer and a war veteran. It is these qualities that have brought you to my attention."

Escoffier lets his words settle and raises his hand to pause Hemingway's response. He continues.

"Before I get to the point, I want you to understand that what I will share with you this evening carries significant weight. I say this as if it will be easily understood, yet even someone like you—well-traveled and aware of the demons lurking in men's hearts—cannot fully grasp the danger that will shadow you and your loved ones for the rest of your life."

Hemingway interrupts.

"Auguste, you speak in riddles about dangers I cannot comprehend."

Escoffier continues.

"You're right, Ernest, but I wanted you to explain the depth of the waters you'll soon swim in."

Escoffier pauses, sensing Hemingway's impatience.

"I bear the burden of a dreadful secret uncovered during a visit to Germany in 1914. A secret that, unless prevented, could reduce our world to ash or enslave everyone into servitude."

Watching Escoffier's internal battle with himself, Hemingway begins to feel the weight of what he still does not fully understand.

"Ernest, I am old and can no longer bear this burden alone. I must find someone young, strong, and capable to share it with to live out my days knowing that I have done my best."

Escoffier considers his words carefully.

"But you should know, Ernest, that the information I want to share with you is controlled by the rich, powerful, and corrupt, and they are determined to see it through."

Escoffier looks down at his silver-tipped cane, remembering the cost of a young boy's life at the hands of Devereux.

"They already claim to have numerous bodies in their desire to remain secretly hidden until they are ready to reveal themselves."

Hemingway sits up in his chair, attempting to process Escoffier's choice of words. He reaches for an empty glass and pours himself some cognac. After a few sips, he places the glass on the table and turns slightly in his chair.

"I perceive the inner turmoil as you struggle with yourself to pass this burden along. Yes, I am young and strong and, as you say, "capable" of managing the knowledge you wish to unload from your shoulders. But tell me, Auguste, how can I be so reckless as to accept this information that could harm me and those I love?"

Escoffier takes a moment to consider Hemingway's words.

"A burden like this is neither trivial nor confined to those it may harm. Regardless of whether you accept this information, the threat to you and your loved ones will endure. If I have accurately evaluated your worth, you seem to be a man who possesses courage. By embracing this information, you will acquire the knowledge and capability to ensure that the worst never happens."

Escoffier takes another sip of his drink.

"Make no mistake, Ernest. If I were a man of your age and experience, I would do everything I could to stop it, even if it meant sacrificing my life. There is no other option but cowardice, and you and I do not possess an ounce of it in our blood."

After emptying the glass, Hemingway takes a large drink and slams it down on the table.

"Before I accept. Tell me everything."

Escoffier begins with his meeting with Carl Correns, during which he learns about Correns' research on weaponizing a plant pathogen and using it to destabilize governments.

"By controlling food production, it will be used to manipulate the will of people around the globe."

It is then that Escoffier speaks of his act of revenge against Devereux, and his eyes fill with tears as he remembers the loss of his son at the hands of the German Army.

Escoffier explains the ongoing barrage of fraud charges being brought against him and the relentless surveillance he endures daily. Once he finishes, Escoffier takes his napkin from his lap and places it on the table, signaling that the meal has concluded. He allows Hemingway to process the information.

Hemingway's intellect kicks into high gear.

"I may not be a man of science, but I acknowledge that if something like this were to happen, those behind it could not be trusted to use the science for the betterment of humanity, especially considering we are talking about fascists or, at the very least, industrial opportunists. And since you decided to share this with me in a locked room, it suggests that those who have you under surveillance might also be employed at this very hotel. Perhaps even one of the men who delivered this meal."

Hemingway observes Escoffier's shoulders have straightened, making him sit taller in his chair. Sharing his secret has lifted a great weight from his shoulders.

"Auguste, what do you think I can do? Besides, perhaps becoming a comrade in arms?"

Escoffier's face remains a block of stone. Unreadable.

"Ernest, it's enough to know that others know Correns' secret. How you choose to handle that knowledge is your decision. However, those who own this secret have extensive resources and a decade-long advantage. Their methods are subtle; they leave innuendos and complicate your life so you cannot keep their actions at bay. But they are also lethal when needed, approaching you first with a handshake."

"I must confess, Auguste, this is not what I envisioned when Scott brought me here tonight. As you said, I am capable, but I worry I may not meet your expectations."

Escoffier's stone visage relaxes.

"Ernest, I expect you to write. It's what you do best. People come and go, but words can last forever. Eventually, I believe others will take up the cause as well."

As Escoffier speaks those words, a feeling in the pit of Hemingway's stomach rises, and his eyes widen as the stark reality emerges.

"I am already the keeper of this secret. It is not a choice I made. You placed it in my lap like a live grenade. All I can do is hope it doesn't go off."

"Or you could find a way to defuse it."

Escoffier's words are cold and honest.

"Auguste, I will take my leave for now, for I have much to consider."

Hemingway puts his napkin on the table and rises. Escoffier stays seated and looks up at Ernest with intense eyes.

"Ernest, my offer to provide you with financial support remains, regardless of your decision. I have already purchased an obscure publication company and will send you a monthly stipend to use as you wish. It is the least I can do now that you bear this heavy burden."

Hemingway rises and begins scanning the area for Hadley and Fitzgerald.

"Your wife and friends are dining in a private room beside the kitchen. I will have the server take you to them."

As Hemingway heads to the private dining room, he runs into Sophia, who is making her way to the ladies' waiting room.

"Fair Sophia. It seems our day must come to an end."

Sofia's face is hard to look away from. She looks back towards the room where Hadley is.

"Perhaps we will meet again in Paris?"

"Then I will stay in Scott's good graces to ensure it happens."

Hemingway smiles, kisses her hand, and heads to the room where Hadley awaits. Sophia feels a great ache in her heart. She has fallen in love with a married man, and nothing good can come of it.

Moments later, the group reassembles in the lobby, where a photographer approaches them.

"Monsieur Escoffier, it is an honor to have you at our hotel. Management politely asks for a portrait."

Escoffier agrees, and the group comes together. As customary for the time, everyone stands for the photo with stoic looks—everyone except Sophia and Hadley. Sophia looks wantonly at Hemingway, as Hadley stares daggers at Sophia.

After the group goes their separate ways, the photographer walks back into the kitchen and calls his Curtain Group handler in Paris.

Lausanne, Switzerland - One Month Later

Since his conversation with Escoffier, Hemingway's lifestyle has dramatically improved. He has received a very satisfactory salary for the work submitted to Escoffier's publishing company. The money, alleviating much of the strain he had been experiencing, has enhanced his relationship with Hadley. After all, it meant he could wager on the horses without worrying about whether he could afford to eat.

It is a cool November morning in Paris when Hemingway receives a commission for a temporary assignment from a local newspaper in Lausanne, Switzerland. The journey takes 4 hours by train from Paris, allowing Hemingway time to work on other stories he has in development. He sends word to Hadley to meet him in Switzerland and to bring the manuscripts and notes from his fictional work. A few days later, Hadley arrives in Lausanne, distraught. As she steps off the train platform, she is sobbing and falls into Hemingway's embrace.

"My dearest Ernest. Our luggage has been stolen."

There's a moment when Hemingway cannot believe the words coming from her mouth. He pulls her away to gaze at her face.

"Was my work in the luggage?"

Sobbing uncontrollably, Hadley shakes her head, telling Hemingway that the luggage had contained his notes and carbons. Hemingway cannot believe what he has heard. His temper flares, and he lashes out.

"That was my work! How did this happen!?"

Hadley's eyes are streaming with tears as she looks up at Ernest, whose face shows deep anger.

"I was helping a woman with a baby carriage get up the stairs, and when I turned around, my luggage was gone."

Ernest rolls his eyes and steps away from Hadley, trying to calm his anger. He turns to her.

"Did you see this baby in the carriage? Was it crying?"

Hadley stops momentarily to think and then realizes the terrible truth. She was conned. There was no baby in the carriage. She falls back into a chair in the kitchen and buries her face in her hands, sobbing.

"Ernest, I am sorry."

Ernest's anger is rising, and he decides to walk it off instead of unleashing any more of it on Hadley. He grabs his hat and jacket and storms out of the apartment. Walking has always been a comfort to Ernest; however, since the injuries he received while driving an ambulance in WWI, it doesn't take long before he feels the pain returning to his legs and lower back. Looking around, he spots a pub and sits at the bar.

Moments later, two men, each wearing a dark suit, enter the pub and sit on either side of Ernest at the bar. Neither orders anything to drink. The man on Ernest's left turns and begins speaking. He has a thick Austrian accent.

"Sir. You wear the face of a man who has lost much. Is this so?"

Hemingway can feel the prickling of uneasiness crawl up his back. He turns his head to the man.

"And you, sir, look like a man who should mind his business."

The man sits back slightly, takes a badge from his jacket pocket, and shows it to Hemingway.

"I am a private detective. I know that look, for I have seen it many times."

Hemingway can tell that there is something off with this man.

"My good sir. What you do for a living does not give you cause to interrupt my privacy."

The man in his chair turns towards Hemingway, as does the man on Hemingway's right. Ernest feels fear creep into his mind and decides to leave. He reaches into his jacket to pay the bill. However, the man sitting on his right removes a small-caliber pistol and places the barrel against Ernest's back.

"Monsieur Hemingway. Please take your hand out of your jacket slowly and place it on the bar. My friend behind you believes you are about to do us harm."

Stunned that the man knows his name, Ernest slowly removes his hand. The man on his left quickly continues.

"Both hands, if you please."

Ernest complies, and the two men relax.

"You see, Monsieur Hemingway, we are here only to deliver a message to you. Nothing more. However, if your anger gets the best of you and you were to overpower us somehow, your wife, Hadley, will be found dead in your apartment, and you will be charged with her murder. Understand?"

Hemingway nods, and for the first time, he notices the man wearing a brightly colored lapel pin with a swastika.

"Monsieur Hemingway. Allow me to speak candidly. We represent a group that requests you cease working for Escoffier's publishing company immediately. We also require that you never mention anything about his irrational fears that he may have shared with you, as they are simply the scattered dreams of an old man who has slowly been losing his mental faculties."

Hemingway stares at the man and is resigned to his fate. His posture changes, and his shoulders slump. The man notices the change in Hemingway's demeanor and rises from the bar.

"You should know that we took your luggage and have individuals at your accommodations in Lausanne. Agree to our terms, and you will never see us again. If you fail to comply, it will result in serious harm to your wife."

Hemingway nods in agreement. The man rebukes him.

"No, sir. A situation such as this requires you to answer verbally."

Hemingway pauses and then speaks.

"You have my agreement. I will not work for Escoffier or mention what he told me to anyone."

The man rises as does his companion.

"We are going to keep your notes and manuscripts as insurance. I am certain you understand. Good day, Monsieur Hemingway."

The two men exit through the door, leaving Hemingway at the bar. Before returning to the apartment, Hemingway locates a gun dealer and purchases a Colt Woodsman pistol. From that point on until the day he took his own life in 1961, Hemingway was never without it.

Brasserie Lipp - Paris, France - One Month Later

After his return from Switzerland, Hemingway cannot shake the feeling of the danger lurking in the shadows, waiting to harm those he loves. The events in Lausanne have deeply affected Hemingway. Payments from Escoffier's publishing company have ceased, and Escoffier is seldom seen outside his Villa in Monaco. Even Fitzgerald has become a recluse, and his wife Zelda's mental health is beginning to decline. Today, Hemingway sits at a table in Brasserie Lipp, nursing a rum, when he notices his friend Sylvia Beach approaching. Sylvia owns Shakespeare & Company, located near the Luxembourg Gardens. Hemingway stands as she comes to his table. They exchange the traditional French greeting of "faire la bise" (a kiss on each cheek).

"My dear Ernest, how have you been? You haven't visited the bookstore in over a month. Is everything okay?"

Hemingway cannot look directly into the eyes of the woman who recognized the potential in his writing and loaned him books from the moment he first entered her store.

"Sylvia, it's good to see you, but I have reasons for my absence. I have been hired as a foreign correspondent. I will be traveling quite a bit more."

"Ernest, this is wonderful news! I'm happy for you. So, why the long face?"

Ernest scans Boulevard St. Germain, his gaze drifting to his Sophia's apartment building.

"I already miss this place that has brought me so much joy—even the dreadful Gertrude Stein. I may miss her the most."

Sylvia gazes intently into Hemingway's eyes as if peering into his soul. She looks away from Hemingway towards Sophia's building.

"My dear Ernest, whatever is troubling you will pass with time, as it will also for the woman waiting for you in that apartment."

Ernest looks sheepish.

"You know of Sophia?"

Sylvia smiles knowingly.

"We all know about her, including your beloved wife. She understands just as Sophia will. As women, we learn at a young age about men's hearts. We recognize the price that must be paid when you commit to a man. This has been true since the dawn of time. Of this, I am certain."

Sylvia rises and places her hand on Hemingway's shoulder.

"I wish you all the best, Ernest, and I look forward to reading your next novel. I'll leave you to your conversation with Sophia."

Before leaving, Sylvia looks up at the apartment and again at Ernest.

"She is much stronger than you realize."

Hemingway watches Sylvia walk away. From his table, he faces directly east. He knows he must go to the apartment of his beloved Sophia, yet he cannot summon the courage to do so. Reluctantly, he rises from his table, taking much longer than expected to reach her apartment. Overwhelmed with guilt, Hemingway knocks on the door.

Sophia answers the door with fear in her eyes, as if she senses the fate that awaits her from his demeanor. He enters her apartment, takes off his coat, and walks into the waiting arms of his beloved Sophia. They share a long embrace. Eventually, Sophia pulls away and leaves the room, and moments later returns with two small glasses of bright orange Aperol. They sit at a small table near the window, and Hemingway can feel the sun's warmth on his face. After an awkward silence, Sophia speaks, looking deeply into her lover's eyes.

"My dear Ernest, what is troubling you so?"

Hemingway attempts to speak, but guilt constricts his throat. Sophia leans back, letting the moments slip by. Whatever he needs to say, she understands it will be challenging for him. She displays patience as only a woman in her position can.

Hemingway reaches into his soul and finds the strength to utter the following words.

"I will travel more and be gone for quite some time."

Sophia's heart drops, yet her expression remains stoic.

"Where will you be going?"

"For now, Spain and Portugal. Afterward, I do not know."

She always knew the direction their relationship was heading. Mistresses are often left behind for the sake of the marriage. Sophia secretly had hoped that Ernest would lose interest in Hadley and move on. She removes her hands from the table and places them in her lap. Confused and scared beyond words, her eyes dart around the room. Sophia's heart begins to sink, yet her face glows with hope.

"Ernest, I understand this was always a possibility. After you returned from Lausanne, I noticed that something had changed in you. You have been distant and distracted."

Sensing there is more, Sophia pushes.

"Is there anything else upsetting you?"

Hemingway relaxes a bit and leans forward. He decides to lie.

"I have had a falling out with Escoffier, and he is no longer paying me to write."

Sophia's face changes to one of confusion. She sits back in the chair as her beloved Ernest continues. It takes him a long moment to utter the words.

"I think it is best that you leave Paris and return to your home in Marseilles. There are disreputable men to whom I owe money. I would not want anything to happen to you."

Sophia breaks in.

"My dearest. I am and will forever be in love with you. Whatever you ask of me, I will do it."

Hemingway smiles sadly as Sophia reaches up to take his face. They gaze deeply into each other's eyes, and then, slowly, Hemingway takes her hands and holds them in his lap.

"I hope there will come a day when I will return to Paris alone, and we can be together."

Consumed with guilt, the heartbroken Hemingway abruptly rises and leaves. Sitting at the table, Sophia begins to cry, realizing that Hemingway will never know that she, too, is pregnant. Her heart sinks as she continues to sob, thinking that her baby will be lost to Hemingway forever.

She gathers the strength to rise from the table, and with determination, she sits at her writing desk and begins to pen a letter to her mother—one she can no longer postpone sending. As she reaches for the inkwell, she notices that one of Hemingway's notebooks has fallen behind the desk. She picks it up and reads an entry from the night they were in Monte-Carlo.

"Tonight, Escoffier has shared a terrible and troubling secret..."

After she reads the entire entry, the book slips from her hands onto the floor. It takes her a moment before she picks it up, as she understands more than ever that Hemingway is trying to keep her safe. Reaching for a piece of paper, she pens a letter to her mother.

Two Weeks Later..

Racked with guilt, Hemingway and Hadley set off for Spain. He has spent the past two weeks reflecting on his cowardice in leaving Escoffier, the secret, and his beloved Sophia behind, struggling to justify it to himself.

"It is better than having harm come to anyone for a secret that may never come to pass."

However, in his heart, a deep sadness takes hold of Hemingway. A sadness that would haunt him throughout his life.

Chapter 8

The Discovery

Home of Chef William Laurent - Upstate South Carolina, United States - Current Day

William kisses his wife, Rebecca, good morning and heads to the coffee bar, only to find his favorite Villeroy & Boch white porcelain coffee cup waiting for him in front of the Nespresso machine. He pours himself an Americano—one shot of espresso, 170-degree hot water, and a splash of whole milk. Rebecca's gentle voice brings him back to the moment as she greets him, speaking French.

"Bonjour, mon amour." (Good morning, my love)

After 30 years of marriage, the look in her husband's eyes as he glances her way fills her with immediate joy and contentment. Carefully picking up his hot Americano, William approaches her and stops abruptly in front of a full-length mirror in an adjacent room. He chuckles and turns to Rebecca, seated in the breakfast nook.

"Need I remind you of our solemn oath to each other when we met?"

Rebecca smiles, looking up from her iPad at her husband's bed head.

"You look fine, my love. Besides, I like it when your hair is a little messy."

He turns back to the mirror. As a trim man in his early sixties, he likes to think of himself as 6 feet tall when, in fact, he's closer to 5'11". His thick salt-and-pepper gray hair, a gift from his French heritage on his father's side, perfectly matches a close-cropped, neatly trimmed beard. His hazel eyes, now beginning to show the wisdom of age, are alert and constantly observing the details around him. However, his thick hair defies gravity this morning and sticks up in multiple directions. He walks over to the kitchen sink and starts wetting and combing his hair with his fingers. Then, grabbing a towel from the counter, he wipes his hands and unconsciously flips the towel over his shoulder—a habit formed from being a chef. The tone he directs at Rebecca is one of sarcasm.

"My hair was not messy. It's borderline Albert Einstein with a tinge of crackpot."

Rebecca smiles but doesn't look up from her reading. Before sitting at the breakfast table, William leans down to her and gives her three kisses with his coffee in hand. She looks up and pokes a little fun at him.

"You love Einstein. That is why you have his quote in your notebook. What was it again?"

Rolling his eyes for effect, William replies.

"Great spirits have always encountered violent opposition from mediocre minds."

He runs his hand through his hair to mess it up again and turns his head towards her.

"But that doesn't mean I want to look like a mediocre mind."

The stunt makes her giggle in a way that lifts his heart. He stares at every feature of her perfect face as he brings the coffee cup to his lips. However, before sipping, he inhales the aroma of the freshly ground beans through his nose. It has taken him years to develop his palate, and this "smell first" process allows him to discern flavor notes hidden inside the coffee beans. Breathing in the steaming coffee, hundreds of receptors in his nose, each capable of identifying thousands of odor molecules, begin sending information to his brain that he is smelling hazelnuts, chocolate, fruit, and caramel. A moment later, he figures out the coffee blend he is drinking. He looks over his cup, smiles, and makes an educated guess in his morning voice.

"By the way, thank you for buying the Kona coffee. It is fabulous."

Rebecca smiles, knowing her husband's keen sense of smell. She returns to the matter of his hair.

"You are dashing when your hair is out of sorts."

He is quick to retort.

"I look crazy, is what I heard you say."

He turns to the magazines next to the breakfast table and pulls out an issue of Bon Appétite. Rebecca stops her reading and turns to her husband of 30 years.

"You were up late last night. More menu work for your upcoming event?"

He pauses on a page featuring a decadent pheasant dish and looks up, taking another sip of his coffee. Rebecca continues to probe.

"This event seems more challenging for you."

She allows her words to hang in the air for a microsecond and then continues.

"You've been distracted lately, and it's affecting your sleep. You tossed and turned all night. What's bothering you?"

He puts down the magazine and looks back at the stairs leading to his studio kitchen.

"I'm a lucky man. I've transitioned from a successful career in public speaking to a flourishing culinary practice. I've developed an enviable list of clients, including business leaders, foreign heads of state, and even a few A-list celebrities. I should be happy, but it's getting difficult to outdo myself continually."

William's thoughts scatter as Rebecca sets aside her iPad and shares the advice he offered her years ago.

"Look, you've always said everything has a beginning and an end. I'm stepping back from my business, so why not do the same for yours? René is an incredible chef in his own right."

William uses his sarcastic voice.

"Well, you've already used up our only child to run your business, and René has told me countless times he'd rather go back to dishwashing than speak to clients."

He reflects for a moment.

"I believe his exact words were... oh yes. If given the choice, he would rather be in the coffin than give the eulogy."

After 30 years of marriage, Rebecca knows her husband well. She returns to her iPad, allowing him to fill the next few moments with silence while his brilliant mind processes his feelings. Picking up the magazine again, William looks at the page showing the Pheasant dish. In silence, they listen to French jazz from the Bluetooth stereo in the living room. The breathy voice of Stacey Kent drifts lightly into the breakfast area as the sun struggles to break through the new leaves on the property surrounding their home. Peering over the top of her reading glasses, Rebecca can see the wheels turning in her husband's mind. Long, quiet moments pass until his eyes go wide. He flips the magazine around and points at the Pheasant recipe.

"This is it!"

Taken aback by his outburst, Rebecca gazes at the magazine with a questioning expression.

"But you already have Pheasant on your menu."

"No, my love. It's the change I've been looking for. Pheasant is served everywhere, but the dish Pheasant Under Glass was left behind decades ago. What if I stop trying to create new recipes and instead reintroduce old ones? It would feel like going back in time."

Rebecca's face shows loving acknowledgment. With a wry smile, she looks back down at her iPad.

"And I think it would also allow you to provide a brief history lesson to your clients."

William smiles back at Rebecca lovingly.

She notices William's eyes scanning the room, recognizing this as her husband's quick way of evaluating an idea—another sign of the intelligence she fell in love with all those years ago. Excited, William continues.

"I can change direction in the menus I create. Instead of focusing on the future of culinary arts, I'll bring back dishes from the turn of the century!"

He starts examining the recipe more closely. He leans back in his chair and explains it aloud.

"This pheasant could be prepared using a method from the 1900s. I recall seeing it in one of my cookbooks downstairs."

He pauses as Rebecca catches up to his thoughts.

"I can see it. You can revive long-forgotten recipes and present them to your clients. To them, these dishes will feel new."

William finishes her thought.

"...and I can reintroduce time-tested culinary techniques also long forgotten."

Rebecca rises from the breakfast table, cups her husband's face in her hands, and gazes deeply into his hazel eyes.

"See. I knew you'd find your way."

Talking Over Food Home Studio Kitchen - Later That Day

William sits at his desk and begins reviewing his rather large cookbook collection with renewed inspiration. After spending a couple of hours on this, he steps away to review his choices. Bourdain, Keller, Boulud, and Beck each include elements in their recipes that feature one of two classic techniques as part of the process. However, he sets them aside and focuses only on three standout books of classic cuisine.

The first book was written by culinary experts Vincent and Mary Price. An American actor known to work on stage, radio, and television, he was best known for portraying villainous roles in the 1940s and 1950s films. However, his most famous work is the narration of Michael Jackson's song "Thriller." In 1966, Vincent and his wife, Mary, published a cookbook titled "A Treasury of Great Recipes," which chronicled their experiences in America's finest restaurants of that time. There, William discovered the recipe for Faisan Sous Cloche, or in English, Pheasant Under Glass.

The second book he chooses is by the first female chef awarded a Michelin star—not once, but three times—in the 1930s. To this day, La Mère Brazier's recipes remain essential for any chef looking to transform simple ingredients into extraordinary dishes.

However, he begins his research with the last of the three books on his desk: Escoffier: Le Guide Culinaire Revised (English), published in 2011. Before he died in 1936, Escoffier codified French cuisine in four editions, which have endured as the bible for chefs worldwide. A book that will soon change William's life in ways he could never have imagined.

As if issuing a warning, the book's binding cracks loudly when he opens it. He starts reading the introduction of Escoffier's book and senses a presence behind him. Turning his head, he is startled to find his Sous Chef, René, looking over his shoulder. René, seemingly unfazed by startling his boss, looks down at the open book.

"Chef. With a cracking sound like that, I can tell you've not spent much time in Escoffier's Bible."

William, unsettled from being startled, retorts.

"And I can tell that you're wearing your ninja slippers. You nearly scared me half to death."

Looking down at his OluKai wool slippers, René smiles.

"These babies sure are comfy and quiet! Again, thank you for the gift."

Without looking up, William responds blankly.

"You should expect a bell to be placed around your neck shortly."

Thinking about it, William grudgingly acknowledges René's comment. In the last few years, he hasn't taken the time to read the book since receiving it as a gift from a client. René notices the other books on the desk.

"I understand that you've been struggling to find a theme for our next event, but is ancient food the direction you want to take?"

As he gazes at the spines of the three books, René suddenly stops.

"Vincent Price! The actor?! Are you kidding me?! Where did you find this ancient tome?"

William waves off the comment.

"I found it online years back. It is full of 'old school' culinary recipes and techniques."

William points to the inside cover.

"Look there. Vincent himself signed it."

René, unimpressed, has a questioning look on his face. William notices it.

"Before you choke on your question, you might as well spit it out."

William continues leafing through Le Guide Culinare.

"Don't get me wrong, Chef. I've seen you do impressive things like forced aging and par-cooking techniques. Does this mean we'll start creating recipes that are older than both of us combined?"

The chef pauses, shuts the book, and faces René with a serious expression.

"René, what defines a chef?"

René holds William's stare.

"Their palate and cooking style."

"You are correct. What is my style?"

"Chef, you are a master of plating and presentation. You help your guests appreciate the inspiration behind each dish and its roots, so to speak."

"Exactly, René! But instead of discussing the roots of a dish—or more accurately, its provenance, we will guide our guests through each dish as it was prepared back in the day."

René steps back and starts pacing the floor. William notices that he is calculating the implications of his statement. René's face brightens with recognition.

"What is old is new!"

William replies in French for added effect.

"Exactement!" (Exactly!)

William returns to scanning Escoffier's cookbook.

"The tough part will be recreating older dishes using present-day tools and techniques."

René's face turns sour.

"Chef, does this mean we can't use electricity?"

William breaks out in laughter.

"No, René, we're not returning to the Stone Age. The period from the early 1900s to the 1960s should suffice. However, we still need to research precisely how the cooking processes were carried out. This will give me something interesting to discuss when serving our clients."

Satisfied that William hasn't completely lost his mind, René retreats to the kitchen to continue preparing for the event on Friday. William casually pages through Escoffier's Le Guide Culinaire to get the lay of the land. He stops on a page dedicated to strawberry recipes. William grew up next to numerous strawberry farms in Southern California. He smiles, reminiscing about the many times local farmers chased after him while he frantically raced to collect as many of those delicious red berries as he could carry.

As William turns the page, he notices the recipe for Fraise Wilhelmine—a dessert made of strawberries, caster sugar soaked in orange juice, and sweet Kirsch brandy. While reading, he sees a set of initials listed after the last ingredient: K.W., C.C., and E.H. Eventually, the thought in his mind reaches his mouth.

"How very strange. Is that a footnote or reference of some kind?"

William makes a mental note of the page number. Looking back at the previous pages and a few that follow, William sees no other initials on any recipes. He leans back in his chair, feeling a familiar tickle at the back of his mind, rooted in his deep fascination with solving puzzles.

As a child, whenever he ran out of puzzles to solve, William would go into his father's garage and start taking apart anything mechanical to see if he could put it back together. Although his father wasn't as enthusiastic about his son's curious mind, he ensured William continued until the machine was reassembled and functional. William smiles as he recalls it, but his attention quickly shifts to the initials.

"This is odd. Perhaps this is a bibliographic reference?"

After a glance, he realizes Escoffier's book lacks a bibliography. William settles back into his chair, remembering the process of solving large jigsaw puzzles.

"The first step in building a jigsaw puzzle is identifying the corners and edges. Let's find out how many pieces I have to work with."

When William turns to the book's last page, he's blown away. Escoffier's Le Guide Culinaire is 646 pages! William scolds himself.

"OK. This is beginning to smell like work!"

A frown forms on his face, and then an idea occurs.

"It's time to go digital on this."

William opens a browser to download a digital version of Le Guide Culinaire. As he scans the results, he discovers that the book is available only in hardcover. He grits his teeth and rolls his eyes.

"OK then. Let's do this the analog way."

He shuts his laptop and decides to develop a process. Turning to the Table of Contents, William sees 17 chapters. However, his heart sinks when he discovers this Edition includes over 5,000 recipes. The itch at the back of his mind propels him forward, and he gives himself a pep talk.

"You can do this. Take each Chapter one at a time and skim each page. The other initials you found stood out even though you weren't consciously looking for them."

William begins by determining how long it should take him to scan the pages in the book. He takes out his phone and starts the stopwatch. It takes him 5 seconds to scan one page. He does the mental math. At 5 seconds per page, scanning 646 pages will take 3,230 seconds or about 54 minutes. He begins by asking the most challenging question when starting any puzzle.

"Do I have the time to finish?"

William looks at his phone.

"It's 3 p.m., leaving me 3 hours before I go upstairs and prepare dinner for Rebecca. Even if it takes twice as long, I should be fine."

William turns to page 1 of Escoffier's book and starts to scan. A few moments later, René pops his head into the kitchen office. William halts at page 7.

"Chef, don't we need to pick up the proteins for Friday's event?"

Without looking up, William responds to René's question.

"Would you mind picking them up for me? I've got my head into something here."

René rolls his eyes, grabs his keys, and heads to the garage. William keeps scanning the end of each recipe page by page. From Chapters 1 to 12, there's nothing to record, and just as doubt starts to creep into William's mind, he stops suddenly. On page 486, the initials E.H. are linked to the section on POTATOES.

By the time René returned with the groceries, the chef had completed scanning the book. René knocked again on the door. He could tell the chef was wholly absorbed in his research.

"Chef, I'm heading home. I've cleaned up and stored the proteins and vegetables. If you need anything, just let me know."

René stands there waiting for William to reply, but his head is buried in Escoffier's book.

"Chef, I'm leaving and never coming back."

Without taking his eyes off Escoffier's book, William responds.

"Great, thanks, René. See you tomorrow."

René shakes his head, aware that nothing will distract him except his wife, Rebecca, when the Chef dives into his research.

After another 15 minutes, William reviews the results:

- Three initials in Escoffier's book: K.W., C.C., and E.H.
- On page 497, the initials C.C. were associated with the entire section on Peas.
- On page 502, the initials E.H. were associated with the section on Potatoes, specifically, Pommes l'huile.

- On page 554, the initials K.W., C.C., and E.H. were associated with a recipe called Fraises Wilhelmine.

William pauses to reflect on the results.

"Escoffier includes three sets of initials in his book while leaving others unmarked. Why? And what do the initials K.W., C.C., and E.H. represent?"

With his curiosity piqued, William settles into his chair and begins his research. As the initials K.W., C.C., and E.H. are assigned to a single recipe, he decides to search there. Logging into his computer, William starts scouring the internet. However, after several attempts, the only promising lead comes from a food etymologist who describes how Escoffier named his famous strawberry dessert after Kaiser Wilhelm II.

Escoffier made a habit of naming dishes after famous people. William also discovered that Escoffier's decadent peach dessert, Peach Melba, was named after the Australian operatic soprano Dame Nellie Melba. Oddly, the other recipes Escoffier named after famous people did not include their initials. William begins to doubt his thought process and vocalizes his feelings.

"Escoffier named Fraise Imperator after Kaiser Wilhelm II. But why single out this one recipe and not others? And why would he include two other sets of initials?"

He continues his online search but still seeks other recipes named after the Kaiser by Escoffier. William returns to the food etymologist article and discovers additional articles referencing a dinner Escoffier hosted for the Kaiser at his Silver Jubilee in 1924. The event took place aboard the Hamburg-Amerikan cruise liner SS Imperator. As William continued researching, he found Escoffier designed the ship's kitchen after the Carlton Hotel kitchen in London. William's mind is now racing. After another few minutes of research, he learned that the Kaiser bestowed the title ' The King of Chefs' on

Escoffier during that celebration cruise. William jots this information into his culinary notebook. He leans back and reviews the reasoning.

"If the K.W. initials stand for Kaiser Wilhelm II, then the other two sets of initials must also represent people."

William leans back in his chair, letting the logic unfold.

"OK. Since the initials C.C. and E.H. were also associated with Fraises Wilhelmine, it stands to reason that the Kaiser, C.C., and E.H. must somehow be connected."

William pauses, letting his mind absorb the last statement. Behind him, he hears his wife Rebecca's voice.

"Are you talking to yourself again?"

William's heart jumped from the surprise.

"You and René have to stop sneaking up on me! The worst gift I ever gave you two was those damn OluKai slippers."

Rebecca smiles lovingly, ignoring her husband's comment. She then leans into his screen, looks at his notes, and asks the same question within seconds.

"Why would Escoffier put the initials of three people in recipes in his book? How odd."

As Rebecca starts to look through Escoffier's book, William brings her up to speed.

"After our conversation this morning, I searched for the best cookbooks to create a new menu inspired by traditional recipes."

Rebecca interrupts after noticing the cookbook by Vincent and Mary Price on William's desk. She begins to read the dedication.

"Oh, I love this book! Where were you hiding this?"

William makes a face that conveys, "RIGHT!?" and returns to his research.

"As I was thumbing through the pages of Le Guide Culinaire, I found a recipe called Fraise Whilimine, and next to it were three sets of initials."

Rebecca makes a face that displays confusion.

"Initials?"

Her mind begins processing the information. William continues.

"I looked up Escoffier and learned that he dedicated the dessert to Kaiser Wilhelm II at his Silver Jubilee dinner aboard the S.S. Imperator."

With Rebecca's interest now piqued, she starts reading William's journal and the recipe for Fraises Wilhelmine from Escoffier's book. She then looks at the other initials William has already discovered before returning to his notes. She places her hand on his shoulder and gazes into his eyes.

"I have to concede that the initials probably belong to people who are somehow connected. Now let's go eat."

William's face is clouded with confusion. Rebecca throws him a lifeline.

"René brought up a delightful Faroe Islands salmon for two. It's warming in the oven. Let's eat and discuss this puzzle you've found."

The Chef grabs his phone and sends René a thank-you emoji. Rene responds with a rolling-eyes emoji.

Going upstairs, he cannot stop thinking about the initials in Escoffier's book. His mind is a flurry of disconnected thoughts, but one thought persists at the top of his mind.

"Why would Escoffier put the initials of three people in Le Guide Culinaire?"

Mattisse Apartment, Cours Seleya - Nice, France

While relaxing in her apartment, the Woman With Auburn Hair receives a hyper-encrypted text.

Tracking AI: "Target actively researching breadcrumbs."

The Woman With Auburn Hair walks over to the window, looking at the Bay of Angels and the Mediterranean Sea. Sipping a cup of tea, her brilliant mind plays out every possible scenario for the next few weeks. Many aspects of her plan could go wrong, and she knows it will take a fair amount of luck to succeed. She smiles, recalling a quote from the famous French chemist Louis Pasteur.

Luck favors the prepared...a variation of the quote 'Chance favors the prepared mind.'

Chapter 9

Deciphering Escoffier's Code

Chicago ORD Airport - United States

It has been two weeks since William discovered the initials in Escoffier's Le Guide Culinaire. Unable to work on Escoffier's puzzle due to a packed calendar of dining events, Chef William and Rebecca are taking a much-needed break to spend time with friends in Paris. In truth, William is looking forward to using the flight time to research Escoffier's puzzle.

William places their carry-on luggage in the overhead compartment as they settle into their First Class pods for the 8-hour flight from Chicago O'Hare to Paris Charles de Gaulle. He grabs his copy of Le Guide Culinaire along with his laptop. Already seated, Rebecca scowls at William as he gets comfortable in his pod.

"Are you seriously going to spend the entire flight trying to figure out Escoffier's puzzle?"

William presents his argument.

"My love, you'll be asleep 15 minutes after they serve us dinner. You won't even know I am here."

Rebecca's expression conveys her dissatisfaction with her husband's plans. She pauses to give him a stern warning.

"I know how you get when you find a puzzle, so don't come crying to me about being tired once we land. And for heaven's sake, try to avoid talking to yourself out loud."

William rolls his eyes and smiles sheepishly. True to his prediction, minutes after the dinner service is over, Rebecca is fast asleep. William opens his laptop and connects to the plane's Wi-Fi. He chuckles to himself, thinking,

"There was a time, not so long ago, when expecting an Internet connection on an airplane was laughable."

Nevertheless, here he is, able to watch movies and surf the Internet while traveling over 400 mph at 36,000 feet. His laptop boots up instantly, and he's already using his search engine. He glances back at his notebook and devises a strategy to solve Escoffier's puzzle. He begins by researching Escoffier and soon discovers that his home is located just outside Nice, France, in a village called Villeneuve-Loubet. He jots down a note to visit the house, turned museum, of the most renowned Chef in history.

William scolds himself for not taking the time to get to know the man who codified the entire French culinary industry. As he reads in the seclusion of his pod, he learns about Escoffier's beginnings as a cook working for his uncle at a restaurant in Nice and how disorganized, unsanitary, and chaotic the conditions were. Later, Escoffier joined the army and became a chef at the headquarters of the Army of the Rhine in Metz during the Franco-Prussian War. Afterward, Escoffier found himself in London with renowned hotelier César Ritz, and they opened the Ritz Paris on the Place Vendôme and finally the Carlton Hotel in London.

Their partnership would last for 17 years and end unceremoniously, with Ritz succumbing to a mental breakdown. Escoffier would later move to Monte-Carlo, where he would live out his life. William smiles as he reminisces about the Ritz Paris he and Rebecca visit whenever they travel through Europe. He then remembers the bar inside the Ritz, named after the renowned American author Ernest Hemingway. The coincidence catches him off guard as his mind plays out the link.

"No way. Could E.H. be Ernest-fucking-Hemingway?!"

William cannot help but say the words out loud. He looks over the partition separating their pods and sees Rebecca sleeping soundly. He then opens a new browser tab and begins researching Hemingway more thoroughly. Specifically, he looks for anything related to Hemingway and Kaiser Wilhelm II. After another 30 minutes, he finds nothing linking the two men. He continues making notes, saving each URL in a bookmarked folder. There is more information than he can digest in the few hours left on the flight. He takes a moment to summarize his findings.

- Hemingway, injured in Italy moved to Paris with his wife, Hadley Richardson, in December 1921.

- Hemingway returns to the States in 1923 where hiss son is born.

- Returning to Paris a year later, Hemingway would leave in 1928 and doesn't return to Paris until the end of WWII (1944)

- Embedded with troops on D-Day, Hemingway collaborated with resistance fighters outside Paris.

- Hemingway doesn't return to Paris until 1956, when a forgotten trunk stored at the Ritz since 1928 was returned to him.

- Soon after, he would write 'A Moveable Feast' using notes he found in the trunk.

Sitting back in his seat, William considers other significant pieces of information he found while researching Hemingway.
- While traveling in the Congo in 1957, Hemingway survives two consecutive plane crashes in as many days.

- In 1961, Hemingway died from a self-inflicted gunshot wound at his home in Idaho.

- No information directly links Hemingway to Escoffier, except for the loose connection to the Hotel Ritz.

- Regrettably, there is only a slim chance that Hemingway and Escoffier might have met before the publication of Escoffier's book in 1923.

Feeling somewhat energized by possibly identifying Hemingway, William focuses on the only person he recognized in Escoffier's puzzle: Kaiser Wilhelm II. Here, he discovered numerous pages of information about the Kaiser, including a substantial amount of detail regarding his involvement in a scientific institute he founded in the early 1900s, known as the Kaiser Wilhelm Society (KWS). William smiles, sensing that he is onto something.

"This looks promising..."

He clicks on the hyperlink, which directs him to the pertinent Wikipedia page about the KWS, ultimately leading him to the current-day Max Planck Society. William's enthusiasm quickly shifts to repulsion as he learns about the horrific scientific discoveries made by scientists and the leadership of the Kaiser Wilhelm Society during both World Wars. However, the one discovery that hits him closer to home is Chemist Fritz Haber, who discovered Mustard Gas, which was used to clear trenches of Allied Soldiers in WWI.

William closes his eyes, allowing himself time to process his feelings. He recalls Rebecca telling him how her grandmother raised her, but never met her grandfather because he died of complications from Mustard Gas poisoning after her mother was born. William sits back in his seat.

"Why am I just now learning about the existence of the Kaiser Wilhelm Society?"

CIA Black-Ops location near the French Maritime Alps

The Woman With Auburn Hair receives another notification from her AI tracking bot on her hyper-encrypted device.

"Asset has researched Kaiser Wilhelm II and the Kaiser Wilhelm Society."

She smiles at the encouraging news.

"Chef, if you maintain this pace, you should have everything you need by the time you arrive in Paris."

United Flight - Somewhere Over The Atlantic Ocean

William jots down his thoughts and reopens his laptop. Putting his emotions aside, he reads through the content continuously. After reviewing the content a third time, William begins taking notes on the essential details he has learned about the Kaiser Wilhelm Society.

- The Kaiser Wilhelm Society originated from Adolf Harnack, a theologian and president of the Berlin Academy of Arts, who sought to prepare Germany for the impending Second Industrial Revolution.
- Shortly after the Society was founded, World War I broke out. The Director of the Institute of Chemistry, Fritz Haber, begins collaborating with the German Army High Command to develop a gas that could help clear trenches of enemy soldiers. He would go on to discover "Mustard" gas and supervise its use against French, British, and American troops. He would later be known as the Father of Chemical Warfare.

- The science Haber created for Mustard gas was used to create a gas called Zyklon B, which was used in prison camps to kill millions of Jewish prisoners in WWII.
- Scientists at the KWS Institute of Biology also carried out experiments on live prisoners in WWII.

This new information visibly shakes William. He begins to close his laptop and stops. At the bottom of the wiki page is the name of the director of the Institute of Plant Biology, geneticist Carl Correns. William's heart jumps as he scans the background on Correns' wiki page. His heart leaps as he reads that Correns' work focuses on the genetic makeup of pea plants. William quickly grabs his notebook and flips to the page in Escoffier's Le Guide Culinaire, where he notices the C.C. initials were also linked to recipes that included peas. William leans back in his seat, allowing the emotions of the last thirty minutes of research to wash over him. He cannot recall ever feeling so elated and horrified in such a short time. Before shutting down his laptop, he writes Correns' name in his notebook.

"Gotcha, Carl!"

CIA Black-Ops location near the French Maritime Alps

Another notification from her AI tracking bot is received on the Women With Auburn Hair's hyper-encrypted device.

"Asset has connected Carl Correns to Kaiser Wilhelm II and the Kaiser Wilhelm Society."

She smiles again at William's persistence. She congratulates herself on choosing him for this part of her plan and makes a mental note to ensure her assets in Paris are in place.

United Flight - Somewhere Over The Atlantic Ocean

Rising from his pod, William places his research materials and laptop in the overhead compartment. Emotionally drained and craving a stiff drink, he glances down the aisle and spots Chief Steward Tony in the galley near the front of the plane. He remembers meeting Tony on a flight to Paris after the COVID outbreak had subsided. Tony's face betrays worry. William rises from his pod and walks to the galley, where Tony already holds a serving tray with a glass of Highland Scotch and offers it to him.

"Perhaps this will help you sleep."

William smiles back, accepting the gift.

"Tony, I apologize for intruding, but you seem upset. Perhaps we both need a drink?"

The Chief Steward gives William a sideways glance and smiles.

"No, Chef, I have proposed to a beautiful Parisian woman, and I'll finally be able to start a family."

Speaking in hushed French, William congratulates Tony by extending his hand.

"This is great news, no? Why the long face?"

They shake, and Tony's smile returns in full force.

"Thank you. We are happy, but I am uncertain how to support my new family as I can no longer fly. The schedule of a Chief Steward isn't how I want my new life to begin."

William considers and then replies in French.

"My friend, I know the perfect job for you at the Ritz Hotel in Paris. You are a formidable Chief Steward, and your skills will be welcomed there. I will send a note to the evening manager. You will have your chance to persuade them to hire you, but I believe it will likely be them trying to persuade you."

Tony is stunned and very thankful for the opportunity. The two continue to chat quietly, and after washing up, the chef returns to his seat to find that Rebecca has awakened. William reaches across the partition and kisses her, which she reluctantly accepts, whispering...

"Be careful when you kiss me. I've been sleeping, so my mouth probably smells like your socks."

For the rest of the flight, William reclines and starts reprocessing the information he has just uncovered about the initials in Escoffier's book. He now knows the initials belong to Ernest Hemingway, Kaiser Wilhelm II, and Carl Correns. He also learned about the atrocities committed by the Kaise William Helm Society. However, he has no idea why these initials are in Escoffier's book. He takes out his notebook and writes Escoffier's name at the top, followed by Hemingway, the Kaiser, and Correns beneath it.

Soon, the plane's staff begins preparing breakfast. William hasn't slept a wink but is happy that Rebecca seems energized. She raises her seat to an inclined position just as Tony arrives to serve the meal. Rebecca glances at William and whispers to him.

"You didn't get any sleep, did you?"

William puts on a brave face.

"I got some rest, but the good news is that I figured out the initials in Escoffier's book."

Rebecca's face displays mild surprise.

"I knew you wouldn't sleep. You'll be a zombie when we get to the Hotel d'Aubusson."

She pauses as if expecting him to say something.

"So, will you tell me who the initials belong to?"

William walks Rebecca through his research just as the meals are served. They spend the rest of the flight engaged in a back-and-forth conversation, with Rebecca playing the role of devil's advocate. However, William cannot shake the feeling that this puzzle isn't what it seems.

Chapter 10

The Revelation

Hotel d'Aubusson - 6th Arrondissement Paris, France

It is a 40-minute drive without traffic to reach Paris from Charles de Gaulle airport, with the Uber dropping them off in the 6th Arrondissement at the Hotel d'Aubusson. Within minutes, they are greeted at the curb by the hotel's manager, Charles, along with two bellhops who assist with their luggage.

"Madame and Monsieur Laurent. Welcome back!"

Charles leans into Rebecca, and they exchange "faire la bise," a kiss on both cheeks. He then turns to William and does the same, shaking his hand with the strength of a bear.

"I am so happy to see you, but you both must be tired from such a long trip. Your room is ready, the bed is turned down, and the staff has been instructed not to disturb you."

Rebecca, feeling the effects of the flight, smiles broadly at the thought of the hotel linens and cozy bed enveloping her. Within a few minutes, they are lying on the bed in the room. Rebecca falls asleep instantly, while William, unable to rest, decides to continue his research at the lobby bar. He grabs his laptop, leaves Rebecca a note, and heads to the elevator.

William exits the elevator and passes an empty dining room set for afternoon service. He recalls spending most of his days in that room preparing for meetings while working in the technology industry during the early 1990s. After retiring early from tech, William, now one of the most sought-after chefs, shakes off those memories like snow from a jacket and continues walking through the iconic seating area.

The Hotel d'Aubusson's sitting area features a large, open fireplace and the original, rough-hewn overhead beams from the original structure, dating back to the 17th century. However, this morning, William's destination is Café Laurent (no relation to William's French heritage), once a speakeasy and now transformed into the hotel's bar and lounge. The hotel has maintained its vibrant jazz history and was known in 1947 for staying open throughout the night. Before Café Laurent, it was known as Tabou and hosted the era's writers, authors, and jazz greats. Today, the hotel d'Aubusson is named after a town in southwest France renowned for some of the world's finest tapestries. William walks into the lounge with his computer under his arm and is greeted by the bartender.

"Good morning, sir. If you're working, I suggest the tables away from the windows. We have many tourists pressing their faces against the glass."

Smiling, William selects a seat near a baby grand piano. He remembers that on Wednesday evenings, the d'Aubusson still hosts live jazz. Moments later, the bartender approaches with a selection of nuts and olives, placing a single napkin on the table. As he looks up, William speaks to the barman in perfectly accented French.

"Monsieur, I need another setting as my wife will soon wake and join me."

The barman smiles.

"As you wish, Monsieur Chef."

William is slightly taken aback. Despite staying at the bar numerous times on business, he has never met this barman. The barman recognizes William's confusion and recovers.

"Monsieur Chef, you are highly regarded at this establishment for your kind words on social media and the clients you have sent us over the years. We always know when you're coming."

The server bows slightly.

"My name is Julian."

He lays down a notecard.

"Here's the passcode for the internet."

"Thank you, Julian. If you could, I would like a Noisette and a Madeleine."

A 'Noisette' is an espresso with a bit of frothy milk. The word 'noisette' refers to the English word 'hazelnut', the color the coffee takes on when the milk is added. The two men quickly finish exchanging pleasantries as William is eager to get back to working on Escoffier's puzzle. It takes a few seconds to boot up, and he returns to the same screen he had during his flight. William gathers himself and opens his culinary notebook to review his progress. A chill runs through him as he contemplates what he has learned about the KWS. He shakes it off, refocuses on the puzzle, and reviews his findings.

"So why would Escoffier put the initials of a German King, an American Pulitzer Prize-winning author, and an Austrian plant biologist in his book of recipes?"

William quickly glances up to ensure he isn't speaking his thoughts aloud again. With no one watching or sending him disapproving glares, he breathes a sigh of relief and continues his train of thought. Then, Rebecca exits the elevator and enters the lounge, taking the same route as William. She walks up behind him and places her hand on his shoulder near his neck. Without looking up, William casually starts speaking.

"I keep telling you not to do that in public. What will my wife think if she sees us? Besides, the staff already knows who I am. This is scandalous behavior, madame!"

Rebecca comes around her husband, dragging her hand across his shoulder. She is dressed in a loose-fitting jogging outfit that accentuates her figure. William smiles in a way that makes Rebecca blush. He rises and offers her a chair.

"Please join me while we wait for my wife."

She notices his computer and notebook as she takes a seat. William gestures to Julian while Rebecca begins flipping through his open notebook. Julian approaches with a cup of coffee, two sugars, and a splash of cream—Rebecca's favorite. Without looking up, she thanks the bartender.

"Thank you, Julian. You are a dear."

Julian heads back to the bar, and William is astonished that Rebecca knows his name. He casts a sly glance her way.

"And how exactly do you know the bartender's name?"

As only a gentlewoman can, Rebecca waits as if she hasn't heard his question, bringing her lips to the warm coffee. After taking a sip, she replies.

"But why wouldn't I know his name, dear? It is on his badge."

William smiles and rolls his eyes as Rebecca shifts her gaze back to the notebook. After she finishes reading his notes, her expression turns serious. He recognizes this look on Rebecca's face as the one she wears while researching. As a multi-decade film production veteran, Rebecca has reviewed numerous scripts to identify potential legal issues that could impact production. She quietly sets down her coffee—a simple act that reflects her upbringing—and requests to be brought up to speed.

"Okay, walk me through it. You've managed to decipher the three initials in Escoffier's Le Guide Culinaire." She stops abruptly and starts reading his notes on the KWS. Her expression sours.

"What on earth is the Kaiser Wilhelm Society? This is horrific. How did you come across this?"

Rebecca can see the terrible impact this knowledge has had on William by the look on his face. She places a hand on his arm and gazes intensely into his eyes.

"Are you alright, my love?"

William pauses for a moment, letting his emotions settle.

"I am **_not_** at all okay. I am starting to regret ever discovering these initials. It appears that the scientific society, established by Kaiser Wilhelm II, was responsible for millions of deaths, including the use of mustard gas on Allied troops during World War I."

William takes a moment to gather himself. He turns to talk directly to her.

"I remember you mentioning that your grandfather passed away due to complications from mustard gas exposure in World War I. How is it that I never learned about the KWS in school?"

Rebecca leans in and hugs her beloved husband. She can tell that William's lack of sleep is affecting him, and he continues.

"How can I focus on Escoffier's puzzle when it involves a tragedy that claimed so many lives, including your grandfather's?"

After a moment, she leans forward and cradles his face.

"I don't know why you found the initials in Escoffier's book, but you did. The only thing left to do is figure out what they mean. Once we learn that, we can decide what needs to be done. So, tell me, where are you in the research?"

William shakes off the last of his emotions.

"I know who the initials belong to, but I lack evidence connecting them to Escoffier. Aside from Escoffier and Kaiser Wilhelm II, for whom ample information is available online regarding their connection, everything else remains conjecture."

Rebecca leans back while closely examining William's face. She chooses to continue the conversation and hands him the notebook.

"Tell me about the Correns connection."

William turns a few pages in his notebook and finds what he wants.

"Correns was a plant biologist studying the genetic makeup of pea plants at the Institute of Biology for the Kaiser Wilhelm Society. This is why Escoffier linked Correns' initials to the section on peas in Le Guide Culinaire."

"What about Hemingway? How did you find that?"

William sits back in his chair and shakes his head.

"That was a guess, but it felt too coincidental to dismiss. The idea popped into my head because we always visit the Bar Hemingway at the Ritz on our trips to Paris. Then, I discovered that the Bar Hemingway didn't open until Mohamed Al-Fayed purchased the hotel from the Ritz estate in 1994. Before that, the bar was called The Petite Bar. Dodi renamed it after Hemingway because of the time Hemingway spent at the Ritz at the end of World War II. That was long after the last printing of Escoffier's book in 1923."

Rebecca's face lights up as a thought occurs to her.

"I saw in your notes that Hemingway returned in 1956 to the Ritz, where he found a trunk he had forgotten containing journals from the 1920s. You noted that he used them to write *A Moveable Feast*. Remind me again of the other reference to E.H. in Escoffier's book."

"It was for a recipe for Pommes L'huile. A recipe of potatoes drizzled in olive oil."

Rebecca saddles up to William's laptop and starts typing furiously. After a few more minutes, she turns it around for William to see. He is taken aback.

"You have to be kidding me. Really?! You found confirmation that it is Hemingway!?"

Rebecca rolls her eyes at William as she leans back in her chair, sipping her coffee with a satisfied look. She sets down the cup and walks him through it. She shows William the page where she found the connection.

"Look here. In his book, *A Moveable Feast*, Hemingway describes all the incredible culinary delights in Paris. Specifically, he recounts enjoying Pommes l'huile at the Café Deux Magots. It was the only thing he could afford. And if Escoffier linked Hemingway's initials to a recipe for Pommes l'huile. It's therefore reasonable to conclude that Escoffier knew Hemingway well enough to know his favorite meal."

William smiles at his wife's brilliance as Rebecca makes an obvious statement.

"Now, we need to determine *why* Escoffier included those initials in his book."

Rebecca looks through the rest of William's notes. Turning to an empty page in his notebook, she draws a rhombus and inserts Escoffier's name. She then creates a rhombus for each of the three remaining names. She turns to William and points to Escoffier's rhombus.

"It's Escoffier's book, so let's start there."

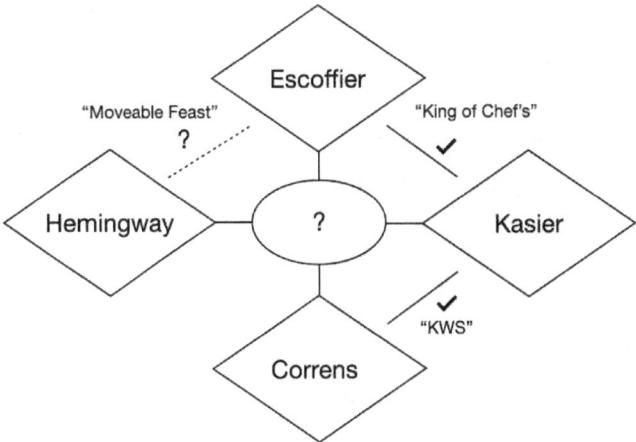

Rebecca draws a line from Escoffier to Kaiser Wilhelm II and then from the Kaiser to Correns.

"The connection between these three is backed by evidence. Escoffier prepared a few dinners for the Kaiser. After naming a dessert called Fraise Wilhelmine in honor of the Kaiser, he awarded Escoffier the informal title of *King of Chefs.*"

William rolls his eyes.

"Yeah, a real bromance going on there."

Rebecca continues her line of thought.

"The connection between the Kaiser and Correns is thin, but it's there nonetheless. We have to assume that Escoffier had his reasons for making the connection. It will take more information that we clearly do not have."

William grimaces at the Correns/Kaiser connection just as Julian arrives with fresh coffee. As he finishes pouring, Julian notices the names on the sheet of paper and hesitates. At that moment, William notices Julian staring at the page and feels a strange sensation, just as Julian realizes he has been gazing at it far too long.

"I apologize for eavesdropping, Monsieur Chef. It's not often that you see the name Escoffier nowadays."

An uncomfortable silence fills the air, and then Julian excuses himself. Looking at Rebecca, William recognizes the same bewilderment on her face.

"Okay. That was weird."

Rebecca looks across the room and sees Julian heading toward the kitchen. She looks back at William.

"Yes. It was."

They return to Rebecca's drawing as she draws a dashed line from Escoffier to Hemingway. After pondering momentarily, she places a check mark on the line linking Escoffier to the Kaiser and from the Kaiser to Correns, indicating plausible evidence connecting them. Once satisfied, she draws an oval in the center of the diagram and links it to each of the four names. Within this, she adds a question mark.

Shaking off the weird interaction with Julian, William looks back at the new drawing. He points to the oval in the center of the diagram where Rebecca had placed the question mark.

"What's that?"

"It's the missing piece of the puzzle, and it answers the question as to _why_ the initials are in Escoffier's book."

William picks up the journal and gazes at it for several minutes. He looks for a connection that might make sense of this puzzle—a process that could unravel it. He decides to construct a narrative that could connect the initials in Escoffier's book. He turns to Rebecca and begins telling a story.

"OK. Work with me on this."

Rebecca puts down his notebook.

"In 1908, the KWS was created to advance work in the natural sciences in Germany. Carl Correns became the director of the Institute for Biology in 1913, where he worked on genetic research associated with pea plants."

William pauses to collect his thoughts and continues.

"After 1913 but before 1921, Escoffier learns of Correns' work through his connection to the Kaiser."

William winces at the stretch he just made in the story. Glancing at Rebecca, she signals him to keep going and begins nibbling on William's pastry.

Hemingway and his wife moved to Paris in 1921. Sometime before they returned to America in 1929, he met Escoffier, who told him about Correns' research. Escoffier then includes the Kaiser, Hemingway, and Correns' initials in the final edition of his book, Le Guide Culinaire."

William finishes. Rebecca's analytical mind already has questions. She quickly begins typing on William's laptop. A few moments pass, and she looks back at him with troubled eyes.

"Escoffier's first edition of Le Guide Culinaire was published in 1903, the second in 1907, the third in 1912, and the fourth and final edition was published in 1921. However, Hemingway and Hadley didn't arrive in Paris until December 1921. Hemingway's initials shouldn't be in the book. If Escoffier and Hemingway had met, it could only have happened *after* the fourth edition was already printed."

Rebecca and William stare at each other without speaking. It is Rebecca who breaks the silence.

"You found the initials in Escoffier's book?"

William walks over to his satchel, takes the book, and hands it to Rebecca.

This isn't an original Le Guide Culinaire. It's a translation of his book into English, published in 2011."

William chastises himself for making such an obvious mistake.

"I've been using the wrong book. I'm an idiot."

Rebecca brushes his comment aside.

"We need to see if the initials are also in an original Le Guide Culinaire."

Rebecca begins typing on the computer, but William stops her.

"None of Escoffier's books are digitized. We'll have to try and locate one."

After a lengthy time researching, Rebecca stops and closes the laptop.

"I found an original volume for sale and sent the owner a message. Hopefully, we'll hear back soon."

Within seconds, her phone vibrates, indicating she has a message.

"Thank you for your interest in the book.

I must say that I found your request quite

odd. However, I looked at the pages you

provided and found no initials associated

with the recipes. Sorry."

In defeat, William rises and walks to the window.

"So, it's some kind of hoax."

Rebecca rises and walks over to him.

"I'm not so certain. It's too elaborate and specific to be a hoax."

William casts her a skeptical look. Rebecca continues.

"Plus, it somehow supports Escoffier and Hemingway's meeting in Paris."

William turns away from the window, clearly upset with himself.

"As far as I am concerned, this puzzle can go fuck itself."

He returns to his computer and puts everything back into his satchel. Rebecca comes over, places her hand on his arm, and turns him to her.

"William. I know you too well to let you stop working on this. You will not stop beating yourself up, and it will be me who ends up getting angry. If you think it's a hoax, then prove it. It's the only way you'll be able to move on. Now sit down and work the puzzle."

It takes William a while to get his head back into it. Rebecca takes the reins and begins asking the obvious first question.

"If the initials in Escoffier's translated book are fake, then why do they point to actual people?"

William half-heartedly replies.

"It could be I found people I wanted to find."

Rebecca digs in.

"You only deciphered and confirmed two of the initials. You guessed at Hemingway, and I independently confirmed it."

William's temper rises.

"Well, since the initials are in a book published in 2011, then obviously somebody else, other than Escoffier, put them there. Therefore, this is no longer Escoffier's puzzle. It belongs to whoever put them in that book."

Rebecca pauses at the simplicity and exactitude of William's statement.

"William. You are absolutely correct."

Surprised, William doesn't know what to say. After a few moments, he gets out five easy words.

"Wait. You agree with me?"

Rebecca rolls her eyes.

"I agree. Escoffier didn't put those initials in the book."

William feels a "but" coming.

"Your logic is sound, but it doesn't prove the initials in Escoffier's book are a hoax. It only proves that Escoffier didn't put them there. We're making progress."

William begins feeling the tickling in the back of his head that he felt when solving puzzles as a child. Looking at Rebecca, he asks the next obvious question.

"So, if Escoffier didn't put them there, who did?"

Rebecca looks back at William with her eyebrows raised as if he should already know the answer, and then it dawns on him.

"Somebody else who also wants Correns' research to come out."

Rebecca leans into William and kisses him hard.

"See. I knew you were in there. Now, let's keep going. Nothing changes except the identity of the person who put the code into the book."

Distracted by the taste of her lipstick, William sits quietly, unable to speak. Rebecca continues as if nothing happened.

"Okay. Let's start at the end of your story and work backward. First, why would anyone leave clues in _Escoffier's_ book?"

William finally breaks the spell of Rebecca's kiss and thinks for a moment.

"They wanted others to know about the secret that connects the three men."

Rebecca's eyes narrow.

"No. Why didn't they use other methods of getting the information out, like reporters and news agencies? Why not just go to one of them?"

William blurts it out.

"Short answer. They were afraid."

Rebecca makes a frown.

"But why be afraid? The KWS was dismantled at the end of WWII."

They both sit there in the lobby and watch people walk by the window facing the street. A few moments later, William turns to Rebecca.

"In my research, I found that the KWS was funded by industrialists and private investors who were making money from those discoveries. Those people remained even after the KWS was dismantled. Perhaps they wanted to keep Correns' discovery to themselves."

Rebecca's face is still lined with questions.

"But that still doesn't answer why Escoffier's puzzle was put in a later publication of _his_ cookbook. Why not put the code somewhere else where more people could find it?"

William begins thinking out loud before Rebecca has a chance to answer. He speaks the words like he should have known the answer from the beginning.

"They need a chef."

Rebecca stops dead in her tracks and looks deeply into William's eyes. William looks over to the people walking by the window and continues.

"Chefs approach things with a different perspective. We see possibilities and connections that others might miss. We are highly focused and pay close attention to detail. We live in a fast-paced and demanding environment, which helps us to be quick thinkers and adept at creative problem-solving. We can adapt to unexpected situations and find innovative solutions to challenges. We are also sensory aware and notice things that others might not perceive. They need a chef."

Rebecca is at a loss for words. She allows the moment to pass, knowing that William is coming to terms with this revelation. Eventually, she places her hand on his arm. He slowly turns his head to her.

"I'm still not convinced about the Hemingway connection, but I feel in my heart that the clues are real."

Kitchen - Hotel d'Aubusson

After leaving William and Rebecca, Julian entered the kitchen and took out his phone, selecting an app given to him by the mysterious and gorgeous auburn-haired woman. There is a delay as the call is routed through a highly encrypted voice service. It goes straight to voicemail.

"Madame. It is Julian from the d'Aubusson. I have information about the American Chef that you will find most interesting. He is working on a diagram with Escoffier, Hemingway, and Correns. I await your call."

Once Julian hangs up, and without knowing, the app automatically deletes all call records from Julian's phone, including his cellular provider's database and the cell tower it was connected to.

Commune Sophia Antipolis - Nice, France

The fashionably dressed Woman With Auburn Hair enters a nondescript office building in the business park of Sophia Antipolis, a neighboring commune near Nice, France. She notices her phone buzzing inside her black leather Chanel bucket bag. She stops walking, looks around, pulls out the phone, and notes the number. Moments later, she listens to the message from her asset at the d'Aubusson Hotel. Her face lights up at the news. She ends the call and uses the same app to erase all digital traces of the message she received. Taking a moment, she processes the new information.

"The American chef is on the scent. Well done, William."

Chapter 11

Working Escoffier's Puzzle

Luxembourg Gardens - 6th Arrondissement, Paris,

France

The Luxembourg Gardens, commonly referred to as 'Le Luco' by Parisian residents, was built in 1612 as the home of Marie de 'Medici, widow of King Henry IV.   Today, her home, the Luxembourg Palace, is owned by the French Senate, which uses it to conduct governmental business. However, the grounds surrounding the Palace are open to the public, and it is here that Rebecca and William are slowly strolling to clear their heads of yesterday's revelations.   They've been walking without speaking as they make their way to their favorite place in the garden, La Fontaine Medicis, initially constructed in 1630. After falling into disrepair, Napoleon had the grotto refurbished, removing a statue of Venus and replacing it with the giant Polyphemus as he discovers the lovers Acis (a mortal) and Galatea (a sea-nymph). It is a quiet and peaceful place as William and Rebecca share a bench at the pool's edge.

Moments pass until Rebecca turns to William.

"A penny for your thoughts."

William smiles and gazes at the three carved figures in the grotto.

"I didn't sleep well last night.   Haunted by dreams of dark figures lurking in shadows."

He turns to look at her.

"In full disclosure, my brain is 100 percent committed to solving the puzzle if for no other reason than learning of Correns' discovery. But this affects us both, so I need to know how you feel about it before we go further."

Rebecca measures her words.

"My feelings land somewhere else. We know the book you have was altered. I want to know why and by whom."

William turns his gaze to the grotto and points to the statues.

"I remember coming here for the first time and seeing this place. The giant Polyphemus looks down at the mortal Acis and his sea-nymph lover Galatea. Out of jealousy, he hurls a rock and kills Acis."

William's words die out, and he takes Rebecca's hand.

"I cannot help but wonder who our Polyphemus is and if we will see the rock coming our way."

The two sit silently contemplating their future. William continues.

"What if I had never opened Escoffier's book? What then? Whoever is pulling the strings is playing 3-dimensional chess."

They exchange knowing looks as they share the same feelings about fate and destiny. They remain sitting there until Rebecca rises.

She reaches for William's hand, and the two turn north towards the Twilleries.

"I've got a surprise for you."

8 Rue Duputren - 6th Arrondissement - Paris, France

William and Rebecca love immersing themselves in the magic and majesty of Paris by simply taking long walks, as they have done since their first visit years ago. Paris offers the best in romance, museums, architecture, and culinary arts. Since that first trip, they have gone out daily, walking for hours and ending wherever their feet lead them.

After leaving the gardens, Rebecca leads them up the Rue de Condé, turning right onto Rue Monsieur le Prince and then right onto Rue Dupuytren. Rebecca stops in front of an unremarkable storefront at 8 Rue Dupuytren. William looks around and notices a small group of tourists gathered by a storefront. He turns to Rebecca, his face clouded with questions.

"And we are standing here because...?"

Rebecca looks lovingly at the man whose head has been under a cloud since discovering his error about Hemingway.

"I have a surprise for you."

Rebecca extends her arms toward a small group of tourists standing before a white-washed storefront.

"Ta-dah!"

William looks at the tourists and can hear the tour guide talk about the building's significance to a group of Americans. William's face shows confusion and minor irritation.

"Why am I looking at a group of tourists?"

Rebecca frowns.

"It's not the tourists; it's the storefront, my love. This is the original Shakespeare & Company. The very one that Sylvia Beach started! This is where Hemingway and the Lost Generation hung out. I thought seeing the real Shakespeare & Co would make you feel better."

William becomes distracted as the tour guide continues speaking to her group about F. Scott Fitzgerald.

"...Shakespear & Company became a second home to the members of the lost generation, including Hemingway, Fitzgerald, Stein, Joyce, and others. For a while, Hemingway and Fitzgerald were often seen together with Sylvia. It is well known that Fitzgerald thought of Hemingway as his artistic conscience."

The tour guide continues.

"This is the original location of Shakespeare & Co., founded by Sylvia Beach in 1919. It would later move a few streets over to 12 rue de l'Odéon. Eventually, however, the store would close its doors in 1941 due to World War II."

A tourist raises their hand.

"So the Shakespeare & Co. near Notre Dame isn't the original?"

The tour guide welcomed the question as it pertained to the group's next destination. She then leads the group north towards the Seine, heading to the newer version of Shakespeare & Co.

"No, it's not. The Shakespeare & Co. today was opened in 1964 by American George Whitman on the 400th anniversary of William Shakespeare's birth. He chose the name Shakespeare & Co. in honor of Sylvia Beach... let's keep walking."

William still has a distant look in his eye. Rebecca pulls him back.

"You're somewhere else entirely."

Rebecca watches silently as William stands as a statue, looking at the storefront and the marker displaying the name Shakespeare & Co. As another tour group walks up, William steps back, letting the group experience the building for themselves. He then looks at Rebecca, noticing that over half the group isn't interested in the empty building.

"I know what you're trying to do, and I appreciate it. "

She takes William's arm and starts walking north toward the Louvre.

"Let's keep walking. Who knows what else we might find before we reach the Ritz?"

Neither William nor Rebecca speaks at length, except for the occasional "look there". Their stroll takes them across the Pont des Arts bridge, which links the Institut de France with the Musée du Louvre over the Seine. Everything in Paris seems to connect the dots as you walk along narrow side streets or wide boulevards, and before you know it, you find yourself at your destination, as if time hasn't moved forward all that much.

As they enter the Tuileries, the famous gardens leading to the glass Pyramid of the Louvre, they come across Rue St. Honoré. They can also see the obelisk in Place Vendôme, home to the Ritz Hotel and the Bar Hemingway. Once they reach the Place Vendôme, Rebecca's heart leaped at the haute couture boutiques of Chanel, Gucci, Cartier, Louis Vuitton, and Van Cleef & Arpels that encircle the legendary obelisk. As William and Rebecca approach the Ritz, they spot an enormous bright red Flying Dragon sculpture by Alexander Calder standing guard in the square. They turn and head in the direction of the Ritz lobby.

William and Rebecca are well-known at the Ritz. The Ritz security personnel at the front entrance allow them to enter with only passing concern. The chef thinks to himself...

"Gaining entry anywhere is easiest when you _know_ you belong."

The inner security guard nods slightly, recognizing William with Rebecca on his arm. Moments later, the hotel host greets them at the top of the stairs with the French "faire la bise" greeting.

"Madame Rebecca and Monsieur Chef, welcome back to the Ritz."

It is the familiar face and firm handshake of Jean-Pierre, the late afternoon host. His English perfectly blends his French heritage with his American education.

"I see you are on our dinner list for 8 p.m. We anticipated your early arrival, as we are used to the routine of enjoying time in The Hemingway Bar. A table is reserved for you."

As Jean-Pierre begins escorting them, he stops as he is reminded of something.

"Monsieur Chef, just last week, management received the resume of the Chief Steward you recommended. They are eager to speak with him and expect that he will exceed the recommendation you kindly provided on his behalf. If all goes well, he should begin training within a month."

"You are most kind, Jean-Pierre. Before you leave us, I have something for you."

William reaches into his jacket and hands Jean-Pierre a charcoal-colored linen envelope that appears to absorb the light around it. The envelope has 'Z embossed in 24-karat gold leaf. Jean-Pierre is noticeably flustered. 'Z is an exclusive invitation-only culinary experience open only to celebrities, high government officials, and the wealthy. It has been said that an invitation immediately elevates the person to the highest level of social status.

"Please accept this invitation from a client of mine at your leisure."

"Monsieur. This is too extravagant a gift. I cannot accept!"

William puts his hand on Jean-Pierre's shoulder.

"Jean-Pierre, it is far less than all the many times you have shown kindness to us. Chef 'Z insists you bring your lovely wife, Claire."

After shaking his hand, the Chef and Rebecca turn and head through the lobby to the hallway of mirrors. They leave Jean-Pierre standing in the lobby, mouth agape, looking down at the envelope in his shaking hands.

"Putain de merde!" (French curse word loosely translating to Holy Shit!)

The Bar Hemingway - Vendome Plaza, Ritz Paris

The walk down the Hallway of Mirrors at the Ritz always takes Rebecca's breath away. Illuminated by hundreds of tiny LED lights, this antique mirrored hallway showcases the season's haute couture, featuring extravagant jewelry and branded attire. However, before entering the hallway, the chef pauses at the stairs leading down to the renowned Escoffier kitchen and culinary school, where he has spent countless days learning his craft from culinary masters.

Rebecca pulls at William's sleeve.

"Honey, let's get to our table. I need to get off my feet."

She knows William would spend the rest of the evening lost in his thoughts if left to his own devices. Turning to her, William summons his best impersonation of Westley from the movie 'The Princess Bride'.

"As you wish."

They arrive at Bar Hemingway in just a few moments, and the bar manager, Michel, is already waiting for them.

"Madame and Monsieur. It is a pleasure. Your table is ready."

Michel leads William and Rebecca through a heavy set of drapes to a solitary table in the back corner of the famous bar. William notices how Rebecca's face lights up, almost luminescent, as she admires the rich history on the walls around them. Rebecca rests her hand on William's arm.

"This is my happy place," she whispers, kissing William's cheek.

The Bar Hemingway features an eclectic mix of items owned or used by Hemingway himself. It boasts a magnificent collection of notes and typewriters, along with many pictures of Hemingway displayed around the room and a bust of him positioned behind the bar.

The staff at Hemingway provides impeccable service, and each member speaks multiple languages fluently. Michel pulls the table out to make room for Rebecca as she sits. After pushing it back in, he sets two linen napkins on the table.

"Would you like to have your favorite cocktails, or do you have something else in mind for tonight?"

William looks up to reply when, out of the corner of his eye, he notices a picture above the table next to them that he hasn't seen before. Slightly distracted, William points to the table beside them in response.

"Yes. Michel, the usual will be fine. By the way, is that photo new?"

Michel gazes in William's direction and turns to respond. Rebecca is freshening her makeup with a small mirror from her purse.

"Why yes. You have an excellent eye for detail, Monsieur Chef. It features Hemingway, Fitzgerald, and Escoffier. It was discovered among some storage in the newly renovated kitchen last month. It was nearly thrown out if not for the quick action of one of the kitchen staff. I believe it was taken at an event in Monte-Carlo after Escoffier retired."

The Chef and Rebecca stare at the picture in stunned silence. Neither of them says anything, but they are thinking the same thing. On the wall beside them is physical evidence connecting Hemingway and Escoffier. The two men were decades apart in age and never traveled in the same circles. Rebecca places her hand again on William's arm.

"Today, the stars are aligning for us."

William turns to Rebecca and, after a brief pause, whispers.

"I think I'd like to take a picture of it."

Without another moment's thought, and before Rebecca can stop him, William stands up from their table and walks over to two men sitting at the table in front of the photo on the wall. William speaks fluent French to the two men.

"I apologize for the interruption, gentlemen. I want to take a picture of the image behind you. Is this acceptable?"

The interruption gets the attention of the gentleman closest to the Chef. He scowls at William.

"Sir, you'll have to speak American if you want me to understand you!"

William smiles politely and starts to step back from the table. He switches back to English.

"I apologize, but I was hoping to photograph the image behind you. Would you mind?"

The gentleman lifts his napkin from his lap and tosses it onto the table for effect. After years of encountering this personality while he was in sales, William already knows exactly where this is heading. He glances over at Rebecca for moral support. She merely shrugs as if to say:

"You are on your own."

The American continues to express his outrage.

"We were in the middle of a business discussion when you rudely interrupted us. Therefore, the answer is yes, we do mind."

The other man at the table, clearly French, turns his gaze towards the bar. Michel notices his expression and quickly approaches to help resolve the situation. William begins to turn on the charm, speaking again in fluent French, but this time addressing the Frenchman directly.

"I sincerely apologize for upsetting your guest. I acknowledge my mistake and will make amends. The drinks will be on me; I insist."

The rude American starts to stand as Michel arrives and addresses him.

"Sir, is there a problem?"

The American gestures to William with his thumb and loudly begins to rant about being interrupted. William turns to Michel, who is still speaking French.

"It seems I've disturbed your guests. I'll cover their drinks, and we will excuse ourselves. I'm truly sorry for causing such a scene."

At that moment, the Frenchman rises from the table and grabs his coat. He speaks to Michel in French but then stops, takes a closer look at William, and a look of recognition washes over his face. His words flows off his tongue like a true child of France, aged like fine wine and silky to the ears.

"You are the one they call Le Chef, Oui?"

William extends his hand, and the Frenchman readily accepts it. William, smiling, continues in French.

"Yes, I'm afraid it's true."

At this point, the American stops criticizing Michel and, upon hearing the name "Le Chef," turns to acknowledge William.

"Well, damn, son, if you had just said that from the start, I wouldn't have been so rude. Even I know who you are by reputation."

William smiles politely at the American while the Frenchman explains his guest's outburst in French.

"Please excuse my companion. He's a bulldog of an attorney, but doesn't know when to ease up. However, you served my wife a meal last year, and to this day, she insists you're a Frenchman pretending to be American."

The two men laugh as William tells him a Frenchman would never want to be an American.

"Thank her for me, but could I ask your name?"

The Frenchman begins putting on his jacket.

"I am Jean-Claud Delsier, and my wife is Georgia."

William recalls the meal held at a chateau in Provence, where he met Georgia.

"Yes, I remember. She was a pleasure to serve, and her palate is highly refined."

The Frenchman smiles, and they begin saying goodbye when the Frenchman turns.

"You should come by for drinks. Georgia will be delighted to see you again, and perhaps we can convince you to test our kitchen. Here is my card."

With his phone, William accepts his card and snaps a picture of the image on the wall behind the table. He turns and apologizes to Michel.

"Monsieur Chef, it's not your fault. That particular American is here too often for our liking. However, Monsieur Delsier is a valued guest, so we must do what we can."

Feeling sheepish, William walks back to the table as Rebecca scowls at him. She uses her quiet but firm voice.

"Sometimes, I worry about your impulse control. Can you remind me again what you do for a living?"

Already distracted, William zooms in on the picture he just took. He glances over at Rebecca and shows her the image of Escoffier, Fitzgerald, and Hemingway standing with stern, unsmiling expressions, typical of photographs from that era. Next to Hemingway is his wife, Hadley, and next to Fitzgerald is a beautiful younger woman.

"It's proof that they at least met... and if Michel's timeframe is correct, the picture must have been taken after 1924."

Rebecca states the obvious.

"So we can add Hemingway back into our Escoffier conversation."

Looking more closely at the picture, she points at Hemingway.

"Is it just me, or does Hemingway look like he has swallowed a bug?"

Rebecca continues to look at the picture and enlarges it further. William cuts in.

"Well, Hemingway was known for being unlikable, and like you said, nobody smiled in photos back then."

As the photo enlarges, Rebecca's keen eye spots something else. She points to the woman standing with Fitzgerald.

"Who is that woman next to Fitzgerald?"

William moves the image over and centers it on Fitzgerald and Hemingway. The woman standing next to Fitzgerald is looking at Hemingway. William makes an obvious guess.

"I don't know. Perhaps it is Fitzgerald's wife, Zelda."

Rebecca stops, takes out her phone, opens a browser, and quickly finds an image of Zelda Fitzgerald. They compare the two images. The woman in the photo is not her. She points at the woman on William's phone/

"That, my dear, is the look of a woman in love, and she is looking directly at Hemingway. Also, Hadley is staring daggers at the woman."

"How could you tell all that just by the look on the woman's face?"

Rebecca brushes off William's question with an 'It's a woman thing' look and returns to the photo, examining Hemingway's face more closely. She lowers her voice to a whisper and points to Escoffier.

"I feel that whatever happened in Monte-Carlo must have something to do with Escoffier's puzzle."

Rebecca's logic confounds William.

"How does that make sense?"

It's Rebecca's turn to roll her eyes at William.

"It confirms Hemingway's connection to Escoffier. Additionally, by Hemingway's expression, it would appear he has learned something dreadful."

Rebecca watches as William processes the information. He turns to her, takes the phone, turns it off, and sets it on the table.

"The look of fear on Hemingway's face haunts me. He was a veteran of World War I and a war correspondent. Whatever Escoffier told him must have been horrific."

Rebecca replies matter-of-factly.

You mean like the Kaiser Wilhelm Society, horrific?"

From that moment, they both continued quietly working on the details of this discovery. They finished their drinks, paid their bar tab, and returned to the Ritz restaurant for their 8 p.m. reservation. They both deeply contemplated William's revelation and rarely spoke while they dined.

Their server comes over as they are about to finish with a troubled look on his face.

"Monsieur and Madame. Is there something wrong with your meal?"

William looks down at his plate and realizes he has only had a few bites. Rebecca's plate is the same. He looks to the server.

"By all means, no. The meal is beyond exceptional. Unfortunately, our minds are somewhere else. Please let the chef know that we apologize for being so distracted. This meal deserves more than we gave it."

As they leave the Ritz, John-Pierre calls for the hotel's car to take the couple back to the Hotel d'Aubusson. In the back seat of the blacked-out Maybach sedan, Rebecca looks at the flower she received when she ordered her drink at the Hemingway. She recalls that it commemorates Bar Hemingway as the first establishment in Paris to serve women drinks. Glancing over at William, she notices him lost in somber thought.

"What are you thinking about?"

William takes his time to respond.

"I am having difficulty coming to grips with the reality of Escoffier's puzzle. I fear we are walking into something we may never truly understand."

Rebecca takes his hand, and the two remain quiet for the remainder of their journey back to the d'Aubusson.

Chapter 12

A Plan Is Hatched

Hotel d'Aubusson - Next Day

William wakes from a restless sleep, and over coffee, he recalls a famous quote from Marcel Proust, one of the most influential French authors of the 20th century:

"The real voyage of discovery consists not in seeing new sights, but in looking with new eyes."

William takes a moment, allowing the words to sink in.

"New eyes indeed. What have I gotten us into?"

William hears Rebecca making her way from the bathroom. She has just woken up and is wearing a robe and slippers. William points to the hot cup of coffee with light cream and two sugars sitting at the table across from him. Next to it, he places her fully charged tablet and cell phone, as is her ritual each morning.

The view from the small table in their room looks out over Rue Dauphine as Parisians head to work. Rebecca takes a sip and smiles, appreciating the awaited caffeine boost. William waits for Rebecca to gather her thoughts. She sets down her cup, opens her tablet, and starts checking her email as part of her daily routine. She senses something and looks up at William with a questioning gaze. He gazes into his love's eyes and pauses before responding.

"I had a fitful night's rest. I am sorry if my tossing and turning kept you up."

Seeing the sadness in her husband's eyes, Rebecca places her hand on his arm, attempting to lift his spirits.

"My dear. I am also troubled, but we now have evidence of the connections in Escoffier's book. It won't be long before we discover why they were put there."

William isn't as optimistic as Rebecca, and his face reflects it.

"That is what has me concerned. The KWS discovered Mustard Gas, created the Gas Chambers, and performed live human experimentation that killed millions of people. That's a very high bar of terrible. Even if Correns' discovery is only a fraction as bad, it's still really horrific."

They both sit in silence, reflecting on William's words. Eventually, it is William who speaks.

"When I got up, I researched Escoffier and learned his former home in Villeneuve-Loubet, now a museum and only 15 minutes from Nice. Maybe we should check it out. Perhaps there will be more clues."

Rebecca's heart jumps at the thought of going to Nice. It is her favorite place in the world. She quickly agrees, opens her laptop, and searches for flights and hotels. Seeing the joy on her face, William cannot help but tease her.

"I hear there are two or three new hotels in Nice. Maybe we should try one of them."

Rebecca isn't having any of it.

"I already have a confirmed reservation at Le Negresco. Keep it up, and I'll start making fun of your hair again."

William smiles back at her as she makes the necessary preparations. However, he also contemplates his genuine desire to visit Escoffier's museum.

"Escoffier was renowned for maintaining detailed journals while writing his books. Perhaps he shared more insights about Correns' discovery in one of them."

Rebecca catches the look on William's face and calls him out on it.

"OK. What are you thinking about, my love?"

Caught, William tells her of his idea.

"I thought there might be something in his museum that could shed more light on Correns' discovery. Perhaps it is one of his journals."

Rebecca throws a wet blanket on the idea.

"So you think they will let you thumb through his journals?"

Rebecca quickly finds images of Escoffier's museum on her iPad. In his office is a glass-enclosed bookcase filled with journals. William is looking over her shoulder.

"Look there! Just as I thought, Escoffier's relentless pursuit of order would have ensured that each journal had a date on it."

Defeatedly, Rebecca responds.

"Yes, they do, but we don't know which journal contains the information we want. Is it the journal from when he hosted the Kaiser's Jubilee dinner? Or when he met Correns? Or when he first spoke to Hemingway? Or when he published his last book?"

Understanding her reasoning, William sighs and leans back in his chair. Rebecca offers him a lifeline.

"But I agree that if he wrote about the secret in more detail, it should be in one of those journals. All we need to do is determine which one."

Without thinking, William blurts out the words resting on the end of his tongue.

"...and steal it."

Rebecca snaps her head toward her husband, making William regret not pausing before voicing his thoughts.

"Are you out of your lovely mind?"

William defends his statement.

"We already believe that the secret must be something terrible. If it is, we will need physical evidence to show the authorities. I agree that the staff won't likely let us thumb through the documents in his office. So, the only alternative is to steal whatever we find."

Rebecca's analytical mind discovers another flaw in their thinking.

"It's been over a century since Correns' discovery and over a decade since it was translated in 2011. What if Escoffier's code was already broken along with Correns' discovery?"

The statement physically deflates William. He had spent all his effort trying to solve Escoffier's puzzle, and it never occurred to him that it could already be out in the world. He turns to Rebecca while he keeps looking for an opening.

"When we steal the journal, one of two things should happen: people start chasing us, meaning the secret isn't out, or nobody chases us, which indicates the secret was probably lost or is already out there. Either way..."

Rebecca finishes his statement...

"To know for certain, we must find and steal the journal."

Rebecca continues...

"You left out another obvious alternative. You steal it and spend a few days in jail, and nobody will chase you because it's a hoax."

Blacked Out Sedan - Nice, France

Within minutes, Rebecca confirms airline and hotel reservations to Nice while simultaneously, the Woman With Auburn Hair receives a text message from her AI tracking bot.

"Targets have confirmed reservations on Air France flight 129 from CDG to NICE, arriving at 13h55 with hotel reservations at Le Negresco for two weeks."

The Woman With Auburn Hair smiles at her good fortune. She considers her options and begins making a few calls.

Hotel Le Negresco, Nice, France - Next Day

When staying in Nice, William and Rebecca usually stay at an apartment in the Carré d'Or (The Golden Square) district. However, since this was a last-minute decision to go to Nice, they booked a room at Hotel Le Negresco, which always makes Rebecca smile.

With its iconic pink and green dome from the 'belle époque' era, the famous Hotel Le Negresco is a prominent landmark on the French Riviera. Since its opening in 1913, it has welcomed artists, royalty, and celebrities, and was envisioned by Romanian confectioner Henri Negrescu, who brought it to life with architect Édouard Niermans.

When it opened, the hotel had 400 rooms, each with a private bath. However, one of its most stunning features is a massive Baccarat chandelier comprising 16,309 crystals adorning the massive circular Royal Lounge. Madame Jeanne Augier, who purchased the hotel in 1957, also contributed an eclectic collection of over 6,000 works of art.

Even though William and Rebecca are exhausted from their experiences in Paris, glancing at Le Negresco's façade makes the weight of their burden feel lighter. As the Uber approaches the lobby entrance, they are greeted by door attendants dressed as 18th-century elite bourgeois servants with red-plumed postilion hats. As they're welcomed into the hotel, Rebecca squeezes William's arm excitedly at their return to her favorite place. The concierge greets them as they approach the lobby.

"Welcome back, Monsieur and Madame Laurent. Your registration has been processed, and I will ensure your bags are unpacked. If you would like, our bartender is eagerly waiting to see you both. Relax and enjoy some complimentary champagne while your room is prepared."

William accepts the key to the room as Rebecca walks forward to view the magnificent Baccarat chandelier. Within moments, William joins her and leads her towards Le Bar 1913. Within seconds, their dear friend Benjamin, the bar manager, enthusiastically greets them.

"Monsieur Chef and Madame Rebecca, it is such a nice surprise."

Benjamin turns to Rebecca, exchanging the traditional greeting of 'faire la bise' as do Benjamin and William. Benjamin pulls out her chair and signals the bar to bring a bottle of chilled Deutz champagne and two crystal champagne glasses.

"I have the honor of serving you champagne. Please take a moment to unwind, as I can see that both of you look exhausted. I'll be right back."

Benjamin walks away, and Rebecca's face brightens with all the attention. Even William feels better. He leans toward Rebecca, reading her mind.

"My love. This, too, is my happy place."

Rebecca surveys Le Negresco's Bar 1913 with a two-story tapestry-covered oak-paneled wall. A jazz quartet plays in the corner, and Rebecca feels a sense of peace for now. She casually reaches over to take William's hand.

"I could live here."

William hears the melancholy in her voice.

"I've been thinking. I'm going to put an end to this nonsense with Escoffier's puzzle. We have another two weeks before we head back to America. Let's make the most of it."

William can see a noticeable improvement in Rebecca's mood. She smiles back at him, knowing that he means well, but she knows well enough that he will not quit before solving the puzzle.

"One day at a time, my love. For now, let's savor the tranquility of this beautiful place."

Chapter 13

Stealing Escoffier's Journal

Henry Matisse Apartment - Cour Seleya, Vieux Nice -

Next Day

The Woman With Auburn Hair is reading a report on the life of Chef William Laurent when she receives a hyper-encrypted text.

"Asset on the move."

She rises quickly and heads downstairs to her waiting blacked-out Sedan.

"Take me to Spyglass, quickly."

She then texts the CIA station chief to confirm her other assets are in place. Arriving at a nondescript apartment building in Sophia Antipolis, she quickly enters and heads to the basement.

The Escoffier Museum - Villenueve-Loubet, France

It is unseasonably warm for an early spring day in Villeneuve-Loubet, a commune in the Côte d'Azur region of southeastern France. The Mediterranean's typically cooler breeze feels unusually warm. William unbuttons his denim jacket and rolls up its sleeves as he gazes at a somewhat comical-looking statue of Saint Fortunat, the patron saint of cooks, perched in an alcove on what may have been the carriage house of the Escoffier family home. As the statue looks down at him, William cannot shake the guilt for deciding to steal Escoffier's journal alone. Having left Le Negresco early and leaving a note for Rebecca, he knows she will be upset.

He shakes his head, thinking to himself...

"Don't kid yourself. She may never forgive you for doing this on your own."

William looks up sheepishly at the statue and lets a thought escape his lips.

"I don't suppose you could just tell me what the initials are hiding in Escoffier's book?"

William pauses in silence, hoping for an answer that will never come. He looks away from the statue and turns toward the museum entrance behind him. His phone starts buzzing. It's a text from his driver, Eitan.

"I am parked around the corner in front of the hotel near the street. Text me when you're ready to leave."

Eitan is a driver for one of William's closest clients who lives outside Nice in Villefranche-sur-Mer. When William and Rebecca are in town, his client makes his car available. William replies with a thumbs-up emoji, returns the phone to his jacket pocket, and walks a few steps to the entrance of a structure that was once Escoffier's family home but is now the Escoffier Museum.

He observes the ancient building, beautifully patinaed in sunflower yellow, with clay-tiled peaked roofs reminiscent of Italian architecture. Each building along Rue de Escoffier, including most in the center of Villeneuve-Loubet, shares this style. The voices of these silent sentinels, closely packed together on both sides of the street, speak to a time when this region of southeastern France was under Italian rule.

As William turns away from the street, his mind races with questions. Will there be evidence of the Correns' discovery? If so, how will he manage to steal it? William takes a moment to mentally review his notes on Escoffier and the initials placed in his book.

"Escoffier leaves a trail of breadcrumbs in his culinary bible consisting of three distinct sets of initials: KW, CC, and EH, which he identifies as Kaiser Wilhelm II, the last Emperor of Germany; plant geneticist Carl Correns; and American author Ernest Hemingway."

Realizing he is once again talking to himself out loud, William quickly glances around to see if anyone passing by has noticed. His head turns toward the museum entrance as a woman emerges from it. Committing to the task, he follows her in and steps into the museum's small entryway, eyeing the woman who has just returned behind the counter after opening the door. She is petite, a few years older than William, and has close-cropped hair. She smiles and looks up at him, speaking beautiful French.

"Welcome, sir, to the Escoffier Museum. How can I assist you?"

William replies in French.

"Yes, Madame. A ticket for the tour, if you please."

William takes a 10 euro note and waits as the friendly receptionist counts his change. As he approaches the counter, he notices a security camera out of the corner of his eye, which is pointed directly at where he will buy a ticket. He turns his head towards the interior of the museum. Moments later, William follows the red arrows painted on the floor throughout the building, indicating the path one should take to explore the story of the greatest French culinary masters. He smiles to himself, thinking:

"If only life were as easy to navigate..."

The ground floor of the former Escoffier house was used for cooking and food storage—a pragmatic design choice, as the ovens in his day were used to heat the home. As William looks around, he notices various culinary artifacts on the walls, including a deep hand-cranked kettle mixer and Escoffier's ancient wood-fueled stove. He pauses along the way, intrigued by multiple objects, artifacts, and pictures while reading the detailed notes beneath each one. However, it is a stalling tactic as he secretly knows that what he seeks can only be found in Escoffier's office. Still, the artifacts pique his interest, and as he progresses through each room, he carefully observes the positioning of any security cameras without looking directly into them.

As he makes his way through the ground floor, William becomes aware of the limited space inside the museum. After all, it was Escoffier's home at the turn of the century, and possibly old enough to have been someone else's residence before that. Large open floor plans, common today, were not a consideration back then. Each room served a distinct purpose. Looking around, he smiles, realizing that he is walking in the very footsteps of Escoffier.

Continuing with the self-guided tour, William can barely wait to reach the second level, which houses Escoffier's office and a library filled with memorabilia. There, he expects to find the evidence of the initials he discovered in Escoffier's Le Guide Culinaire—a puzzle whose purpose he has yet to uncover.

A few moments later, he enters a room adorned with Escoffier memorabilia. Along the wall hang posters of various dining venues that Escoffier hosted throughout his storied career and advertisements from that era. In the center of the room, he notices glass cases showcasing menus from notable dining events organized by Escoffier. As he meanders through, peering into the glass, William suddenly halts and fixates on a menu featuring an image of Kaiser Wilhelm II. This menu is from the very event aboard the ocean liner SS Imperator! The event where the Kaiser bestowed on Escoffier the informal title of 'The King of Chefs'. William's heart races, and he feels his blood pounding in his ears. His mind rejoices, realizing this is an actual menu from his Kaiser's Silver Anniversary cruise! He snaps a photo of the menu. William once again reminds himself of the task he is there to accomplish.

"Quit being a tourist and get back to uncovering evidence of the Correns' discovery."

However, as William is about to move on, he stops, noticing something handwritten in the lower right corner of the Silver Anniversary menu. The handwriting is faint from age and slightly obscured by the glass covering it. He takes another picture using his phone, zooming in on the menu's foxed corner. He brings the image up on his screen and enlarges it. At the bottom, written in pencil, are the numbers 27-6-14. William thinks momentarily and recalls that Europeans write dates differently from Americans. They begin with the day, month, and year, while Americans start with the month. His mind races as he considers the implications of those numbers. His eyes return to the menu and the date printed on it. ***Tuesday, June 23, 1914***

"Escoffier did leave a reminder of the journal entry, and it was 4 days after the dinner on 27 June, 1914!"

Unsure of the significance of that specific date, William steps back from the cabinet and bumps into a young woman holding a mop and bucket. The collision causes her to drop the bucket and dump the soapy water in it.

"Monsieur, please excuse me." She immediately grabs a towel from her shoulder and begins wiping up the spill. William replies in French.

"Mademoiselle. Please excuse me."

In that moment, another woman enters the room to assist. With both women busy cleaning up the mess, William takes advantage of the accident and moves toward the next room that holds Escoffier's office. He politely excuses himself, and upon entering, he notices Escoffier's desk in the back corner and, behind it, the bookcase filled with his journals. He pauses at the entrance and scans the room for cameras, spotting one directly above Escoffier's desk.

It is then that William takes note of the moment he is in. Standing in front of Escoffier's desk, William imagines Escoffier sitting behind his desk and writing the entry into the journal regarding Correns' discovery.

William is startled as he hears the floorboards creak from the weight of the woman returning to Escoffier's office. William lowers his head and swiftly approaches the case containing Escoffier's journals. Quickly scanning the journals, he finds the one dated 27 June, 1914. With adrenaline coursing through his veins, William rises and looks around the room, listening to the women complain about the spill. He takes a deep breath and encourages himself.

"It's now or never, William."

Reaching into the case, he carefully removes the notebook and opens it.

Exact Moment - CIA Safe House (code name: Spyglass) - Nice, France

The Woman With Auburn Hair looks up at a sophisticated array of monitors as a young computer tech feverishly types away at the keyboard in front of her. She leans over to examine a real-time black-and-white image of William standing in Escoffier's office in the museum. However, he looks down, and she cannot see his face. The tech notices the gorgeous auburn-haired field agent leaning in beside her, her blouse slightly open, revealing a glimpse of her cleavage. Her perfume is intoxicating, and the tech tries to impress her.

"Madame, this is happening in real-time. I accessed their video feed by spoofing an internet-connected coffee pot in the museum's break room. Forensically, they could trace the hack, but we will be long gone before that."

The Woman With Auburn Hair smiles when William opens the cabinet and takes out the journal. As William looks around, the technician's face reveals a look of confusion.

"Why is he just standing there? Those cleaning people are close to finishing up."

The Woman With Auburn Hair allows a smile to escape her calm demeanor.

"He senses a trap. Very good indeed, William. I'm impressed."

The two women watch as William opens the journal and flips through its pages. Even without sound, the tech and the Woman With Auburn Hair can see that he is cursing at himself. The Woman With Auburn Hair quickly stands back and grabs her purse.

"I'm heading to the Curtain Group offices. They, too, will soon be aware of the intrusion. Please send me updates on my secure line. Oh, be a dear and remove any image you find of his face, both coming and going."

The computer technician smiles brightly as the intoxicating auburn-haired woman turns and heads toward the stairs.

Back Inside Escoffier's Office in the Museum

William opens the journal and immediately notices the pages are blank. He is furious but must hold back his anger for another time.

"The journal is fake!"

In just two beats of his heart, he understands the truth about his current situation. He quietly chastises himself.

"This is a fucking trap!"

William hears the cleaning staff returning to the office and is determined not to look up. He quickly heads to the nearest exit, turning his head away from the surveillance cameras.

Tech Industries Ltd. (A subsidiary of The Curtain Group) Sophia Antipolis, Nice

A computer technician is playing an online game and notices an alarm at the Escoffier Museum. He calls his supervisor, who then contacts the Head of Covert Ops for the Curtain Group.

"Sir, our technician in section 3 has an alarm at the Escoffier Museum."

There is a slight pause as the supervisor listens to instructions.

"Yes, sir. An alpha response team is seven minutes out."

[short pause]

"No, sir. We reviewed the camera footage, but the subject kept his face out of frame.

[short pause]

"He is a white male of average height, possibly in his late fifties, and wearing a denim jacket."

[short pause]

"Yes, sir, all files have been downloaded to field assets."

Chapter 14

The Chase

Escoffier Museum, Villeneuve-Loubet, France

As William reaches the street to the village square, he grabs his phone and sends an urgent text to his driver, Eitan. Looking around, he notices several cameras outside the museum and makes an effort to walk directly underneath them, where their field of vision is limited. Moments later, his executive driver sees William hurriedly approaching and pulls the car up to the traffic circle. William jumps headfirst into the back seat of the Range Rover Sentinel SUV and gives Eitan his instructions in tightly controlled and urgent English.

"Eitan, it's time to go. Quickly, if you please."

Before becoming a private driver, Eitan worked as a Mossad agent, where he learned to read his clients' emotions. He wastes no time getting the car out of the parking lot and onto the streets of the quiet village of Villeneuve-Loubet, heading toward the A8 autoroute and the city of Nice.

William sits in the back seat, collecting himself as he continually turns his head to check if anyone is following them. Relaxing slightly, he flips through the empty pages of his journal, angry at himself for being so foolish. He looks up and notices a questioning look on his driver's face. Just then, William is startled by his phone buzzing in his jacket. It's Rebecca; her voice carries an edge that William recognizes as anger.

"Imagine my surprise when I get up and find you've already gone. Please tell me you didn't just steal the journal?"

William shares with Rebecca the discovery of the fake journal and his escape from the museum.

Rebecca gets right to it.

"Is there anyone following you?"

William looks back through the tinted glass.

"No, it doesn't appear we're being followed."

William notices Eitan pick up his cell phone and starts speaking in Hebrew. Rebecca, acknowledging what's done is done, shifts her focus to the future.

"Okay. I'll be downstairs when you get here. Are you going to get arrested?"

William has no idea how to answer.

"No, I don't think so. I will see you in a few minutes. I love you. Bye."

William sits back heavily into the seat. The drive from the museum in Villeneuve-Loubet to the Le Negresco Hotel takes just under twenty minutes, which William believes will give him ample time to devise a plan. However, five minutes into the drive, his thoughts are interrupted by a car racing alongside with blacked-out windows. William's heart races as he instinctively sinks into his seat to stay hidden. Eitan finishes his call and looks back at William through the rearview mirror.

"Sir, the windows of our vehicle are also tinted, reflective, and bulletproof. No one can see either of us. You're safe... for now. Is your seatbelt fastened?"

William buckles up and notices his hands shaking from the adrenaline after racing out of the Museum. He takes a few deep breaths and relaxes as Eitan continues speaking.

"Sir, I have just learned from my sources that those following us have canceled police intervention."

William pauses for a moment, suddenly overwhelmed with the meaning of his words. Eitan completes the thought for him.

"If they can do that, they are either the French government or something far less pleasant."

Looking back, William sees the cars slowing down. He then looks up at Eitan.

"Eitan, why have they stopped following us?"

Eitan steals another look at William in his rearview mirror.

"Monsieur Chef. The other car is falling back if we make a last-minute turn that the front car cannot manage. What do you wish me to do?"

Unfamiliar with the situation, William takes a moment to compose himself, thinking...

"You knew that taking the journal could trigger a response. At least now it's likely the secret hasn't been revealed yet."

William dials back Rebecca. She immediately picks up, and he blurts out the answer they were not hoping for.

"Alright. So the secret is _NOT_ out."

Rebecca's heart races with fear.

"So people _are_ chasing you!"

"Yes. Two cars."

Eitan breaks in.

"Sir, if I may ask. Did you take something? It might have a tracking device."

"You mean like a bug?"

Rebecca, hearing the conversation, jumps in.

"You've been bugged!!?"

William's mind is racing. Rebecca's voice is shaky.

"Look, William. You handle your situation. I'll call our attorney and figure out our options. I'll reach out once I know something. Stay safe, and don't do any more reckless things like leaving me out of the loop."

The line goes silent, and William slips his phone back into his jacket. Eitan, gazing at the traffic, replies matter-of-factly.

"Sir, it doesn't have to be a bug; it's more likely an RFID tag."

William recalls using such tags during his previous career in the technology industry. It was an innovative and cost-effective method to reduce shoplifting. A small circuit board that emits a weak radio signal is attached to an item, and as it passes by an RFID reader, it triggers an alarm. The devices were even integrated into car tires to monitor tire wear and usage.

Eita breaks in once again.

"It is small and thin enough to remain mostly unnoticed."

William pulls out the journal and starts searching for the tag. It takes some time, but he feels it is just beneath the inside cover, near the bottom corner. He quickly lifts the corner of the journal's cover, exposing the RFID tag concealed in the lining. William rolls down the window slightly and tosses the device out.

Eitan glances back at William.

"Monsieur Chef, I'm sorry to say there are other ways to track us without using RFID."

William smiles.

"Agreed. But now it's a game of cat and mouse, and I assume it's a game you're quite familiar with."

Smiling back, Eitan gets on the phone with his security company.

Executive Suite, The Curtain Group - Sophia Antipolis Technology Park

"THIS IS UNACCEPTABLE!"

A loud, heavily accented British voice echoes through the door, easily heard by anyone passing by. The shouting from inside the room continues without pause. The secretary outside the door continues typing, seemingly unaffected by the outburst.

"HE JUST WALKED OUT WITH IT?! WHERE IS HE NOW?!"

There is a brief pause as the veins in his neck bulge with his mounting anger. As Operations Director for The Curtain Group, Herman Dashil has relished the benefits of his position on the French Riviera for the past 20 years. A graduate of a prestigious military academy at 17 and with two tours of duty serving his native Great Britain, Herman epitomizes tall, brooding, and intimidating. Standing over 2 meters tall (6'7" US), he commands every room he enters. When anything threatens the certainty of his business, it is met with all the emotion his body and temperament can muster. He listens for a moment longer, rolls his eyes, and interrupts.

"My Turkish friend, you must detain the person who took the journal for questioning. It's time to earn your pay. If I were you, I'd do so quickly."

Herman slams the receiver down on the phone, walks to the door, and opens it. Sitting in the luxuriously appointed reception area outside his office is the Woman With Auburn Hair, relaxing in a white leather Barcelona chair. She is reading a text she just received from the cute young technician at the CIA ELINT (ELectronic INTelligence) unit, informally referred to as Spyglass.

"CG assets are currently monitoring the target."

She looks at Herman and puts away her phone as he waves her into his office. The Woman With Auburn Hair is dressed in a form-fitting pencil skirt paired with a billowing white translucent top and Saint Laurent stilettos. She epitomizes fashion and beauty while carrying herself with the poise of a consummate professional. She has striking red hair and intoxicating pale green eyes that conceal a razor-sharp intellect that supports more degrees than most Rhodes Scholars. Fluent in over seven languages, including the ability to read lips in each of them, she strides confidently into the office.

Herman shuts the door behind her and walks over to his desk.

"I suspect you heard all that?"

It wasn't a question. The Woman With Auburn Hair remains standing.

"Yes, sir. This is unexpected. However, I wonder why…"

Herman interrupts her mid-sentence. His voice was still tempered with anger.

"Does the _why_ matter?!"

The Woman With Auburn Hair also notices the condescending tone of his interruption.

"Herman, I was just going to say, why _now?_ We've always anticipated this happening, but the timing feels suspicious."

Herman nods in agreement and mentally notes her knowledge of his business. He relaxes slightly and sits behind his desk, looking at her dispassionately.

"You're our fixer, so fix it."

The Woman With Auburn Hair shakes off the comment like it was a piece of lint from her sleeve. She rises.

"Herman, I like you, but remember who I work for."

Herman dismisses her comment and begins providing her with an update she is already aware of.

"We're tracking the man, and he's heading to Nice. Let's hang back and see if he meets anyone. We have three units on their way to pick him up. Keep me updated on the situation in real-time. You must catch up since the Turk is already handling the retrieval."

Without responding to Herman's instructions, the Woman With Auburn Hair turns and starts toward the door, but stops and looks back at Herman.

"Herman, once the Turk loses the target, have him meet me at the Le Negresco Hotel. I'll be in the lobby bar."

Herman rolls his eyes at her inability to follow an order. With only a sly glance, the Woman With Auburn Hair leaves the room, trailing a cloud of perfume that even Herman finds hard to ignore; a gift from a talented CIA biologist specializing in covert fragrances crafted to elicit various emotional responses at a molecular level.

A Range Rover Sentinel - Speeding Along The A-8

Built by Land Rover Special Vehicle Operations, the Sentinel SUV is a mobile fortress featuring the latest technology in occupant protection, including armoured glass, roof blast-protection, and an emergency escape system. It has a supercharged V8 engine, capable of 0-100km/h in 10.4 seconds (0-60mph in 9.8 seconds). Oblivious to these facts, William begins to experience genuine fear, which comes across as a metallic taste in his mouth. He gathers what little courage he can muster and sees Eitan looking back at him in the rearview mirror.

"Eitan, if you wanted to capture us, how would you do it?"

Eitan's response is immediate.

"Sir, I would direct you to a capture box. It would require multiple teams to approach us from all directions at once. I believe that is what our pursuers are trying to do now."

William's mind races to formulate a plan that keeps him one step ahead of his pursuers.

The Lead Pursuing Car

A serious-looking man of Mediterranean descent takes his phone from his jacket and hits a pre-programmed speed dial for Herman Dashill. The call is picked up immediately. His thick Turkish accent fills the car.

"Sir, we have fallen back. [Pause] No, sir, we do not know who is in the SUV. It is a Range Rover Sentinel, which can obscure our view and passively block infrared FLIR (Forward Looking Infrared) imaging. I've positioned spotters on the A8 leading into Nice, and our assets are ready to converge once we have the target in position. [Pause] Yes, sir. It will be done."

The Range Rover Sentinel - Speeding Along The A-8

William gathers his thoughts and glances at Eitan in the rearview mirror. He doesn't appear confident, which only heightens William's concern. He takes a moment to think aloud.

"Ok, William. You still have 15 minutes before you reach Nice. Maybe now is a good time to devise a strategy that doesn't end up with you being captured."

As Eitan continues driving, William's mind wanders back to his first time in Nice (pronounced like the English word "niece"). He was drawn to it by its culinary scene. Throughout the ages, Nice has been home to many cultures that, over time, have melded to create culinary dishes no longer belonging to any of them. They have become something unique. They have become Niçoise. This is why William and Rebecca think of Nice as their second home. They enjoy learning something new about it every day, as William reflects.

"Every day except today."

A few moments pass, and William notices that a decision must soon be made. Should they continue on the A8 or exit onto M6098, better known as the Promenade Des Anglais? William looks up at Eitan in the mirror, noticing that he, too, has the same question on his face. Eitan voices his thoughts as they speed toward the exit.

"Sir. Which way would you like me to go?"

William needs more time to think. A plan is beginning to form in the back of his mind.

"Eitan, let's stay on the A8 and circle in from the north. I need time to think."

He gazes at the journal resting on the seat beside him. He places it back in his jacket, if only for evidence.

In a few moments, they arrive at exit 54 for Boulevard Paul Rémond, named after the former Bishop of Nice. William instructs Eitan to exit, but Eitan takes it a step further. As soon as he exits the A8, he starts making random turns, beginning at Le Parc Du Ray. Eitan, seeing the questioning look in William's eye, explains.

"The more turns we make, the more our pursuers will be confused, making it extremely difficult to box us in.

The Pursuit Turns Analog

No longer able to digitally track the car's direction, William's pursuers change tactics and begin positioning assets above several main roads leading into Nice. These assets hold binoculars and scan the road for the SUV. A spotter reaches for his phone as their SUV passes one such location. A man with a thick Turkish accent answers as the scout reports.

"Sir! I have them on Route de Turin, turning onto Voie Romaine and heading west. Spotters are being rerouted as we speak."

Two minutes into the pursuit, Eitan looks back at William apologetically in the rearview mirror. His eyes reflect the resolve of the Mossad, and he will do his best to stay ahead of our pursuers, though this will not change the fact that they will ultimately be caught. William instinctively vocalizes the beginning of a plan lurking in his mind.

"Eitan. Let's find a route to Vieux Nice instead."

Pronounced like the English word (view), Vieux (Old) Nice is filled with tourists, but its tiny streets do not allow such pursuits. Smiling in recognition, Eitan changes course, turning East onto Rue Gioffredo and heading toward the Museum of Modern Art. Eitan notices William's face shows concern, so he looks back at him in the rearview mirror and offers some advice.

"Monsieur Chef. This level of pursuit indicates that these individuals are military-trained. My company has just informed me that the Gendarmerie has not been notified about your actions at the museum. What these people want remains unclear, but they are determined and capable of taking you into custody."

William's mind races. Whatever the outcome, if his pursuers are willing to put in this much effort to capture him, his life and that of his family will undoubtedly be in danger. Looking back through the dark-tinted bulletproof glass, William sees his pursuers just a few cars behind. He silently resolves to take action. He voices his thoughts aloud.

"They haven't seen me and can't connect me to this car, so my family should be safe as long as I avoid getting caught. However, I need to throw off this pursuit and disappear."

At that moment, William recalls a childhood memory. William was short and stocky as a young boy and wore thick glasses to correct a crossed eye. This made him an easy target for elementary school bullies seeking to establish their reputation. William's main bully was a kid named Georgie, who also happened to know karate. It took only one jab-punch from the little brat to teach William a valuable lesson.

"Use your brain, not your brawn, and especially not your mouth, to avoid a beating. It's better to stay out of reach of their fists."

Whenever little Georgie came looking for him at school, which was far too often, William would head straight to the playground monkey bars. A semi-circular metal structure, Monkey Bars, are as tall as they are wide, featuring a web of bars to crawl on and through. Imagine it as a spider web with wider openings. This maze of openings provides an ideal spot for a smaller, more agile child to stay out of reach of a slower, much larger bully. William finds inspiration in this memory because he recalls a similar area near their current location. He looks up at Eitan.

"Keep going and turn right onto Rue Alfred Motier toward the Promenade du Paillon. Let's see if we can create more distance between us and them."

The ancient area of Vieux Nice was founded by the Phocaeans from Marseille (a colony of Greek mariners) around 350 BCE. It is a maze of narrow streets lined with tall multi-story buildings dating back to the 16th century. The streets of Vieux Nice showcase the passage of time in the region. Like many paintings by French masters, the structures feature open windows with billowing clothes drying in the gentle Mediterranean Sea air.

Most buildings in Vieux Nice are at least six stories tall, painted in umber tones, weathered over the centuries, and arranged to create a maze. The good news is that William knows these streets like the back of his hand, having spent countless hours as a chef buying ingredients from local vendors and visiting the many delightful restaurants there. More importantly, he knows all the exits to the maze, including a few that many people aren't aware of. And like his childhood bully, once he's inside Vieux Nice, his pursuers would never lay a hand on him.

To the blaring horns of local Niçois drivers, Eitan swiftly moves through heavy traffic, which jerks William in his seat and causes him to grab the door handle. The Niçois, who call Vieux Nice home, are very aggressive in their driving habits. There is little patience for timid drivers, and Eitan demonstrates his skills to keep up with the best of them.

As Eitan arrives at the intersection of Rue Gioffredo and Rue Alfred Motier, William observes that Eitan has created some distance from their pursuers. He slows down as he approaches the intersection, still deciding whether to turn. Instantly, the cars behind him begin honking their horns, aware that the light will soon change. Eitan waits deliberately and, with perfect timing, makes the turn just as the oncoming traffic starts to flow through the intersection. Meanwhile, the pursuers, now many cars back, are trapped in the traffic and have to wait for the light to turn green again. Eitan flashes a rare smile, which William reciprocates with one of his own.

"Eitan, your skill amazes me."

Thinking quickly, Eitan jumps back on the phone with his company. He starts speaking in Hebrew, which to William sounds like he's arguing with himself.

"Do we have other Black Sentinels in Nice or not? It is a simple question!"

There is a pause. Eitan continues

"We do? At the Plaza? Excellent. Have all of them converge on my location immediately!"

William knows the Plaza is an area where many luxury hotels are located. He is thoroughly impressed with Eitan's move. Many of the guests at those hotels will likely use Eitan's company for transportation. Having more SUVs that look just like the one he is in should confuse the pursuers enough for him to escape. William nods at Eitan in the mirror, acknowledging his efforts. Eitan is distracted by movement in the cars behind them. William sees a man from a pursuing vehicle trying to open his door to follow on foot. However, the line of parked cars on the street prevents the door from opening completely, trapping him in his seat. The man returns to the car and grabs his phone.

"Car Three. Return to the Promenade and pick up the Sentinel as it merges into traffic."

The man listens to the response, anger raging in his eyes. Then, he begins shouting into the phone in his Turkish accent.

"I do not care how many Sentinels you now see. Pick one and ram it!"

Thanks to Eitan's driving skills, they arrive at Avenue Saint-Jean Baptiste, where their pursuers can no longer track them visually. William seizes the chance to exit the sedan.

"Eitan. Thank you for keeping me safe. I owe you!"

Eitan is a consummate steely-eyed professional. He nods while checking the mirror to see if anyone is on foot. He signals an all-clear as William exits the car and crosses the street amid the blaring horns of frustrated Niçois drivers forced to stop for him. Upon reaching the checkered steps at the Greenbelt entrance to Vieux Nice, William glances back to see Eitan turning onto Ave Saint-Jean and racing toward the Nice Downtown Center.

Looking up at the church towers rising above all else in Vieux Nice, William gains his bearings and starts heading toward Place Saint-François at a dead run. As a chef, William has spent long hours on his feet, but he knows that his aging body won't hold up for long at this pace. He smiles as he notices the familiar group of ancient buildings that will help him evade his pursuers.

"It's time to enter the monkey bars..."

Chapter 15

The Monkey Bars

Place Saint-François - Vieux Nice, France

Place Saint-François is the northern part of Vieux Nice, just a hundred yards from the steps where William had entered. As he slows his run, he begins to feel the pulse in his ears pounding loudly while his heart struggles to deliver oxygen to his legs. Upon reaching Place Saint-François, he notices it is packed with tourists and local Niçois people. He feels pleased with himself for the moment, thinking,

"This should even the odds a bit."

William chose the Place Saint-François because he knew the area would be bustling with locals buying food to take home at this time of day. Another reason William selected this particular entry point into Vieux Nice because it is home to the Fishmongers of Saint-François. As he rushes into the square, he momentarily stops and locks eyes with his longtime friend, an older fishmonger known to the locals as Luca. The two men briefly stare at each other before William looks back towards the Promenade he just ran through as multiple vehicles begin to arrive.

A dark sedan that William recognizes from the A8 quickly pulls up to the curb as men gather at the Place Saint-François entrance. They are all looking around in different directions, fingers jabbing at their cell phones, and one man is speaking loudly to them; even from this distance, William can hear his thick Mediterranean accent. The man waves his arms in various directions, issuing orders. William turns once more to his friend Luca, shrugs his shoulders, and smiles awkwardly as he moves swiftly through the crowd and away from the men on the street. Luca's face reveals concern, and he approaches his grandsons, speaking to them in Niçard (pronounced Knee-sard), the ancient language of Vieux Nice.

"Our friend Ordures (an ancient Niçard word meaning "trash") seems to have people chasing after him. Go find out why, and do so quickly."

Luca's grandsons wink at each other, glad to let others handle the fish packing. They dash toward the men, who have increased in number, at the entrance to Place Saint-François.

William also has a tactical reason for choosing Place Saint-François as his entry point to Vieux Nice. The square provides numerous directional options, forcing his pursuers to split up in their search for him. If he plays his cards right, this should confuse and slow them down. Now, feeling the cold sting of sweat dripping freely down his forehead and into his eyes, William reminds himself that he cannot maintain this pace. Thinking quickly, he decides to revise the plan.

"Okay, you're in the monkey bars, but now you need to find some high ground."

He leaves Place Saint-François, turning right onto Rue Pairoliere, using its narrow passage to his advantage. He continues down it, looking up ahead at an intersection crowded with people buying groceries. The street sign shows Place du Carret, and he remembers it having access to the upper levels of Vieux Nice. This is also where the town's cannon is located. It fires a blank at midday, startling pigeons and tourists for miles.

The upper levels of Vieux Nice are also home to the Chapelle De La Visita Saint-Claire, constructed in 1669 for Italian-born Saint-Claire of Assisi. The structure could provide him a place to hide or, at the very least, give him the advantage of seeing his pursuers coming from a long way off. The trouble with this part of his plan is the many stairs he must climb to reach the Chapelle. Jokingly, William chides himself.

"At least your iPhone Health tracker will show some stairs today."

The thought doesn't boost his confidence much, but the new plan gives him purpose and a more substantial advantage, so he starts climbing the stairs two steps at a time. Reaching the top takes longer than expected and requires more effort than his 6-decade-old body can handle. As he clears the top landing, he notices a group of men hurrying down the Rue Pairoliere beneath him, resembling salmon trying to swim upstream. William smiles to himself.

"The more people in the monkey bars, the easier it is to hide."

It takes William just a few more minutes to reach the high ground. Turning right onto Rue Jovan Nicola, he navigates through a passageway to the intersection of Rue Guigonis, where he suddenly stops. At the bottom of the street, he notices three men on their cell phones, looking around in all directions. They appear to be receiving instructions. Seeing a public water spigot in a covered passageway, William moves further into it.

Once at the spigot, William wets his hair and slicks it back, which has the added benefit of cooling him down. Happy with the results of his physical transformation, he drapes the jacket over his shoulder, holding it casually like a local. Subconsciously, appearing calm should also provide him with some cover, as his pursuers are looking for someone afraid for their life. He takes a few deep breaths to slow his heart rate and emerges from the passage, acting like an older man taking a stroll. Immediately, he notices the men turn in his direction, but just as quickly, they turn away, dismissing him. William crosses the intersection to take a quick, casual glance back as the men continue down Rue Pairoliere.

William quickens his pace down Rue Jovan Nicola, passing the Cappelle Saint-Claire, which, to his surprise, has undergone a complete renovation. Its towering facade is an empty shell with wooden supports in each window to ensure its structural integrity for what will soon become a museum, business, or residential building. William curses his luck.

"So much for me hiding out or using it as a lookout."

Now that William has the high ground, he notices fewer people around him. Quickening his pace, he finds himself on Rue St. Claire, where a quick right and then left onto Rue Serruriers will lead him back down to the lower levels of Vieux Nice.

Without incident, he walks the short distance to Rue Saint Joseph, his jacket still draped over his shoulder. He turns right at the end of the street, leading him to Rue Rosetti and his friend's kitchen, Chef Rosa Jackson of Les Petits Farcis. He hopes to find her there, but as he steps off the street, he notices her kitchen is closed. Most likely, she is busy with one of her famous destination events in some fantastic country abroad.

As his heart sinks at his bad luck in not finding a suitable hiding place, William notices two men walking toward him on Rue St. Joseph. He takes out his phone to capture images of Rosa's closed kitchen, the street, and other historic buildings. After putting the phone back in his pocket, he walks past them. His inner voice kicks in, and he chastises himself.

"Stupid move taking the pictures. Now they know you are not a local."

However, the ruse works because the two younger men pay little attention to the "old" man. William keeps moving as if he hasn't a care in the world, and the pace of his pursuers creates distance between him without much of a glance in his direction. It is clear to William now that they have no idea what he looks like. With newfound confidence, he stops to devise a plan to escape this mess in one piece.

Continuing his slow walk, William arrives at Rue Rosetti, a major pedestrian thoroughfare in Vieux Nice that descends a long, sweeping hill. The narrow cobblestone street barely accommodates even one of those tiny Twizzy cars seen throughout downtown areas of European cities. Although he loses the benefit of the higher ground, William notices that the Place Rosetti at the bottom is bustling with people. This spot is a popular destination for incredible gelato and is home to the beautiful Cathedral Sainte-Reparate de Nice.

As he enters Place Rosetti, he sees a man on his cell phone outside the Cathedral Sainte-Reparate. The man speaks French with a strong Middle Eastern accent, and his head swivels as he scans the crowds around him.

"...the target entered Vieux Nice at Saint-François. We have a general description of him from the staff at the Escoffier Museum, but we have not yet managed to locate him. We need more personnel to contain him in the kill box."

Wincing at the words "kill box," William desperately hopes it's a metaphor. He also chuckles at the thought of his driver, Eitan, referring to it as a "capture" box, likely trying to avoid scaring him further. Standing there, feeling both his mortality and confidence slipping away, William begins to recognize the accent, which he concludes must be Turkish. As he pretends to be a tourist, William and the Turkish man are distracted by a large group of Americans exiting the Cathedral Sainte-Reparate after a recently completed tour. Surprised by this stroke of luck, William looks up at the visage of Sainte-Reparate towering above and blows the Saint a kiss, silently thanking him.

"Thank you, blessed Saint. It's time to get lost in the crowd...again."

William easily blends into the primarily American group, where his pursuers cannot tell one person from another. Now walking with them, William quickly starts a conversation with a few people next to him and realizes he is heading in the wrong direction. Uncertain whether to ditch the tour group, William suggests to a few in the group that they join him for gelato near a souvenir shop. A few peel off from the leading group, and with this new vantage point, he can see up and down Rue Sainte-Reparate.

Not noticing the Turkish man or any obvious pursuers, William quickly walks toward the open market when he hears a commotion behind him. A shopkeeper is scolding a younger man for knocking over his street display. The younger man tries to speak into his phone when his eyes lock onto William's. Immediate recognition crosses the young man's face as he realizes that the person he is looking at is the one they are searching for. The young man pushes the shopkeeper to the ground and starts shouting into his phone.

"I found him on Rue Saint-Reparate, heading east. I repeat, heading east."

However, before the young man can take a single step, he is swiftly surrounded by an angry crowd that begins to restrain him while others shout for the police. Taking advantage of the moment, William bolts down Rue Sainte-Reparate, straining to hear the footsteps he fears will soon be upon him. Once again, William's inner voice kicks in.

"You've been made. It's time to find a place to hide."

As William runs, he recalls that one of the best fromageries (cheese makers) in Nice, whom he has relied on numerous times for his culinary events, is not far ahead. It takes only a few more moments before William notices a light coming from the side door of the fromagerie. When he reaches the door, he glances behind him, opens it, peeks inside, and closes it securely while setting the latch. He quickly enters what turns out to be a small storeroom filled with dried goods and turns off the lights.

Moments feel like hours as he strains to hear any hint of his pursuers, and without warning, the doorknob in his hand begins to jiggle. Nearly jumping out of his skin, William catches his breath and stands motionless like the saintly statue in the nearby Place Rossetti. The handle stops moving, and after a few seconds, the footsteps continue down the alley in opposite directions. Breathing a sigh of relief, William turns to find the room beyond, which is also lit, where two sets of eyes look at him quizzically. The two older men standing there began speaking in Niçard.

"Monsieur Chef, is that you?"

William steps forward, flashes his signature smile, and in perfect Niçard, greets the two familiar faces.

"Arthur et Carlo! Enfan e can counouissoun qu ben li fan, n'est-ce pas?!" (Loosely translates as "My friends! Children and dogs recognize those who love them, is this not true?!")

Arthur and Carlo, the owner and son-in-law of the Fromagerie, respond by giving William a hearty slap on the back, laughing loudly, and welcoming him into their cheese shop.

Moments Later - The Fromagerie - Vieux Nice

As they enter the now-closed store, William pauses to call Rebecca. He reaches for his cell phone and notices several texts from her, each saying, "CALL ME NOW!"

William excuses himself and dials her number. He barely hears it ring before she begins speaking.

"Where are you? Are you okay? Where have you been? I've been going out of my mind with worry. Your driver came by earlier, saying that you were being chased on foot into Vieux Nice."

William pauses, gathering his thoughts, and tells Rebecca the story of the monkey bars.

"I'm fine. I'm with Carlos and Arthur at the Fromagerie. I'll wait a bit to ensure I'm not being followed."

Rebecca's voice is cracking. She is on the verge of tears.

"I promise I'm fine. I've called Eitan, and he said he'd pick me up himself. I should be back at Le Negresco within the hour."

Eventually, William and Rebecca say their goodbyes as he hangs up and turns to his friends.

"My friends, catching up with you has been a delight. However, I have overstayed my welcome and must let you finish closing up. Please allow me to help by sweeping the floor."

Carlo is the first to respond.

"You won't do that, Chef. Our shop has flourished since we met you and the many others you've sent us. We owe you a debt too great to repay."

William has not shared why he broke into their storeroom or waited so long to leave. He feels ashamed but fears what might happen if they discover he is being pursued. Arthur speaks up cautiously.

"Chef, it is clear that you were hiding from someone earlier, and as much as we love your company, we can see the fear in your eyes. What can we do to help?"

William cannot look directly at them, but he gathers his courage to tell them a lie he hopes will explain.

"My friends, I'm embarrassed to admit that I was chased by a man who thinks I'm having an affair with his wife." William lets the silence grow between him and his friends. Carlos is the first to respond.

"Chef, we will not interfere with your affairs. When you need our help, we will be there."

Arthur then cuts in.

"And Chef. Leave the lying to us. We are much better at it than you."

Sheepishly, William shakes his friend's hand just as he receives a text from Eitan informing him that two of his men are waiting outside the Fromagerie to escort him to an SUV. It takes William just a few minutes to make his way to the Promenade des Anglais, which leads directly to the Negresco. As he turns onto the famous rue de la Poissonnerie, he glances up at a building featuring an Italian bas-relief of Adam and Eve holding clubs dating back to the 16th century.

The Chef pauses to reflect on the sight of the couple poised to attack each other with clubs raised above their heads. He has often encountered this bas-relief, yet it still makes him chuckle. William glances at his escorts for a moment longer. He resumes walking, navigating through the Cour Selaya market, passing the apartment of the renowned French artist Henri Matisse, and through a short tunnel leading to the Promenade des Anglais. "The Promenade," as the locals call it, is a pathway that starts at Nice's airport and runs along the coast of the Bay of Angels, stretching about 7 kilometers (approximately 4 miles). It is the quickest route to Le Negresco.

As they make their way through the passage, a black Range Rover Sentinel pulls up, and he sees Eitan in the driver's seat. The two exchange knowing looks. Eitan speaks first as William enters the Sentinel.

"I must say, Chef, I'm impressed by your skills. It's no small feat that you managed to escape capture."

William thanks the two escorts and closes the SUV's heavily armored door.

"Eitan, you must be thanked for seeing that I did not end up at the bottom of the Bay of Angels."

They exchange glances like brothers in arms. Smiling, Eitan chuckles at William and shakes his head.

"I will never forget the lesson you taught me about monkey bars, Monsieur Chef."

Chapter 16

Meeting The Enemy

Le Negresco Bar - Nice, France

William smiles as he gazes up at the brightly lit entrance of Le Negresco Hotel. He recognizes the doorman, Stefan, the grandson of Luca, the fishmonger at Place Saint-Francios.

"Bonjour Ordures! How was your running tour of Vieux Nice today?"

Stefan has a powerful handshake as he winks at William.

"Don't turn your head, but two people are in the car just across the street. I think they're waiting for you. Would you like me to help make their day less pleasant?"

William resists the urge to look.

"Thank you, Stefan. That won't be necessary. It will only delay the inevitable. Besides, the hotel's security should keep things civil. Please tell your grand-père I'll be by to thank him very soon."

The Bar 1913

Le Negresco hosts 2 bars directly off the lobby: Facing the ocean is The Versailles (pronounced Ver-Sigh), a marble-floored area for drinks and hors d'oeuvres with painted ceilings and a fireplace the size of a small apartment, and The Bar 1913, a walnut-paneled room filled with ancient tapestry and hosts live music.

As William is about to enter the bar, he receives a text from Rebecca saying she is heading down to meet him. He quickly responds.

"Hang tight. There were people outside waiting for me."

Rebecca replies with a shocked emoji. William quickly types his response.

"It's best that you keep an eye on me from the bar. I will let Benjamin know you are coming."

Rebecca sends him an "exclamation", "thumbs up", and a "prayer" emoji.

As William enters the Bar, he is greeted by the Bar Manager, Benjamin, and the two exchange Le Bise. Benjamin is first to speak.

"My friend, you usually tell me when you are coming."

William apologizes.

"It was a last-minute decision. Rebecca is heading down, and I asked her to sit at the bar while I meet some guests. I would be in your debt if you would look after her."

Benjamin changes gears.

"Certainly. I will have a glass of Deutz Champagne for her immediately. Rest assured, Madame Laurent will be well cared for."

William has a last-minute thought.

"Would you mind if I take the back table near the windows?"

Benjamin shows him to the table and removes the "reserved" placard.

"I will be back to take your drink order."

William leans in to Benjamin.

"In full disclosure, I do not know the manners of my guests. Best to bring me a scotch and two glasses of your least expensive wine from your cellar."

"Very good, my friend. I will see to it."

Lobby of Le Negresco Hotel

Rebecca arrives at the bar through the back entrance and is seated by Benjamin just as two people enter from the main lobby. The two are as different as night and day: a tall, thin, athletic-looking Mediterranean man in a Gorgio Armani pin-striped grey suit and a gorgeous auburn-haired woman dressed in classic Chanel. The man looks around the room and leans into his auburn-haired companion.

"So how is it that we are going to know who..."

Before he can finish the question, the concierge promptly approaches the auburn-haired woman and greets her in the French tradition of "faire la bise" (a kiss on both cheeks).

"Madam, it is always a pleasure to welcome you here at Le Negresco. Are you and your guest here for dinner? I would have been better prepared had I known you were coming."

"Thank you, Louis. Could you be a dear? We're here to meet a client, and I think I see him over there in the corner."

"Oh, you mean Le Chef! Naturally, a person of your stature would know such a distinguished guest of Le Negresco. This way, please."

Louis guides the two to William's table just as Benjamin arrives with his 25-year Dalmore Scotch and two glasses of red wine.

The concierge Louis walks the two guests to William's table. William decides not to get up, making Louis feel like he's made a mistake.

"Le Chef. These are the guests you were expecting, are they not?"

William glances at Louis and eases his concern.

"Louis. It is fine. I am certain they won't be staying long."

William becomes distracted by the auburn-haired woman as she looks down at the table and notices the scotch and the glasses of wine. Her voice is melodic and refined.

"Are we interrupting something?"

William notices the cold stare from the Mediterranean-looking man in the Giorgio Armani suit and ignores her question.

"Please, have a seat. I took the liberty of ordering a lesser wine for the occasion."

The Mediterranean-looking man breaks in.

"We are not here on a social call."

Having taken cooking lessons in Greece a year ago, William quickly identifies the man's accent as Turkish from a northern province. He also remembers the man as the one who was trapped while trying to exit his car near Vieux Nice. William greets him with the same cold stare.

"Sit down, walk away, or get tossed onto the street. It makes little difference to me."

The auburn-haired woman indicates her intention to stay by sitting across from William. The Turkish man settles into the empty chair beside her.

Benjamin quickly arrives and delivers the Bar's signature amuse-bouche.

"Thank you, Benjamin. Your kitchen is as enchanting as always. This looks incredible."

"You are very kind, Monsieur Chef. I will leave you to your guests."

However, before Benjamin walks back to the bar, he recognizes the auburn-haired woman.

"Madame! I was not told you would be joining us. Otherwise, I would have had your table reserved."

Intrigued, William looks over at the woman, who shrugged back at his surprise. He then leans in, grabbing one of their signature smoked salmon bites, and speaks to the Turkish man without making direct eye contact.

"It seems I wasn't too hard to find after all. I was, however, genuinely concerned when I saw you pursuing my car. I feared the worst and instructed my driver to do his best to shake you. Nothing personal. You understand."

The Turkish man starts to respond as William decides to make another stab at his pursuers. He turns to the auburn-haired woman.

"Madame, it is a pleasure. How does a woman of your obvious stature find yourself in the company of such disreputable individuals?"

The auburn-haired woman smiles slightly and recovers while looking at the Turkish man.

"I assure you our relationship is strictly professional. We are colleagues."

William feigns shock. He looks at the Turk.

"Can you tell me why you were chasing me?"

Looking at a mirror against the wall, William notices Rebecca sitting at the bar, staring intensely at the auburn-haired woman. The Turkish man cannot hold back his anger.

"You know very well why we were chasing you. You stole Escoffier's journal. We have recordings of you doing it."

William calmly replies.

"Then why are you here and not the Police or the Gendarmerie?"

The Turkish man's anger is getting the best of him. He has already envisioned a hundred ways to take William's life. He can no longer sit still, and as he rises from his seat, William bumps the table, sending the wine into the Turkish man's lap. Noticing the look of surprise on his face, William quickly begins speaking to the Turkish man in French. Quick reflexes from the auburn-haired woman allowed her to catch it before it could spill. William rises from his seat and begins speaking in fluent French.

"Excuse me, sir. You startled me, and I am afraid I spilled wine on you. Please allow me to have your suit cleaned."

William notices that the auburn-haired woman has the oddest smile on her face. She is entertained by the sudden turn of events for her companion. The Turkish man looks down at his clothes and starts to brush off the wine.

Benjamin hurries to help, and William notices the Turkish man's phone lying under his chair, clearly having fallen from his pocket when the wine was spilled. Quickly standing up, William grabs a nearby napkin and hands it to the Turkish man. Then, with his foot, he pushes the phone back under the seat where he's been sitting.

The Turk is feeling exposed and finally loses his temper. William continues speaking in French.

"Please, sir, I am a Chef, and I know how to keep wine stains from setting."

William turns to Benjamin.

"Please give me a tall glass of club soda and a clean bar towel."

The Turkish man pushes William away harshly with a look of disdain on his face.

"You're as clumsy as you are naive. Do you think this will make a difference? I have dozens of suits that are even more expensive than this."

William's gaze turns icy, yet his tone stays apologetic.

"Again, sir, I do apologize. When you rose so quickly, it startled me. I am sorry to have bumped the table."

Several nearby bar patrons, overhearing the heated exchange, begin showing concern. The Turk starts to realize that he has been baited into acting foolishly. William continues to offer his sincere apologies as security approaches. The Turkish man regains his composure but doesn't notice his phone on the floor. As Benjamin returns, the Turkish man turns toward William, and his demeanor softens.

"Monsieur, this was my fault. As you say, I startled you. Please accept my apology."

The man is speaking loudly enough for the tables around them to notice that he is being gracious. He looks at Benjamin and hands him a credit card.

"Sir, please bring my friend a bottle of the hotel's finest wine."

He steps slightly towards William to shake his hand. William accepts it as the man draws him closer in and whispers.

"This will not end well for you, Chef."

William increases the grip and, leaning in even closer, he whispers back.

"Monsieur. I led you here so that I might meet my enemy."

William looks the Turkish man up and down.

"I am not impressed."

The Turkish-accented man looks over at the auburn-haired woman, who is now gathering her bag.

"Come, it is time to leave."

As she picks up her belongings, she glances at William, who notices a familiarity in her face. She drops her napkin and looks toward it, then up at William. The man and the auburn-haired woman leave without incident through the lobby of the Negresco, closely followed by hotel security.

William steadies himself and smiles at those who are now resuming their conversations. Everyone in the bar breathed a sigh of relief that cooler heads prevailed. William picks up the Turkish man's phone and the napkin left behind by the woman. He walks over to the bar where Rebecca is seated and orders a €35,000 bottle of Petrus 2011 using the card the Turkish man gave to Benjamin. Smiling at Rebecca, William casually responds,

"He did say to order the finest wine at the hotel."

William turns off the Turkish man's phone, takes out the SIM card, and slips it into his jacket pocket. He then reads the napkin discarded by the auburn-haired woman.

"Le Tire Bouchon 10P."

As William reads the napkin, he can't shake the feeling that he has seen the auburn-haired woman before. When Rebecca touches his arm, he is pulled back to the present moment.

"My love, where were you just now?"

She looks at the note on the napkin and immediately begins feeling anxious. She looks over at William.

"You aren't considering going there? It's clearly a trap."

William disconnects from the feeling of déjà vu about the auburn-haired woman and gazes into Rebecca's eyes.

"I have this strange feeling that I've seen her before."

Rebecca's eyes flash briefly with jealousy, but then she relaxes and begins to search her feelings about the auburn-haired woman.

"You know, now that you mention it, I'm also experiencing a bit of déjà vu about her. Her face looks familiar, but I can't figure out who she reminds me of."

William and Rebecca exchange a glance of recognition, and Rebecca is the first to voice it.

"She resembles the woman next to Hemingway in the photo we discovered at the Ritz!"

William grabs his phone and pulls up his photo at Bar Hemingway. Rebecca notices she closely resembles the woman next to Hemingway. Rebecca quickly opens her phone and realizes that the picture she took of the woman while she was sitting with William isn't on it.

"That's odd. None of the photos I took of her are on my phone."

William reflects on his time in the technology industry.

"I cannot comprehend the level of technology necessary to accomplish that in real-time."

That's when Benjamin steps forward with the 2011 Petrus.

"Should I send this up to your room?"

Without a second thought, William glances at Rebecca as she shakes her head in approval with a knowing expression.

"Benjamin, please accept this bottle for the Le Negresco's Children's Hospital Foundation dinner auction."

Benjamin smiles, and the two men shake hands. He also reaches over to kiss Rebecca's cheek.

"This is why you are our favorite guests."

Rebecca recalls the earlier moment and looks sideways at William.

"You're not planning to meet her, are you?"

William considers it carefully.

"Yes, I am. Something about her doesn't align with the man she was with. I want to discover why she reminds us of the woman in the Hemingway pic."

Rebecca's expression reveals uncertainty. William is quick to calm her anxiety.

"Look, I will ask Eitan for a small security team to take me to and from the restaurant. Plus, I hear the chef at Le Tire Bouchon is extraordinarily talented."

Rebecca isn't happy but agrees. She quickly outlines her conditional agreement to the meeting.

"Keep your phone on at all times. I'll text you every 10 minutes, and I expect a "heart" emoji each time. If you send me a "crazy" emoji or don't reply, I'll send in the troops."

"...and if I catch a whiff of her perfume on you, there will be hell to pay."

Curtain Group Headquarters - Sophia Antipolis

Technology Park - Nice, France

The Turkish man paces the floor just outside Herman Dashil's office. He feels uncomfortable in such an enclosed space. He turns and gazes longingly out the window, but only his reflection stares back at him—a side effect of the high-density bulletproof glass. When engineers first encountered the molecular flaw, they couldn't find a workaround. So, someone in marketing promoted it as a feature that would enhance anonymity. The Turkish man shifts his gaze toward the Woman With Auburn Hair. She looks back without revealing the loathing she feels for him. Both heads turn as Herman's booming voice quickly escapes the confines of his office.

"A thirty-five-thousand-euro bottle of wine!?"

The Woman With Auburn has a face that reveals amusement. She greatly enjoys the audacity of William's actions.

"Alright. They're just outside. I'll ask them myself."

Herman's administrative assistant glances at the two individuals in the waiting area.

"Mr Dashil will see you now."

The Turkish man is the first to enter before the Woman With Auburn Hair can rise from her chair. He begins speaking to Herman before she even makes it into the room.

"I should have just shot him in the lobby and been done with it, but you said we only needed to scare him."

Herman's sarcasm oozes with disdain.

"So, you bought him the priciest bottle of wine at the Negresco? How intimidated do you think that made him feel? Oh, and by the way, that wine will not be reimbursed."

The Woman With Auburn Hair enters the office, and through force of habit, she takes her usual seat closest to the door. Herman directs his venom at her.

"And you just sat there doing nothing?

The Woman With Auburn looks back at the Turk before responding.

"Your man instructed me to stay silent during the interaction. So, I did what I was told. Once the altercation happened, it was too late to do anything."

Herman shoots her one of his "This is my world, and you're lucky to be in it" stares. She deflects it by opening her purse to touch up her lipstick. Herman glances at both of them and recalls something the Woman With Auburn Hair said before the chase began. He locks eyes with her.

"You mentioned earlier today that you would be waiting at Le Negresco once the Turk lost track of our thief. How did you know where the target would be staying?"

The Woman With Auburn Hair returns a blank stare as if it should already be evident to him.

"Once the alarm was triggered, I began live-streaming the museum's security feed in real time. It showed a man getting into a Range Rover Sentinel. Your typical Uber driver doesn't offer that luxury fortress on wheels. So, the person who left the museum must have been someone of wealth or status. And we all know where those individuals stay in Nice."

The Woman With Auburn Hair drops the bomb she's been waiting to deliver.

"Oh, I'm having dinner with our thief later tonight."

Herman and the Turk both turn their heads toward her simultaneously. Herman is the first to speak.

"What did you say?"

"You heard me. Tonight in Vieux Nice."

She turns toward the Turk and gestures in his direction.

"While he was acting like a troglodyte in the Negresco bar, I slipped the target a note inside my napkin. My sources at Le Negresco told me that the target picked it up after we left. I expect to meet him this evening. That is, if we can wrap this meeting up."

The Turk shoots her a nasty look. It bounces off her without effect. He turns to Herman.

"Perfect. I'll pick the target up and take him to the warehouse."

Herman starts to reply, but the Woman With Auburn Hair interrupts.

"You'll do no such thing!"

Herman turns to the bewildered Turk to explain.

"If the target is wealthy, he must also have connections. It is prudent to determine how connected he is before we make a decision that could backfire on us."

The Woman With Auburn Hair has already gathered her things and is moving toward the door.

"I will submit a detailed report once our meeting is over. After the staff has had a chance to review it, we can make a more informed decision about the target's outcome."

The Turk turns to watch her leave and begins walking toward the door. Herman raises a hand, stopping him.

"Stay a moment so we can discuss our next steps."

The Turk flashes his signature cruel smile and strolls to Herman's liquor cart, pouring himself a single malt Scotch of some note. The two wait until they are certain she is out of earshot.

"She still doesn't suspect our plan?"

Herman rolls his eyes.

"Of course not, but that doesn't mean her ignorance will last. She's brilliant, and I believe she senses something already. Keep her on a short leash, and let's see how this unfolds over the next few days."

The Turks drain his glass, place it on the cart, and head out the door. Reaching into his jacket for his phone, he realizes it is missing. A cold chill creeps up his spine.

Chapter 17

Dining With The Enemy

Le Negresco Valet Parking - Nice, France

After leaving Rebecca in the capable hands of Benjamin and his staff, William is greeted outside by his driver, Eitan, and two other men standing next to the Range Rover Sentinel SUV. He quickly notices the worried expression on Eitan's face. As he settles into the back of the SUV, Eitan updates him on the research he conducted after dropping him off after the chase.

"Sir, I spoke with my contacts in Mossad. They inform me that you've captured the attention of the Curtain Group. I took the liberty of hiring two men to serve as your bodyguards."

William looks confused as Eitan explains.

"Sir, the Curtain Group is a multinational security services company that works with a select group of high-profile clients, most notably the UN Food & Agriculture Organization and a few dozen mining operations in the Congo."

William's expression is one of disbelief. The words escape his mouth before Eitan finishes his statement.

"It seemed odd that such a company would also be managing the surveillance system at the Escoffier Museum. Am I missing something?"

Eitan nods his head in agreement.

"Yes, it would be like using a bazooka to kill a squirrel."

William shakes off the image of a squirrel being blown up and tells Eitan about his meeting with the Turkish man and the auburn-haired woman. He explains how the pictures they took were deleted from their phones. Eitan listens intently and then lowers his head.

"Sir, the Turkish man you described is known by many names. He is a ruthless contract killer who is wanted in many countries and protected by even more. As for the Woman With Auburn Hair, very little is known about her, except that she is a "fixer' with numerous high-level connections. It seems the Curtain Group employs them both."

Eitan sees fear building in William's eyes.

"Sir, I don't believe they plan to kill you—at least, not yet. Why would they sit down and talk with you if they wanted to kill you? They will likely want to determine who you know and how much you know before committing to a course of action. They will likely try to locate something or someone to intimidate you. It is far more effective and efficient than having you killed."

Seeing the look of shock on William's face, Eitan quickly continues.

"Not to worry, sir. I have ordered a security detail for Madmae Laurent as well."

William leans back in his seat, trying to process the information he has just received. His emotions swirl wildly as the reality of the situation sinks in. He pulls out his phone, ready to call Rebecca, but manages to rein in his fear. Glancing at Eitan, he searches for something to shore up his courage.

"What about the auburn-haired 'fixer'? Is she also a ruthless assassin?"

Eitan smiles.

"No, sir. She is a non-lethal asset. She moves pieces around instead of removing them from the board."

William chuckles nervously at the chess metaphor as he gazes out the SUV's window.

"So there's no harm in meeting with her? She left me a note inviting me to Le Tire Bouchon."

Eitan's eyes go wide in shock.

"Sir, she wants to meet you at a location of her choosing? I strongly advise against this."

William nods to Eitan, remembering how he first met the auburn-haired woman in the bar. A feeling in the back of his mind is telling him he can trust her. He glances up at Eitan.

"When I met the auburn-haired woman, there was something familiar about her, as if I had seen her somewhere before. However, I never sensed that she would harm me. The Turk, on the other hand..."

At that moment, a plan takes shape in William's mind.

"Eitan, let's test the auburn-haired woman's reputation? I wonder how long it will take her to find me at a restaurant of my choosing? Let's head over to Le Plongeoir."

Eitan smiles at his American client as he pulls away from the curb.

"Sir, I am beginning to think you might be very good at espionage."

Blacked-Out Mercedes Sedan Parked Outside Curtain Group Headquarters - Vieux Nice, France

The Woman With Auburn Hair sits in her car as her phone vibrates.

"AI Tracking bot - Target deviating from expected destination."

The Woman With Auburn Hair opens the AI tracking app on her phone. It connects her directly to the malware she remotely installed on the chef's cell phone when they met at Le Negresco bar. She listens to the conversation he is having with his driver. She disconnects the app and leans forward to the driver.

"New route. Take me to Le Plongeoir in Port Lympia."

The driver nods as the car pulls away from the curb.

Le Plongeoir Restaurant, Port Lympia, Nice, France

It takes Eitan 18 minutes to drive from Negresco to Le Plongeoir's restaurant. Since their earlier adventure, Eitan has become hyper-aware of being followed and ensures they cannot be boxed in. The outcome of his efforts would have added another 10 minutes to the average driver's commute. However, they arrived on time at 60 Boulevard Franck Pilatte, just north of Port Limpia and home to Le Plongeoir restaurant, in record time.

The iconic restaurant in Nice is perched atop a rock outcropping along the shoreline. At the end of the nineteenth century, a stylish fishing boat was moored on the rock where, during "La Belle Époque," guests could enjoy meals and sip tea six meters above the Mediterranean. The restaurant, linked by a walkway to a charming gazebo typical of that era on the French Riviera, quickly became a symbolic part of the city of Nice.

Today, the restaurant Le Plongeoir (which loosely translates to "diving platform") is a renovated version of that iconic structure and offers diners a breathtaking panoramic view of the port entrance and the Mediterranean Sea. William recalls having been to Le Plongeoir on his first visit with Rebecca to Nice many years earlier. He has always appreciated how the staff presents skillfully crafted, Mediterranean-inspired dishes.

As William exits the SUV, he notices his two bodyguards standing by the curb and surveying the restaurant's entrance. With one ahead and one behind William, they soon make their way down the stairs, passing a kitchen where he sees the chef diligently preparing a dish that emits an aroma of saffron and herbs. At one point, the two chefs exchange a knowing glance. Moments later, the manager and his dear friend, Christophe, greet William in the traditional "faire la bise" greeting.

"Monsieur Chef, it's an honor to have you with us tonight."

Noticing the bodyguards, he glances around before returning to William.

"But where is Madame Rebecca?"

William smiles.

"I'm afraid this is a business meeting. However, Rebecca sends her love and has threatened me with serious bodily harm if we don't return and have dinner by the end of the week."

Christophe smiles broadly as he picks up two menus. However, he halts suddenly.

"Your dinner guest has already been seated in the private dining platform."

William's face is filled with surprise.

"She called ahead and asked for privacy; since it was her, we were happy to accommodate. Please follow me."

Christophe realizes that William hasn't moved and turns back to him.

"Chef. Is there an issue?"

William tries to clear out a few thousand questions swimming in his head. He decides to ask the simplest one.

"So you know the auburn-haired woman?"

Christophe chuckles.

"Chef. She is well-known throughout France and has been a guest here numerous times. However, she prefers to be called 'Madame'. But I have also heard her referred to as the Woman With Auburn Hair in certain circles."

Christophe begins ushering William to the divining platform where his guest awaits. William realizes that one guard remained behind at the kitchen while the other accompanies him to his table. Moments later, they cross the platform leading to the rock outcropping and the private dining area. Upon reaching the table, Christophe seats William and hands him a menu. With his trademark smile, he heads back to the kitchen.

At that moment, William is again struck by a sense of déjà vu about the woman sitting across from him. Without looking up from the menu, she speaks first.

"You were wise to bring backup."

William sarcastically replies while looking at his menu.

"Who knew Nice was such a hotbed of assassins and fixers?"

The Woman With Auburn Hair smiles at his wit.

"I agree. This is a much better spot for our conversation. Did I pass your test?"

William leans back in his chair, sensing a hint of sarcasm in her voice.

"Madame, I must say you truly live up to your reputation. Oh, and thank you very much."

She gazes at him curiously as William takes out his cell phone and hands it to the bodyguard.

"I believe my phone has been infected with malware."

The bodyguard speaks into the microphone concealed in his sleeve. Moments later, the other bodyguard arrives, places the phone into a signal-dampening Faraday bag, and returns to the entrance. William continues.

"You repeated almost the exact words I said to my driver before arriving here. Since we were sitting close together in the Negresco bar earlier, you must have cloned my phone."

"Well, you're full of surprises, Chef. Or may I call you William?"

Ignoring her question, William places his napkin on his lap just as the server arrives. William looks up at him.

"Please let the Chef know that we would be delighted with whatever he serves, including the wine pairing."

As the server steps away, William returns to her question.

"No, Madame, you may not. I reserve my first name for close friends and loved ones. You are neither. Chef will suffice."

Without emotion, William continues.

"And what should I call you? 'The Woman With Auburn Hair' is quite the mouthful."

She smiles, delighted that William has done his homework.

"Madame will do for now."

William gets down to business.

"So, Madame, why are we here?"

The Woman With Auburn Hair takes a moment to evaluate William.

"I'm curious why you took Escoffier's journal?"

William frowns.

"And I want to understand why an assassin and fixer are working for an organization of mercenaries called the Curtain Group. However, I fear there is not enough mutual trust to answer those questions with complete transparency."

The Woman With Auburn Hair is rarely surprised or impressed.

"Well done, Chef."

William returns a blank stare and waits for her to continue as silence envelops the space between them. William raises his eyebrows in anticipation.

"Madam. It was you who called this meeting. Was it not?"

She relaxes her posture.

"You are correct, Chef."

She takes a moment to collect her thoughts, even though she already knows what she wants to say.

"I thought it would be good for us to get to know one another."

Recalling the advice he received earlier from Eitan, William decides to stab at her with it.

"So you can use what you learn to intimidate or manipulate me?"

The Woman With Auburn Hair can see that William can hold his own in a conversation, and she raises her hands in surrender.

"Chef. Allow me to try this again."

William considers her surrender and rejects it.

"Madame. It was not but a few short hours ago that people you work for were trying to take me unlawfully into custody. The only reason I agreed to meet with you is that I had a feeling that we had somehow met before."

She does not like where this is going. She tries to interrupt as William is about to continue, but both are interrupted as the server arrives at the table.

"Sir. The chef has selected a delightful Sancerre to pair with the meal. If you wish, I will pour it for your tasting."

William smiles up at the server.

"Thank you. Tasting a Sancerre is _never_ required. Please extend my gratitude to the Chef for the selection."

The server acknowledges pouring each of them a glass, and William takes in the aroma of the Sancerre's bouquet and decides to switch topics.

"Madame. Don't you find it odd that a multinational security firm like the Curtain Group is monitoring the alarm for the Escoffier Museum? It seems somewhat excessive, particularly considering its clientele?"

The Woman With Auburn Hair is happy to have the topic changed and responds without hesitation.

"Yes, I do. However, I'm under contract with them and can only speculate on the rationale."

He looks up at her while enjoying another sip of the Sancerre.

"Since you brought up your employment, that same multinational security firm hires a renowned auburn-haired 'fixer' along with an internationally wanted contract killer to track down an _alleged_ shoplifter. Again, it feels like overkill. My driver likened it to killing a squirrel with a bazooka."

The Woman With Auburn Hair smiles as she raises her glass and gently sips from it.

"I'm not a fan of the term 'fixer,' but I see your point. Perhaps there's more to this journal?"

"Perhaps indeed, Madame. But then it would likely have more in it than blank pages."

William takes out the journal and places it in front of her plate. He swiftly shifts gears.

"I am curious. Am I, or is anyone in my family or circle of friends, at risk of being abducted or murdered by you, the assassin, or your _actual_ employer?"

William's bluntness surprises her just as the server returns with their first course.

"Madame and Monsieur. The chef presents poached cuttlefish with capers and chives in a mustard velouté sauce. Bon appétit."

As is customary, the server places a dish first in front of the woman and then in front of William. The Woman With Auburn Hair watches William's face transform. He is fully present, absorbing the aroma and presentation of the dish as if nothing else matters. He looks up at her, inviting her to take the first bite.

"Madame. After you."

She takes a bite and notices the delicate texture of the fish, complemented by the smooth mustard velouté sauce, which finishes with a briny, salty note. She closes her eyes to savor the moment and finishes sipping her wine. The two of them eat in silence as they complete the dish.

Dabbing her mouth with the napkin, the Woman With Auburn Hair answers his question by picking up where they left off.

"I imagine it would depend on how committed you are to your cause."

The two lean back in their chairs as the server returns to clear the plates. After he leaves, William continues.

"So the more committed to my 'cause', the more people around me die? That seems an odd way to frame your response. Wouldn't you agree?"

The Woman With Auburn Hair tries to deflect.

"I was speaking generally..."

William interrupts her.

"No, Madame. You were not. Your threat was clear. Keep going, and my family and friends become pieces on the board. Pieces that can be forcibly removed"

William stares intently at her. She stares back. William moves on.

"So, working for the Curtain Group is just a transactional relationship for you? They pay you, and in return, you serve me and my family on a platter. Good to know."

The Woman With Auburn Hair smiles back at William as though someone would if a door had been held open for them. Leaning forward, she looks at him with similar intensity. She needs to understand his willingness to see this through. She decides to put him to the test.

"Chef, you are clearly out of your depth. It would be in your best interest to step aside. Think of your wife and daughter."

William's expression darkens, and she immediately regrets her words. After taking a sip of wine, he allows the moment to pass in silence. He sets down his wine glass and glares at the auburn-haired woman.

"Madam, you go too far. I suggest you focus your threats on me. You don't know my wife, but I assure you she wouldn't think twice about making you eat your words."

The Women With Auburn-Haired retreats

"I only meant it as a precaution."

William advances.

"Madame, let us not pretend there's a way to walk this back. I have discovered something that requires a team of mercenaries to take me into custody. No, I believe I will continue working on Escoffier's puzzle. Hopefully, I can stay one step ahead until those pulling the strings are identified and held accountable for whatever they are planning."

William sits back and pauses for effect.

"Unless, of course, you're planning to wipe out my entire bloodline to keep their secret safe."

In that instant, William detects fear in her eyes when mentioning the word "bloodline" to her. She tries to recover.

"Chef, I do not condone violence in any form. However, I am not leading this team, so I cannot control the actions of others."

William pauses and then pushes Escoffier's journal closer to her. His voice is contemptuous.

"Madame, I believe this belongs to your client. I discarded the RFID chip, but it damaged the journal's inner lining. I am willing to reimburse the owner for their losses, but since the journal is fake, I doubt those costs would be substantial. He leans back in his chair, a look of disappointment on his face, as a father would to his child.

"Fortunately, there's no reimbursement for someone losing their soul."

The remark profoundly impacts the Woman With Auburn Hair, but she collects herself and, using his name, speaks to him with desperation.

"William, tell me _why_ you took the journal."

Later, William would recall not knowing exactly why he chose to be honest with her. His eyes begin to fill with tears as he starts speaking.

"Very well, Madame. But know this. Anything less than complete honesty in return will mark the end of this meeting."

She nods in acceptance. William takes another sip of wine and leans into the table.

"At first, I viewed the initials in Escoffier's book as a puzzle to solve. However, something inside me snapped when I discovered the connection to the Kaiser Wilhelm Society. My wife, whom you so callously and casually threatened, never knew her paternal grandfather because he passed away from complications related to mustard gas exposure in World War I—a grim legacy from Chemist Fritz Haber and the Kaiser Wilhelm Society."

William takes a moment to hold back his emotions. She senses loathing in his voice.

"Years later, during World War II, millions of Jewish prisoners were subjected to live experimentation, murdered in gas chambers, and starved to death. Also, gifts from the Nazi-controlled Kaiser Wilhelm Society."

William pauses, unable to hold back his emotions. He takes another sip of wine.

"I don't know what Escoffier's code will reveal, but if it's even a tenth as horrific as the other atrocities connected to that vile organization, then I feel compelled to see it through."

William turns his head towards the vast Mediterranean Sea, lost in his thoughts. The Woman With Auburn Hair's voice, filled with legitimate concern, brings him back to the moment.

"The Curtain Group has protected its secrets for over a century. Many have died simply for knowing of its existence, and even more have faced financial ruin or imprisonment."

William studies her.

"You're the fixer, so fix this. You appear to have the resources and connections to finish it, yet you stand aside while this secret could change the world forever."

William notices a look of shame on her face. He decides to probe further.

"Madame, have you ever heard of cultural anthropologist Margaret Mead?"

The Woman With Auburn Hair immediately recalls the quote from memory and recites it to him verbatim.

"Never doubt that a small group of thoughtful, committed individuals can change the world. It's the only thing that ever has."

At that moment, the server brings out the next course, and as though they are boxers in a ring, they each return to their respective corners.

"Madame and Monsieur, the chef has prepared his famous mushroom risotto."

William is once more in the moment, savoring the appearance and aroma of this famous dish. He bites into the risotto and then sips the wine.

"Tell me, Madame, why are you working for an organization that has protected a society that has carried out so many terrible acts?"

She is about to respond when William raises his hand and interrupts her.

"Madame, please understand, I have laid my soul bare to you. Anything less from you, and this meal is finished."

The auburn-haired woman pauses momentarily, reaches into her bag, and retrieves her phone. Unlocking it, she selects an app and places the phone upside down on the table. Williams's face is a map of questions.

"I have turned off and erased all video security feeds for this restaurant. Electronic countermeasures are now in place, rendering any eavesdropping devices inert."

William relaxes in his chair and remembers that the pictures Rebecca took of her have disappeared from her phone. He is impressed by the depth of the technology at her disposal. He makes a mental note of it and continues.

"Madame. You haven't answered my question."

She bites into the risotto, her eyes rolling back as she savors the dish. After dabbing her mouth with a napkin, she sips her wine.

"Yes, I agree. My agenda does not align with that of my employer. I am here to ensure that the secret you refer to finds a safe home— somewhere it can benefit humanity instead of being used to subjugate it."

"So, you know what Escoffier's secret is. Please enlighten me."

She decides to draw it out of him instead.

"What do you think it is?"

William leans back in his chair, showing significant displeasure.

"Madame, I gave you a chance to provide me with an honest answer. Yet, you continue to play games."

William leans forward and delivers an emotional gut punch to the Woman With Auburn Hair.

"Fine. You want to play cat and mouse? Then it's my turn to play cat."

William notices her demeanor changing.

"I mentioned earlier that you remind me of someone. Allow me to elaborate. You, Madame, are a descendant of a woman who was in love with Ernest Hemingway. I saw her picture at Bar Hemingway earlier this week. It was in Monte-Carlo in 1924. That's the night Escoffier told Hemingway about the secret."

William pauses as he does the math and turns his anger on her.

"That would make the woman in the picture your grandmother. Did the Curtain Group kill her off, too? I mean, after she had Hemingway's baby, of course."

William pauses realizing her the Woman With Auburn Hair's birthright.

"Wait. That would make you a descendant of Hemingway."

The Woman With Auburn Hair is caught off guard. She tries to regain her composure, and for the first time in two decades, the memories come flooding back in vivid detail in her mind. William notices the turmoil boiling beneath the surface and decides to bury the dagger deeper into her soul.

"Oh, so you now are beginning to understand how I felt about your callous death threats to my family?"

The Woman With Auburn Hair attempts to collect herself.

"You have good instincts, Chef, but if you ever mutter those words again, I will rethink my position as a non-combatant."

William looks sideways at her.

"But you still haven't revealed the secret to me."

She takes another bite of the risotto.

"Given your momentum, it won't be long before you figure it out on your own, which will also clarify my intention."

William cannot control the rage he is feeling.

"Madame, you excel at your job, but have you ever considered that I don't care about your intentions? You manipulate people..."

William halts mid-sentence, suddenly realizing that he has been manipulated. He sets down his flatware, wipes his mouth, and stares at the Woman With Auburn Hair as though he has just learned that there is no Santa Claus.

"You placed the date on the menu and put the RFID chip in Escoffier's journal."

She holds up her hands as if to surrender.

"You used me to incite a reaction from the Curtain Group, endangering my family's lives in the process. I'm involved now and can only see it through to the end."

William glances at her with dark, unforgiving eyes. She starts to speak, but immediately decides against it. William leans back in his chair, wrestling with his emotions. Yet another revelation strikes him, and it crushes him.

"The initials in Escoffier's book. You placed them there. You played me like a fiddle, fully aware of what the Curtain Group could do to me and my family. You, madame, are truly a piece of fucking work!"

At that moment, the server comes to clear the plates. William looks up and addresses him in fluent French.

"It appears that my guest has another engagement and must leave. May I please come by the kitchen and speak with the chef? I wish to thank him personally."

"He is expecting you, Monsieur Chef."

William stands, looking down disapprovingly at the seated Woman With Auburn Hair. She has difficulty making eye contact with him.

"Madame, you had no right to use me in your personal war. But here I am, and now I must protect my family. It is best that we never see each other again. Especially if my wife is present, for I will not protect you from her wrath."

After thanking the chef, William says goodbye to Christophe and is escorted back to Eitan and the relative safety of the waiting SUV. He leaves the Woman With Auburn Hair to settle the bill, which she does gladly. Taking out her phone, she releases the hold she had placed on the surveillance devices surrounding the restaurant. She then calls the female technician she had worked with earlier at the CIA safe house.

"I need to secure the social media presence of my asset and his entire family. [There is a pause.] Yes, every one of them, including extended family members. Make the security measures "sticky" and send all results to my server. I want to know the moment someone tries to locate them."

Back at Le Negresco

As they arrive at Le Negresco, William, feeling deflated and emotionally drained from the revelations of the evening, thanks Eitan for his help. Eitan can see from William's face that he carries the weight of the peril he has put his family in. William walks through the lobby and enters the ornate elevator that takes him to his floor, and as it rises, he can't stop thinking about the conversation with the Woman With Auburn Hair. Upon reaching his room, he opens the door and tries not to wake Rebecca, but she stirs anyway.

"I was about to send out a search party."

William leans over, kisses her, and sits down on the bed. When Rebecca returns from the bathroom, she finds William fast asleep in his clothes. She covers him with a small blanket and kisses his forehead.

As Rebecca kisses William's forehead, the Woman With Auburn Hair waits with her driver across the street from Le Negresco. She is deeply troubled by how her meeting with William went at the restaurant. She did not intend to alienate him, especially at this stage of her plan. However, he unintentionally touched a sensitive nerve regarding her lineage, and she feels regretful. Sitting in the dark, parked along Rue De Rivoli across from the Masséna Museum, she looks up through the moon roof at the magnificent pink dome of Le Negresco.

She concludes that William's commitment will likely disrupt her Client's timeline. However, she will also need to maintain her distance from him because of the connection he has established with her family lineage.

The Turk stands in the shadows across from Le Negresco, watching as the Woman With Auburn Hair drives away. The Turkish man smiles ominously and presses the speed dial on his cell phone.

"Our target has returned to Le Negresco."

The Turk pauses to listen to the response on the phone.

"No, she doesn't know I've been following her. I can have a team here in 15 minutes to apprehend the target."

The Turk's face darkens with anger as he listens to the response.

"I understand. As requested, I'll monitor the building and update you on his location."

Frustrated, the Turk angrily disconnects the call.

"Why won't they let me do my job!? I could have him talking in under an hour. Then it is an easy thing to dispose of the body, and who cares after that?"

The Woman With Auburn Hair drives her car back around the street and spots the Turk in the shadows, on his cell phone, across the street. She presses a speed dial number on her cell phone.

"I want you to watch our Mediterranean friend closely. I have a feeling he's about to act impulsively."

She hangs up, contemplating her next move.

Next Day - Hotel Le Negresco, Nice, France

William's sleep was restless, and his dreams chaotic. Dinner last night took the wind out of his sails, leaving him no closer to uncovering the secret or deciding whom he could trust. He lifts his head from the pillow and notices that Rebecca's side of the bed is empty. From down the hall, he sees the light on in the seating area of their suite. William quickly gets dressed and shuffles down the hall loudly to avoid startling her. Rebecca notices him coming and kisses him.

"Well, good afternoon, sleepyhead. I was going to wake you up, but you came in late last night."

William smiles warmly at her and looks at the clock on the wall while Rebecca pours him a cup of coffee.

"I assume you'll want a café Viennois (pronounced Vee-en-wah)."

A café Viennois is made with lungo espresso, 170 degree water, and a generous dollop of Chantilly créme. William and Rebecca discovered this coffee drink during a trip to Paris over the Christmas holiday. It was late afternoon, and they were hungry, searching for a café to grab a quick bite. They had just left the unsettling sight of the burned-out remains of Notre Dame and decided to uplift their spirits by visiting Saint-Chapelle Cathedral, famous for its breathtaking stained glass windows. After crossing the Pont au Change bridge, they stumbled upon a charming café at the corner of Place de Châtelet and Avenue Victoria called Le Sarah Bernhardt, named after the celebrated 19th-century French stage actress, "the queen of the pose and the princess of the gesture." Interestingly, the drink is available in two versions: coffee and rich chocolate.

William's smile returns.

"Yes, a Viennois would be perfect. Thank you, my love."

As William glances at his Viennois on the kitchen table, he notices his open notebook. Rebecca observes his puzzled expression.

"I took the liberty of reviewing the notes we made at the d'Aubusson bar, but we aren't doing anything until we discuss what happened at your dinner last night. Tell me everything."

Rebecca pats the chair's seat next to her. William lovingly complies.

William summarizes the evening's discussion with the Woman With Auburn Hair, including the venue change to Le Plongeoir. He also tells her that he confronted her about the woman in the Hemingway Bar picture and the ensuing argument that followed shortly after.

Rebecca acknowledges.

"So, she _is_ linked to the woman in the picture. Just like we thought."

William gives a nod.

"I'm certain of it. I first sensed it when I asked her if the Curtain Group would erase our bloodline to keep the secret safe. Her reaction when I made the connection to the woman in the Hemingway picture confirmed my suspicion. What I said frightened her, and that's when she issued a thinly veiled threat against our family."

William quickly regretted mentioning the threat, seeing Rebecca's face displaying rage.

"She threatened our family!? Who does that bitch think she is? And who is the Curtain Group?!"

Sitting in front of her laptop, Rebecca starts searching for the Curtain Group. William quickly shuts her laptop, nearly pinching her fingers in the process.

"What are you doing!?"

"I'm sorry, my love, but as Eitan was dropping me off last night, he warned me that the Curtain Group monitors all activity on its website. He said he would reach out to his contacts in Mossad and send me relevant information about it, along with its major clients, via WhatsApp."

William's phone begins to chime as if in a queue. He then forwards the information to Rebecca's phone, and they spend the next few minutes absorbing it.

Monsieur Chef, I have compiled a synopsis of information about the Curtain Group, The Turk, and the Woman With Auburn Hair.

- The Curtain Group was founded in 1913 in Berlin-Dahlem, Germany
- There purpose was to secure the discoveries made within the Kaiser Wilhelm Society. At that time, they reported to the Board of Trustees.
- Today, they are a multi-national security services firm with a presence on every continent.
- While providing traditional security and protection services, they are more recognized for their off-the-book capabilities.
- Their largest single client is the UN FAO, and in this capacity, they overlap with a consortium of companies that manage 65% of the planet's seed production.
- The Woman With Auburn Hair is a ghost with no digital presence. She can be a formidable enemy or ally.

- The Turk has over 25 confirmed kills associated with governments in the Middle East and Asia. He is a blunt instrument asset, and at least six sovereign nations protect him.
- No evidence of a connection between Escoffier, Hemingway, Correns, and other currently identified players.
- The woman in the picture you provided is Sofia Mormant. She hails from a wealthy merchant family in Marseilles. Interestingly, all traces of the Mormant family vanished after 1923.

Rebecca looks up from her phone after quickly reading Eitan's report. She leans back, sipping her coffee, and absorbs the new information. After a moment of thought, Rebecca grabs William's notebook, opens it, and starts another diagram. Moments later, she flips the notebook around for William to review. Then, she stands up and walks around the room in silence. William senses a storm brewing inside her. She halts her pacing and stops in front of the window, her voice laced with melancholy.

"This is quite a mess we're in."

William rises and holds her.

"It is worse."

Rebecca looks into her husband's eyes and sees an enormous burden on his face. He returns her gaze.

"I've been deceived. The Woman With Auburn Hair placed the initials in Escoffier's book."

Rebecca closes her eyes to stifle the anger she's holding back.

"So, are the Curtain Group, KWS, Correns' discovery, Hemingway, and the secret all nonsense?"

William waits for Rebecca to come to a realization. It takes two heartbeats.

"The secret *is* real, and she needed you to trip the alarm."

William feels Rebecca's legs give way. He supports her and sits her in the chair. He kneels beside her as she processes their fate. Tears begin to form in William's eyes.

"My love, this is my mistake. I will do everything I can to keep you and our family safe."

Rebecca looks at William with loving eyes.

"No, it is not your fault. She played you without considering the damage it could do to our family. It's all on her—every last bit of it. Before this is over, she will know what it's like to feel my hand across her face."

She rises from her chair, grabs Williams's notebook, and rips the pages out, throwing them in the trash. Then, with a stern look, she turns to William.

"From this moment on, we play _our_ game, and if the Woman With Auburn Hair gets in the way, we run her over with a bus. Am I clear?"

William smiles.

"I couldn't love you any more than I do right now."

Rebecca states the obvious.

"Does the Woman With Auburn Hair have a name?"

It's William's turn to roll his eyes.

"She asked me to call her Madame."

Rebecca's analytical mind is running at full speed.

"...and you believe she's linked to Hemingway's mistress?"

William's response is definitive.

"I am certain of it. There was fear in her eyes for only the briefest moment. But it was there."

Rebecca sits back down at the table and sips her now cold Viennois.

"She doesn't want anyone to find out who she is connected to. We can use that against her."

William gets up and refreshes Rebecca's coffee.

"I agree, but she's playing three-dimensional chess while we're playing checkers. We need to uncover the connection to

Hemingway's mistress. That information will provide us with the leverage to deal with her."

Rebecca smiles after taking another sip of her Viennois.

"So tell me what else she said."

William chooses to steer the conversation in a different direction.

"First, let me discuss what I think the Woman With Auburn Hair is capable of."

Rebecca perks up.

"I like where your head is at. Tell me everything.

William takes a deep breath.

"First of all, she has access to advanced technology."

Rebecca's face wrinkles in confusion.

"Why would you say that?"

"She was already sitting at Le Plongeoir when Eitan and I arrived, which indicated that she likely had my cell phone cloned during our meeting at the Negresco bar yesterday."

Rebecca begins to speak, but William cuts her off.

"...and before you ask, I gave my phone to Eitan's team, and they removed the malware."

Rebecca cannot hold it back.

"She's a sneaky bitch."

Smiling, William continues.

"That's the least of it. While we were eating at Le Plongeoir, she used her phone to send out a signal that disabled the security at the restaurant and other nearby businesses. The only organization I can think of that can do this is the CIA. So she must somehow be connected with our government."

Without warning, Rebecca grabs a pen and starts writing on a new page in William's notebook.

"COULD SHE BE LISTENING TO US NOW?"

William leans back. He spots Rebecca's purse, walks over to it, and takes her phone. Then, he grabs the Faraday bag he had kept from Eitan's bodyguards and places their phones inside it. He returns to the table.

"That should do the trick for now."

William hugs Rebecca.

"We will need allies. I believe it's time to visit our friends in Vieux Nice."

Rebecca catches William's attention.

"We also need to have a call with the kids. It's time to circle the wagons."

CIA Safe House in Sophia Antipolis

The Woman With Auburn Hair removes the headphones she used to listen to William and Rebecca's conversation. No longer intercepting their phones, she goes old school and plants listening devices in their hotel suite. Leaning back in her chair, she begins to rethink her assessment of William. He is highly perceptive and saw through her from the moment they first met. She congratulates herself on selecting him as her asset. She rises from the chair and walks through security to retrieve her personal belongings.

It takes her about 20 minutes to reach her apartment on the Cour Seleya. Once inside, she realizes that William may be the first person she has met who is as intuitive as she is.

Chapter 18

The Fishmongers of Saint-François

Place du Saint-François - Vieux Nice, France

It took only a few minutes for Eitan to meet William at the entrance of Le Negresco. During the drive to Vieux Nice, he updates Eitan on the recent encounter with the Woman With Auburn Hair. William notes that Eitan seems to have relaxed for the first time since this nightmare began.

"Sir, I know you don't see this from your perspective, but if she said those words, it was meant to see how easily it would be to scare you off. It also means she has plans for you, making you an asset to her. There is no better position for you to be in. She will protect you at all costs."

William leans back in the Range Rover Sentinel and relaxes a bit. They don't exchange words, and within a few minutes, Eitan stops in front of Place Saint-François in Vieux Nice. He speaks as William exits the car.

"Monsieur Chef, I have men in Vieux Nice who will watch over you. Do not fret if you don't see them. Because, if you do, then something has gone horribly wrong."

Place Saint-François, Vieux Nice - Côte d'Azure

France

Minutes after being dropped off, William's keen olfactory senses immediately pick up the aroma of fresh fish being carried by the gentle Mediterranean breeze. Remembering his history with Luca, William reflects on his first trip to Nice, where he met the well-known fishmonger. A native Niçois, Luca did not immediately warm up to William, who confidently approached him, asking for a job selling fish. However, it didn't take long for Luca to realize that an American chef who spoke fluent French and could interact with locals was better suited at the counter than at the fillet table.

William recalls how fiercely competitive fishmongers can be on his first day of work. Throughout the week, the Place Saint François hosts at least three to five families of fishmongers selling their catch. Each one offers the same fish brought in daily from the fishing areas in the Mediterranean. They are dedicated workers, and even the youngest family members, whether male or female, assist with daily tasks such as transportation, setup, display, sales, and cleanup. Fishmongers have a rich heritage in France that dates back centuries, and they take pride in continuing this vital part of Niçoise tradition. However, if you cross them or are openly rude, you might quickly find a very sharp fillet knife pointed at your face or, worse, between your legs.

In his first year, William worked for Luca without pay. Through hard work and skill, William and Luca quickly became friends, and William eventually earned the nickname "Ordures," which in Niçard (the ancient Nice language) loosely translates to "Trash." Years later, William still makes time on each trip to Nice to return to the open fish market and visit the Fishmongers of Saint-François.

Today, however, is different because it was only yesterday that he ran through Place Saint François, being chased for stealing a journal from the Escoffier Museum. As William enters the Place, he hears a friendly voice calling out.

"Bonjour Ordures!" (Good day, Trash!)

Luca spots William from a distance much farther than his aged eyes should be able to see. William pretends not to hear him and starts looking around the beautiful square. It takes only a moment before the severed head of a freshly filleted Durade lands right in front of him. However, before William can pick it up and throw it back, a gull descends and makes off with its catch.

William calls out to his friend Luca.

"Last year, you struck me with a Durade. Now I believe you're growing weak from age."

With a scowl on his aged and wise face, Luca reaches for another fish head to toss while William quickly raises his hands.

"Okay. Okay. I surrender!"

Walking over to his dear friend, he greets him in the traditional French style of "faire le bise". Turning around, he notices Luca's grandsons approaching, and they, too, exchange greetings with him. William continues their ritual by teasing Luca, giving him a playful pat on his stomach.

"Luca. I can see that you are eating your profits again."

They all laugh and tease each other more until his wife, Sylvie, comes over and scolds them all for not selling fish. She tosses an apron to William, and he grabs a fillet knife, getting to work at the back tables, filleting fish while chatting with tourists. The smile on William's face says it all; it's as if he's never left.

While chatting with customers, William scans the Place Saint-François to see if he can spot Eitan's security team. Noticing William's cautious demeanor, Luca gives him a wink.

"Ordures, your babysitters were too obvious, so we asked them to go. My family is better equipped to keep you safe."

William begins to unwind, and before long, they have sold all the fish. A very pleased Sylvie brings out a bottle of limoncello, and Luca and William move to the tables closest to the fountain to sit and catch up on each other's lives. Luca is a stout and strong man with a weathered face and aged gray eyes that reflect extraordinary life experience and a wry sense of humor. The two men start sipping the homemade limoncello as Luca's expression grows serious, and he leans forward in his chair. William interjects before Luca can begin to speak.

"My friend, I apologize for hurrying through the Plaza yesterday without greeting you and your family."

William lowers his head, unable to meet Luca's gaze.

"I was in a hurry."

Luca pauses, waiting for Ordures to glance back up at him.

"There are stories out there about you, Ordures. They are not pleasant ones."

William is neither surprised nor offended by his comments. Luca is known for always sharing his thoughts, no matter who his words are directed toward.

"Perhaps you could share with me what is happening to you?"

William leans back and surveys the open market. His expression is troubled, and he hesitates to talk about it, fearing he might drag Luca and his family into the darkness that is quickly engulfing him.

"It's true my family and friends have been threatened. I came here today to escape it all and do what truly makes me happy, but I fear that doing so also puts you and yours in peril."

Luca leans back in his chair, gazing at his drink while reflecting on William's words. He glances at Sylvie, who encourages her grandsons to put more effort into cleaning up. Then, he turns to William.

"You need to understand something, Ordures. We have known each other for many years, and you are the only foreigner we consider part of our 'Famille' (family). If something is troubling you, it also troubles us."

William is amazed to be called family. It is something sacred that the Niçoise people don't take lightly, as people do in America. Luca considers him part of his family, which is the greatest compliment of his life. William's eyes begin to tear up, and Luca is quick to admonish him.

"There's no time for tears, Ordures. We are men responsible for our families. If even half of what I've heard is true, then you're in grave danger, and we will not stand idly by while others threaten our family."

Sylvie approaches with her grandsons, Stefan and Tein. She rests her hand on William's shoulder, and with her aged eyes, she gazes deeply into his soul. Her French is thick and rich, and her melodic tenor almost sounds like singing.

"You are fortunate to have us, Ordures, just as we have you. Stefan is starting his culinary training with Chef Phillip from La Merenda because of your support. Thanks to your generosity, Tein will soon own a vessel, and his wife is expecting twins. What Luca says about family should not be taken lightly."

William draws strength from her words.

"Thank you, Sylvie. I value your words more than you know, and due to the potential harm that could come to you, I must avoid involving you in the mess I've created."

Sylvie glances down at Luca and encourages him to speak.

"Ordures, we're already involved. How do you think we discovered the trouble you're in? As you know, Stefan is a doorman at Le Negresco, and he heard of a young Niçoise man working there who has made many poor choices and is associated with those who seek you. He was reluctant to speak with us, so his family encouraged him to do so."

William is confused by the Niçard word Luca just used.

"He was *encouraged*?"

The grandsons chuckle as Sylvie sends them off, while Luca wears a wry smile.

"It is enough to know that the young man has been welcomed back into his family, and in return, he shared everything he knew about his employer. He also explained how they communicate and provided us with their equipment. That's how we came to learn about your troubles."

Luca's expression darkens as he continues.

"You should know that the man who showed up at Le Negresco is known as the Turk. He is a contract killer and a former mercenary. The other person appears to be a woman who has no past. However, she is well-known and has allies and enemies in high places."

William starts to interrupt. Luca raises his hand.

"Ordures. One is a wolf with your scent, while the other is a ghost."

"My friend, I already know this. They work for Curtain Group."

It is Luca's turn to be surprised, and he continues.

"The Turk has ceased using his equipment, but we know his whereabouts and how to locate him. More importantly, he doesn't know who you are... yet."

William experiences a massive wave of relief.

"You keep amazing me, Luca."

Luca brushes off the compliment.

"If you want, we can bring the Turk here, and you can speak with him yourself."

Luca sees the astonishment on William's face.

"Ordures, you need to understand that we are not a people who wait for help to arrive. We take action!"

William notices a tear starting to well up in Luca's eyes. It takes him a moment before he continues.

"Ordures, I was just a young boy when my parents were involved with the Maquis (rural French resistance fighters during World War II), and I learned a secret that organized military forces fail to comprehend."

Luca leans into me and whispers.

"Determination, driven by love and anger, can inflict great physical and psychological damage on an enemy 100 times its size. Every bomb that exploded, every man and woman killed, only deepened our love for one another and sparked a growing anger that empowered us to defeat the Nazis and the Vichy regime."

Luca turns his head to the side, wiping his eyes with the back of his weathered hand. William is beginning to see his longtime friend for the first time and gets to know him like a brother.

"This is why we are tough on family when they ignore our generation's sacrifices and associate with the wrong crowd."

William leans forward to place his hand on Luca's shoulder.

"I am honored, my friend, that you shared this with me. You have pointed out the flaws in my thinking, and I would be grateful and forever indebted to you if you could help me avert this impending danger."

William begins to get up, but Luca raises a hand, asking for one more thing from him. He sits back down again.

"Ordures, the trouble you are in is worse than you can imagine."

The weight of his words leaves William bewildered.

"The people looking for you are ruthless individuals who will, without hesitation, throw your body into a pit. But there's something else you need to know."

Luca allows the words to sink in before he drops a bomb on William.

"As I mentioned, my family was part of the French Resistance. One day, our group encountered a German SS unit carrying a suitcase filled with top-secret documents. Our commander, my father, recognized the briefcase's contents, which included a secret dating back before World War I. I believe this is the very secret you were looking for when you visited Escoffier's museum."

William leans back in his chair, clearly shaken.

"How did you learn about the museum?"

"Ordures, I told you we have the devices they use to communicate with each other. We know that and much more, but I need you to confirm that the satchel is what you're looking for?"

William cannot believe what he is hearing.

"My friend. I'm not certain what I am looking for. I thought I was searching for the answer to a mystery left behind by Escoffier. But that was before I realized I was being manipulated by the Woman With Auburn Hair so that I would set off alarms within the Curtain Group."

Luca's eyes widen, and then he sits back and reflects on his words.

"Ordures, I have a story to share that requires more time and privacy than we can manage here. Let's grab the limoncello and head to the boat."

Just as Luca is about to stand up, his grandson Tein leans in and whispers in his ear. Luca turns back to William.

"Ordures, two men working for the Turk were spotted entering the Greenbelt near our location. They've now been invited to check out our storage cellar."

He winks and smiles at William.

"Since we're unsure how much information they have shared with their friends, we'll take a different route to the boat."

It's a 15-minute walk from Vieux Nice to Port Lympia. Luca leads William down into a cellar, and from there, they pass through an ancient tunnel beneath the ruins of the old fort, whose history dates back to 300 BC. Once they emerge, William spots the famous #ILOVENICE sculpture behind them and to the west. Moments later, they arrive at Luca's boat, and he goes below deck, returning shortly with a worn leather satchel marked with Nazi insignia.

"Ordoures. Pour us more limoncello and get comfortable. There's a story I must tell you."

Chapter 19

Luca's War

April 1944 - Outskirts of Rambouillet, France

"I was too young to remember life in the village of Rambouillet before the Nazi invasion. However, as I approached my 10th birthday in the spring of 1944, we could feel the war was nearing its end. Allied troops had advanced after landing in Normandy, and for the French and Belgian Resistance, known as the Maquis, it was a time when we began to receive direct aid from Allied forces."

William looks at his friend Luca's face and sees a deep sadness in his eyes. Luca wipes away the tears again with the back of his hand.

"The reality I grew up in left me no time to be a boy. Yet, even at such a young age, I was viewed as a capable young man and became well-known for my stealth and ability to hide in plain sight. Not a day went by without dreaming of the scent of fresh herbs, grass, and flowers from the rural countryside. However, this was a different time, when the air was filled with the acrid smell of sulfur, smoke, and death."

William notices Luca gripping the satchel on his lap as if someone might take it from him. Luca continues speaking.

"One morning, as a young boy, I woke up, sensing something was wrong. Everything felt eerily still in our house, and as I strained to hear the sounds of insects or any movement from my family in the cottage, I heard nothing at all. Not even the distant sound of gunfire from the Vichy (Nazi collaborators) or other resistance fighters. I knew this could mean only one thing: danger was near."

William sees a fire igniting in Luca's eyes.

"I quietly put on my tattered clothes, shoes, and the scabbard that held my hunting knife. As I was about to enter the hallway, I noticed my grand-père standing very still. From the look on his face, I could tell that danger was actually upon us. I followed him into our main living area, noticing that my mother and sisters were not in their rooms, which meant they were likely already hidden away."

With a far-off look in his eyes, Luca continued.

"I tugged at my grand-père's shirt tail and mouthed the word 'Papa.' My grand-père shook his head "no" and put his finger to his lips, signaling the need for complete silence. I then realized that he and I were the only two standing between whatever danger lurked outside and my mother and sisters. I remember reaching for my belt and unfastening the strap that held my hunting knife, a gift given to me just a few weeks earlier for my birthday. I never went without it, and touching the knife's hilt made me feel invincible."

"It was then that my world changed forever. Suddenly, my grand-père looked deeply into my eyes and handed me his pistol, directing me back to the barn. Due to my fearless talent for climbing, my father entrusted me with repairing the barn's thatched roof. I spent countless days scaling the rafters and tiptoeing across the ledgers to lay new straw on the leaking spots, never once falling, mind you. Eventually, the barn roof became my favorite hiding spot. It also gave me a clear view for miles as I waited for my father to return from his patrols."

Luca paused the story, and William saw the distant look in his eyes. He placed his hand on Luca's arm.

"Are you alright, my friend?"

Brushing away tears from his eyes, Luca continues.

"I did as I was told and made it to the barn roof without being seen or heard. From there, I counted three men standing at the cottage windows, looking for signs of life. Without warning, my grand-père dashed from the cottage, knocking down two of the men as he ran into the thicket. A few moments later, I heard shouting and several gunshots, followed by silence. For the longest time, I believed my grand-père would return with my mother and sisters. But that was just a young boy's dream, and I would never see any of them again."

Luca's eyes fill with tears as he continues telling the story.

"The men eventually found where my mother and sisters were hiding, and they proceeded to rape them inside the cottage. I was beyond afraid, and their cries live in my nightmares to this day. Afterward, the men bound and gagged them, making plans to sell them to the Nazis. I watched helplessly from the barn roof and felt sick from my fear. In that moment, I recall feeling my fear transform into a blinding rage that fueled the strength I would need to grow into a man. Perhaps even a man who would kill."

Luca shakes his head as though to dispel the memories.

"I waited on the roof for my father to return for two days. Thirst and starvation drove me to come down, as I searched through the house for hidden food supplies. Another day passed, and a young man I recognized from town arrived at the house and began to look around. He even thought about checking for me on the barn roof. However, I had moved to a thicket of dense trees and scrub brush near the main entrance of the cottage, keeping my pistol aimed at him the whole time. I watched as the young man took a piece of cloth from his pocket and started waving it. I immediately recognized it as my father's scarf. I raised the gun to fire, but then the young man opened his mouth and spoke our family's safe word, *"Ordures!"*

William is visibly stunned by this revelation. Only now does he comprehend the true significance of the nickname his friend gave him—a sacred title that, in that moment, William silently vows to earn. Luca places his hand on William's arm, and they share a quiet moment of reflection. After a few more moments, Luca continues.

"As a family involved in the resistance, you learn two words— simple, everyday words used to signal safety or danger. The word the young man spoke to me was our family's word for safety, signifying that whoever uttered it could be trusted. I emerged from hiding, standing right behind him, and he nearly jumped out of his skin when I touched his tunic."

"After looking around, the young man instantly realized what had occurred. I recall him telling me how my grand-père loved me, that he sacrificed himself to save me, my mother, and my sisters."

Luca gazes into William's eyes.

"There is no greater act of love than willingly laying down your life for someone else. Wouldn't you agree, Ordures?"

All William can do is nod, and deep down, he begins to worry that the path he has chosen for his family may lead to a similar deadly conclusion.

"The young man eventually reunited me with my father, who was a few kilometers east of our farm. Once we were together again, I spent long minutes embracing him and crying. After that, I finally felt the weight of sleep take over me, and I lay on the floor and drifted off. It was early dawn the next day when I awoke, stiff and sore from the journey. We found ourselves in a small village on the outskirts of Rambouillet. As I quietly made my way to the kitchen, I heard voices whispering inside. Everyone turned in surprise when I entered the kitchen."

Then, Luca downs his Limoncello in one gulp and pours himself another. He also fills William's drink, which he hasn't touched much since Luce began speaking.

"I remember running over to where my father was sitting, unable to hold back my tears. He comforted me and discussed going after the men he believed were responsible. Eventually, he pulled me away, and as I stood before him, I will never forget his words."

Luca takes another sip from his glass, and William does the same.

"Young Luca, what you experienced isn't right. However, know this. The time for revenge will come. You should know that your mother will protect your sisters with her life, just as your grand-père has done for you."

"I stood there, wiping the tears from my eyes, as my father rose and proudly patted me on the shoulder, bragging about my stealth to the people in the room. After eating something, I listened to the others continue their discussion. It was the young man who brought me there who spoke first."

"There are reports of many farms being raided by other Frenchmen. It seems they are exploiting this situation to seize land and shift the blame onto the Nazis."

My father, always the more strategic thinker of the group, sat back and listened while the young man continued.

"If this is the case, we must return and reclaim what is rightfully ours."

I focused my gaze on my father. After a moment, he rose from his chair and faced the young man.

"One enemy at a time, Pierre. Our land isn't going anywhere."

I found comfort in hearing his father speak with authority.

"Members of the group began to discuss an American captain assisting them. My father noted that he had promised to send guns, but nothing had arrived yet. The group appeared deflated, but my father quickly reminded them of all they had achieved to free their land from the Nazis."

Luca halts the story here and leans toward William with a wry smile.

"Ordures. There's something you must know. The American captain my father was talking about was Ernest Hemingway."

William has to get up from his seat as goosebumps spread across his body. A thousand questions form in his head, but only one exits his lips.

"Luca, did you meet Ernest Hemingway?"

Luca chuckled a bit while scratching the back of his neck.

"I can't say I met the man, but he was there. However, I need to keep telling the story because I also have something you'll need to keep you safe."

William swiftly returns to his seat and waits with bated breath. Luca continues talking.

"I woke up early the next day to relieve myself outside. I found a well-trodden path and walked far enough to ensure the privacy I needed. As I retraced my steps back to the cottage, I heard soldiers approaching from the north. All I could do was scramble up a thick stand of poplar trees and wait. The approaching soldiers were German, and from the insignias on their uniforms, at least some were SS. I counted a squad of five soldiers, the highest-ranking of whom carried a satchel. The Germans, weary from an evening of walking, decided to make camp, and within minutes, they were lying down with a lone sentry leaning against the tree I was in."

William is captivated and struggles to remain seated.

"Sometime later, my father notices my absence. He wakes the group, and they immediately set out to find me, knowing I'm likely nearby. It's still early, but the sun is beginning to illuminate the wooded area. Shortly after, my father finds the bootprints of a small group of soldiers crossing my path. They decide to split up and surround the soldiers from each compass point—north, east, west, and south—hoping to catch them off guard."

Luca halts and glances at William, a subtle grin on his face.

"Are you okay, Ordures? You look uneasy."

William takes a large sip of his limoncello and leans back in his chair. Luca continues and also takes another sip of his limoncello.

"From my vantage point in the tree, I can see my father and his group advancing toward the soldiers. At that moment, the sentry beneath my tree rises, stretches, and wakes another soldier to take his place. The noise they make causes my father's patrol to freeze as the new sentry has to relieve himself before taking his position beneath my tree. I realize that if my father's patrol were to attack, the others would still be asleep, but not the new sentry. So, I decided on a course of action. I quietly climb down from the tree and find a hiding spot in the nearby shrubs, within arm's reach of where the soldier will return. I take out my father's hunting knife from its sheath and wait for what is sure to be an attack from my father."

"Within moments, the soldier returned from relieving himself and found the same spot to sit against the tree. I am now less than a foot away, staring at the side of the sentry's head with my knife in hand. Just then, a breaking twig from my Father's group brings the new sentry to alert, and he waits to see if he can hear it again. It is at that point that I thrust my knife directly into the soldier's throat, severing his carotid artery and windpipe. Images race through my mind of my mother, sisters, and grand-père. With almost no sound, the soldier sinks back down against the tree with a look of surprise. Standing there over the dying Nazi, I realized it was my 10th birthday."

William's mouth is agape. He closes it and leans back in his seat.

"Moments later, my father, the American Captain, and the others converge on the sleeping soldiers, and each is killed using knives. The resistance used this tactic since it could be weeks before more ammunition was found or taken from the enemy. The entire group of 5 soldiers lay dead in a growing pool of blood as I emerged from the brush, surprising my father and startling the American Captain."

Luca now leans back as he finishes his story.

"My father rushes over, drops to one knee, and hugs me like only a father can. We don't say a word, but I can't help sobbing and shaking uncontrollably. The American captain and the others begin searching the soldiers, taking away any weapons and ammunition. Then, my father finds a satchel containing research documents from the Kaiser Wilhelm Society."

William's eyes go wide. Luca casts another wry smile at him.

"It's interesting that when Hemingway first saw the documents, his eyes widened like yours are now, Ordures."

Since their arrival, Luca has kept the satchel in his lap. He now offers it to William, who accepts it skeptically and places it beside him like a menacing omen. The look on William's face tells Luca he needs clarification.

"Ordures. What is troubling you?"

After a brief moment, William looks over at his friend.

"I am astonished by how many events had to have taken place to bring this satchel with us on this boat today."

Luca has his own thoughts on the matter.

"Whether you believe it or not, it's fate. What else could it be? Don't waste time overthinking it; accept it has happened and focus on what comes next."

William nods in agreement.

"But Luca, how is it that you have it now?"

Luca finishes his story.

"My father and Hemingway talked about what to do with the satchel. Hemingway shared his connection to the information in the satchel. He admitted his cowardice in not staying in Paris to see it through with Escoffier. Feeling ashamed, Hemingway asked my father if he could return it to the American military command to make amends for letting Escoffier down."

Luca looked away as his eyes looked past William.

"Something about Hemingway unsettled my father; he thought it best to keep the documents among us. The two disagreed, and Hemingway stormed off. After that, I hardly remember much except my father deciding it was time for me to live with a relative, a fishmonger, and his wife here in Nice. The young man who found me after my Grand-pere was killed took me to where my uncle lived. However, before I left, my father handed me the satchel and told me to guard it carefully."

Luca again stares off, and his eyes begin to water this time.

"A few months later, I received word that my father had stepped on a land mine and died. I never found out what happened to my mother or sisters. After I grew up, I met Sylvie, and we got married. Years later, I met you, and yesterday, I discovered that dangerous people were searching for you because you knew about their secret. Once again, it is fate; we are just feathers on a windy day, having landed next to each other."

William is still in shock that Luca is connected to Escoffier's secret. They share long moments of silence until Luca finally breaks it.

"You see, Ordures, you're in more trouble than you realize. Perhaps it is time we devise a plan to handle this once and for all."

William leans back, allowing the new information to sink in. It becomes evident to him that the only person who could have known about this is the Woman With Auburn Hair. Somehow, Hemingway must have written something about Escoffier's secret, and whatever notebook he wrote in now belongs to the Woman With Auburn Hair. William glances over at Luca.

"My friend, I agree that we need to devise a plan, but we still lack much information. Maybe it would be better to take more time to figure out who is pulling the strings of those chasing me?"

Luca is quick to reply.

"Ordures, time is not your ally. I fear the intensity of those pursuing you, which confirms that. And what if you get caught? What then?"

William reflects on Luca's words and, with steely-eyed resolve, turns to him.

"What if I were caught indeed?"

Luca takes a moment to stare into William's eyes, seeing his resolve. He stands and starts to make his way up to the deck. William stops him.

"Luca. I have not killed another person in my life. There is no way for me to understand the aftermath. And even though I've experienced the death of a loved one, I have never felt the burden of knowing that my actions had somehow contributed to their passing..."

William allows those words to settle on the floor like dust. He then continues.

"But I'll tell you this: I am a man of resolve, and if taking a life or sacrificing my own is required of me, then I can only hope not to hesitate in my decision."

William looks away, and Luca approaches and places his hand on his shoulder.

"Ordures. Keep those words close to your heart; I know you'll be ready when the time comes."

Luca takes out his phone and dials Sylvie.

"My dear, we have guests for dinner. Set a place for two."

Sylvie doesn't miss a beat.

"What has taken you so long? The table is already set, and dinner is cooking."

Luca & Sylvie's Apartment - Port Lympia, Nice, France

"Welcome, my dear Rebecca, welcome."

Sylvie reaches forward, and the two women embrace in a long, firm hug. They pull back and hold hands while Sylvie looks deeply into Rebecca's eyes. Tears flow from both women's eyes as they stand in the doorway. Luca calls out from the kitchen.

"If you are going to cry, do it in the kitchen. We have towels in here."

The women wipe their eyes, and Sylvie casts a scowl toward the kitchen. She winks at Rebecca.

"I have a place on the terrace where we can talk. Come, let's sit and catch up."

As they pass the kitchen and head to the terrace, William quickly mouths, "I love you." Rebecca returns it with a smile, and the two women proceed to a lovely terrace with many plants and a small Parisian table with two chairs looking out to the Mediterranean. The two women sit as Luca brings out a tea kettle, cream, sugar, and a setting for two. He kisses Sylvie on her head and leaves without saying a word. With the tea now poured, Sylvie breaks the ice.

"My dear. What a mess you and dear William have found yourself in."

Rebecca sips her tea and looks out over the blue water of the Mediterranean. She then looks over her shoulder at the men sitting at the table, eating Sylvie's famous tomato galette, and turns back to Sylvie.

"I am afraid it is a mess of our own making. Don't get me wrong, but there are times when I wish William could rein in his impulse control."

Sylvie's voice is quiet after sipping her tea.

"We love our men for who they are. It can be no other way. What brought you here was more than his impulse. I think you know that, too."

Rebecca's eyes tear again, and she wipes them with her napkin.

"Yes, for he and Luca to meet those many years ago in Place Saint-Franciose was more than chance. It was fate."

Sylvie, too, looks off across the Mediterranean.

"Yes, a cruel fate that Luca, a boy 10 years old, must witness the atrocities inflicted on his family. But Luca is stronger for it. So it will be with Ordures."

Rebecca cannot hold back the tears.

"Sylvie, I am afraid for him and our family, and I do not trust that wretched auburn-haired woman."

Sylvie puts down her tea and reaches across the table to take Rebecca's hand.

"My dear. You are not alone. Our men are strong in character. We will be sitting here looking out at the sea for many years. Trust me when I say we will look back at this time with our families."

It wasn't just the words Sylvie spoke but how her energy seemed to flow from her arm into Rebecca's hand—a strength that she could feel. Rebecca straightened her back, sat up in her chair, and took in the sweet afternoon air. She realized she was no longer afraid.

"You are a dear friend, Sylvie. Thank you."

With a wink, Sylvie begins to rise.

"I think it is best if we join our men, or there will be nothing to eat or drink for dinner."

As Sylvie and Rebecca enter the kitchen, the two men immediately rise from their chairs at the table. Sylvie turns to Rebecca, giving her a knowing smile as she prepares their dinner.

"You see, my dear. It's like I said. Strength of character."

Chapter 20

Planting The Seed

Bell V-280 Valor - Vertical Lift Long Range Assault Aircraft

Master Sergeant "Winny" Winslow looks out the portal at the lights on the northern coastline of Egypt. Technically, no longer in the US military, her rank and nickname stuck when she was hired by the Curtain Group's Military Operations Division. Her focus returns as she hears the flight Captain transmit their status over the internal comms.

"We have entered Egyptian Airspace. We are comms dark from here on out. ETA to LZ in 20 mikes."

Her team of operators consists of three men and one woman. They reach up and double-tap their microphone buttons in sequence, indicating they acknowledge the message. However, the 'Germ Nerd' in the back of the cargo hold is, once again, not wearing his communications equipment. Winny rolls her eyes and heads over to the mission's science tech, Dr. Leo Cline, a plant biologist recently hired by the Curtain Group's Science & Technology division. She taps him on the shoulder, and the man jumps in surprise, unable to hear her coming because of the noise of the engines.

"Shit! You scared the piss out of me."

Unamused, Winny points to the tech's headset lying on the deck of the cargo hold.

"This is the last time I'll tell you to wear your comms at all times. If I have to remind you again, you will be coming home in a body bag. Am I clear?"

The tech nods and quickly puts on his headphones and microphone. Winny continues staring at him. The tech finally realizes he hasn't turned it on and promptly resolves that issue. Turning away, Winny heads over to her fire team. She speaks loudly to the group.

"We do this right, you'll each have an all-expense-paid two-week vacation in Cairo. Mess it up and I'll see to it that you spend time in a Libyan prison. Is that sufficient motivation?"

The team chuckles and nods their heads in affirmation. They have been together for three years with the Master Sergeant and have come to appreciate her unique form of motivational speeches. The female member of the fire squad, a former CIA Lioness, speaks up.

"What if the 'Germ Nerd' goes off book?"

Winny looks over at the female operator.

"He even farts while you are out there. Feel free to deliver physical motivation."

The group chuckles again, but now that Dr. Cline has his comms working, he doesn't feel the same about his particular motivation. The copilot reaches over his console in the cockpit and turns on the yellow warning light. The team immediately responds by preparing their gear. Dr. Cline quickly rises after noticing their movement. The Lioness looks over to the rest of the team with a smile.

"Looks like he's not as much of a dumbass as I thought."

Winny moves across the interior and releases the ramp just as the orange indicator lights up. She brings the group together.

"We have a short 3-klick walk to our mission objective. Once there, our 'Germ Nerd' plants the seed, and we head to the extraction point. Any questions?"

Everyone looks at the 'Germ Nerd'. He quickly shakes his head no.

2300 GMT - Qena Governorate - South Eastern Egypt

The Qena Governorate (pronounced Gena by the locals) is one of Egypt's most southern wheat-producing regions. An impoverished area on the banks of the Nile, it supplies farmers with water to feed its sparsely planted hectares of wheat in an otherwise barren region. For this reason alone, the Curtain Group decided to make this area the testbed for the Exodus Seed as the 'Germ Nerd' explained on the 3-kilometer walk to the less-than-eager audience of the operators.

"When it germinates, even if the wind blows it in another less desirable direction, there will still be other plants for the blight to cling to."

The group arrives on time at the 3-hectare field designated as ground zero for the test. Dr. Cline immediately gets to planting the Exodus Seed as the operators scout the location for anyone accidentally stopping by for a chat. Once completed, he feels the need to share his brilliance with the operators over an open channel.

"With the seed planted and supplemented with a liberal amount of nutrient-rich soil, germination will take around 45 days. After that, anything downwind should begin to wither in under three days and die off completely in another two days."

He reaches into his satchel, grabs his phone, and takes a picture of the location. Master Sergeant Winny, noticing his actions, walks over to him, takes the phone away, and smashes it under her boot. Dr. Cline jumps up.

"What the hell did you do that for?!"

She grabs the tech by his shirt, throws him to the ground, and points to the freshly planted Exodus Seed.

"Two reasons. First, you used an open channel to inform anyone listening about exactly what we are doing here, and second, you took a geotagged photo of it. Do you think your employer wants either of these things to happen in their top-secret mission?"

The Master Sergeant pulls out her pistol and points it at Dr. Cline. Cowering, Dr. Cline throws up his hands in surrender. The Lioness operator comes over and pulls him to a standing position.

"You should buy a lottery ticket when you get home. You're the luckiest nerd in the world. The Master Sergeant rarely pulls her gun without firing it."

The former Lioness releases him and turns to the rest of the squad.

"I was wrong. He is still a dumbass."

Moments later - CIA Data Center - Langley, Virginia

In the labyrinth of the CIA's data center sits a locked server rack housing a single server belonging to the Woman With Auburn Hair. The server's amber processing light begins steadily flashing. After a few seconds, the orange light goes dark and its Bluetooth indicator activates. Soon after, the Woman With Auburn Hair receives a text message from her asset, a former Lioness now under cover in the Curtain Group. Looking at the hyper-encrypted phone, she sees the following coordinates.

"E-seed 26.1551° N, 32.7160° E @ 02:32 GMT"

Realizing the Exodus project is on the clock, she sets a mental timer inside her brilliant mind. They have less than a month to finish the task at hand. She begins typing a text to a waiting SEAL Team, who are cooling their heels on the Greek island of Crete. She gives them the coordinates of the Exodus Seed and awaits their acknowledgement. Within seconds, she has her reply.

"Message received. Seed extraction team is a go. Confirmation of mission status in 7 hours."

Exactly 7 hours later, she receives confirmation from the SEAL team that they successfully replaced the Exodus Seed plant with a replicant and sprayed the surrounding area with a normal blight that would make anyone believe the Exodus Seed was viable. On their return trip, they also burned Exodus Seed plant in an enclosed chamber and dropped its ashes into the Mediterranean.

Executive Suite, The Curtain Group - Sophia

Antipolis Technology Park - Moments later

Second-in-Command Delya Morris of the Curtain Group is relaxing in her office in the early morning hours. She is waiting for confirmation from Dr. Cline that the seed has been planted. She rises from her chair, stretches, and walks to the window with her coffee. While looking over the hills surrounding Nice, dotted with thousands of lights, she smiles cruelly, thinking to herself.

"It has taken over a hundred years to see the completion of the Exodus seed project. How much time and money have been spent? How many lives were tossed aside so that the vision of the KWS could be finally realized?

She takes a moment to sip her coffee and allows the words to escape her lips.

"Time to take a few pieces off the board."

Chapter 21

Loose Ends

Office of Herman Dashill - Curtain Group

Headquarters - Sophia Antipolis, Nice, France

Herman stands at the window, looking out to the Mediterranean Sea. Having just received word of the successful mission to plant the Exodus seed in Egypt, Herman should relax, but he cannot. There is still no resolution to the man who stole Escoffier's journal. His thoughts are interrupted by the voice of his assistant coming through his phone.

"Sir, they have arrived."

Herman walks back to his desk.

"Thank you. Send them in."

Moments later, two men and The Woman With Auburn Hair enter the room. The first to enter the room is an asset named "The Turk". He moves to a wall and leans against it. He learned long ago to keep his back to the wall. The Woman With Auburn Hair approaches the conference table as a young Ethiopian man pulls out a chair for her. He then finds another seat for himself and boots up his computer.

Herman moves around to the front of his desk, leaning against it, waiting as the connecting door to the next office opens. The last to enter, his second-in-command, Delya Morris, steps in and sits at the conference table across from The Woman With Auburn Hair. Herman, irritated that she's always last to enter the room, gets right to it.

"We have a problem. I've just gotten off the phone with our client, Madame Chairperson."

He allows his words to settle in.

"She has lost faith in our ability to resolve the Escoffier issue. Her feelings have merit."

Herman looks over at the Turk.

"Care to explain how you were unable to capture the target?"

Uncharacteristically, the Turk becomes uneasy.

"The team did its best under the circumstances. The target had greater situational awareness due to his knowledge of the labyrinth that makes up Old Nice. We were also working with poor intel on his appearance."

Looking over at the Woman With Auburn Hair, Delya Morris jumps in.

"Yet our 'fixer' accurately predicted where the target would go to ground."

She looks at the Woman With Auburn Hair with a questioning gaze.

"How *did* you know to go to Le Negresco?"

Calmly, the Woman With Auburn Hair responds to Delya's query.

"It was an educated guess."

Delya probes.

"Which part? When you told Herman that the Turk would lose the target or that the target would end up at Le Negresco."

"The second part, madame. The first part about the Turk losing the target was simple math. The Turk is the one who shoots the target *after* it has been caught. He lacks the skill to catch a fleeing turtle."

Nigel cannot help but chuckle at the comment, but quickly recovers after receiving an evil glance from the Turk. Nigel joins the conversation.

"In fairness to our Turkish contractor, the target is getting assistance."

This captures everyone's attention, including the Woman With Auburn Hair. Nigel opens a new file on this laptop.

"First, the SUV used in the escape is a Range Rover Sentinel. It is a rolling luxury fortress capable of defeating most countermeasures. It is registered to an Israeli attaché stationed in Nice, making the driver likely a Mossad agent. This would explain our team's failure to direct the target into a kill box."

Nigel continues.

"As to the foot pursuit, the target's ability to effectively utilize the labyrinth of Old Nice suggests he has spent much time in the area. This is likely why he had the upper hand evading the Turks' assets."

Lastly, Nigel looks over to The Woman With Auburn Hair.

"Our electronic forensic team also discovered a hack of an internet-connected coffee pot at the Escoffier museum. However, its cache has already been deleted, which taints the video footage and explains why we didn't have a more detailed target description."

The Woman With Auburn Hair looks around the room as everyone's eyes settle on her. She turns her focus and words on Nigel.

"Perhaps you can explain why the cameras were not repositioned after the museum's remodeling last year. Nearly every piece of furniture has been moved in Escoffier's office. Hack or not, your cameras were in the wrong place to see anything, Nigel."

She pauses for effect.

"And if you were to find one of my hacks, it's because I wanted you to find it."

This announcement unsettles Nigel, and he mentally notes that he will never look her way again in any meeting. Herman and Delya exchange looks, realizing the depth of the Woman With Auburn Hair's tradecraft. There is an uncomfortable moment of silence before Herman redirects the conversation.

"The hack notwithstanding, we know very little about the target or his motivation. Nigel, I believe your team has put together an analysis."

Nigel opens another file on his laptop.

"The security footage suggests that the theft was spontaneous. However, the target was skilled at avoiding the camera angles, indicating that he may have prepared for the crime beforehand or had received coaching."

Looking at the footage, the Woman With Auburn Hair is pleased with the edits the CIA technician made to the video. She completely edited the moment when William realized that Escoffier's journal was a fake while maintaining the accuracy of the timestamp throughout. She makes a mental note to send the tech a gift. Herman cuts to the chase.

"Nigel, what is your team's recommendation?"

Nigel gathers himself and brings up a risk assessment worksheet.

"The first option is to deploy a team to extract the target forcibly. The risk associated with this option is extremely high, as security at Le Negresco is highly trained, and the target always has a Mossad-trained security detail. If the extraction fails, it could expose us and jeopardize the project deadline."

Herman nods in agreement as Nigel continues.

"Our second option is to have the Woman With Auburn Hair lure the target to a location of our choosing, where we can have assets ready to extract. Our risk in this scenario is manageable."

Herman turns to The Woman With Auburn Hair.

"Madame, do you have any thoughts on the second option?"

The Woman With Auburn Hair acts as though she is collecting her thoughts when, in fact, she is already prepared for this particular option.

"As I mentioned in my report, my meeting with the target did not end well. When I clarified his options, he became angry and left. I doubt he will be willing to meet with me again."

Delya takes a shot at the Woman With Auburn.

"So, at last. There is something our 'fixer' cannot fix."

Brushing off Delya's insult, the Woman With Auburn Hair acts as though she has another idea when, in fact, it is the next phase of her plan.

"There is a third option. Since we can agree that the target already knows the nature of Escoffier's secret to some extent, why not give him what he's looking for?"

Herman becomes greatly agitated and responds sarcastically.

"Why don't we just put him on the payroll and give him an office next to mine!?"

The Woman With Auburn Hair rolls her eyes and explains.

"The target believes that Escoffier's secret is worse than anything the Kaiser Wilhelm Society has ever created. Who better to persuade him of our intentions than the person who hired us? In the worst case, we can contain and extract him if required. If she talks him down, we proceed without disrupting the timeline."

Delya cuts in.

"You've already established that the target is on high alert. What makes you think he will meet with her if he won't meet with you?"

The Woman With Auburn Hair quickly answers.

"Because she is the only person he will *want* to meet.

Delya jumps back in.

"What makes you think she will want to meet with *him*? I cannot believe you would suggest such a thing. What of our client's safety?"

Herman looks over to Nigel.

"Nigel, does your team feel that the target poses a threat to Madame Chairperson?"

Nigel confidently responds.

"No, sir. The target is a non-combatant. His actions reflect someone trapped in a situation he is trying to understand. If there is anyone he would be willing to meet, it would be the person he believes holds the answers to his questions. Harming that person would not facilitate that outcome."

Thinking to herself, Delya's face lights up with anticipation, betraying her intent.

"At last, a way to eliminate the Madame Chairperson."

Herman turns to the Woman With Auburn Hair.

"Speak with your employer and set up a meeting. I needn't remind you of the time crunch we are in."

The Woman With Auburn Hair leaves the meeting and gets into her waiting sedan. She enables electronic countermeasures and sends a hyperencrypted text message to the Madame Chairperson.

"They've taken the bait. I need to confirm the meeting between you and my asset."

Moments pass, and she receives a reply.

"Excellent. I will make the necessary arrangements."

Delya returns to her office and sends a hyper-encrypted text to an unknown recipient.

"Client in play. Set up Boscolo"

After Nigel leaves the office, Herman and the Turk walk over to the window after pouring themselves a Scotch. Looking down at the street, they see The Woman With Auburn Hair's sedan pull away. Herman turns to the Turk.

"You have a green light on the target and the trophy."

The Turk takes a sip of the 25-year-old Dalmore and smiles.

"I recently learned that our target is traveling with his wife."

Herman's face shows surprise, and he updates his orders.

"So now you have _two_ targets and the trophy to kill."

Chapter 22

The Revelation

Le Negresco Hotel - Nice, France

Since 5 a.m., William has sat at a small table near the balcony. A calm early morning Mediterranean breeze wafts in with the open windows, causing the sheers to billow inward. He ordered room service and tried to be quiet so Rebecca could sleep. At the moment, he sits enjoying an Americano and looking at the documents from the satchel. His head is a little cloudy from all the Limoncello he and Luca consumed yesterday.

Moments later, he feels Rebecca's warm hands on his shoulders as she leans down and kisses him three times. William repeats the words they've spoken since starting the three-kiss tradition when they first met.

"One kiss for yesterday, one for today, and one for tomorrow."

Now seated in front of the open laptop, Rebecca begins looking through the pages as William serves her an Americano with half an almond croissant. He sits next to her and starts nibbling on the other half. William reflects on yesterday's revelations.

"It was nice to spend time yesterday with Luca and Sylvie."

Rebecca pauses her reading, smiles, bites into the croissant, sips her Americano, and leans back in her chair.

"I am amazed by the circumstances that brought us together. But now that we are here, I can't imagine it happening any other way."

William sinks deeper into his chair while sipping his Americano.

"I don't like dwelling on the unexplainable, but I must admit this situation with Luca and Hemingway has me scratching my head."

Rebecca leans forward and scans several pages of Correns' research. Beside his laptop, she spots a German-English dictionary, which she picks up.

"Why not just look the words up on the…"

She stops herself in mid-sentence as it hits her.

"Because there is likely some person or program monitoring searches for terms related to genetically altered plants."

William rises and brings her a notepad he has been using with three pages of notes.

"I had the concierge go to the bookstore, where I gave her cash to purchase the dictionary and notepad. I also had her purchase a book on algebra and two manga comics."

Rebecca nods in understanding.

"So, if anyone's watching, all they'll notice are things a 20-something college student studying German might purchase. Well played."

Rebecca begins reviewing his notes. William smiles, knowing Rebecca's superpower is in quickly condensing research into a hypothesis. William attempts to justify his reasoning.

"There were too many technical terms, so I focused primarily on Correns' personal notes."

Rebecca quickly finishes reading and sips her coffee. She turns to him.

"They are making a plant bomb."

William's facial expression is one of surprise and curiosity. Rebecca explains.

"Correns discovered a genetic mutation of a particular type of pea plant that, when it germinates, it releases a strong mutated version of a blight pathogen. Anything downwind of it is quickly covered in the weaponized pathogen, killing everything it touches. Correns discovered a genetically modified plant bomb."

William and Rebecca sit silently until William recalls his conversation with the Woman With Auburn Hair.

"At dinner, the auburn-haired 'fixer' said her focus was to ensure the secret finds a safe home—a place where it can benefit humanity rather than subjugate it. If they are making a plant bomb, then she is either being used by her employer, or she is complicit in their plans."

Rebecca sips her coffee as she continues to work on the rationale. William rises from his chair just as Rebecca comes to another conclusion. She looks up at William with a questioning face.

"We're missing something."

Rebecca sits back and sips her coffee. She smells the aroma and remembers William telling her that the beans were grown in Ethiopia and that most coffee beans are distributed through London before making their way to France and the rest of the world. At that moment, her eyes go wide with an epiphany. She looks over at William.

"Didn't you say that the Curtain Group's largest client was the UN FAO?"

Already knowing the answer, Rebecca pauses, running the details through her brilliant, research-trained mind.

"This isn't about stopping them from making a plant bomb. It's about stopping them from distributing it!"

Rebecca goes over to William's laptop and then stops midstride, remembering they shouldn't use the computer. William smiles and walks over to her.

"You've figured it out."

At that moment, Rebecca's phone rings, startling them both. She breaks away from William and sees the initials 'WWAH' on the screen. She shows it to William and then answers, her voice dripping with loathing.

"Well, if it isn't the auburn-haired fixer."

The Woman With Auburn Hair allows the sentiment to pass without a response. After a tense pause, she addresses her.

"Madame, I know what you must think of me, but we have things that need to be discussed, woman to woman."

Rebecca shuts her eyes and envisions choking the life out of the auburn-haired woman. She eventually answers.

"If you were a man, I'd say you have quite the set of balls for suggesting that."

The Woman With Auburn Hair responds without emotion.

"Madame, you will have your reckoning with me, but it will have to wait until we figure out how to end this ordeal in a way we can both live with."

As Rebecca considers her choice of words, William paces the floor like an expectant father.

"*Living* being the operative word. However, I am afraid, Madame, that we no longer need your assistance."

The Woman With Auburn Hair interrupts.

"Yes. You do. And before you argue your point, you should know I've already got a person working on the distribution element of the plan."

Rebecca pauses and puts her cell phone on mute. She looks at William.

"She's listening to our conversation in real time."

William begins looking around the room. Rebecca takes the phone off mute. The Woman With Auburn Hair continues talking.

"The thing you should know about my app is that once it is on a phone, the only way to remove it is to destroy the phone. Oh, and the Faraday bag you've been using isn't real. It just looks real. By the way, that was a nice piece of logical reasoning, figuring out the distribution element."

The Woman With Auburn Hair keeps her momentum going, but Rebecca interrupts her with deep anger and sarcasm.

"What audacity, Madame! What more can this family do for you? Let me get a pen so I can write your instructions down."

"Madame Laurent. I chose William because of his tenacity and intuition to be able to read between the lines. We still need to draw out those who remain in the shadows."

Rebecca has had enough, but before she can speak, the Woman With Auburn Hair continues.

"Madame, you should know that since meeting your husband at Le Plongeoir, I placed an electronic blanket on your family's online presence—yours and your daughter, her family, your nephew, and your business. If anyone tries to search for an image of you or anyone in your family, no information will be returned.   Additionally, Langley is actively monitoring these systems to mitigate any potential threats. Go ahead and try searching for anyone in your family on the Internet. I'll wait."

William's face reflects confusion as Rebecca walks over to her laptop and begins browsing the internet. After about a minute, she closes it and returns to the phone.

"And this changes how we feel about you because...?"

The Woman With Auburn Hair measures her words.

"It isn't meant to change anything. However, it should show you my commitment to ensuring your family's safety."

Rebecca's temper flares again.

"So, now you're placing our family on electronic house arrest to make us do what you want?"

The Woman With Auburn Hair takes a deep breath and audibly exhales her frustration.

"Madame, look at your husband. Is he the kind of person who would walk away from this?"

Rebecca looks over into William's eyes. His face is wrinkled with worry.

"No, he wouldn't."

The Woman With Auburn Hair pleads with her.

"Rebecca, join me in ending a secret that has taken the lives of everyone I have ever loved. A secret that, if released, will endanger and/or subjugate billions around the globe, including your family!"

Her words strike a chord in Rebecca's heart.   She pauses while looking into William's eyes.

"Okay. I'll speak with him. So, what is it that you need him to do?"

She listens to the Woman With Auburn Hair and cannot contain her anger.

"YOU HAVE GOT TO BE FUCKING KIDDING ME!"

Chapter 23

Madame Chairperson

Boscolo Exedra Hotel, Blvd. Victor Hugo - Nice, France

It took William nearly the entire evening to ease Rebecca's apprehension about meeting with the Curtain Group's client at the Boscolo Exedra Hotel. William promised to bring Eitan along and to keep his phone on the entire time.

Eitan and William arrive 30 minutes before the scheduled meeting. Eitan is also apprehensive and spends the entire drive between Le Negresco and the Bosoclo reminding William of the dangers he could face. Eventually, they pull up to the hotel's driveway. Eitan makes one last plea.

"Sir, you should have security of your own. At the very least, I should go with you."

William points to the hotel as he responds.

"Eitan, the Woman With Auburn Hair, has assured me that my family is no longer in play. Besides, this is her client's *residence*. She has the home-field advantage. Trust me when I say we don't have enough security to make a difference."

Eitan's response is unsettling.

"Sir. That does not mean that _you_ are not in play."

William turns to Eitan with complete seriousness.

"My friend, I'm not going in unprepared. I have a plan...or at least an idea of one."

As William exits the Sentinel and begins walking towards the hotel, he stops and turns back to Eitan.

"But if you can stay close, I would be even more in your debt."

Eitan smiles and keeps the car running while William walks through the doors of the Boscolo Exedra Hotel and heads directly to the bar.

Genesi Bar - Boscolo Exedra Hotel - Blvd Victor Hugo, Nice, France

Minutes before the scheduled meeting, an austere woman wearing a bespoke Italian pantsuit and jacket that would easily cover the cost of staying at the Boscolo for a few weeks, enters the lobby. She pauses to gain her bearings and notices William standing at the bar. A concierge walks over and takes her coat. As she walks across the white Italian Carrara marble floors, William notices the lobby's slightly off-white walls, reflecting the light from the vaulted stained glass skylight above.

The austere woman is fit, of average height, and relaxed, but her eyes betray her. They dart quickly around the room, gathering tiny bits of information that will inevitably be used later in the conversation. It takes her only a few seconds to notice William standing at the bar with his back to her. Like a chameleon, she alters her demeanor to become an off-putting yet likable person whose sole interest is doing something nice for others. William watches her in the bar mirror as she walks toward him. William's intuition tells him something is off about her.

Still, at the bar, William moves his glass in a circular motion to create enough noise to disrupt the moment. Hearing the sound, the austere woman turns and approaches the bar. Moments later, she stands in front of William with a casual smile.

"Thank you for meeting with me, Monsieur Chef."

William's response is off-putting.

"Madame, I am waiting for someone else."

The austere woman recovers.

"Is that so?"

She pulls out her phone and shows William a grainy black-and-white image from a video camera in the Escoffier Museum.

"Is this not you?"

William scowls at the picture. He hands her phone back, carefully dragging his fingers down the device to blur any fingerprints he might leave behind. Thinking to himself, he silently thanks Eitan for the spycraft. William explains.

"You misunderstand. I am supposed to meet with someone who I have been told is extraordinarily detail-oriented. That person would have greeted me by my real name. You did not, so you are not the person I am here to meet."

William tires of the charade.

"Perhaps you could let the *real* Madame Chairperson know that I am still interested in meeting with her, but I do not appreciate my time being wasted. Good day, madame-whoever-you-are."

William turns his back to the austere woman to ask the bartender for the bill when she digs into her purse and pulls out her phone.

"Yes, Madame. As you foretold, the ruse did not last long. I shall send him over."

The woman taps William's shoulder.

"If you would be so kind as to accompany me to the billiards room."

William signals to the bartender to bring his drink to his destination as the austere woman guides him through the white marble-tiled lobby. As he begins following the austere woman, he notices nearly ten people, all women, positioned between them and the billiards room. Each one is scanning the room, constantly updating their threat assessments. These are the Madame Chairperson's bodyguards. William approaches, lost in thought.

"Now we are getting somewhere."

As William reaches the billiards room, he sees two members of Madame Chairperson's security team move in front of him with such swiftness and grace that it reminds him of a ballet. They block his entrance and glare at him menacingly while another approaches and runs an electronic wand across his body. It beeps, and William is immediately patted down in places that only his wife is familiar with. They remove his phone and hand it to another security guard, who quickly exits the lobby and delivers it to a tech on a laptop in an adjacent anteroom. Moments later, it is returned inside a Faraday bag and given back to the Madame Chairperson's Security Chief. Looking around, William notices the austere woman is nowhere to be seen.

William returns to the moment, looking at the head of security, and sarcastically begins speaking in fluent French.

"Noté. N'apportez jamais un téléphone à un échange de coups de feu." [*Noted. Never bring a phone to a gun fight.*]

She returns a look that William translates into: 'Keep it up, mister, and I'll have your testicles tattooed.'

It is then that William's nose detects a familiar fragrance that he can't quite place. Just then, a woman approaches him, holding a billiard cue. The two guards part, allowing room for the Madame Chairperson to greet her guest. William hesitates, noting that her guards are still within striking distance of at least seven vulnerable areas on William's upper torso. As Eitan taught him, William relaxes his arms, allowing them to drape at his sides. He recalls Eitan's final lesson. No sudden movements.

The woman is dressed in linen slacks, a silk blouse, and Sketchers. She offers her hand and speaks in English with neither emotion nor accent. Standing just a few feet away, William could have felt her presence a mile away. In Hollywood, she would be known as a person who possesses '*It.*' She is slender but not skinny, neither short nor tall, attractive yet not beautiful, and she radiates a confidence that acts as both a force field and a tractor beam.

"You must be Chef William Laurent. It's a pleasure to meet you, but I hear you prefer to be called simply Chef. Is that right?"

William nods in the affirmative and receives her handshake, which is as authoritative as it is feminine. He immediately smells the fragrance he noticed earlier and begins listing the ingredients, which causes the Madame Chairperson some confusion.

"Lavender, vanilla, lilac, and... what is that last element? Oh, cocoa! But not a South American species. It must be Moroccan."

The woman is somewhat surprised by William's olfactory skills. William blushes a bit, feeling embarrassed by his outburst. She mentally notes it. William regroups.

"It's a pleasure to meet you. You must be Madame Chairperson and a client of the Curtain Group. Is there a name to go with your title?"

She lets go of his hand, and her response is definitive as she turns toward the billiard table with the cue in hand.

"No, I do not."

In that instant, William's intuition kicks in as he realizes that there is also something familiar about her. It's the same feeling he had when first seeing the Woman With Auburn Hair. However, the Madame Chairperson does not resemble her or the woman in the picture with Hemingway in the least. Without thinking, William speaks the words in his head.

"You remind me of someone..."

She turns her head sharply toward William. A flash of anger and fear flickers in her eyes, only to vanish just as quickly. He recalls noticing the same emotions when he said the same thing to the Woman With Auburn Hair at Le Plongeoir. The Madame Chairperson glances at her security captain, and the security line moves back, allowing William to join her. William walks over and stands with his back against the wall, providing him with an unobstructed view of the lobby and her entire security detail. William has always preferred to have his back to the wall. However, he still cannot help but glance toward the ceiling to ensure the Sword of Damocles isn't hanging over his head.

Madame Chairperson turns away and begins to study the remaining billiard balls on the table before lining up her shot. At the last moment, she looks up directly at William as she strikes the cue ball. The ball bounces off two of the blood-red velvet rails of the pool table, and as it slowly reaches the eight ball, it touches it with just enough energy to sink it into the corner pocket. She walks over to William as the ball drops into the pocket. She hands the cue to a nearby security guard, who then hands her a drink.

"So you think I look like someone you know. Should I take that as a compliment?"

William is embarrassed.

"No, Madame, I said you remind me of someone. You carry yourself like the person who set up this meeting."

William pauses.

"You also wear the same perfume as she."

She stares at William with unfeeling eyes for an uncomfortable amount of time. William deflects.

"Madame, I often react to my feelings without thinking. If you ask my wife, she would tell you it's her least favorite of my many character flaws."

Madame Chairperson smiles coldly at the self-deprecating humor.

"I think I would like your wife. We already have something in common."

William, appearing disinterested, casually looks around at the security detail as a wall of silence builds between them. William cuts through it with his next question.

"Are you familiar with empathetic mimicry?"

The Madame Chairperson, surprised at the question, nods in recognition.

"Yes. It is when people who, through an emotional connection, begin to display similar mannerisms. So, you believe I am mimicking the Woman With Auburn Hair?

William rolls his eyes.

"Yes, your 'fixer'. The very one who set up this meeting. Or she could be mimicking you. The jury is still out on that one."

Madame Chairperson glares at William, and he can immediately sense a heightened alertness in her security detail. She relaxes her posture just as the bartender approaches with William's drink on a silver tray. Her security team confronts the man. Taking the drink from the tray, they pour it into a plastic cup, but not before inserting a small device, which, seconds later, displays a green LED light. They then bring it over to William, wrapped in a napkin. Accepting the drink, he makes an overly dramatic slurping noise while sipping it. Madame Chairperson smiles again, but this time with genuine emotion.

"Chef, I now understand what our common friend sees in you."

William is quick to correct her.

"Madame. I am no friend of your 'fixer'.

William glances at the serious-looking bodyguards surrounding the billiards room.

"May I approach?"

Madame Chairperson nods in agreement. Without giving an order, her bodyguards bring over two massive blood-red velvet armchairs and a small white marble table to create a separation. As they take their seats, Madame Chairperson hands the cue stick to a departing bodyguard, signaling that the formalities are complete and they can get down to business.

William sits back in his chair and takes the offensive.

"I know why I am here."

She concedes and leans back in her chair, folding her arms.

"And yet you still came. Tell me why?"

William's response is intentionally vague.

"Personal reasons."

Madame Chairperson realizes he is baiting her, and a part of her respects him for it.

"Chef, we are each here for the same personal reason. Our family."

It is William's turn to set down his drink and carefully watch Madame Chairperon's response. She continues.

"I want to commend your intuition earlier. The Woman With Auburn Hair and I share more than a professional relationship. She is my stepdaughter."

William does his best to curb his emotions.

"I met and married her mother soon after the two of them were driven apart by the Curtain Group. After she passed away, I took over her mission to bring down the Curtain Group. However, I did something she never thought to do. The one thing the Curtain Group would never see coming. I gave them the Exodus Seed."

William cannot believe what he is hearing. She raises her hand, asking him to delay his response.

"It was my wife, the Woman With Auburn Hair's mother, who worked out the science. She spent all her vast resources over the years controlling the research so that her company alone managed its development and countermeasures. Once she revealed she had the science, she knew those looking to use it would come out of hiding. Once in the open, she planned to expose them. However, by then, she was too frail from age, and once she passed, I realized that the Curtain Group was merely the teeth of the beast. So, with the help of the Woman With Auburn Hair, we hatched our plan."

William can no longer remain silent. But now, having more understanding, he backs off his emotions and affirms his knowledge to her.

"You needed an unknown element to threaten the project at the last possible moment so that those hiding in the shadows would have to get involved."

The Madame Chairperson relaxes her posture and smiles back at William. He continues.

"Which is why I am here, meeting with you. Our coming together allows them to kill two birds with one stone. How could they resist?"

"Precisely, William. Even when a lamb is staked to a tether, a wolf will still be a wolf, even when it knows it is a trap."

William considers her words.

"Madame, there was a time when this was simply a puzzle for me to solve. I discovered an odd set of initials in Escoffier's Le Guide Culinaire, and through research, I made the connection between people who shouldn't have known each other. Now, I realize that it was never a game or a puzzle. It's someone's business plan and an evil one at that. Truth be told, I thought it was yours."

"And now, whose business plan do you think it belongs to?"

William is about to answer when her security team quickly moves from the billiard room towards the hotel lobby. Her security Chief comes between her and William, his face showing confusion.

The Security Chief takes Madame Chairperson by the arm and retreats toward an exit at the back of the hotel lobby. William begins to rise, but the security chief puts out her hand, which is now holding a gun. William, raising his hands, gladly remains seated. The Madame Chairperson looks at William with sympathy in her eyes.

"I'm afraid our time together has come to an end."

Her security chief moves her towards the lobby entry as the Madame Chairperson looks back at William.

"I am glad that she found you, William."

The security captain stops, reaches into her jacket, removes William's cell phone still inside the Faraday bag, and tosses it to him.

As they make their way to the lobby exit, a scuffle ensues as three others from Madame Chirperson's security detail swiftly grab the hotel's concierge, lifting him off the ground and escorting him through a service door behind the lobby desk. William notices that the security chief is now holding a second gun, presumably concealed in the jacket the concierge was retrieving for the Madame Chairperson. In the next moment, the Madame Chairperson is whisked away to a waiting, heavily armored SUV.

Five Blocks Away From The Boscolo Exedra

The austere woman William first met exited the Boscolo hotel moments after William saw through her ruse. She quietly made her way through the lobby doors and down the Boulevard Victor Hugo toward Avenue Jean Médecin. Entering a local department store, the austere woman quickly retrieves an outfit she stashed in a dressing room earlier that day. Waiting several minutes before exiting the store, she walks out onto Jean Médecin toward the Liberation Market dressed as a frail elderly woman returning from buying food. Just as she begins to relax, her situational awareness alerts her that something is out of place. It is then that a blacked-out SUV quickly pulls up next to her, and before she can react, three women of the Madame Chairperson's security detail pull a black hood over her head and push her into the SUV, driving off before anyone can respond.

Speeding Black SUV

The security chief pulls the hood back from the austere woman's head. It takes a moment for her eyes to adjust to the interior light. She hears Madame Chairperson's voice coming from behind her. The austere woman offers a wry smile, even though she cannot turn to look her target in the eyes. The Chief of Security notices the smile and tenses. It is Madame Chairperson who speaks first.

"I understand why you betrayed us, but I would have thought a woman of your experience would have better calculated the odds of success. Delya would be displeased."

The austere woman stares ahead and casually stretches her arms. Just as she relaxes, a slight beep comes from her foot. The motion of hyper-extending her arm triggers a detonator hidden in her shoe. The austere woman looks out the window and calmly speaks.

"No. She won't"

In that very second, the security chief pushes open the SUV's door and throws the austere woman into oncoming traffic. In another second, an explosion rocks the SUV, sending it careening into a steep embankment. The SUV continues to roll down a hill, gaining momentum until it comes to rest against the side of an apartment building, steam billowing from the engine compartment.

There is no movement from inside the SUV. The 'hi-lo' sirens of emergency vehicles begin to wail in the distance.

Outside the Boscolo Exedra Hotel

After the Madame Chairperson is whisked away, William pays his bar tab and walks back onto Boulevard Victor Hugo. Within a few moments, he and everyone on the street hear an explosion coming from up the street. William gets on his phone and dials Rebecca. She immediately begins talking when he picks up.

"Where are you? Is everything OK? How did the meeting go?"

William gathers his wits and tries to calm his voice as he looks toward the smoke. He can now hear many sirens as emergency vehicles make their way up the hill. Eitan quickly brings around the Sentinel and signals for William to get in. William is still on the phone as he enters the SUV.

"There's been an explosion. It may have been the Madame Chairperson."

Rebecca gets on her laptop.

"It says that several vehicles were involved, but not much more."

It is then that William's phone receives another call—this time without any associated number.

"I'm getting a call from the Woman With Auburn Hair. Keep me posted if you learn anything more."

William picks up the call. The Woman With Auburn Hair's ordinarily calm demeanor has been replaced by fear and anger.

"Where are you? What happened after you hung up?! Tell me everything!"

The Woman With Auburn Hair quickly calms down before William can collect his thoughts.

"Scratch that. I can see you have gotten into the Sentinel. Have your driver take you to my apartment on the Cour Seleya. I will send him the address and access code."

William begins looking through the windows and notices cameras outside the Boscolo hotel. Eitan is also on his phone, and once William hangs up, he turns in his seat.

"I was on the phone with a colleague. The SUV with the Madame Chairperson exploded a mile up on the Boulevard Victor Hugo. It doesn't appear that there are any survivors."

The next moment, Eitan receives a text with the address and access code from the Woman With Auburn Hair. Eitan gives William an odd look.

"Sir. This address is the former apartment of the French artist Henri Matisse. Are you sure of the address?

Impatiently, William replies.

"It came from the Woman With Auburn Hair, so let's assume she lives up to her reputation for not making such a rookie mistake."

William then sends a text to Rebecca.

William:

"Meeting up with the WWAH (The Woman With Auburn Hair) to discuss the meeting with MC."

Rebecca:

"Explosion update... several cars were involved. No word yet on casualties."

William:

"WWAH is distraught. I fear the explosion may involve MC."

Rebecca:

[Shocked emoji] "Where are you meeting WWAH?"

William:

"You're never going to believe me."

After William texts Rebecca on the location of the meetup, Eitan pulls up to the Cour Seleya. However, he first drops William off before taking the ramp to the underground parking. As he enters the eastern end of the Cour Seleya, William receives a text message from the Woman With Auburn Hair.

"Good. You're here."

William sends a text to Rebecca before going in.

"I'm here, and I'll call you as soon as I know more. I love you."

William uses the code and enters the lobby.

The Former Apartment of Henri Matisse - The Cour Seleya - Vieux Nice, France

Most of the centuries-old buildings in Vieux Nice do not have elevators. Luckily, the building housing Matisse's former residence is only five stories tall. After getting through the lobby, William climbs the stairs with little effort. As he turns down the hall, he sees only one door and the Woman With Auburn Hair in it. She steps back into the apartment and leaves the door open.

As William enters the apartment, he first notices the pungent odor of linseed oil, the main ingredient in the paint used by artists at the turn of the century. He can hear her moving around in what must be the kitchen and calls out to her.

"How long before you get used to the smell of this apartment?"

The Woman With Auburn Hair looks up from her phone as William enters.

"What smell?"

William looks around the apartment and sees no less than a dozen original Matisse paintings on the walls. He notices a look of worry on The Woman With Auburn Hair's face. He tries to distract her.

"Rebecca was saying there is nothing definitive yet from the news outlets."

Rolling her eyes, she continues viewing information on her phone.

"The news outlets only report what they are told to report. A woman of the Madame Chairperson's stature isn't going to show up on the news. What is troubling is that my sources aren't responding to my outreach."

Putting her phone down, she walks into the kitchen. William follows her.

"Tell me exactly what happened in your meeting with Madame Chairperson. Start from the moment you arrived with your driver."

William takes a seat at a small kitchen table. He goes through the entire story, beginning with the austere-looking woman and ending with Madame Chairperson being whisked away by her security detail. The Woman With Auburn Hair sends another text requesting that the Boscolo lobby video footage be forwarded to her immediately.

William and Rebecca's Suite at Le Negresco Hotel - Nice, France

It has been 15 minutes since William last texted from Matisse's apartment. Rebecca looks down at her phone, hoping to hear from him. She is worried. It is not like him to go dark like this. She begins to write a text to him when an incoming text arrives with no associated number.

"William's phone is dead. Please meet us at Matisse's apartment in Vieux Nice. He said he would fix lunch. I'll text a list of things to pick up at the Cour Seleya market. We have much to discuss. - WWAH"

Rebecca collects her purse and phone and sends a text to Eitan.

"Need a lift to meet with William. He's at the Cour Seleya."

Eitan also doesn't reply. Anxious to meet William, Rebecca calls the Negresco concierge and asks to use the hotel car. She is on her way to the Cour Seleya within a few minutes.

A young man across the street from Le Negresco takes a picture of Rebecca and forwards it on his cell just as Rebecca's sedan drives away.

"Image sent. Target 2 on the move."

The Former Apartment of Henri Mattisee - The Cour Seleya - Vieux Nice, France

The Woman With Auburn Hair looks at her phone impatiently, as she hasn't heard back from her team. William looks down at his phone and notices that it shows no service. He rolls his eyes at the Woman With Auburn Hair and walks to the window to see if he can get better reception.

"Would you mind turning your countermeasures off. I'm not getting any reception."

The Woman With Auburn Hair looks at her phone and runs into the living room, where her hyper-encrypted satellite phone sits near the window. Grabbing it, she sees an urgent text from the tech in the CIA safehouse.

"Updates available on an explosion. Why aren't you responding?"

The 15m Sea Ray Yacht "Manifest Destiny" - Bay of Angels, Nice, France

A young man of military age sits prone on the yacht's aft deck. He is looking through the sight of a Winchester sniper rifle towards the salmon-colored building at the east end of the Cour Seleya. He speaks into a bone mic.

"Trophy confirmed. Repeat Trophy confirmed."

The former Apartment of Henri Matisse - Cour Seleya, Vieux Nice

William follows the auburn-haired woman into the living room.

"I should get back to the hotel. Rebecca is probably worried out of her mind. I'll text Eitan and have him pick me up once you remove your app."

The Woman With Auburn Hair turns to him with a look of dread.

"Cellular comms are down, and it isn't me who is doing it."

At that moment, Eitan can be heard pounding on the apartment door. The Woman With Auburn Hair quickly looks at a surveillance monitor in the kitchen.

"Sir. Are you in there? Are you alright?"

The Cour Seleya Market, Vieux Nice

The Le Negresco driver stops the sedan at the corner of Rue Saint François de Paule and Rue Louis Bassin, which marks the east entrance to the famous marketplace. He looks at her in his rearview mirror.

"Madame Laurent. The building you are looking for is at the far end of the market. I apologize for being unable to take you further. Driving in the Cour Seleya is restricted."

Rebecca collects her things and checks her phone. She notices that she has no service. She looks up at the driver.

"I don't recall the cell service to be this bad here. How is your cell?"

He turns to his device and notices he, too, has no service.

"Madame. This is odd. There must be an issue with the service provider."

Rebecca places her phone in her purse, exits the SUV, and decides to choose the ingredients for the lunch menu herself. Across the street, two men sit watching Rebecca exit the SUV at a cafe. Their eyes have been fixed on the SUV as it displays the Le Negresco logo on the doors. Seeing a woman exit, the spotter looks at the images sent to him by the agent outside the Le Negresco. The lead man speaks into his phone.

"Target 2 confirmed. Repeat. Target 2 is confirmed and heading into the market."

As Rebecca begins navigating the bustling crowds in the Cour Seleya, she pauses at her favorite flower vendor and hears her phone ring. She notices that the incoming call is from William. She picks it up.

"There you are. I was certain my cell would not get service. The driver from Le Negresco just dropped me off, and I'm in the market picking up supplies for lunch. I'll be there shortly."

William's heart drops as he tries to gather his wits.

"Rebecca. Listen to me. You are in danger. Is the Negresco driver still there?"

Rebecca can hear the fear in William's voice, and she begins looking around.

"No. He has already gone down to the underground garage."

At that moment, listening to William's call with Rebecca, the Woman With Auburn Hair dials the Turk's cell phone. William can hear a cell phone ringing very close to Rebecca. He calms his tone but keeps it urgent.

"My love. Do you recall the prefect's office across the street from Le Tire-Bouchon? I need you to throw whatever you are carrying in the direction of where that phone just rang near you and run like your life depends on it to the Prefect's office. Eitan and I are on our way to you. Run, my love. RUN NOW!"

Rebecca reacts quickly, picking up a large bucket of flowers on the ground in front of her. She turns and recognizes the man known as the Turk in the next stall from the Le Negresco lobby when he met with William. He has answered the call from the Woman With Auburn Hair, and the distraction makes him take his eyes off Rebecca. With all her strength, she throws the flowers at him, surprising him and the people around him. She cuts through the stall and is halfway down Rue Louis Bassin, heading toward the Prefect's office before he can recover.

The two men sitting in the cafe cannot see what happened because too many people are blocking their view, but they can hear the commotion. Eventually, they look down Rue Louis Bassin and see Target 2 running. As they leave, a waiter stops them for not paying their bill. One of the men continues running toward Rebecca, leaving the other man behind to settle up.

Rebecca resists looking back but senses that someone is chasing after her. She enters the brocante (flea market) below the steps of the Nice Courthouse. She stops long enough to hear a disruption from behind her. Throwing off her shoes, she turns her fear into anger and begins running as fast as possible.

The Former Apartment of Henri Matisse - Cour Seleya, Vieux Nice

William bolts past Eitan in the hallway, quickly realizing Rebecca is in danger. The two men reach the lobby just as Rebecca throws the bucket of flowers at the distracted Turk. William points toward the Courthouse, while Eitan points toward the eastern entrance to the Cour Seleya. From inside the apartment, the Woman With Auburn Hair calls the Mayor's personal cell phone number from memory.

A few seconds later, William starts scanning the street for signs of Rebecca. At the far end of the street, he notices people shouting at someone who has fallen and knocked over a table. As he turns the corner, he can see Le Tire Bouchon and several men in tactical gear surrounding the door to the Prefect's office. As William runs toward the uniformed men, the Gendarmerie train their guns on him. William stops immediately, raises his hands, and in the most fluent French he has ever spoken, he falls to his knees and begins yelling the words...

"Je suis son mari! Je suis son mari! Je suis son mari!" (I AM HER HUSBAND! I AM HER HUSBAND! I AM HER HUSBAND!)

The Gendarmerie quickly surrounds William. Looking between the officers facing him, he can see Rebecca's beautiful face, creased with worry, staring at him from inside the Prefect's office. Standing beside Rebecca, the Mayor ushers her through the door, instructing the Gendarmerie to stand down. Rebecca rushes over to William, still kneeling with his arms raised. She kneels next to him and wraps her arms around him. Through tears of joy, she whispers into his ear.

"I couldn't love you any more than I do now."

William rises from his knees and stands with Rebecca, holding her close. The Mayor walks over to them, and William reaches out to accept his hand. His words are feeble to the debt he now owes to this man—a debt he could never repay in 100 lifetimes.

"Monsieur, Merci beaucoup (thank you very much) for the protection you have extended to my wife...I am forever in your debt!"

The Mayor breaks into near-perfect, albeit heavily French-accented English.

"Monsieur, the Woman With Auburn Hair is who the debt is owed."

A bit taken aback, William looks down at his phone and sees another message. The text is from Eitan.

"I have an asset of the Turk's in my custody. Perhaps you would like to have words with him?"

By now, people have gathered to see why there are so many armed police in tactical gear in front of the Prefect's office. From behind the crowd, the Turk watches William shake the mayor's hand. He takes out his phone and hits a speed dial. The call is picked up immediately.

"Yes. There was a complication. Target 2 is out of reach for now. Our "Trophy" called in a distraction while my team attempted to capture her. One of my spotters was captured, and we've lost valuable time. Yes. I will await further instructions."

The Turk hangs up and watches as the chef's security detail arrives at the Prefect's Office. Moments later, they are placed in a car and quickly returned to Le Negresco. The Turk's hatred for the Woman With Auburn Hair is boundless, and seeing the man responsible for delaying the Exodus project pushes him over the edge. He places another call to a yacht sitting just outside the entry to Port Lympia....

"Trophy is in play. Take the shot."

The Former Apartment of Henri Matisse - Cour Seleya, Vieux Nice

The Woman With Auburn Hair contemplates the attempt to kidnap Rebecca and the assassination of the Madame Chairperson. Her mood changes quickly as she taps into her brilliant analytical mind while tamping down the emotional interference.

Rising from her chair, she looks out the window and notices a yacht anchored just past the entrance to Port Lympia. Somewhere deep within her brilliant mind, she recalls a moment when Navy SEALs, while towing a lifeboat with Captain Phillips aboard, simultaneously shoot two Somali pirates from 40 yards away. In that instant, a synapse connects, sending glutamate molecules (neurotransmitters) to her hypothalamus, releasing adrenaline and triggering her autonomic nervous system. In that instant, her heart rate and blood pressure increase, preparing her body to respond quickly.

Her eyes catch a reflection from the boat, and she instantly drops to the ground just as a high-velocity round shatters the window pane and hits the wall behind her. Three more rounds strike the wall just above her, forming a golfball-sized hole between the eyes of Amélie Noellie Matisse-Parayre (Matisse's wife) in his masterpiece, The Green Stripe. Lying prone on the floor, she takes out her hyper-encrypted satellite phone and dials a number she never thought she would use. It connects after the first ring.

"Coucou (an informal way to say "hi" or "hey," often used between close friends and family). There are people on a boat near Port Lympia shooting at Matisse's apartment. Would you be so kind as to look into it?

There is a pause while she listens and then thanks the caller.

"Merci, beaucoup." (Thank you)

Frigate USS Adelline, International Waters -

Mediterranean Sea

After ending the call from the Woman With Auburn Hair, Vice Admiral William Becket Hall, commander of the US Northern

Atlantic fleet operation, turns to a junior tech officer who is scanning a drone screen. He is feverishly typing commands on his keyboard.

"Acquiring target now, sir."

There is a short pause.

"Image on screen, sir. Zooming in."

The Vice Admiral looks over his shoulder and sees the image of what appears to be a small yacht, perhaps 15 to 18 meters in length, making a sharp turn back to wherever it came from.

"Sir, FLIR imaging confirms three male individuals on board. Signature imaging has detected what appears to be a high-powered rifle."

The Vice Admiral contemplates his next move.

"Do we have assets in the area?"

"Yes, sir, a drone."

The Vice Admiral frowns. It is unlawful to have armed surveillance drones inside the territorial waters of an ally.

"What is its payload?"

"No ordinance, but it does have a Seat Heater."

The "Seat Heater" is a passive response technology designed for operating in or near allied territory. It is a tightly focused, low-intensity laser that superheats its target to nearly 700 degrees Kelvin. It is ideal for overheating an engine or causing someone to spontaneously combust. The Naval scientists who developed the weapon affectionately referred to it as "heating someone's seat," which led to the nickname "Seat Heater" becoming permanent.

"You are authorized to disable the engine and notify the French Coast Guard so they come prepared."

"Yes, sir."

The Vice Admiral hits a speed dial on his phone and begins speaking to the Woman With Auburn Hair. Moments later, he reflects on the call and smiles, thinking to himself.

"It's always good to have the Woman With Auburn Hair owe you a favor."

15m Sea Ray Yacht "Manifest Destiny," Bay of Angels, Nice.

The Curtain Group asset on board the yacht places a call to his handler, the Turk.

"No, sir. Trophy is alive. Our shooter says the woman was aware of the incoming round. We are not certain how."

There is yelling from below deck as the spotter comes over.

"The engines are overheated and have stopped working. We are adrift."

In a few minutes, the men on the Manifest Destiny notice a French Military Vessel heading in their direction at full speed. The Curtain Group asset already knows what he must do. He sends the shooter and the spotter below deck and locks the door behind them. Returning to the deck, he retrieves the scuba gear he had stowed in a forward locker along with an explosive device. A few minutes later, he is in the water with plenty of air to reach Port Lympia. Moments later, the 15m Sea Ray "Manifest Destiny" explodes.

Chapter 24

Hiding Out In Provence

Castillon-Du-Gard - Provence, France

After returning from events in the Cour Selaya Le Negresco, William and Rebecca decide to find a spot where they can see people coming from a long way off. Their choice is the ancient village of Castillon-du-Gard. The drive takes almost three hours, but it gives them time to let the previous day's events settle down in the comfort and protection offered by the Range Rover Sentinel.

As they arrive at their destination, Eitan begins scanning the area while his security team helps William with the luggage. As William and Rebecca enter the hotel lobby, the concierge greets them. He looks up and immediately notices Rebecca.

"Madame Rebecca, it is so very nice to see you!"

He looks down at the register and notices he cannot find Laurent's name. Rebecca, seeing his confusion, explains.

"We had our service put together the reservation. It is under the name Mr. Anderson."

His eyes find the records.

"Yes, here we are. We understand your request for privacy and will notify our staff accordingly. I have booked one of our more remote rooms with a terrace and close to the spa, as we know Madame prefers."

The concierge tries to assist with their luggage, but thinks twice about it once he sees the icy cold stare from Eitan's security team. After William and Rebecca have finished unpacking, Eitan posts a guard in the sitting area outside their room. Going to a small table, William grabs a bottle of chilled Rosé and two glasses and heads out to the terrace. Looking out across the magnificent landscape of

Provence, William's mind drifts to a short quote he wrote in his latest cookbook, 'Talking Over Food'.

"Wine is an elixir that the universe delivers to many places on Earth. However, among all such places, Provence is especially blessed."

William sits at a small table on the terrace of the second-floor suite at the luxurious Le Vieux Castillon. The hotel, situated in the Provence region of France, is part of the ancient walled city of Castillon-du-Gard. From his second-floor vantage point, William spies several white Camargue horses wandering carelessly through the vineyards at the base of the walled city. He is lost in thought and does not hear Rebecca approaching. She walks up to him, kisses his forehead, takes his glass of wine from his hand, and takes a sip. William looks up at her as she walks over to the balcony railing.

"You are the only woman I know who truly understands the art of taking wine from a man."

Smiling, Rebecca looks over the hectares of vineyards as the afternoon sun shines through her billowing linen cover-up. The fabric silhouettes her figure, arousing William's hope. She knows he is looking at her, and she looks back at him with a seductive look that only a woman in love can produce.

As she looks back at him, William produces a second wine glass filled with the same Rosé. Rebecca has a surprised look on her face.

"So, you saw me coming?"

"No, but I expected it. Like I expect the sun to set this evening."

Rebecca turns to William and leans back with her elbows on the railing.

"Are you ever going to come out from under that cloud of yours?"

William takes a sip of the wine and savors it for a moment. He looks deeply into her eyes.

"I almost lost you, and I cannot bear the thought of it."

Rebecca sees the guilt William is carrying, but has yet to help him find a way past it.

"At least we now understand exactly what we got ourselves into."

William rolls his eyes.

"Or more accurately, what I was suckered into and then dragged you in with me?"

William rises and stands next to Rebecca at the railing.

"We still have the Turk to worry about. He's taken his shot, and you can bet it won't be his last. That much I am certain of."

There is a knock at the door. William walks over, hearing Eitan's voice in the hall. William opens the door.

"What's up, Eitan? Is everything OK?"

"Sir, there is an elderly fisherman at the front desk, and he says he knows you. He wishes to speak with you and Madame Rebecca. How is it that this man knows you are here, and why didn't you tell me you were expecting him?"

"That is because we were not expecting him, but now that he is here, please send him up."

Just as Eitan turns to leave, William calls back to him.

"Be careful not to anger him, Eitan, or you may find the pointy end of a knife close to your genitals."

Moments go by, and just as Luca walks into the room, Rebecca comes in from the terrace. They exchange "faire la bise" and sit in the living room.

"Ordures. Your Israeli friend is very rude."

William smiles and relaxes back into his chair. Luca's face shows concern.

"You are very relaxed for a man with a target on his head. As I drove in, I saw you and Rebecca standing on the terrace. Even with my aging eyes, I could have shot you both where you stood from a kilometer away."

Rebecca's face shows worry. William's face doesn't.

"You forget, my friend, that I know you have family stationed around the entire walled city. I am relaxed because I trust you."

Luca tries to swat away William's words by waving his hand in the air.

"Be that as it may, we have much to consider. The Turk has gone dark, and we do not know where he is hiding."

Rebecca's fear begins to show itself as she rises from the chair and walks over to the window.

"Luca, do you think he will come back?"

The look on Luca's face gives her the answer Rebecca was not hoping for. He speaks the words anyway.

"It is unlikely that he will walk away from the money they are paying him."

As William considers speaking, Rebecca turns away from the window.

"Do not think for one moment, William, that you will let yourself be found by him."

Both Luca and William look at each other with surprise.

"Yes. I know about the plan you both hatched on the boat. So forget it. There has to be another way."

At that moment, they hear knocking from the door connecting to the next suite. Everyone rises as William walks over to it. Rebecca's whispering voice is tense.

"You're not going to open it!?"

William looks back at her.

"I don't think the Turk would announce his entrance."

He unlocks and opens the door. The Woman With Auburn Hair walks in and takes a seat on the couch. She looks over at Rebecca, whose face is beginning to show the signs of a building rage. The Woman With Auburn Hair pats the seat next to hers.

"Rebecca. Sit by me. We have much to talk about."

Everyone else in the room looks at each other with questioning looks on their faces. It is William who speaks up.

"How did you get past security?"

The Woman With Auburn Hair responds rather coyly.

"I own a room at the Castillon. After the Cour Seleya incident, I reactivated the malware on your phone. Once I knew where you were headed, I had the owner open my suite."

Rebecca cannot contain her anger any longer.

"Madame. There are no words to describe how morally corrupt you have become."

William, Luca, and Rebecca return to their seats, but Rebecca chooses the one furthest from the Woman With Auburn Hair, who begins looking around the room.

"Where is Eitan? He will also need to hear this."

William texts Eitan, and within seconds, there is a knock at the door. He enters and cannot believe his eyes. Before he asks, William fills him in.

"It would seem the 'fixer' has a residence here and decided to crash our party."

Eitan casts a wry smile towards the Woman With Auburn Hair and remains standing as she continues.

"Since losing my client, I believe it is time for us to close our endeavor. However, to do so, we still have a few outstanding issues that need buttoning up."

She turns to William and Rebecca.

"Your intuition, William, is well-honed. I am indeed a descendant of Ernest Hemingway. My grandmother met him while attending school in Paris, and the two fell in love. However, by then, Escoffier had already told Hemingway about Correns' research, which also put him and my grandmother, Sophia, in the crosshairs of the Curtain Group."

The Woman With Auburn Hair continues her story until she finishes with William meeting with her stepmother, the Madame Chairperson, at the Boscolo. She turns her gaze to Rebecca.

"Madame, I realize you and I have unfinished business, but I am asking that we set that aside so we can put an end to the Curtain Group and the evil people who are running it. Can we agree on this?"

Rebecca holds her gaze, and as she answers, William hears a tone that says much more than her words convey.

"Yes. I can."

The Woman With Auburn Hair looks over to Eitan.

"My good man. You will shortly receive a text from an asset of mine inside the CIA. Once the people involved in this nightmare are identified, I will require assistance from your former employer to collect them before they scatter like bugs into the walls. Would you be so kind as to set that up? I'm afraid I haven't had the time to properly introduce myself to the Mossad."

Eitan nods his head. She turns to Luca.

"I will also need to ask for your help, dear Luca. The Turk will undoubtedly return to complete his assignment, and when he does, I will make certain that it will occur at the Port of Antibes."

Luca also nods. She then turns to look at William.

"You and I have several tasks to complete that will require that we separate ourselves from the group for the time being."

Before Rebecca can speak, the Woman With Auburn Hair cuts in.

"...and yes, Rebecca. I will return him in the same condition as he left in."

Rebecca slightly relaxes as the Woman With Auburn Hair feels a pang of guilt in her gut for lying to her just then.

Thinking to herself:

"William may physically be the same, but emotionally he will be very different."

The Woman With Auburn Hair receives an incoming text. Reading it, she rises from her seat.

"It seems our time has run out. The Curtain Group is preparing to distribute the Exodus seed. I will keep everyone informed individually."

Looking again at her phone, the Woman With Auburn Hair turns to William.

"It's time to go. Our car is waiting outside."

Rebecca rises, not waiting to be recognized by the Woman With Auburn Hair.

"Perhaps you can enlighten us on how you will keep the seed from being distributed?"

The Woman With Auburn Hair answers matter-of-factly.

"I have an asset inside the UN Food & Agriculture Organization who is a brilliant biologist, computer programmer, and a chess grandmaster. He is a consummate professional and able to handle any situation that may arise."

Chapter 25

The Mad Hatter of Svalbard

Svalbard Seed Bank - Norwegian Island of

Spitsbergen

Svalbard Seed Bank is located on the tectonic permafrost covering the Norwegian island of Spitzbergen in the Svalbard archipelago in the North Sea, some 1,300 kilometers north of the Arctic Circle. Its purpose is to collect, protect, and share a wide variety of seeds to ensure the biodiversity of crops worldwide for future generations.

A seed bank acts the same way as safety deposit boxes work in financial institutions. The bank owns the building and vaults securing the deposits, and the depositor retains ownership of the materials stored in those vaults. In this instance, the materials are plant seeds. The facility houses three separate vaults, each with its own individual and duplicated cooling systems, ensuring that the seeds remain dormant at a temperature of -18 °C (-4 °F) for their predetermined time in the vault. Each vault is accessed by a central corridor ending at 'The Cathedral', which houses several maintenance areas, including a Spartan series of sleeping areas, a standard room for cooking and eating, and an anteroom for communications and security.

As the station Director for the Svalbard Seed Bank, Yeltzen Oldigart, known not so affectionately by his fellow scientists as "The Mad Hatter of Svalbard", has worked at the Svalbard facility since its opening in 2008. He is a recluse and a brilliant scientist dedicated to protecting the seeds entrusted to him. He is also a disheveled, socially awkward man in his early 50s, possessing a keen wit and wicked sense of humor. He has also received three doctorates in horticultural sciences with specialty studies in plant chemistry and viral immunity. Most importantly, he would die for his seeds. This morning, Yeltzen is on a Zoom call with his mother. He has his earbuds in.

"Mother, you cannot keep calling to tell me I am overworked! I am now the boss. It's official. Nobody cares what I think!"

Yeltzen is pacing the floor of the Svalbard Seed Bank kitchen in his prized Star Wars pajamas. He is about to drink from a glass that holds a dark green liquid. He raises the glass to his nose and is repulsed.

"Certainly, Mother! Are you trying to kill me with these concoctions of yours?"

Grudgingly, he gathers enough courage to take a sip. His face contorts.

"Mother, What is in this?!"

As she tells him, he spits out the smoothie, covering the wall in front of him with the gelatinous, dark liquid.

"Did you say cow urine?!"

With the dark-colored liquid dripping from his scruffy beard, his heart sinks as he realizes his prized collection of Danger Girl comics is now covered in a cow urine smoothie.

In that moment, his mother quickly logs off their Zoom call, allowing another Zoom call to begin. Without looking, Yeltzen, while cleaning his beard, continues speaking, not realizing his mother has logged off.

"Mother. I told you to stop calling me!"

Yeltzen is interrupted by a balding man in his late 60s staring at him with an odd look on his face.

"I am not your Mother, Yeltzen, and we've talked about using corporate assets for personal use."

The man on the other end of the video call abruptly stops talking and begins staring intently at his screen.

"For Christ's sake, Yeltzen, are you wearing pajamas?"

Still wiping the cow urine smoothly from his unkept beard, Yeltzen looks up at the caller and nonchalantly spins in his chair for dramatic effect.

"No, they most certainly are NOT pajamas! This is a limited edition lounging robe and joggers from the Star Wars Mandalorian universe! It helps me stay warm in this frozen seed tomb."

The balding man on the Zoom call is not impressed.

"Seriously, Yeltzen, if you were not such a brilliant geneticist, I would see to it that you spent some time on the couch with the best psychiatrists in the world."

Yeltzen replies, matter-of-fact.

"Been there. Done that. Oh, and remind me why you called?"

"You haven't read your emails this morning, have you?"

"It depends."

"It depends on what?"

"Which morning are we talking about? There are at least 4 time zones where it is still yesterday, and if memory serves me, there are a few where it is tomorrow."

"Whatever day it is, check your email now. We need to discuss an urgent request for a seed deposit."

Yeltzen frowns. The balding man knows what is coming next.

"...and before you start ranting about procedure, Yeltzen, may I remind you of your responsibility to the oversight committee?"

Yeltzen, reading the email while his boss was moving his lips (he muted him), looks up at the caller, smiling and then frowning.

"Unfortunately, you only have three of the seven required signatures. Therefore, your request is denied. Come back to me when you have a majority."

Yeltzen drops the Zoom call before the balding man can argue the point—a point that Yeltzen was correct in making. Getting up from the computer, Yeltzen begins the arduous task of cleaning his Danger Girl comic book collection. Picking up a favorite issue depicting Danger Girl naked in a hot tub, he watches as dark, urine-smelling sludge slides down the plastic cover protecting it. He congratulates himself on investing in the plastic covers, thinking...

"Money well spent."

As Yeltzen continues to clean his comic books, he begins humming a Viking song of dubious Norwegian origin. Eventually, his comics are clean and hanging on the wall again. Yeltzen returns to his computer to see who else the email he was sent was copied to.

"Let's see who wants this seed deposit so much..."

Electronic mail (Email) services offer various options when sending email. However, the most common features are (cc) Carbon Copy and (bcc) Blind Carbon Copy. The term "carbon copy" is left over from manual typewriter days, where a piece of carbon paper was inserted between two sheets of paper. When the typeset keys hit the paper and the ink ribbon, they were also pressed on the carbon sheet, effectively making a copy on the second piece of paper without having to retype. As a bonus, IBM introduced the (bcc) feature to its email application in the 1980s, allowing additional copies to be sent to people without notifying the other 'copied' recipients.

A brilliant and creative computer coder, Yeltzen designed and built a 10th-generation laptop computer that can access any email server connected to the Internet and extract all (bcc) information sent. Within moments, Yeltzen's computer displays the email addresses that were blind copied on his boss's email.

"Let's see...yes. There you are. Now, let's see _who_ you are?"

Yeltzen points at three email handles, none belonging to the UN FAO. He opens a console screen and types in an algorithm he wrote to locate the server from which the email addresses are securely stored.

"Gotcha! Oh my..."

Yelzten sits back in his chair and raises his hand to his bearded face. Momentarily distracted by a dried piece of dark liquid still holding onto it, he flicks it into the trash bin while considering the newly uncovered information. Looking at the screen, Yeltzen captures the illegally obtained data and, just to be safe, he sends it to a secure 12th-generation custom-built server in his mother's basement in Hamnøy, a picturesque fishing village in Lofoten, Norway.

Yeltzen rises from his chair and heads over to a cabinet where he removes a false back and takes out his stash of mjød (mead), a liquor made from fermented honey with a heritage dating back to the days of ancient Viking kings. While Yeltzen sits in front of his computer considering his next move, another email arrives; however, this one is from a brilliant and attractive auburn-haired woman whom Yeltzen met at a UN FAO conference some years back. He looks up at his favorite auburn-haired Danger Girl comic on the wall as she seductively sits topless in a hot tub full of bubbles and begins typing a reply to the Woman With Auburn Hair.

"My Dearest Danger Girl. It is an interesting coincidence that you are reaching out to me..."

3 Blocks from the Curtain Group Headquarters -

Sophia Antipolis, Nice

After reading Yeltzen's email reply, the Woman With Auburn Hair turns to William, who has been hydrating since leaving the Le Vieux Castillon.

"It's time to take the meds. My contact at the Svalbard Seed Bank believes a UN security detail will soon arrive at the seed bank."

William smiles.

"Looks like we're still a half step ahead of them."

He then looks at the rather average-looking pill and swallows it with the last bottle of high alkaline Waiākea water. He looks at her quizzically.

"I'm not going to like this, am I?"

She looks at him as the pill begins to take effect.

"It's like a three-day hangover...while an elephant sits on your head."

William's focus lapses, and his head falls back against the seat. The Woman With Auburn Hair puts Plasticuffs on him and then begins the drive to the parking garage in the Curtain Group Headquarters basement. Once there, she starts texting with Herman Dashill, the President of the Curtain Curtain Group.

"Herman, I know we have our issues, but you have a problem that I am willing to solve for you. At Delya's request, she had me pick up the Chef and bring him to your offices. Hopefully, you are already aware of this. However, the Chef has information he recorded that links her to the attack in the Boscolo against my boss and your client, the Madame Chairperson. Play your cards right, and you'll have Delya out the door in Plasticuffs before lunch."

After reading the text, Herman's mind begins racing. If she is telling the truth, it solves a big problem. If she is playing him, and he is confident that somehow she is, then what is her angle? Herman decides to let things play out. He turns to his phone and enters a code that activates the microphone on Delya's desk phone.

Svalbard Seed Bank - Norwegian Island of Spitsbergen

"Keep up, BB-8. We have lots of work to do. Danger Girl needs our help!"

The remote-controlled droid named BB-8 is from the Star Wars sequel 'The Force Awakens'. It was produced in a limited release by a company called Sphero. Although no longer being made, Yelzen had purchased many of them and recoded them to respond only to him. Yeltzen looks down at the BB-8 droid, which now looks back at him.

"But first, we must be more presentable for our guests!"

He runs into his sleeping quarters as BB-8 follows close behind, making a series of chirping sounds.

Curtain Group Headquarters, Sophia Antipolis, France

Delya looks up as a call comes into her line.

"Madame Delya. I am bringing in the Chef for questioning as requested."

Delya is surprised and a little confused.

"You have the Chef?"

"Yes, Madame. Although he is still feeling the effects of the drugs I slipped him."

Delya still needs clarification.

"I asked the Turk to take care of this. What happened?"

"I do not know. For obvious reasons, the Turk is no longer accepting my calls."

Delya puts her on hold and quickly does a trace on the Turk's cell phone. It shows him getting off at the tram stop at Nice International Airport, but actually, it is an AI-generated signal spoofing the Turk's phone. The Woman With Auburn Hair continues explaining.

"Madame. It's been a difficult few hours for me since the Boscolo incident, but foremost, I still work for the Madame Chairperson, and the Chef is still key in keeping her project on track. I am leaving now and will require assistance getting him inside the building. I will be in the car park, sublevel 3. Please send a couple of agents to assist me in getting him upstairs. He is drugged."

Delya's management skills kick in autonomously.

"I have texted Samula and Lithe. They will be there in moments."

"Thank you, Madame."

The Woman With Auburn Hair hangs up the call, and within minutes after arriving at the car park, the two agents arrive with a wheelchair. They begin pushing William into the elevator leading to Delya's office.

Svalbard Seed Bank - Norwegian Island of Spitsbergen

Before long, Yeltzen is sitting at his computer, remotely accessing the secure server in his mother's basement. He now wears a Star Wars C3PO three-quarter-length robe with matching slippers as his BB-8 robot randomly circles the room. He begins streaming the bcc email data he collected from his supervisor's email.

"Gotcha, you sneaky little pricks. Now, let's see who you are talking to."

At that exact moment, his monitor begins flashing, indicating an electronic brute force intrusion is being attempted on the Svalbard UN FAO network. Unflustered, Yeltzen types in a string of commands that mirrors his computer onto a virtual drive of an air-gapped computer in his lab. With the Svalbard network secure, Yeltzen sends a priority security breach email to the UN Electronic Crimes Division.

"Our network is undergoing a brute force intrusion that appears to be coming from a security services firm called The Curtain Group."

Yeltzen's brilliance as a biologist is matched by his skills as a computer programmer and hacker. Skills that he likes to keep quiet about. After speaking with the Woman With Auburn Hair, Yeltzen redesigned his honey pot to resemble the systems at the Curtain Group. Anyone looking would think they were responsible for his attempted breach of their secure communications. In moments, he has traced the actual source of the intrusion to the United Nations. Yeltzen sits back in his chair, pondering the significance of this revelation.

"So who at the UN is involved..."

Yeltzen types another series of algorithms from memory, making his presence on the UN network appear as if he were a UN computer security specialist conducting scheduled maintenance on communication servers. Yeltzen begins flipping through communications logs until he finds the target. It is then that BB-8 rolls up next to Yeltzen and whistles, indicating that people are arriving at the Seed Bank entrance.

Delya Morris' Office - Curtain Group Headquarters, Sophia Antipolis, France

"Welcome, Chef. I am glad to see you awake."

William is just beginning to gather his wits as he tries and fails to sit up.

"Madame, clearly you have never been drugged before."

There is a metallic taste in his mouth. He is disoriented, thirsty, and has the mother of all headaches that can only be explained as nearly unbearable. As he attempts to open his eyes, he is rewarded by a light that burns the back of his retinas. He rasps out a few short words from the depths of his soul.

"Perhaps a couple of Motrin?"

Delya looks at William momentarily and begins speaking to whom William hopes is the Woman With Auburn Hair, who is standing behind him. As he lies on a couch on his stomach, he realizes that the sofa is soft on his face, velvet perhaps, and he can feel the liquid of his drool on it. In another moment, a hand is extended in front of his face with two pills that appear to be what he asked for. William hesitates nonetheless. He hears Delya's voice.

"I assure you those are Motrin or, at the very least, some brand of ibuprofen. I will take one if it will put you at ease."

It takes extraordinary determination to get William's muscles to comply with his brain's commands. In fairness, his brain has little to no idea what commands it sends to his muscles. He eventually rolls over and accepts the pills being offered. His wits begin to return as he quotes a line from 'The Matrix'.

"Take the blue pill, and you can go back to the world you know, or you can take the red pill and see just how deep the rabbit hole goes..."

Delya looks confused as William's movie trivia knowledge kicks in.

"The Matrix? Keanu Reeves? Carrie-Anne Moss? Lawrence Fishburne? The Wachowski brothers...or are they sisters now?"

The woman continues to look blankly at William, displaying no emotion whatsoever. She turns to the person standing behind him and issues more orders. In moments, a bottle of electrolytes and a sandwich are presented. Delya sets the plate on the table in front of William.

"You are incoherent, Chef. Perhaps something to replenish your body chemistry."

He accepts the sandwich and bottle willingly and replies with a mouthful of food.

"I would thank you, but I seem to recall you having me drugged and kidnapped, so....fuck you."

Delya's upbringing kicks in.

"How crass, sir!"

William, ignoring her comment, continues chewing and swallowing...loudly. Some crumbs from the sandwich fall on the rug. He changes to a sarcastic tone.

"Excuse me. But would it be possible to have a napkin? How could anyone with an ounce of civility ever deliver food without a napkin? Madame, a woman of your obvious education and apparent upbringing. How crass indeed."

Then, her office line rings. After seeing the number, she walks over to her desk and picks up the phone. Her voice is sharp.

"We did no such thing. [She pauses, listening to the response.] I gave no order to hack the UN FAO. I don't care what your security team thinks; you're mistaken. [pause] Do me a favor, speak to our IT staff, and never call me again."

She slams down the receiver. It takes all of his will for William to move his head around to view the room slowly.

"Did somebody download porn again?"

Svalbard Seed Bank - Norwegian Island of

Spitsbergen

Yeltzen, distracted by the motion sensors, begins recording the search while he walks over to the monitors facing the road leading to the Vault. He rewinds the video feed for 20 seconds and begins replaying it. His brilliant mind recoils as he sees his boss's balding head and face in the leading SUV's passenger seat. He also notices two other vehicles, each carrying four men who appear to be military personnel. Yeltzen heads back to his computer and quickly changes the codes that allow entrance to the facility.

Moments later, he is back in front of his computer, replaying the computer search he had been recording before he was distracted. The final name on the screen is a mid-level assistant working directly for the UN Secretary-General. Yeltzen's thinking is again interrupted by the phone ringing on his desk. He lets it go to voicemail and smiles at the approaching vehicles.

"I hope you all brought warm clothes because you will be out there awhile."

The average temperature on the Norwegian Island of Spitzbergen at this time of year is a balmy -0 degrees C, and a wind speed of 24 kph, making it feel like -2 C. Yeltzen's boss is sitting in the passenger seat of the lead SUV. He picks up his cell phone and tries redialing Yeltzen while mumbling with clenched teeth.

"Pick up, you little prick."

From inside, Yeltzen hears the phone ring again, but this time, he sends it directly to a new voicemail he just recorded. After a maximum of five rings, Yeltzen's boss is forwarded to voicemail. He hears Yeltzen's voice.

"I'm sorry, but I am busy saving the world. If you would be so kind as to leave a message, I will be certain to return your call sometime in the next millennium. If you are the soulless shell who is my boss, I hope your balls are freezing. May I remind you that

UNFAO Protocol S310.1-A stipulates that all visits to the Seed Bank must be scheduled at least one month in advance. No exceptions."

Curtain Group Headquarters, Sophia Antipolis, France

After hanging up the phone about the fake hack of the Seed Bank by the Curtain Group, Delya's face begins to show signs of stress. Even in his current sedated state, William can tell their plan to keep Delya distracted is working. They must give Yeltzen more time to find those hiding in the shadows. William gathers strength knowing that this part of the plan is working. Delya, shaking off the call, turns her attention back to William.

"This is pointless, Chef. Perhaps we can start over."

From his prone position on the couch, William wholeheartedly agrees.

"I'm all for that, but how far back are you asking to go? Do we go back to when you had me drugged and kidnapped by the redhead, or perhaps before that, when you conspired to capture and kill my wife, or we could go back to when you had your people chase me through the streets of Vieux Nice? Where shall we begin anew from?"

Her look back at William was like a parent watching a child acting out.

"Why don't we start at the beginning when you stole Escoffier's journal. How does that sound?"

William puts down the empty bottle and tries to rise. The result of which lands him back on the couch. His legs aren't ready to accept commands from his brain yet.

"OK. I'll play nice. Why don't you begin? It's clear the drugs in my system haven't quite been flushed out by the delightful cuisine you so magnanimously prepared for me."

Delya's look at William could chill molten lava. However, William's face still betrays the whole "fuck you" feeling. Now becoming more coherent, William notices she is a woman comfortable with power. Her hair is pulled tightly back into a very tight bun. Her jawline is tight and square, if not Germanic in appearance. She carries herself with pride and confidence. She begins speaking without caring what William might be thinking.

"You seem to think that some grand conspiracy is underway. Is that accurate?"

William responds without looking into her eyes.

"No, Madame, it is not. A grand conspiracy is about to be *revealed*. A conspiracy that requires the utmost secrecy until it is too late for anyone to do something about it. Wouldn't you agree?"

The two lock eyes as William awaits her response. She flinches.

"I agree. Your statement is more accurate. I applaud your intuition, sir. You are far more cunning than you appear."

William turns to the Woman With Auburn Hair, looks at her disdainfully, and returns the look to Delya.

"Yeah. I seem to get that a lot from you people."

Svalbard Seed Bank - Norwegian Island of

Spitsbergen

The lead SUV arrives at the seed bank's main entrance. Yeltzen looks at the front entry monitor and sees his boss throwing his cell phone down onto the tundra, shattering it into pieces. He storms around in circles briefly and flips his middle finger at the camera—the camera that Yeltzen has had in record mode since his boss's arrival. Yeltzen pushes the button near the monitor, activating the two-way speaker.

"Sir, I regret to inform you that, because of your recent outburst and subsequent actions, I am now afraid of being physically harmed by you. I have sent the video footage of your unscheduled arrival and threatening behavior to the Norwegian government, as well as to the HR department of the UN Secretary-General. I suggest you return to town, as I have just been notified that the weather will soon worsen."

Yeltzen mutes the microphone at the entrance and watches his very pissed-off boss yell and fume while making obscene gestures at the camera. It is like watching a silent Charlie Chaplin movie if Mr. Chaplin were old, balding, and extraordinarily stupid. Yeltzen smiles as his microwave dings. He gets up, grabs the popcorn bag, and returns to his seat to see if his boss is continuing with his performance.

Noticing a military-looking man taking out a satellite phone and beginning to dial, Yeltzen jumps over to his computer and starts scanning for encrypted frequencies. He finds one and begins his de-encryption algorithm. Within five seconds, he listens to a conversation between the soldier outside and his commanding officer (CO).

Soldier: "Sir, our liaison cannot access the facility."

CO: "What are our options, Captain?"

Soldier: "The Vault is designed to withstand nuclear fallout. Internal systems are autonomous and controlled from the inside. The person inside is citing protocol and not allowing entry to the facility. Our liaison has blown a gasket and is now in the SUV cooling down...uh, strike that. Warming up."

CO: (pausing) Very well. Your orders are clear. We must gain access immediately. Have your team review the building schematics to determine if there are countermeasures we can employ. I am sending an aide to the UN Security General's office to defuse any fallout our liaison has created. Dig in and wait for further orders.

Soldier: "Yes, Sir. Out"

Yeltzen sits back, considering his options.

"No system is 100% secure. These boys will take about a day, perhaps two, to make it inside. Let's see if I can help them do it in 5. By then, it will be too late."

Yeltzen scoots his chair to the control board that operates the security doors, lights, air purification, and temperature systems. He types on his computer, shrouding all the online controls under a secure, randomly morphing algorithm so that even if they dig down the 20 meters of permafrost to reach the comms conduits, they still wouldn't see the control systems on their computers.

Then, he notices the audio controls for the internal and external speakers. A wicked smile creases his bearded face, and he rifles through a nearby desk drawer. He removed an ancient Apple iPod and connected it to the comms console via its outdated USB port.

"Let's go old school on these boys."

Curtain Group Headquarters, Sophia Antipolis, France

William continues distracting Delya, hoping Yeltzen can hold off the UN security team and locate those hiding in the shadows.

"Madame, please stop with the subliminal insults. Let's pretend that we respect each other's position of power. That would go a long way toward finding common ground. Wouldn't you agree?"

Delya acquiesces.

"I agree, William. I hope you don't mind me using your given name. Everyone seems to refer to you only as Chef."

William raises an eyebrow.

"Chef will be fine, and what should I call you? We have not been formally introduced, or if we have, then I must have been drugged."

She comes around in front of her desk and leans against it in an informal gesture of compliance.

"I am Delya Morris, second in command of the largest and most powerful multinational security firm in the world."

William takes another long sip of water and shakes his head at Delya.

"I thought you worked for an organization secretly created to protect the science discovered at the Kaiser Wilhelm Society? That same group of German Nationalists, who would later become Nazi's, would unleash some of the most horrific science the world has ever seen."

He directs his disdain for the Curtain Group at Delya,

"And here I thought we just agreed to be forthright, respecting each other's position of power."

William's response surprises Delya.

"Chef, I must commend you on your depth of knowledge about us. I apologize. Old habits die hard."

William begins to feel his leg strength returning. He continues eating away at the clock.

"If you would excuse my curiosity, Delya, why was it necessary to use such measures to get me here? Why not simply ask?"

She stops and looks William square in the eyes.

"Because we do not have the luxury of time..."

Raising his hand as though he were in school, William interrupts her mid-statement.

"I am sorry for asking, but why would time be a factor for a plan hatched over a century ago?"

Delya coyly smiles.

"Let's call it 'right place at the right time.' And leave it at that."

William catches the turn of phrase.

"Oh, I see. The Curtain Group is the right place, and it's the right time for _you_. But for that to be true, you'd have to..."

William turns towards the auburn-haired woman.

"How did the Turk put it back at the Negresco? Oh yeah. I remember."

William turns back to Delya.

"You must remove a few pieces from the board."

Looking puzzled, William turns back to the auburn-haired woman, who cannot hide her grin.

"Did I say that correctly? It didn't sound as bad-ass when your Turkish friend said it."

He turns back to Delya.

"You cannot have anyone higher up the food chain fucking with your plan. Which makes me wonder..."

It takes all of William's strength to rise to a standing position. Delya retreats behind her desk.

"What part are you wondering about? The place or the time?"

William nonchalantly sets the hook.

"Neither. I already know that information."

Her cold smile returns as the viper William has been expecting, finally shows itself.

"Excellent Chef. We both see each other for who and what we are..."

William interrupts her again.

"No, Madame, you don't see me at all. People like you never do. But I _do_ see you."

Delya's curiosity is piqued.

"How so?"

William pauses a beat.

"If you are going through the trouble of removing a piece, you have tipped your hand. The only person left in your way is your boss."

Exterior Entry Door, Svalbard Seed Bank

The soldiers assemble in an antechamber leading to the vault's entrance. It is covered and well-lit; his men have already unpacked their gear. There is even coffee brewing. The Captain has his men scanning online documents given to them by an asset inside the UN. They are looking for a way to gain entry. Scouring the anteroom area, the men find buckets, which they now use as makeshift seats, with power supplied by a few outlets near the vault entry. Each has a military-grade laptop on their lap.

The Captain addresses his people.

"Let's make this quick. We are on the clock."

The soldier closest to him stands up from his bucket.

"Sir, I have located the air duct specs. There is a service access on the north side of the..."

Without warning, the soldier's words are lost as the music of AC/DC's hit single "I've Got Big Balls" from their Back In Black Album begins blaring from the outdoor speakers. Each seated soldier falls off their bucket, sending their laptops skidding across the icy floor. The men put their hands up to their ears and must retreat to the SUVs to hear themselves think.

Yeltzen then turns off the power to the entry receptacles and the artistic lighting of the entryway. His bearded, round face frames a big smile.

"Hope you boys enjoy the music. It's all you are going to hear until you leave."

Later, the townspeople nearest the Seed Bank would recall hearing rock music played for three days straight. Yeltzen records the entire incident while providing short and random interludes in the playback. He shares the live feed with an online news organization under the caption:

"The Siege of Svalbard Seed Bank"

Yeltzen, relieved that it will take the men outside at least 3, possibly 4 days to gain entry, returns to the email logs to see what else he can learn. He quickly writes an algorithm to connect identified cell phones to names on the list. Within another minute, Yeltzen has a complete list of all the devices, their email addresses, and their associated names and telephone numbers.

Immediately, the algorithm begins drawing lines between names. At first, the connections seem random, but as the Yeltzen's algorithm taps into call logs, a clearer picture emerges, revealing a short list of three people who receive the most calls and texts from the other phones. Yeltzen's mind starts racing.

"There you are. The Butcher, The Baker, *and* The Candlestick Maker."

Yeltzen organizes the data and summarizes his findings using an AI he created in 1997. He sends the data to the Woman With Auburn Hair within seconds via a hyper-secure email server.

Curtain Group Headquarters, Sophia Antipolis, France

The Chef looks around Delya's office and notices two security people, one male and one female, entering the room on her silent command. He cannot help himself, so he makes fun of the situation.

"And here I thought we were becoming fast friends. So, it's the wood chipper for me, is it?"

Delya walks around her desk and doesn't look up at William. She is disconnected from her humanity. William is no longer a human being. He is nothing more than a bug under her shoe.

"No, Chef, that would be too easy an out for someone like you. You will live knowing what your actions have done to those you love."

Williams's heart turns cold in that instant.

"Madame, you should be careful of whom you threaten."

Delya allows his threat to fall without taking the bait.

"Chef, I control a multinational security organization that employs thousands of mercenaries, capable of taking out anyone I see fit, including the first-in-command. However, you will not be among them. You will remain to live out your life knowing you caused the excruciating deaths of your family and friends."

William smiles inside, realizing she has finally said the words that will end her career and possibly her life. He mimics her emotionless face and delivers the final blow.

"Madame, have you ever wondered why I've always been able to stay one step ahead of you? As you say, I am an amateur and nobody, but how long did the redhead take to find and secure me?"

Delya pauses, thinking it through.   William delivers the final blow.

"What if the First-in Command has been playing _YOU_ all this time?"

Exterior Entry Door, Svalbard Seed Bank

Yeltzen opens a command screen on his computer. In it, he types the words "Waste Management Interface."   On queue, three video screens come alive as lights come on in the facility's somewhat vacant warehouse area. A few keystrokes later, a red strobe light begins flashing, indicating movement in the room. From the corner of the video monitor, Yeltzen sees an automated hand truck slowly progressing across the warehouse's open space and towing a large container emblazoned with biohazard stickers.

Yeltzen looks down at his BB-8 droid and smiles as it begins beeping and whistling.

"Yes, yes, my little friend. Not to worry. This will be in place long before we open the door."

As programmed, the automated hand truck begins lifting the biohazard container on its 6-foot-tall scissor lift. Yeltzen scoots his chair over to the monitors to see that a number of the military contractors have gathered near the warehouse's entrance. This area of the 'Cathedral' is the least secure, as it must be accessed monthly to dispose of the organic waste, including both human and non-human waste, from the facility. It is also the point of entry that Yeltzen knew would be their first point of attack.

Hurrying back to his computer, Yeltzen adds another code sequence that allows the facility door to open. However, he abruptly stops it, only 15 centimeters (6 inches) off the floor. This leaves just enough room for the men to see into the area if they lie on their bellies, which is precisely what they do.

At that moment, Yeltzen sends a command to the hand truck to empty the contents of the container in front of the door opening. Yeltzen scoots over to the video monitor just in time to see 30 days of human fecal matter and food scraps come spilling out on the floor and into the waiting faces of the entire UN security detail. As a bonus, Yeltzen's boss got there just in time to get a face full himself. Rolling back to his computer, Yeltzen closes the warehouse door and plays "Dirty Deeds Done Dirt Cheap" by AC/DC over the loudspeakers.

As BB-8 begins spinning into a dance, Yeltzen screams.

"Pink eye for everyone!"

Curtain Group Headquarters, Sophia Antipolis, France

And right on queue, Delya's phone buzzes. William turns quickly to see the look on Delya's face as the call is coming from Herman Dashill's office, the First-in-command at the Curtain Group. The blood rushes from Delya's face. She lifts the receiver; her face is ashen, and she begins to shake. William plunges the virtual dagger in deeper and begins twisting it.

"Madame, if you wish to play the game, it would be wise not to fool yourself into thinking you are the smartest one playing."

At that moment, the two security guards simultaneously raised their hands to the micro communications devices in their ears, confirmed their new orders, and began walking towards Delya. Within moments, she was in Plasticuffs. Delya's brain cannot process what is happening.

"Wait! Who? What? How?"

Her eyes have become dilated. She has become disconnected from reality. William has the final words.

"Luckily, Madame Delya, I don't think it will be a wood chipper for you either. But if I had any say in it, I would ask that it be a meat grinder and have you watch as each piece of you is put through it. And in a perfect world, they'd let me crank the handle. Au revoir, Madame."

William slowly begins walking out of her office, the Woman With Auburn Hair trailing slightly behind him

"Well played in there, William."

William turns to her.

"How is our Viking doing?"

The Woman With Auburn Hair's face lights up with a large smile.

"He has outdone himself. Not only did he successfully repel the invasion by the Curtain Group Security team, but he also identified the people complicit in the plan to store and distribute the genetically altered seeds."

William stops and places his hand on a nearby wall to steady himself.

"You weren't kidding about the whole 'elephant sitting on my head' thing."

She takes him by his arm and guides him down the hall to her waiting car.

"Take it slow, William. We still have one more piece to remove from the board."

Chapter 26

The Lamb & The Wolf

Undisclosed Location in the South of France

The Woman With Auburn Hair is sitting outside, enjoying the afternoon breeze of the French Riviera, as William walks over to join her. He is still feeling the effects of the drug he was given, but he was also happy to report to Rebecca that he expects a full recovery. The Woman With Auburn Hair looks over at him.

"I am certain Rebecca did not take the news well."

William drinks another long swig of bottled water and looks over at her.

"Ya think!? Why do I get the feeling that you enjoy torturing her?"

"Not at all. I work alone and am not used to explaining everything I do."

William looks at her sideways.

"You know. You're not making this any easier on me."

She rolls her eyes, speaking sarcastically.

"Oh, tsk, tsk. The happily married couple of 30-plus years has something to work out. How terrible for you."

Just then, her phone begins to ring, and as she looks at the incoming caller ID. Realizing it is from Geneva, she hesitantly takes the call.

"Yes?"

The woman on the other end of the line is all business.

"Madame. My name is Ms. Green. I am the attorney of record for the Madame Chairperson and have been tasked to inform you of the Madame Chairperson's status."

The Woman With Auburn Hair holds her breath.

"Please, go on."

"Madame, I am sorry to report that Madame Chairperson did not survive her injuries."

Ms. Green pauses, allowing her words to sink in, and then continues. The Woman With Auburn Hair closes her eyes and listens while her brilliant memory records each word.

"Madame. At 23:24 GMT, the Madame Chairperson was taken off life support due to a lack of brain activity. As is customary, the committee's president has stepped in as interim Chairperson to continue operations. As Madame Chairperson hired you outside the committee's knowledge, they voted to terminate your contract immediately. However..."

The Woman Auburn Hair anticipates her following words.

"You are about to tell me that she also named me as her successor to the board and has left me her ownership stake in the company in her will. Am I correct?"

"You are correct."

The Woman With Auburn Hair allows the information to sink in. She collects herself as Ms. Green continues.

"The Board has instructed me to meet with you regarding her affairs. I will send you my contact information."

After she hangs up with Ms. Green, her hyper-encrypted communications device buzzes, indicating a text message has arrived. It is a variation of a quote often attributed to Mark Twain.

"The reports of my demise have been greatly exaggerated. Finish the job."

The Woman With Auburn looks over at William and allows a huge smile to escape.

"Good news, I take it?"

"It is. Grab more water. We are heading to Antibes. It's time to settle the score with our Turkish friend."

William rolls his eyes, grabs another 6-pack of water, and turns to the Woman With Auburn Hair.

"You know, this qualifies for hazard pay...just saying."

Curtain Group Headquarters

After taking Delya into custody, Herman Dashill sits at his desk, reviewing Delya's communications. As is protocol, communications are automatically forwarded to the Chief of Station whenever a company's senior director is released from service. He does not like what he sees. Delya has been forwarding his reports to people outside the Curtain Group. Names he knew but was sure she did not. She has also been directing the actions of the Turk and making it appear that the direction was coming from him.

As he weighs his response options, he notices an incoming call on Deyla's phone. He picks up the line and notices that the caller ID is missing. He waits for whoever has called to begin speaking.

"Herman. It's time we talked."

He immediately recognizes the Woman With Auburn Hair's voice.

"Well played today, Madame. It would seem that not only Delya, but also I have seriously underestimated your abilities."

"Don't take it so hard, Herman. I, too, get that a lot."

"Why are you calling?"

The Woman With Auburn Hair allows a moment to pass before she speaks.

"I need a favor. It has to do with the Turk."

"And in return for this favor..."

"You get to keep your job."

Herman's skepticism kicks in.

"You're overplaying your hand, I think."

It is then that Herman hears another voice on the line. This one is male, and he recognizes it.

"No, sir. She isn't. This is Deputy Director Willis of the Central Intelligence Agency. I believe we have met on several occasions."

Herman is quick to respond.

"Yes, we have, Deputy Director. I was not aware that you were involved."

"Be that as it may, The Woman With Auburn Hair has presented us with an extraordinary opportunity. One, I believe, you will find equally interesting."

Herman is confused.

"Sir, you said 'us'. To whom are you referring?"

The Deputy Directors for Mossad, MI-6, and Europol, including a few attorneys from The Hague, then introduce themselves. The Woman With Auburn Hair takes the opportunity to finish her conversation with Herman.

"So, Herman. About the Turk..."

Bastion Shipyard, Antibes, France

William is sitting on the parapet of the Bastion Shipyard, the port outside the walled city of Antibes. The shipyard is the former home of the 'Calypso', the boat made famous by the French oceanographer Jacques Cousteau. William is looking east with the sun on his back. Behind him is 'Le Nomade', an enormous 8-meter-tall faceless sculpture by famed Catalan artist Jaume Plensa. Le Nomade is a giant figure of a man, made of a lattice of stainless steel letters welded together and painted a brilliant white. The faceless sculpture sits atop the parapet with knees drawn up to its chest as it gazes across the Mediterranean Sea.

Seeing the sculpture for the first time years ago, William had been inexplicably connected to it in many ways. Today, however, William sits alone and looks out at the sea with his faceless friend, mimicking the giant's pose with his knees drawn to his chest and his arms wrapped around them. Together, they are looking out onto the vast blueness of the Mediterranean Sea, and for this moment, William is content. However, it doesn't take long before his moment is ruined by the sound of approaching steps from behind him. He hears a man with a thick Turkish accent begin to speak.

"It was unwise for you to come here."

William decides to play along, but cannot help but mock Turk.

"I could say the same about you. Oh, and thank you for the bottle of wine. I expect it to go for 3 times the price at Le Negresco's charity auction."

The Turk chuckles in a way that makes William's skin crawl. As he steps closer to William, the Turk turns his head around slowly as though it were on a swivel.

"I would not have thought of you as the type to act as a lamb tied to a stake. A critical error made by the Woman With Auburn Hair."

Learning from Eitan that the Turk prefers to look in the eyes of the target as their life fades at his hands, William continues to speak with his back turned as the Turk slowly moves closer.

"Because she is so well known for making errors? Hardly."

The Turk reaches into his jacket and takes out a knife laced with a lethal poison.

"You should know that the people watching out for you at the entrance and on the back wall are no longer there. Let's say they were persuaded to find other employment."

Without turning his head, William replies in a calming tone.

"You couldn't have killed them because they are better at it than you. So what did you do? Bribe them? How much may I ask? We have a bet going."

The Turk continues rotating his head in all directions, checking his situational awareness.

"I do not wantonly kill someone without a contract. It is unprofessional. All it took was a few thousand each. The younger one seemed very happy."

William audibly exhales in relief and then lowers his head as a sign of defeat. The Turk taunts William further. Hearing the Turk speak, William can tell the Turk has just stepped into the kill box.

"I am afraid you cannot find good help these days. But soon, it will not matter to you and those you hold dear. For you will all be dead."

At that moment, something in the air spooks the Turk. William, slightly turning his head, sees the Turk through his peripheral vision as he prepares to lunge forward to embed his knife in William's back. William laughs, breaking the Turk's concentration.

"So you finally figured it out. I expected better."

Frigate USS Adelline, International Waters -

Mediterranean Sea

A Northrop Grumman RQ-4 Global Hawk H.A.L.E. (High Altitude, Long Endurance) Unmanned Combat Aerial Vehicle is circling at 15,000 feet outside French airspace. US Navy Specialist Talbert is operating the control console. His backup, Lt Michaels, monitors the UCAV's flight controls and location as Vice Admiral William Becket Hall looks on. Specialist Talbert addresses the Vice Admiral.

"Sir, I have target lock. Waiting for orders."

The Vice Admiral looks over at Lieutenant Michaels, who returns a nod, affirming that everything is ready.

"Very well. Let's test the 'Seat Heater' to ensure all systems are functional. You may proceed, specialist."

"Aye. Aye. Admiral. Systems test is underway."

Specialist Talbert smiles, knowing a short burst of the laser will only render a human target unconscious. However, anything metallic they possess will quickly become too hot to touch.

Vice Admiral Hall takes another sip of his coffee just as his phone buzzes, indicating a text message has been received.

"Dinner is on me. WWAH"

Bastion Shipyard, Antibes, France

In less than 3 seconds, the Turk drops the knife as it becomes too hot to hold. He also feels lightheaded and falls to the ground unconscious. William leaves his seated position, walks over to the unconscious Turk, and looks down at him without feeling.

"Monsieur Turk. Fortunately, we need you alive. But I do not envy the next few days of your life. Bonne chance, (good luck) you wretched man."

As William walks away, he waves up to the sky to what he hopes is the US NAVY drone that the Woman With Auburn Hair coordinated. A moment later, Luca appears from the stairs leading to the entrance to the ancient walled city of Antibes, along with his grandsons and a large duffel bag with wheels. Luca winks at William as he approaches.

"You see, Ordures, it is as I said. The wolf will always be the wolf, especially when a lamb is tied to a stake."

The Turk, now regaining consciousness, becomes incensed, but he can only drool from the aftereffects of the laser. Luca's grandsons begin binding the Turk's hands and feet with knots only fishermen can make. They then lower him into the duffel. William turns to both grandsons.

"Thank you, boys. I told you it would be the easiest money you will ever make."

They both laugh and begin hauling the Turk away. Luca remains.

"Ordures, are you certain you want him to live?"

William places his hand on Luca's shoulder.

"Yes, my friend, I want him alive, for he knows those pulling the strings. But I did not say he needed to be comfortable."

Luca's smile broadens.

"I know just the place!"

After Luca and his grandsons depart, William reaches into his pocket, retrieves his phone, and dials Rebecca. She picks up immediately.

"Are you alright? Did they catch the Turk?"

"Yes, my love. The Turk is no longer a threat to us."

An idea pops into William's head.

"Pack our things. I'll call Eitan and have him bring you to me. Let's take the time to savor this moment. Bring some Rosé, and we can watch L'heure Bleue (the blue hour) in Antibe with Le Nomad."

The Fishing Vessel "Tempest," Port Lympia, Nice, France

It is early morning the next day in Nice. The Chef has returned to Le Negresco with Rebecca. Luca is with his two grandsons above deck, preparing to get underway. The Turk is below deck and still recuperating from the effects of the Seat Heater. Ropes aged by the sea bind him to a sturdy wooden chair. They are coarse and strong and do not give way under pressure.

Above deck, Luca tosses the last line securing the Tempest to the dock as his grandson increases power and maneuvers the boat past the tightly packed port. It will take another 20 minutes before they find the open ocean and another 4 hours to reach their fishing area in the Mediterranean Sea. As Tempest is a fishing vessel, it and its captain are well known to the local French Coast Guard.

As they reach their destination, the engines are cut, and the ship drifts. A thought runs across Luca's mind that makes him smile. Luca's grandson catches his smile.

"Grand-pere, why are you smiling?"

He winks back at his grandson.

"It is rare to have caught the fish before actually setting the lines."

Luca's grandson acknowledges the irony with a small laugh.

"But we must set the lines nonetheless, as we must bring back enough fish for our hungry customers."

Luca's other grandson pokes his head from the gangway leading below deck and addresses Luca.

"Our guest has awakened from his slumber and asks when his breakfast will be served."

Everyone above deck laughs loudly. Luca's grandson has a wicked sense of humor.

"Please tell our guest that we will set out a chair for him on the deck where he may relax."

Luca's grandson smiles and disappears below deck. With his bonds, the two grandsons drag the Turk up the gangway with little effort. He then lashes the Turk to the Samson Post, a heavy vertical post that supports the booms used to load diesel fuel and heavy cargo and, in the case of this type of vessel, the fishing nets and lines. The Turk's clothes are removed, and his feet are lashed in opposite directions to cleats set into the heavy deck.

As Luca's nephew places a wide-brimmed hat on the Turk's head, he snarls at the Turk.

"If it were up to me, you would bake in the sun like a Turkish date."

The Turk's expression is one of acceptance, but his eyes burn deep with hatred. Luca walks up to him next, and seeing the Turk's eyes follow him, he turns his head around and begins the interrogation.

"There is only one question that needs answering, and it requires specific names of the people who stand in the shadows. The sooner you supply that information, the sooner your torture will end. Make no mistake. It is death that you should be looking forward to, not life, and it will be given to you sooner when you speak the truth."

The Turk looked around at those standing on the deck.

"I cannot give what I do not have."

Luca shakes his head and removes the wide-brimmed hat from the Turk.

"Very well."

Luca gags the Turk as he and his grandsons set the fishing lines. He looks back over at the Turk.

"We will be fishing for three days. During that time, you will receive no food or water. If you are lucky, it may rain, but the radar shows no sign of it. Here, you will remain to bake until your life is drained by the sun from your miserable hide."

It takes the Turk two days of unrelenting sun to crack. He provides detailed operational knowledge of Curtain Group, including several instances where he oversaw security personnel for high-level government officials and other wealthy individuals. Luca's grandson passes the information on to the Woman With Auburn Hair for confirmation.

On the morning of the third day, Luca approaches the weak and nearly incoherent Turk. He recognizes Luca and flashes him a sadistic smile. Luca turns away from him and removes an old hunting knife he has had since he was a boy growing up in Rambouillet, France. Luca thinks back at the first and only time he used this knife when the Nazis nearly captured his family, and with tears forming in his eyes, he thinks of his Mother, Sisters, and Father, who lost their lives to Nazi evil.

In one swift and decisive motion, Luca embeds the knife to the hilt in the soft side of the Turk's temple. The Turk's eyes go wide in surprise, and with dilated pupils, his life is over. Luca removes the knife and begins cleaning it. His grandsons come over and remove the bonds securing the Turk's body to the Samson post while Luca unties the Turk's feet and attaches a cinder block to his waist. They throw his body overboard without another thought. In seconds, the Turk's body is lost in the darkness of the sea, and it is then that Luca drops his Father's knife in the Mediterranean, watching as it too is lost to the darkness of the sea.

Luca's grandson, watching his grand-père drop the knife, removes his phone and sends a text to William.

"Theose hiding in the shadows are identified."

Chapter 27

The Reckoning

Le Negresco Plage - Nice, France

The beaches in Nice are continually occupied with culinary activity. Like an intricate and well-rehearsed daily ballet, each restaurant's menu offers dishes inspired by the many countries surrounding the Mediterranean Sea.

Their job, however impossible, is to try and match the scenic beauty of the azure blue sea with flavors that complement the climate and the diverse population of locals and tourists that make up this legendary city.

Today, William finds himself at Le Negresco Plage, the namesake beach restaurant of the Cerulean blue and pink-domed Belle Époque Hotel that looks down at it from across the Avenue Des Anglais.

William turns his eyes to the table of people who have gathered in the aftermath of the events in Svalbard. In a moment, William feels the presence of a person standing beside him. It's the Woman With Auburn Hair. He turns his head, and immediately, his eyes widen with mild shock as he notices a change in her hair color.

"It would seem that you are going through a rebellious phase. Looks like you'll need a new name."

The Woman, once known for her beautiful Auburn-colored hair, now stands next to William with perfectly silky, understated, highlighted light brown hair. She smiles out of the side of her mouth while rolling her eyes.

"Is that all you got?"

William continues staring out onto the waters of the Mediterranean.

"Why don't I just call you by your given name, Miller?"

The once auburn-haired woman, only slightly surprised by hearing her name spoken for the first time in decades, turns towards the table where their friends are gathered.

"So, how did you learn my real name? Let me guess. Rebecca somehow figured it out."

There is a noticeable pause as the two take in the most beautiful place in the world. William turns to her and holds up his hands in surrender.

"It was an informed guess by yours truly. One that you, just now, so nicely confirmed."

Miller reaches into her Hermes tote and retrieves a small, slightly tattered black journal. She hands it to William, who raises his eyes in disbelief.

"Is that what I think it is?"

Miller casts him a wry smile.

"Yes. It's Escoffier's actual journal. You'll need it when you visit Escoffier's family vault in Villanueve-Lobet."

William asks her how she knew he would go to Georges Auguste Escoffier's final resting place, but thinks better of asking silly questions. Miller turns her attention to where Rebecca is sitting, then returns to looking out over the Mediterranean.

"I'd better get this over with. No use drawing it out."

William turns his head to her as she begins to leave.

"Cut her some slack. What has happened to us was never on her bingo card."

Miller nods and begins walking towards the Negresco Plage's ivy-covered canopy. On the way, she passes Daniel, the Le Plage manager, who is delivering drinks to a guest on a lounge chair at the shoreline. He nearly drops the tray when he realizes who the woman is. Miller smiles at him and keeps walking. As she approaches the canopy area, Rebecca and Sylvie are finishing up a conversation. Sylvie smiles at Miller and rises to join the others. Rebecca is the first to speak.

"The new hair color looks good on you. What will you be called now that the Woman With Auburn Hair is no more?"

Miller smiles knowingly while extending her hand.

"Rebecca. Allow me to introduce myself. My name is Miller-Catherine Domrémy of the family Mormant."

As Rebecca is ready to accept her hand, she instead slaps Miller hard across her face. Miller, holding her cheek and looking back at Rebecca, regains her stance.

"I deserved that."

Rebecca's face softens as though nothing had happened.

"It's a pleasure to know your real name, Miller. Please, please sit and have some tea."

Still holding her cheek, Miller offers another suggestion.

"Tea is too civilized. I'm going to have an Aperol Spritz. Care to join me?"

Daniel returns. He takes their order and tells the rest of the staff to leave them be. Miller begins speaking.

"Rebecca. I want to start over if we can."

Rebecca holds up her hand.

"Miller. That won't happen. Not ever. In truth, I hope never to cross paths with you again."

Miller lowers her eyes as sadness crosses her face. Rebecca reaches out and touches her hand.

"Miller. I know why you did what you did, and on some level, I think I may have done the same. I also realize the trouble my loving, incredibly reactive, naive husband brought on us. But he was just being himself. You, however, knew what you were doing, and you played us."

Miller looks up at Rebecca as she continues.

"Unfortunately, every time I see you, I am going to remember the sight of my husband on his knees begging the Gendarmerie not to shoot him."

Miller nods her head, acknowledging Rebecca's feelings. Daniel then arrives with the drinks momentarily, winking at the former

Woman With Auburn Hair. He leaves promptly. Rebecca has a question for Miller.

"Have you decided what you're going to do now?"

Miller sips her drink and then thinks a moment before answering, even though she already knows.

"I've played the Woman With Auburn Hair role for so long that I fear I have lost whoever I was before this all began. I no longer have any use for the anger over what was done to my family. Perhaps I will find a place to settle down."

Rebecca passes off her last comment. Miller notices the look on her face.

"So you don't think that's a good idea?"

Rebecca chuckles a bit.

"No, I don't. You are, without a doubt, one of the most intelligent and influential people on the planet, complete with a network of contacts that spans the globe. And from what I can tell, you are blessed with at least three types of long-term memory. Not to mention your various doctorates in criminal science and psychology. So, settling down and raising a family sounds like copping out."

Miller hasn't been called out like this since she parted ways with her mother.

"So what would you have me do? Run for political office?"

Rebecca rolls her eyes.

"Are you serious? That would be like entering a cheetah in a slow-walking contest. Excuse my crass words, but our world needs to wake the fuck up. We need complex and influential thinkers to start turning the tide on our evolutionary path before it is too late. I would think that would be something a mind like yours could sink its teeth into."

Miller is taken aback at Rebecca's words. She realizes that Rebecca has touched something deep within her soul. A sleeping giant lies dormant, and in the wake of her comment, it triggers her hypothalamus to send a rush of adrenaline through her system, causing the tiny muscles attached to her hair to tighten. Within seconds, the hairs on her arms become rigid, pulling the skin at their base upward.

"Rebecca, you may be on to something. I just got goosebumps!"

The two women spend the next few minutes brainstorming ideas until each has consumed their drinks. Miller rises from the table.

"Thank you, Rebecca. I deserved much worse for what I did."

She turns and leaves, and without another word, Rebecca breathes a sigh of relief, knowing that Miller's world will no longer be part of their life. Miller enters the Le Negresco Plage kitchen, and she is gone before anyone notices.

Soon after, William walks to the ivy-covered canopy dining area and sees Rebecca staring at the Mediterranean. William looks around.

"She has left?"

Rebecca looks up at her husband, and he knows the answer to his question by the look of peace on her face.

"I was hoping to say goodbye. Perhaps this is best."

He sees that Rebecca is still looking out to the shoreline. William intrudes on her contemplation.

"A penny for your thoughts."

It takes Rebecca a long moment to clear her mind of her recent conversation with Miller. Now, in the present, she looks up at her husband.

"I may have just unleashed the former Woman With Auburn Hair onto the world."

William's face is a jigsaw puzzle of questions.

"Never mind, my love. She has gone to live her new life, and we are here with our friends to celebrate surviving this part of ours."

The two of them turn their heads toward the large table where Luca, Sylvie, their grandchildren, and several staff members are talking and laughing while listening to the music being spun by a local DJ. William extends his hand to Rebecca, who rises and takes it.

"Let's join the party before the food and alcohol are gone!"

Later That Night, Still At The Table In The Negresco Plage

The ladies have all excused themselves to retire into the loving arms of the Le Negresco Hotel. They were undoubtedly in the Bar 1913, enjoying drinks and being pampered by the bar manager, Benjamin, and his capable staff. All that was left to do was to talk amongst men. Men who risked everything.

Sitting across from William is his friend Luca, and at his side sit his grandsons. Daniel, the Plage Manager, walks over with a rare bottle of vintage Scotch and crystal glassware. He looks at the men of various ages, each with the same look of solemn judgment on their faces. He recognizes the look and places a hand on William's shoulder.

"My friend, this is for you from the staff here at Le Negresco. I will leave you now, but before I do, I must say this: I do not begin to understand the gravity of the situation you now seem to be past, but I recognize the look that each of you wears, and it is with deep respect that I thank you for whatever it was that you accomplished. Wearing those faces meant it had to come with a great sacrifice."

Without another word, Daniel turns and places two security guards at the top of the stairs, instructing them not to let anyone down without William's approval.

After another few moments of silence, Luca speaks first, as it is his honor as the eldest. He looks at both sides of the table and his grandsons' faces.

"It is a terrible thing to go through life with blood on your hands. I know it all too well. There is no justification, only acceptance of the burden that yours alone can bear. But I will offer this to each of you..."

Luca points his finger at William.

"Especially to you, Ordures. Many men before us have also shouldered this burden. To those around this table, it began over a hundred years ago, and after we have left this world, there will be others who will sit at a table wearing the faces we wear today. Know only that what we have done has made a difference. Know also that the need will surely arise again. This is a certainty. So prepare those who come after you. Your sons and their sons and so on. We must never allow evil to breathe the same air as us."

Luca's eldest grandson opens the scotch, pours each glass, and then raises it to the table. Everyone else raises their glasses.

"To the beautiful heartache we shoulder. May future generations never forget these lessons."

Everyone tosses back the scotch. Luca's youngest grandson coughs as it hits the back of his throat. They all laugh and drink again. William rises from the table, indicating with his hand that everyone should stay seated.

"I am Ordoures. I am of the Family of the Fishmongers of Saint-François. You are forever my brothers."

William raises another glass, taps it onto the table, throws it back into his mouth, and slams it upside down on the table. Each man does the same individually. The youngest grandson picks up the glasses and wraps them in a napkin. The oldest grandson speaks.

"These glasses will never be used until we are all together again or when someone has passed into the next existence."

The grandsons depart, leaving Luca and William to themselves. William is the first to speak.

"Your youngest has taken the only things we can drink from."

Luca picks up the bottle and swigs it, slamming it down on the table and wiping his face with his arm. William follows suit. In another moment, the two lock eyes, and William speaks first.

"My friend, I owe you more than I could ever repay. You took me in and showed me what it's like to be part of your amazing family. For that, I am eternally grateful."

Luca takes another swig from the Scotch bottle and hands it to William.

"I remember the first day you walked into our square asking to be taught how to become a fishmonger. Perhaps you didn't realize what you were asking, eh?"

The two of them chuckle.

"No, my friend. I did not. But I am thankful and would not change anything."

The Chef takes the bottle from Lucas's hand and raises it.

"To the Fishmongers of Saint-François"

Luca takes the bottle back, raises it, and repeats the exact words in his native Niçard dialect.

The Next Day - Le Negresco Hotel Suite

Rebecca puts down her iPad. She'd been reading the news about the aftermath of their entangled events. There was no mention of Miller (a.k.a. The Woman With Auburn Hair). However, there was plenty about the UN FAO, the Curtain Group, and the Svalbard Seed Bank. A very comical picture of Yeltzen standing with a Viking hat and spear in front of the entrance to the seed bank, with the caption:

Local Viking Repels Invading Forces

William returns to the balcony with his Americano coffee and croissant. Rebecca looks up from her iPad.

"Our names have been left out of these articles."

He raises his eyebrows while chewing on the first bite of a supremely perfect buttery French croissant. After finishing swallowing, he turns his head towards Rebecca.

"I wonder who could have accomplished that?"

Rebecca, rolling her eyes, takes the bait.

"You know very well. She is still trying to compensate for all she has done to us."

William shrugs his shoulders as they finish their meal and looks up at Rebecca.

"Would you mind coming with me to visit Escoffier's grave?"

She smiles lovingly.

"Yes, I will."

William texts Eitan to ask if he is available. Eitan agrees to meet but cannot help poking fun at William in his return text.

"You're not planning to steal something again?"

City Cemetery in Villeneuve-Loubet, France - Next Day

Under a cloudy sky, William and Rebecca walk the steep road of Villaneuve-Lobet to the cemetery where Escoffier is buried. Neither has spoken since being dropped off by Eitan, and Rebecca can tell that her husband's mind is entirely elsewhere. As though William is reading her mind, he begins speaking.

"I am sorry to be so quiet. Our destination is hitting me harder than I thought it would."

Rebecca smiles up at him without speaking, allowing the love in her eyes to say everything. William continues speaking as though he is trying to convince himself of something.

"Now that the Exodus Seed is no longer a threat, I wonder what Escoffier would think of me."

Rebecca allows the words to settle on the ancient cobblestones of the street before responding.

"I believe he would think what everyone who knows already thinks. You did your best, and it was enough."

William and Rebecca remain silent until they reach the Escoffier family vault. It is a traditional marble vault that reveals its age with a rusted black iron gate and weathered marble, marked by dark streaks caused by the surrounding city's air pollution. At the center above the vault door is another statue of Saint Fortunat, the patron saint of cooks, and on the ground lies a single withered wreath of faded flowers. He smiles, remembering the first time he met the Saint when he stole Escoffier's journal. Tears begin to fill William's eyes, and he speaks as if expecting the Saint to hear them.

"Thank you for keeping me and my family safe."

In that moment, a stiff breeze comes up, blowing away a buildup of leaves on the marker in front of Escoffier's vault. As William looks down, he kneels and brushes away the remaining debris. There, inscribed in marble, are the numbers 27-6-14—the exact numbers as those written on the menu by Escoffier over a hundred years ago. Rebecca sees the numbers, and she touches William's shoulder.

"Escoffier left a clue after all..."

Reaching into his pocket, William removes Escoffier's original journal, given to him by the former Woman With Auburn Hair. He slowly opens it and begins reading the words penned by Escoffier himself.

"Journal Entry: 27-6-14. Today, I witnessed the callous nature of science and have seen the darkness filling the hearts of men who work to control it."

William returns it to his jacket pocket, unwilling to continue reading the entry. Thinking to himself:

"Best to let sleeping dogs lie."

Chapter 28

The After-Action Report

Undisclosed CIA Debriefing Room - France

The Woman With Auburn Hair is seated in a chair bolted to the floor. She is staring forward, looking into a two-way mirror across a stainless steel table, which is also bolted to the floor. She knows who is behind it, having been the person who has watched many debriefings throughout her career. She also knows the technology employed to record every detail of her reactions to the questioning that will inevitably come. All it would take is one skipped heartbeat or a sideways glance, and she could be spending several years in some black site prison. However, her brilliant mind has already worked out each possible line of questioning, and her visage is stoic and confident. She looks towards the door as if expecting it to open.

In that moment, as if on cue, there is a buzzing sound as an electric deadbolt is released on the door. Two people enter the room, a man and a woman, which is protocol when interviewing a female asset. Miller sizes them up quickly. Carmichael, a male, is the subordinate agent, carrying a thick file and a notepad. The female agent, Nicholes, has a slight limp, likely from an operation that hadn't gone as expected. Now, she's interviewing agents instead of running ops. Miller's brilliant mind absorbs every detail about the two, including the cologne they each wear. His being Dior Savauge. The Woman is wearing classic Chanel No.5. As expected, Nicholes initiates the conversation.

"Good afternoon, agent. I am Special Agent Nicholes, and this is Agent Carmichael. Can we get you something to drink?"

Without waiting for a response, the agents take seats across from Miller, leaving enough space between themselves to allow the recording equipment to capture every angle. Miller replies appropriately.

"Good afternoon, and no, thank you. I hydrated before arriving."

The two agents settle in as Carmichael opens the thick file. Special agent Nicholes begins speaking.

"I've been doing post-operation interviews for years. I commend you for your A.A.R.'s (After-Action Report) thoroughness and detail. It is like you can recall each detail from memory."

Miller nods slightly. Nicholes continues.

"It makes it much easier for us to focus on intent rather than fact. I appreciate that because, as you already know, there is a monumental amount of intent in the operation since it began in the early 1900s."

Miller replies, matter-of-fact.

"11 January 1911, to be exact."

Nicoles also replies matter-of-factly.

"Yes, the inauguration of the Kaiser Wilhelm Society."

She looks over at Charmichael, and he hands her a paper-clipped set of pages, some showing signs of foxing and heavy discoloration from age. She hands them over to Miller.

"Agent. Have you seen these documents before?"

Miller skillfully scans (and memorizes) each document, noting that three of the pages have a Nazi swastika stamped on them. She hands them back.

"No."

Nicoles raises an eyebrow.

"You are certain?"

"Yes, Ma'am. I have not seen those documents before entering this room."

Nicoles continues.

"Do any names ring a bell to you?"

"Yes, Ma'am. In school, I learned of the Alsos Mission and their work at the end of World War II."

"What is your assessment of the documents?"

"Ma'am, are you looking for my judgment or asking me to validate its provenance?"

Nicholes smiles slightly. Miller continues.

"Without forensic testing, my instincts tell me the documents are authentic, which should validate their provenance. Since the documents lack any identifiable Allied government reference labels besides the Alsos Mission, I believe they were overlooked by Alsos ranking officers, which isn't that surprising..."

Carmichael jumps in. Nicholes seems put off by the interruption. An oblivious Carmichael continues.

"Why isn't it surprising?"

Miller clarifies.

"The Alsos mission was in Germany to collect information relating to the Nazi's nuclear program. The Exodus Seed documents you just handed me, although important, looking through the lens we are using today, were not on anyone's radar then."

Nicholes takes the reins back and switches gears. Miller already expected the change in topic.

"Would it surprise you that the Exodus Seed genetic material and all documentation are missing?"

Miller does not hesitate to respond.

"No, it does not."

"Why is that agent?"

"Because I have it on good authority that everything was destroyed."

"Who was that authority?"

Miller looks into the mirror and focuses on the equipment recording her every heartbeat, breath, and temperature. She answers again, matter-of-factly.

"Because it was I who destroyed them. Every document and every last sample that the Curtain Group had in their possession."

Nicoles sits back in her chair with an odd look of inspiration. She leans across the table.

"Why would you do that?"

Miller centers herself.

"Because some discoveries are better off not being rediscovered, and since inheriting my stepmother's position at the company that created the genetically altered seeds, I was within my rights to destroy that which my company owned."

Carmichael, looking to help his performance review, attempts to discredit her.

"I find it oddly coincidental that you obtained an ownership stake in your stepmother's business as you were also working as an asset for the CIA."

Agent Nicholes cringes and sits back, letting Miller loose on him.

"I appreciate your candor, Agent Charmichael, but there are facts involved that are above your clearance level."

Undaunted, Charmichael doubles down.

"I also find it odd that the company you now own is being sold off in pieces to companies throughout the world. It seems rather convenient, wouldn't you say?"

Agent Nicholes senses Miller's response, and as Miller looks over at her, she nods, saying it's OK to let loose on him.

"Agent Charmichael. In our line of work, innuendo can kill. Be cautious when making statements about events outside your authorized clearance level. First, I was always in my stepmother's will to inherit her holdings. Second, her death was the catalyst that moved me into the position. The timing was the Curtain Group's doing, and I doubt my stepmother was happy with the timing or outcome. Third, and this is something you should remember as it relates directly to your climb up the ladder."

She allows a pause before continuing.

"Never, and I mean ever, interrupt a senior agent in the room during an interrogation. Many people down in the basement of Langley learned that lesson the hard way."

Two Days Later - The Former Apartment of Henri Matisse, Vieux Nice, France

Miller walks through the apartment, packing and organizing her things. She has also removed Matisse's paintings from the walls, and a half-dozen cloth-gloved people who are carefully preparing them for shipment and repair.

There is a knock at the door. Without looking at the security feed, Miller already knows who is at the door. She calls out to her visitor.

"The door is open, Agent Nicholes. Please come in."

The door opens slowly, and Agent Nicholes walks into a room full of people standing over several of Matisse's original works. Miller comes into the living room from the kitchen.

"Agent Nicholes. To what do I owe the pleasure?"

Agent Nicholes is distracted by the odor of linseed oil that envelops the room.

"Do you ever get used to the smell in here?"

Miller replies blankly.

"What smell?"

Agent Nicholes' eye catches Mattisse's The Green Stripe being carefully placed in a wooden shipping container. She notices the hole in the center of the woman's forehead in the picture. She looks over at Miller.

"Is that a bullet hole?"

Miller nonchalantly replies.

"Why yes. An assassination attempt that did not turn out as expected for the assassins. And before you ask, it was redacted from my After-Action report. National security concerns. You understand."

Agent Nicholes decides not to press the matter, which would no doubt mean more paperwork and interviews. She continues looking around the room.

"Do all these paintings belong to you?"

Miller laughs.

"My goodness, no. This apartment and its furnishings belonged to my late stepmother. I have donated them to several worthy causes. That is, of course, after some repair and cleaning."

Miller pauses, waiting for Agent Nicholes to finish looking around.

"Is there something I can help you with, Agent Nicholes?"

Miller's tone shakes Agent Nicholes to the present moment.

"Yes. My apologies. I am here to give you this."

Miller accepts the package and places it on the table next to them. "Anything else?"

Agent Nicholes is dumbfounded.

"Don't you want to know what's in the package?"

"It is most likely a copy of the After Action Report. Thank you for bringing it to me, but you could have sent it via secure courier instead. Which begs the question...why are you here?"

Agent Nicholes, surprised by her intuition, squares her shoulders.

"I am here to offer you a commission."

Distracted by the museum curator struggling to fit one of the paintings into its crate, Miller responds without looking at the agent.

"I accept."

Agent Nicholes' eyes go wide again.

"You don't know what it is."

Miller looks at her.

"Yes, I do because you hinted at it throughout the After-Action briefing. Congratulations. I am looking forward to working together. It should be good for you to get back out in the field."

Miller shakes her hand and returns to the kitchen. Agent Nicholes stands there, not knowing what just happened and wondering how Miller knew about her being behind a desk. She then departs, and as she reaches the street, she commits herself.

"I'll need to step up my game to keep up with her."

Looking down from Mattisse's apartment window just as Agent Nicholes considers upping her game, Miller smiles.

"I think you'll do just fine, Agent Nicholes."

THE END

About The Author

James Sevier, American Chef & Author has spent his career in technology as a professional speaker, a career that has afforded him the opportunity to experience the world. It is from his travels that James will immerse you in the culture and flavors of the locations in each novel as though you were there with him. In fact, he often leaves behind "Easter Eggs" in his the storyline, hinting to an element or future element or storypoint. Sevier's interest in writing was propelled by his work and it was in 2022 when he decided to begin writing the Le Chef series.

Le Chef - The Exodus Seed is James Sevier's debut novel, celebrating a lifetime of travel, public speaking, and love of the culinary arts. Sevier is inspired by the works of John Scalzi, Lee Child and Danial Suarez.

www.ingramcontent.com/pod-product-compliance
Lightning Source LLC
Chambersburg PA
CBHW070917260626
47162CB00007B/2699